CW01624540

Night Fears is an outstanding collection of original stories from three of the most talented writers in the field of horror and dark fantasy: Dean R Koontz, Edward Bryant and Robert R McCammon. It has an introduction by bestselling author Clive Barker and is illustrated by Kevin Davies.

Night Fears

Introduction by Clive Barker

All original stories by

Dean R Koontz
Edward Bryant
Robert R McCammon

Illustrated by

Kevin Davies

HEADLINE

Originally published in the United States of America
by Dark Harvest, Inc.
under the title *Night Visions 4*
Night Visions 4 Copyright © 1987 by Dark Harvest, Inc.
Introduction Copyright © 1987 by Clive Barker
Illustrations Copyright © 1987 by Kevin Davies
Miss Attila the Hun Copyright © 1987 by Nkui, Inc.
Hardshell Copyright © 1987 by Nkui, Inc.
Twilight of the Dawn Copyright © 1987 by Nkui, Inc.
Predators Copyright © 1987 by Edward Bryant
The Baku Copyright © 1987 by Edward Bryant
Frat Rat Bash Copyright © 1987 by Edward Bryant
Haunted Copyright © 1987 by Edward Bryant
Buggage Copyright © 1987 by Edward Bryant
Doing Colfax Copyright © 1987 by Edward Bryant
Author's Notes Sections Copyright © 1987 by Edward Bryant
The Deep End Copyright © 1987 by Robert R McCammon
A Life in the Day of Copyright © 1987 by Robert R McCammon
Best Friends Copyright © 1987 by Robert R McCammon

First published in Great Britain in 1989
by HEADLINE BOOK PUBLISHING PLC

All rights reserved. No part of this publication may be reproduced, stored in a retrieval system, or transmitted, in any form or by any means without the prior written permission of the publisher, nor be otherwise circulated in any form of binding or cover other than that in which it is published and without a similar condition being imposed on the subsequent purchaser.

All characters in this publication are fictitious and any resemblance to real persons, living or dead, is purely coincidental.

ISBN 0 7472 3258 X

Typeset in 10/11 pt Mallard by Colset Private Limited,
Singapore

Printed and Bound in Great Britain by Collins, Glasgow

HEADLINE BOOK PUBLISHING PLC
Headline House, 79 Great Titchfield Street, London W1P 7FN

Dark Harvest, Inc. would like to express their gratitude to the following people. Thank you: Dawn Austin, Kathy Jo Camacho, Stan and Phyllis Mikol, Wayne Sommers, Tony Hodes, Dr Stan Gurnick PhD, Bertha Curl, Kurt Scharrer, Ken Morris, Cindy Cargine, Sharon Krisch, Luis Trevino, Raymond, Teresa and Mark Stadalsky, Howard Morhaim, Stephen King, Dan Simmons, George R R Martin, Douglas E Winter and Ann Cameron Williams.

And, of course, special thanks go to the five most important people to this book. Without them, *Night Fears* would not exist: Dean R Koontz, Edward Bryant, Robert R McCammon, Clive Barker and Kevin Davies.

Contents

Introduction

People say prostitution is the oldest profession; but I wonder. Certainly it's got a good long tradition, honorable and dishonorable by turns, and if commerce were to have sprung into being from any particular exchange in the human experience, the sexual exchange is certainly prime material. Accounts of the profession's existence can be found in some of the earliest histories, back to the beginning of the written word; and indeed there are probably creatures for hire in some of the shadier backwaters of our major cities who predate that.

But stories, and their telling, have surely been a means to profit for as long. And stories of fear have always had a central place in any story-teller's canon. Something about them appeals. Perhaps they simply tell the truth of our condition in a way that is palatable, and honest, even in its fictional excesses. After all, we are born into a state of anxiety. *Born*, note; not made. Just as we are surely sexual from our first breath (because physical), so we are afraid (because vulnerable). It makes sense therefore that stories which dramatize our confrontation as spirits with the brutal business of physicality, and – at their best – seek to discover a pattern in our defeats and triumphs, should be of enduring interest.

Stories of the body: the doomed machine in which we awaken, prone to the frailties of age and the corruptions of disease. Stories of the mind: a system striving for reason and balance while the ape and the lizard were – and in our coils, still are – slinking through its darker places. Stories of God and the Devil: the actors we have cast to play our moralities out. Stories heroic or absurd; epic or elegiac: but all, in their different ways, touching upon the fears that we live with day by day.

To some, they may be Freud writ rampant; to others, a dip into the Jungian stream. To many, myself included, they are all these things, and more. Horror fiction, dark fantasy, *grand guignol*: however you choose to describe it, the *genre* fascinates.

But one should probably not be surprised that this area of fictional endeavor is often treated with contempt. The function these stories serve is too *raw*. It requires an admission of vulnerability in the experiencer; a willingness to confess to nightmares, in a culture that increasingly parades banality as feeling, and indifference as proof of sophistication.

But back to prostitution, for a moment; just as there's always been a tradition of husbands indulging, in the company of professional ladies, desires they'd never dare confess to their wives – and wives taking lovers for the same healthy reason – so this kind of fiction is indulged. Behind closed doors, as it were: a secret vice. It's on the shelves in greater and gaudier displays than ever, of course; and on the cinema screen, but it's still perceived, for the most part, as gutter entertainment, ignored by critics who say it's beneath their pen, while reading it beneath their desks.

There must be times in the lives of most who write in the *genre*, therefore, when this profession – despised at best, or condescended to – strikes them as strange. We spend our working days making traps; stories that will corner the reader into confronting, in fictional form, experiences most of humanity spends its time assiduously avoiding. Showing them the body's corruption and the mind's decay; showing them loneliness and cruelty; showing them the world gone mad. There are, it's true, differences in approach from author to author. Some eschew disgust as an objective – preferring to keep the atrocity out of sight; others (myself included) value the full confessional. Some like to keep the world their fiction describes realistic, indulging in only the subtlest tinkering with reality; others go for revolution. But whatever the stylistic or conceptional differences, we're all in the same business at heart: selling fear. This, in those days of the unblinkered eye, when we see what we do with uncommon clarity, may seem perverse.

In a sense it is. That's why I'm the first to applaud the author who comes up with a new twist, a new distressing notion, because perversity, by its nature, withers once it becomes acceptable; it perpetually needs new taboos. But taboo and perversity are not enough in themselves. If we merely celebrate the urge to *appal* we may find ourselves defending mere sensationalism simply because it makes us nauseous. No, we must also have structure to our horrors, and – given that any narrative worth its sweat has some underlying metaphysic – meaning too.

Here, then, the whore and the horror writer finally part company. Our literature may be underbelly literature – fables of the forbidden which will only be indulged in private – but stories of fear have a chance to leave a profounder impression on their readers than any other fictional form, while the most the oldest profession is likely to leave you with is a burning sensation while passing water.

We who write and read and celebrate horror fictions have, I'd argue, our fingers on a pulse which beats where most people won't even look, never mind explore.

And so, to three brave explorers, about to lead expeditions into that region: Mr Koontz, Mr Bryant, and Mr McCammon. I don't believe in giving too much away in introductions. After all, you bought the book for the thrill of discovery, not to have somebody give the game away before you've reached page one. I won't therefore spoil your pleasure by hinting at the contents of these tales. What I can allude to, without giving anything away, is the range of effects these fine writers create.

The *genre* is often condemned – usually by those who don't read it – for the narrowness of its vision and intention. It's a similar argument, and no more valid, than that levelled at erotic literature; that somehow the desire to scare, like the desire to arouse, is a fundamentally shallow one. The stigma touches the purchaser as well as the purveyor. It's seen as a failure of maturity to enjoy such stimulations. The same argument, of course, could be levelled at comedy, which 'merely' seeks to induce laughter, or love-poetry, with only love and loss on its simple mind. Such arguments strike me as nonsensical, and in the face of the kind of works these gentlemen produce should be apparent as such. They deserve better enemies, or none at all. Personally, I'd prefer the former: that is, to be opposed by people who have a thorough knowledge of the *genre*, rather than whined at by born-again Christians who saw an Italian zombie show once, and decided the whole thing was unholy.

It's too much to hope for, of course: informed and intelligent criticism. It's up to us to press ourselves to higher goals – and new perversities along the way; up to us to keep clear in our heads what good horror fiction can do to people – how it can debate matters of great consequence. How it can unveil the once upon a times behind apparent realities. How it can show the nursery-crib and the death-bed as equally haunted places, and every bed between – whether we're sleeping or fornicating there, as touched by the same spirits. At its best it's a visionary literature, with its feet in blood and its eyes on transformation; a literature not blinded by the conventions of 'acceptable' subject matter, a little in love with death, and all the more honest for that; a literature that looks, and looks again, and never flinches.

Here then, are several such tales. Enjoy. Three minds have dug deep to produce these fragments of their personal darkness for you, and loaned them. Imagine these gentlemen, if you will, seated beneath a shady tree, earning their daily bread selling their visions to any who'll listen. They wouldn't go hungry, I suspect. So what if whoring *is* the oldest profession. In the end, they go their way, the ladies of the night. But the man who sells you fear – if it's *good* fear – sells you nightmares for life. There are few better bargains this side of the Devil.

But that's another story . . .

April 1987

Dean R Koontz

Miss Attila the Hun

1

Through frost and thaw, through wet and dry seasons, the thing on the forest floor had waited many hundreds of years for a chance to live again. Not that it was dead. It was alive, aware, always alert to the passage of warm-blooded creatures in the thick woods around it. However only a small portion of its mind was required to monitor nearby animals for a possible host, while for the most part it was occupied with vivid dreams of previous and ancient lives that it had led on other worlds.

Deer, bears, badgers, squirrels, chipmunks, rabbits, possums, wolves, mice, foxes, raccoons, cougars, quail that had strayed in from the fields, dogs, toads, chameleons, snakes, worms, beetles, spiders, and centipedes had passed near enough to the thing to have been seized if they had been suitable. Some, of course, were not warm-blooded, which was one of the strange creature's two primary requirements of a host. Those that did have warm blood – the mammals and the birds – did not meet the other requirement: a high order of intelligence.

The thing did not grow impatient. It had found hosts in one form or another for thousands of millions of years, and it was confident that it would eventually have an opportunity to ascend from its dreams and experience this world, as it had experienced – and conquered – many others.

2

Jamie Watley was in love with Mrs Caswell. He had considerable artistic talent, so he filled a tablet with drawings of her: Mrs Caswell riding a wild horse; Mrs Caswell taming a lion; Mrs Caswell shooting a charging rhinoceros that was as big as a Mack truck; Mrs Caswell as the Statue of Liberty, holding a torch high. He had not seen her ride a horse, tame a lion, or shoot a rhino, nor had he heard of her having performed any of those feats, and she certainly did not look like the Statue of Liberty (she was prettier), but it seemed to Jamie that those imaginary scenes nevertheless portrayed the real Mrs Caswell.

He wanted to ask Mrs Caswell to marry him, but he was not very confident about his chances. For one thing she was well-educated, and he was not. She was beautiful, and he was homely. She was funny and outgoing, but he was shy. She was so *sure* of herself, always in command of any situation – remember the school fire in September, when she single-handedly saved the building from burning to the ground? – while Jamie found it difficult to cope with even minor crises. She was already married, too, and Jamie felt guilty about wishing her husband dead. But if he were to have any hope at all of marrying Mrs Caswell, the worst problem to be overcome was the difference in their ages; she was seventeen years older than Jamie, who was only eleven.

That Sunday night in late October, Jamie sat at the plank-topped, makeshift desk in his small bedroom, creating a new pencil drawing of Mrs Caswell, his sixth-grade teacher. He depicted her in their classroom, standing beside her desk, dressed in the white robes of an angel. A wonderful light radiated from her, and all the kids – Jamie's classmates – were smiling at her. Jamie put himself into the picture – second row from the door, first desk – and, after some thought, he drew streams of small hearts that were rising from him the way fog rose from a block of Dry Ice.

Jamie Watley – whose mother was an alcoholic slattern and whose father was an alcoholic, frequently unemployed mechanic – had never much cared for school until this year, when he had fallen under the spell of Mrs Laura Caswell. Now Sunday night was always the slowest night of all because he was impatient for the start of a new school week.

Downstairs his mean-spirited and drunken father was arguing with his equally drunken mother. The subject was money, but the argument could as easily have been about the inedible dinner she had prepared, his eye for other women, her sloppy appearance, his poker losses, her constant whining, the lack of snack foods in the house, or which TV program they were going to watch next. The thin walls of the decrepit house did little to muffle their voices, but Jamie was usually able to tune them out.

He started a new drawing. In this one, Mrs Caswell was standing on a rocky landscape, wearing futuristic clothing, and battling an alien monster with a laser sword.

3

Teel Pleever drove his battered, dirty, eight-year-old Jeep wagon into the hills before dawn. He parked along an abandoned logging road deep in the forest. As dawn was breaking, he set out on foot with his deer rifle. The gun was a bolt-action Winchester Model 70 in .270 caliber, restocked in fine European walnut, with a four-power scope on Stith Streamline mounts, incorporating windage.

Teel loved the woods at dawn. He loved the velvety softness of the shadows, the clear early light spearing down through the branches, the lingering smell of the night dampness. He loved the feel of the rifle in his hand, the thrill of the hunt, but most of all he loved poaching.

Although he was the most successful real-estate wheeler and dealer in the county, a man of position and modest wealth, Teel was loath to spend a dollar when the same item could be had elsewhere for ninety-eight cents, and he refused to spend a penny when he could get what he wanted for free. He had owned a farm on the northeast edge of Pineridge, the county seat, where the state had decided to put the new turnpike interchange, and he had made better than six hundred thousand dollars in profit by selling off pieces to motel and fast-food chains. That was the biggest of his deals but far from the only one, and he would have been a rich man without it. Yet he bought a new Jeep wagon only every ten years, owned one suit, and was notorious at Pineridge's Acme supermarket for spending as much as three hours' comparison shopping to save eighty cents on one order of groceries.

He never bought beef. Why pay for meat when the woods were full of it, on the hoof, free for the taking? Teel was fifty-three. He had been shooting deer out of season since he was seventeen, and he had never been caught. He had never particularly *liked* the taste of venison, and after having eaten uncounted thousands of pounds of the stuff over the past three and a half decades, he sometimes didn't look forward to dinner; however his appetite always improved when he thought of all the money he had kept in his pocket and out of the hands of cattle farmers, beef brokers, and members of the butchers' union.

After forty minutes of climbing the gently sloped, forested foothills without spotting deer spoor, Teel paused for a rest on a large, flat rock between two tall big-cone pines. After he sat down on the edge of the rock and put his rifle aside, he noticed something odd in the ground between his booted feet.

The object was half buried in the soft, moist, black soil. It was also partly covered by decaying, brown pine needles. He reached down with one hand and brushed the needles away. The thing was the shape of a football but appeared to be about twice as large. The surface was highly polished, as glossy as a ceramic glaze, and Teel knew the object must be man-made because no amount of wind and water abrasion could produce such a sheen. The thing was darkly mottled blue and black and green, and it had a strange beauty.

He was about to get off the rock, drop to his hands and knees, and dig the mysterious object out of the soil, when holes opened in several places across its surface. In the same instant, black and glossy plantlike tendrils exploded toward him. Some of them whipped around his head and neck, others around his arms, still others around his feet. In three seconds he was snared.

Seed, he thought frantically. Some crazy damn kind of seed no one's seen before.

He struggled violently, but he could not pull free of the black tendrils or break them. He could not even get up from the rock or move an inch to one side or the other.

He tried to scream, but the thing had clamped his mouth shut.

Because Teel was still looking straight down between his legs at the nightmarish seed, he saw a new, larger hole dilate in the center of it. A much thicker tendril – a stalk, really – rose swiftly out of the opening and came toward his face as if it were a weird-looking cobra swaying up from a snake charmer's basket. It was black with irregular midnight-blue spots, and it tapered at the top, terminating in nine thin, writhing tendrils. Those feelers explored his face with a spider-soft touch, and he shuddered in revulsion. Then the stalk moved away from his face, curved toward his chest, and with horror he felt it growing with amazing rapidity through his clothes, through his skin, through his breastbone, and into his body cavity. He felt the nine tendrils spreading throughout him, and then he fainted before he could go insane.

4

On this world its name was Seed. At least that was what it saw in the mind of its first host. It was not actually a plant –

nor an animal, in fact – but it accepted the name that Teel Pleever gave it.

Seed extruded itself entirely from the pod in which it had waited for hundreds of years and inserted all of its mass into the body of the host. Then it closed up the bloodless wounds by which it had entered Pleever.

It required ten minutes of exploration to learn more about human physiology than humans knew. For one thing, humans apparently did not understand that they had the ability to heal themselves and to daily repair the effects of aging. They lived short lives, oddly unaware of their potential for immortality. Something had happened during the species' evolution to create a mind–body barrier that prevented them from consciously controlling their own physical being. Strange.

Sitting on the rock between the pine trees, in the body of Teel Pleever, Seed took another eighteen minutes to acquire a full understanding of the depth, breadth, and workings of the human mind. It was one of the most interesting minds that Seed had encountered anywhere in the universe: complex, powerful, yet distinctly psychotic.

This was going to be an interesting incarnation.

Seed rose from the rock, picked up the rifle that belonged to its host, and headed down the forested hills toward the place where Teel Pleever had parked the Jeep wagon. Seed had no interest whatsoever in deer poaching.

5

Jack Caswell sat at the kitchen table, watching his wife as she got ready for school that Monday morning, and he knew beyond a doubt that he was the luckiest man in the world. Laura was so lovely, slender, long-limbed, and shapely that Jack sometimes felt as if he were dreaming his life rather than actually living it, for surely in the real world he would not have merited a woman like Laura.

She took her brown-plaid scarf from one of the hooks by the back door and wrapped it around her neck, crossing the fringed ends over her breasts. Peering through the half-steamed window in the door, she read the outside temperature on the big thermometer mounted on the porch. 'Thirty-eight degrees, and it's only the end of October.'

Her thick, soft, shiny, chestnut-brown hair framed a perfectly proportioned face reminiscent of the old movie star, Veronica Lake. She had enormous, expressive eyes so dark brown that they were almost black; they were the clearest, most direct eyes that Jack had ever seen. You could not look into those eyes and lie – or fail to love the woman behind them.

Removing her old brown cloth coat from another hook, slipping into it, closing the buttons, she said, 'We'll have snow well before Thanksgiving this year, I'll bet, and the whitest Christmas in ages, and we'll be snowbound by January.'

'Wouldn't mind being snowbound with you for six or eight months,' he said. 'Just the two of us, snow up to the roof, so we'd have to stay in bed, under the covers, sharing our body heat in order to survive.'

Grinning, she came to him, bent, and kissed him on the cheek. 'Jackson,' she said, using her pet name for him, 'the way you turn me on, we'd generate so darn much body heat that it wouldn't matter if the snow was a mile higher than the roof; regardless of how cold it was outside, it'd be sweltering in here, temperature and humidity over a hundred degrees, jungle plants growing out of the floorboards, vines crawling up the walls, tropical molds in all the corners.'

She went into the living room to get the briefcase that was on the desk at which she planned her school lessons.

Jack got up from the table. A little stiffer than usual this morning but still in good enough shape to shuffle around without his cane, he gathered up the dirty breakfast dishes, still thinking about what a lucky man he was.

She could have had any guy she wanted, yet she had chosen

a husband with no better than average looks and with two bum legs that wouldn't hold him up if he didn't clamp them in metal braces every morning. With her looks, personality, and intelligence, she could have married rich or could have gone off to the big city to make her own fortune. Instead she settled for the simple life of a school teacher and wife of a struggling writer, passing up mansions for this small house at the edge of the woods, forgoing the luxury of limousines for a three-year-old Toyota.

When she came bustling into the kitchen with her brief-case, Jack was putting the dishes in the sink to wash them. He said, 'Do you miss the limousines?'

She blinked at him. 'What're you talking about?'

He sighed and leaned against the counter. 'Sometimes I worry that maybe . . .'

She came to him. 'That maybe what?'

'Well, that you don't have much in life, certainly not as much as you ought to have. Laura, you were born for limousines, mansions, ski chalets in Switzerland; you *deserve* them.'

She smiled. 'You sweet, silly man. I'd be bored in a limousine. I like to drive; it's *fun* to drive. Heck, if I lived in a mansion I'd rattle around like a pea in a barrel. I like *cozy* places. Since I don't ski, chalets aren't of any use to me. And though I like their clocks and chocolates, I can't abide the way the Swiss yodel all the time.'

He put his hands on her shoulders. 'Are you really happy?'

She looked directly into his eyes. 'You're serious about this, aren't you?'

'I worry that I can't give you enough.'

'Listen, Jackson, you love me with all your heart, and I know you do, I *feel* it all the time, and it's a love that most women will never experience. I'm happier with you than I ever thought I could be. And I enjoy my work, too. Teaching is immensely satisfying if you really try hard to impart knowledge to those little demons. Besides, you're going to be famous someday, the most famous writer of detective novels since Raymond Chandler. I just know it. Now if you don't stop being a total booby, I'm going to be late for work.'

She kissed him again, went to the door, blew him another kiss, went outside, and descended the porch steps to the Toyota parked in the gravel driveway.

He grabbed his cane from the back of one of the kitchen chairs and used it to move more quickly to the door than he could have with only the assistance of his leg braces. Wiping the steam from the cold pane of glass, he watched her start the car and race the engine until, warmed up, it stopped knocking violently. Clouds of vapor plumed from the exhaust pipe. She went down the driveway, out to the county road, and off toward the elementary school three miles away. Jack stayed at the window until the white Toyota had dwindled to a speck and vanished.

Though Laura was the strongest and most self-assured person Jack had ever known, he worried about her. The world was hard, full of nasty surprises, even here in the rural peace of Pine County. And people, including the toughest of them, could get ground up suddenly by the wheels of fate, crushed and broken in the blink of an eye.

'You take care of yourself,' he said softly. 'You take care and come back to me.'

6

Seed drove Teel Pleever's battered old Jeep wagon to the end of the abandoned logging road and turned right on a narrow macadam lane. In a mile the hills descended into flatter land, and the forest gave way to open fields.

At the first dwelling Seed stopped, parked, and got out. Drawing upon its host's store of knowledge, Seed discovered that this was 'the Halliwell place.' At the front door, it knocked sharply.

Mrs Halliwell, a thirtyish woman with amiable features, answered the knock. She was drying her hands on her blue-and white-checkered apron. 'Why, Mr Pleever, isn't it?'

Seed extruded tendrils from its host's fingertips. The swift, black lashes whipped around the woman, pinning her. As Mrs Halliwell screamed, a much thicker stalk burst from Pleever's open mouth, shot straight to the woman, and bloodlessly pierced her chest, fusing with her flesh as it entered her.

She never finished her first scream.

Seed took control of her in seconds. The tendrils and stalks linking the two hosts parted in the middle, and the glistening, blue-spotted, black, alien substance flowed partly back into Teel Pleever and partly into Jane Halliwell.

Seed was growing.

Searching Jane Halliwell's mind, Seed learned that her two young children had gone to school and that her husband had taken the pickup into Pineridge to make a few purchases at the hardware store. She had been alone in the house.

Eager to acquire new hosts and expand its new empire, Seed took Jane and Teel out to the Jeep wagon and drove back onto the narrow macadam lane, heading toward the county road that led into Pineridge.

7

First thing in the morning, Mrs Caswell always began the day with a history lesson. Until he had landed in her sixth-grade class, Jamie Watley had thought he didn't like history, that it was dull. When Mrs Caswell taught history, however, it was not only interesting but fun.

Sometimes she made them act out roles in great historical events, and each of them got to wear a funny hat suitable to the character he was portraying. Mrs Caswell had the most amazing collection of funny hats. Once, when teaching a lesson about the Vikings, she had walked into the room wearing a horned helmet, and everyone had busted a gut laughing. At first Jamie had been a bit embarrassed for her; she was *his* Mrs Caswell, after all, the woman he loved, and he couldn't bear to see her behaving foolishly. But then she showed them paintings of Viking longboats with intricately carved dragons on their prows, and she began to describe what it was like to be a Viking sailing unknown misty seas in the ancient days before there were maps, heading outward into unknown waters where – as far as people of that time knew – you might actually meet up with dragons or even fall off the edge of the earth, and as she talked her voice grew softer, softer, until everyone in the room was leaning forward, until it had seemed as if they were transported from their classroom onto the deck of a small ship, with storm waves crashing all around them and a mysterious dark shore looming out of the wind and rain ahead. Now Jamie had ten drawings of Mrs Caswell as a Viking, and they were among his favorites in his secret gallery.

Last week a teaching evaluator named Mr Enright had monitored a day of Mrs Caswell's classes. He was a neat little man in a dark suit, white shirt, and red bow tie. After the history lesson, which had been about life in medieval times, Mr Enright wanted to question the kids to see how much they really grasped of what they'd been taught. Jamie and the others were eager to answer, and Enright seemed impressed. 'But Mrs Caswell,' he said, 'you're not teaching them the sixth-grade level, are you? This seems like about eighth-grade material to me.'

Ordinarily, the class would have reacted positively to Enright's statement, seizing on the implied compliment. They would have sat up straight at their desks, puffed out their chests, and smiled smugly. But they had been coached to react differently if this situation arose, so they slumped in their chairs and tried to look exhausted.

Mrs Caswell said, 'Class, what Mr Enright means is that he's afraid I'm pushing you too fast, too hard. You don't think that I demand too much of you?'

The entire class answered with one voice: '*Yes!*'

Mrs Caswell pretended to look startled. 'Oh, now, I don't overwork you.'

Melissa Fedder, who had the enviable ability to cry on cue, burst into tears, as if the strain of being Mrs Caswell's student was just too much to bear.

Jamie stood up, shaking in terror, and delivered his one line with practised emotion: 'Mr En-Enright, we can't t-t-take it any more. She never lets up on us. N-n-never. We c-c-call her Miss Attila the Hun.'

Other kids began to voice rehearsed complaints to Mr Enright:

'– never gives us a recess –'

'– four hours of homework every night –'

'– too much –'

'– only sixth graders –'

Mr Enright was genuinely appalled.

Mrs Caswell stepped toward the class, scowling, and made a short chopping motion with her hand.

Everyone instantly fell silent, as if afraid of her. Melissa Fedder was still crying, and Jamie worked hard at making his lower lip tremble.

'Mrs Caswell,' Mr Enright said uneasily, 'uh, well, perhaps you should consider sticking closer to the sixth-grade texts. The stress created by –'

'Oh!' Mrs Caswell said, feigning horror. 'I'm afraid it's too late, Mr Enright. Look at the poor dears! I'm afraid I've worked them to death.'

At this cue, every kid in the class fell forward on his desk, as if he had collapsed and died.

Mr Enright stood in startled silence for a moment, then broke into laughter, and all the kids laughed, too, and Mr Enright said, 'Mrs Caswell, you set me up! This was *staged*.'

'I confess,' she said, and the kids laughed harder.

'But how did you know that I'd be concerned about your pushing them past sixth-grade material?'

'Because everyone *always* underestimates kids,' Mrs Caswell said. 'The approved curriculum never challenges them. Everyone worries so much about psychological stress, about the problems associated with being an overachiever, that kids are encouraged to be *under*achievers. But I know kids, Mr Enright, and I tell you they're a much tougher, smarter bunch than anyone gives them credit for being. Am I right?'

The class loudly assured her that she was right.

Mr Enright looked around the room, pausing to study each child's face, and it was the first time all morning that he had really *looked* at them. At last he smiled. 'Mrs Caswell, this is a wonderful thing you've got going here.'

'Thank you,' Mrs Caswell said.

Mr Enright shook his head, smiled more broadly, and winked. 'Miss Attila the Hun indeed.'

At that moment Jamie was so proud of Mrs Caswell and so in love with her that he had to struggle valiantly to repress tears far more genuine that those of Melissa Fedder.

Now, on the last Monday morning in October, Jamie listened to Miss Attila the Hun, as she told them what medical science was like in the Middle Ages (crude) and what alchemy was (lead into gold and all sorts of crazy-fascinating stuff), and in a while he could no longer smell the chalk dust and child scents of the classroom but could *almost* smell the terrible, reeking, sewage-spattered streets of medieval Europe.

8

In his ten-foot-square office at the front of the house, Jack Caswell sat at an ancient, scarred pine desk, sipping coffee and rereading the chapter he had written the previous day. He made a lot of pencil corrections and then switched on his word processor to enter the changes on the diskette.

In the three years since his accident, unable to return to work as a game warden for the department of forestry, he had struggled to fulfill a lifelong desire to be a writer. (Sometimes, in his dreams, he could still see the big truck starting to slide on the ice-covered road, and he felt his own car entering a sickening spin, too, and the bright headlights were bearing down on him, and he pumped the brake pedal, turned the wheel into the slide, but he was always too late; even in the dreams he was always too late.) He had written four fast-paced detective novels in the last three years, two of which had sold to New York publishers, and he had also placed eight short stories in magazines.

Until Laura came along, his two great loves were the outdoors and books. Before the accident, he often had hiked miles up into the mountains, to places remote and serene, with his backpack half filled with food, half with paperbacks. Augmenting his supplies with berries and nuts and edible roots, he remained for days in the wilderness, alternately studying the wildlife and reading. He was equally a man of nature and of civilization; though it was difficult to bring nature into town, it was easy to carry civilization – in the form of books – into the wild heart of the forest, thereby allowing him to satisfy both halves of his cleft soul.

These days, cursed with legs that would never again support him on a journey into the hills, he had to be content with the pleasures of civilization – and, damn it, he had to make a better living with his writing. From the sales of eight stories and two well-reviewed novels spread over three years, he had not earned a third as much as Laura's modest teaching salary. He was a long way from reaching the bestsellers lists, and life at the lower end of the publishing business was far from glamorous. If he hadn't received a small disability pension from the department of forestry, they would have had trouble keeping themselves housed, clothed, and fed.

He remembered the worn brown cloth coat in which Laura had gone off to school that morning, and he felt sad. But the thought of her in that drab coat also made him more determined than ever to write a breakthrough book, earn a fortune, and buy her the luxuries that she deserved.

The strange thing was that if he had not been in the accident he would not have met Laura, would not have married her. She'd been at the hospital visiting a sick student, and on the way out she had seen Jack in the hall. He had been in a wheelchair, sullenly roaming the corridors. Laura was the most compassionate person Jack had ever known, and she was incapable of passing an obviously depressed man in a wheelchair without making an attempt to cheer him up. Filled with self-pity and anger, he rebuffed her, but rejection only made Laura try harder. He didn't know what a bulldog she was, but he learned. Two days later she returned to visit her student, and she paid a call on Jack as well, and soon she was coming every day just to see him. When he resigned himself to life in a wheelchair, Laura insisted that he work with a therapist every day and that he at least try to learn to walk with braces and a cane. When the therapist had only moderate success with him, Laura wheeled him, protesting, into the therapy room every day and put him through the exercises a second time. Before long her indomitable spirit and optimism infected Jack; he became determined to walk again, and then he *did* walk, and somehow learning to walk had led to love and to marriage. So the worst thing that had ever happened to him – the leg-crushing collision – had brought him to Laura, and she was far and away the *best* thing that had ever happened to him.

Screwy. Life sure was screwy.

In the new novel on which he was working, he was trying to write about that screwiness of life, the bizarre way that bad things could lead to blessings, while blessings sometimes ended in tragedy. He had a feeling that if he could thread that observation through a detective story in such a way as to explore the more profound aspects of it, he would have written not only a big money book but a book of which he could be proud as well.

He poured another cup of coffee and was about to start a new chapter when he looked out the window to the left of his desk and saw a dirty, dented Jeep wagon pull off the county road into his driveway.

Wondering who could be calling, he immediately levered himself up from the chair and grabbed his cane. He would need time to get to the front door, and he hated to keep people waiting.

He saw the Jeep Cherokee stop in front of the house. Both doors flew open, and two people got out, a man and a woman. Jack recognized the man – Teel Pleever – whom he knew slightly. Just about everyone in Pine County knew Pleever, but Jack figured that, like him, most folks didn't really know the man well. The woman was vaguely familiar to him. She was about thirty, attractive, and he thought perhaps she had a child in Laura's class and that he had seen her at a school function. In only a housedress and an apron, she was not properly clothed for the chilly October morning.

By the time Jack caned halfway across the office, his visitors began to knock on the front door.

9

Seed pulled off the highway as soon as it saw the next dwelling, for after centuries of dreamy half-life, it was eager to expand into more hosts. From Pleever, it knew that five thousand people lived in the town of Pineridge, which was where Seed intended to be by noon. Within two days, three at most, it would take over every one of the town's citizens, then would spread throughout Pine County, until it had seized the bodies and imprisoned the minds of all twenty thousand residents in that rural area.

Although spread among many hosts, Seed remained a single entity with a single consciousness. It could live simultaneously in tens of millions, hundreds of millions, in even *billions* of hosts, absorbing sensory input from billions of eyes and billions of ears and billions of noses, mouths, and hands, without risking confusion or information overload. In its countless millions of years of drifting through the galaxies, on the more than one hundred planets where it had thrived, Seed had never encountered another creature with its unique talent for physical schizophrenia.

It took its two captives out of the Jeep and marched them across the lawn to the front porch steps of the small white house.

From Pine County it would send its hosts outward, fanning across this continent, then to others, until every human being on the face of the earth had been claimed. Throughout this period, it would not destroy either the mind or individual personality of any host but would imprison each of them, while it used the host's body and store of knowledge to facilitate its conquest of the world. Teel Pleever, Jane Halliwell, and all the others would be horribly aware during their months of total enslavement, aware of the world around them, aware of the monstrous acts they were committing, and aware of Seed nesting within them.

Now it walked its two hosts up the porch steps and used Pleever to knock loudly on the front door.

When no man, woman, or child on earth remained free, Seed would move to the next stage, the Day of Release, suddenly allowing its hosts to resume control of their bodies, though in each of them would remain a part of the puppetmaster, always looking out through their eyes, always monitoring their thoughts. By the Day of Release, of course, at least half of the hosts would be insane. Others, having held onto their sanity in hope of eventual release from their torment, would be rocked by the realization that even after regaining control of themselves they must endure the cold, parasitical presence of the intruder forever; they, too, would then go slowly mad. That was what always happened. A smaller group would inevitably seek solace in religion, forming a socially disruptive cult that would worship Seed. And the smallest group of all, the tough ones, would stay sane and either adapt to Seed's presence or seek ways to evict it, a crusade that would not prove successful.

Seed rapped on the door again. Perhaps no one was at home.

'Coming, coming,' a man called from inside.

Ah, good.

Following the Day of Release, the fate of this sorry world would conform to the usual dark pattern: mass suicides, many millions of homicides committed by psychopathic madmen, complete and bloody social collapse, and an irreversible slide into anarchy, barbarism.

Chaos.

Creating chaos, spreading chaos, nurturing chaos, observing and relishing chaos were Seed's only purposes. The thing had been born in the genesis explosion at the start of time. Before that, it had been part of the supreme chaos of supercondensed matter in the time before time began. When that great undifferentiated ball of genesis matter exploded, the universe was formed and order began to be established in the void, but Seed was not part of that order. It was a remnant of pre-creation chaos; protected by an invincible shell, it drifted forth into the blossoming galaxies, in the service of entropy.

A man opened the door. He was leaning on a cane.

'Mr Pleever, isn't it?' he said.

From Jane Halliwell, Seed extruded black tendrils.

The man with the cane cried out as he was seized.

A blue-spotted, black stalk burst forth from Jane Halliwell's mouth, pierced the crippled man's chest, and in seconds Seed had its third host: Jack Caswell.

The man's legs had been so badly damaged in an accident that he wore metal braces. Because Seed did not want to be slowed down by a crippled host, it healed Caswell's body and shucked off the braces.

Drawing upon Caswell's knowledge, Seed discovered that no one else was at home. It also learned that Caswell's wife taught at an elementary school and that this school, containing at least a hundred and sixty children and their teachers, was only three miles away. Rather than stop at every dwelling on the road into Pineridge, it would be more effective to go directly to the school, seize control of everyone there, then spread out with all those hosts in every direction.

Jack Caswell, though imprisoned by Seed, was privy to his alien master's thoughts, for they shared the same cerebral tissue, the same neural pathways. Upon realizing that the school was to be attacked, Caswell's trapped mind squirmed violently, trying to slip free of his shackles.

Seed was surprised by the vigor and persistence with which the man resisted. With Pleever and the Halliwell woman, it had noticed that human beings – as they called themselves – possessed a far more powerful will than any species with which it had previously enjoyed contact. Now Caswell proved to have a considerably stronger will than either Pleever or Halliwell. Here was a species that obviously struggled relentlessly to make order out of chaos, that tried to make sense of existence, that was determined to *impose* order on the natural world by the sheer power of its will. Seed was going to take special pleasure in leading humankind into chaos, degeneration, and ultimately into devolution.

Seed shoved the man's mind into an even darker, tighter corner, and chained him more securely. Then, in the form of its three hosts, it set out for the elementary school.

10

Jamie Watley was always sort of embarrassed to ask Mrs Caswell for permission to go to the bathroom. He wanted her to think that he was special, wanted her to notice him in a way she did not notice the other kids, wanted her to love him as much as he loved her, but how could she think he was special if she knew he had to pee like any other boy? He realized he was being silly, of course. Having to go to the bathroom was nothing to be ashamed about. Everyone peed. Even Mrs Caswell –

No! He wouldn't think about that. Impossible.

But all through the history lesson he did keep thinking about his own need to pee, and by the time they were finished with history and halfway through maths, he could no longer contain himself.

'Yes, Jamie?'

'May I have a lavatory pass, Mrs Caswell?'

'Certainly, Jamie.'

The lavatory passes were on a corner of her desk, and he had to walk by her to reach them. He hung his head and refused to look at her because he didn't want her to see that he was blushing brightly. He snatched the pass off the desk and hurried into the hall.

Unlike other boys, he did not dawdle in the restroom. He was eager to get back to class so he could listen to Mrs Caswell's musical voice and watch her move back and forth through the room.

When he came out of the lav, three people were entering the end of the corridor through the outside door to the parking lot: a man dressed in hunting clothes, a woman in a house dress, and a guy in khaki pants and a maroon sweatshirt. They were an odd trio.

Jamie waited for them to pass because they looked as if they were in a hurry about something and might knock him down if he got in their way. Besides, he half suspected they would ask him where to find the principal or the school nurse or somebody important, and Jamie enjoyed being helpful. As they drew abreast of him, they turned suddenly toward him, as one.

He was snared.

11

Seed was now four.

By nightfall it would be thousands.

In its four parts, it walked down the hall toward the classroom to which Jamie Watley had been returning.

A year or two hence, when the entire population of the world had become part of Seed, when bloodshed and chaos were then initiated with the Day of Release, the thing would remain on the planet only a few weeks to witness firsthand the beginning of the human decline. Then it would form a new shell, fill that vessel with part of itself, and break free of the earth's gravity. Returning to the void, it would drift for tens of thousands or even millions of years until it found another likely world, where it would descend and await contact with a member of the dominant species.

During its cosmic journeying, Seed would remain in contact with the billions of parts of itself that it had left on earth, though only as long as those fragments had hosts to inhabit. In a way, therefore, it would never really leave this planet until the last human being had been destroyed centuries from now in a final act of chaotic violence, whereupon the one remaining bit of earthbound Seed would die with him. Or Seed would cease to exist on earth if the human species devolved into a lower lifeform that no longer possessed higher intelligence and was therefore no longer an agent of order in the universe.

Seed reached the door of Laura Caswell's classroom.

The minds of Jack Caswell and Jamie Watley, hot with anger and fear, tried to melt through the shackles in which Seed had bound them, and it had to pause for a moment to cool them down and establish full control. Their bodies twitched, and they made gurgling sounds as they tried to scream a warning. Seed was shocked by the rebellion that, while having no slightest chance of success, was nevertheless greater than any resistance it had ever encountered.

Exploring the minds of Jack and Jamie, Seed discovered

that their impressive, stubborn exercise of will had been powered not by fear for themselves but by fear for Laura Caswell, teacher of one and wife of the other. They were angry about their own enslavement, yes, but they were even angrier about Laura being possessed. They were both in love with her, and the purity of that love gave them the strength to resist the horror that had engulfed them.

Interesting. Seed had encountered the concept of love among half of the species that it had destroyed, but nowhere had it perceived the force of love as strongly as in these human beings. Now it realized, for the first time, that the will of an intelligent creature was not the only important power in the employ of universal order; love also fulfilled that function. And in a species that had both a strong will and an unusually well-developed ability to love, Seed had found the most formidable enemy of chaos.

Not formidable enough, of course. Seed was unstoppable, and by tomorrow night all of Pineridge would be absorbed.

Seed opened the classroom door. The four of it went inside.

12

Laura Caswell was surprised to see her husband enter the room with Linda Halliwell's mother, that old scoundrel Teel Pleever, and Jamie. She couldn't imagine what any of them, other than Jamie, was doing there. Then she realized that Jack was walking, actually *walking*, not shuffling, not dragging himself along stiff-legged, but walking easily like any man.

Before the wonder of Jack's recovery could sink in, before Laura could ask him what was going on, even as her students were turning in their seats to see what was happening, terror struck. Jamie Watley held his hands out toward a classmate, Tommy Albertson, and hideous, black, wormlike tendrils erupted from his fingertips. They lashed around Tommy and, as the snared boy cried out, a repulsive snakelike thing burst from Jamie's breastbone and pierced Tommy's chest, linking them obscenely.

The children screamed and pushed up from their desks to flee, but with astonishing speed they were attacked and silenced. The hateful, glossy worms and the thicker snakes spewed forth from Mrs Halliwell, Pleever, and from Jack as well, and to Laura's horror she saw three more of her nineteen students seized. Then suddenly Tommy Albertson and the other contaminated children were joining in the attack; the worms and snakes erupted from them, too, only seconds after they themselves had first been pierced.

Miss Garner, the teacher in the next room, stepped through the door to see what the shouting was about. She was taken before she could cry out.

In a single minute all but four thoroughly terrorized children had been taken firmly under the control of some nightmare organism. The four survivors – including Jane Halliwell's son Richie – gathered around Laura, two of them stunned into silence and two of them crying. She pushed the kids behind her, into a corner by the blackboard, and stood between them and the monstrosity that wanted them.

Fifteen possessed children, Pleever, Mrs Halliwell, Miss Garner and Jack gathered before her, staring at her. For a moment all were still and silent. In their eyes she saw not only reflections of their own tortured souls but the inhuman hunger of the thing that had taken control of them.

Laura was badly scared, and she was sick at heart to think of that glistening black *thing* curled inside her Jack, but she was not hobbled by either confusion or disbelief, for she had seen her share of the movies that, for decades, had been preparing the world for precisely this nightmare moment: *Invaders from Mars*, *Invasion of the Body Snatchers*, *The War of the Worlds*. She knew immediately that something from beyond the stars had at last found the earth.

The question was: could it be stopped – and how?

She realized that she was holding her blackboard pointer

as if it were a mighty sword and as if the nineteen alien-infected people in front of her would be kept at bay by such a useless weapon. Silly. Nevertheless, she did not cast the pointer aside but thrust it forward challengingly.

She was dismayed to see that her hand was shaking. She hoped that the four children crouching behind her were not aware that she was in the grip of terror.

From the possessed group that confronted her, three moved slowly forward: Jane Halliwell, Jamie Watley, and Jack.

'Stay back,' she warned.

They took another step toward her. . . .

Laura had broken out in a sweat. A bead of perspiration trickled down her right temple.

Mrs Halliwell, Jack, and Jamie advanced another step.

Suddenly they didn't seem to be as well controlled as the others, for they began to twitch and jerk with muscle spasms. Jack said 'Noooo', in a horrible, low, agonized voice. And Jane Halliwell said, 'Please, please', and shook her head as if to deny the orders she had been given. Jamie was trembling violently and holding his hands to his head as though trying to get at the thing inside him and wrench it out.

Why were these three being forced to complete the subjugation of the classroom? Why not others?

Laura's mind worked feverishly, sensing an advantage, searching for it, but not sure if she would recognize it when she found it. Perhaps the thing in Jane Halliwell wanted her to infect her own son Richie, who hid behind Laura's skirts, as a test of its control over the woman. And for the same reason it might want Jack to experience the horror of inducting his wife into this colony of the damned. As for poor Jamie . . . well, Laura was aware of the boy's fierce crush on her, so maybe he was being tested as well, to see if he could be made to attack the person he loved.

But if they had to be tested, that meant their master was not yet entirely certain of its dominance. And where it had doubt, surely its intended victims had hope.

13

Seed was impressed with the resistance that three of its hosts put up when the moment came to infect their loved ones.

The mother was furious at the thought of her son being brought into the fold. She pried at the restraints on her mind and struggled fiercely to regain her body. She posed a mildly difficult problem of control, but Seed squeezed her consciousness into an even tighter, darker place. It pushed her mind down, down, as if it were thrusting her into a pool of water, then it weighted her in that deep place as if placing heavy stones on a woman whom it had drowned and whom it wished not to be found.

Jamie Watley was equally troublesome, motivated as he was by pure, clean puppy love. But Seed reasserted authority over Jamie as well, stopped the boy's muscle spasms, and forced him forward toward the woman and children in the corner of the room.

The husband, Jack Caswell, was the most difficult of the three, for his will was the strongest, and his love was the most powerful. He raged against confinement, actually bent the bars of his mental prison, and would have gladly killed himself before taking Seed to Laura Caswell. For more than a minute he resisted his master's orders, and there was one startling moment when he seemed about to break free of control, but at last Seed squeezed him into full if grudging compliance.

The fourteen other captured children in Mrs Caswell's sixth-grade class were easily seized and controlled, although they also exhibited signs of rebellion. As the teacher backed into a corner, as the three chosen hosts approached her, a flutter of rage went through every child in the room, for they all loved and could not bear the thought of her possessed. Seed clamped down on them at once, hard, and their brief exertions of will faded like sparks on a cold wind.

Under the guidance of Seed, Jack Caswell stepped in front

of his wife. He tore the pointer out of her hand and threw it aside.

Seed burst from Jack Caswell's fingertips, seized Laura, and held her, though she struggled fiercely to pull free. Opening the mouth of its host, Seed shot forth a thick stalk, pierced the woman's breast, surged into her, triumphant.

14

No!

Laura felt it slithering along the paths of her nerves, questing coldly in her brain, and she denied it. With the iron determination she had brought to her campaign to make Jack walk, with the unlimited patience she brought to the instruction of her students, with the unshakable sense of self-worth and individuality with which she faced every day of her life, she fought the thing at every turn. When it cast restraining bands of psychic energy around her mind, she snapped them and threw them off. When it tried to drag her down into a dark place and imprison her there under psychic stones, she threw off those weights as well and soared to the surface. She sensed the thing's surprise, and she took advantage of its confusion, delving into *its* mind, learning about it. In an instant she realized that it was in contact with the minds of all its hosts simultaneously, so she reached out to Jack and found him –

– *I love you, Jack, I love you more than life itself* –

– and she tore at his mental bonds with all the enthusiasm that she had shown when assisting him in therapeutic exercises for his ruined legs. Questing outward across the psychic net by which Seed linked its hosts, she found Jamie Watley –

– *You're a sweet kid, Jamie, the sweetest, and I've always wanted to tell you that it doesn't matter what your parents are, doesn't matter if they're alcoholics and poor; what matters is that you have the capacity to be far better than them; you have the capacity to love and to learn and to know the joy of a fulfilling life –*

– and Seed swarmed over her, trying to draw her back into her own body, where it could restrain her. However in spite of its billions of years of experience and its vast knowledge acquired from a hundred doomed species, Laura examined it and judged it inferior because it did not need love, could not give love. Its will was weaker than human will because humans could love, and in their love they found a reason to strive, a reason to seek order out of chaos, to make better lives for those they cherished. Love gave purpose to will and made it infinitely stronger. To some species, Seed might actually be a welcome master, offering the false security of a single purpose, a single law. But to humankind, Seed was anathema –

– *Tommy, you can tear loose if you'll think of your sister Edna, because I know you love Edna more than anything; and you, Melissa, you must think of your father and mother because they love you so much, because they almost lost you when you were a baby (did you know that?) and losing you would have broken them; and you, Helen, you're one heck of a little girl, and I couldn't love you more if you were my own, you have such a sweet concern for others, and I know you can throw this damn thing off because you're all love from head to toe; and you, Jane Halliwell, I know you love your son and your husband because your love for Richie is so evident in the self-confidence you've given him and in the manners and courtesy you've taught him; you, Jimmy Corman, oh, yes, you talk tough and you act tough, but I know how much you love your brother Harry and how sad it makes you that Harry was born with a deformed hand, and I know that if someone made fun of poor Harry's twisted hand, you'd fight them with every bit of strength you have, so turn that love for Harry against this thing, this Seed, and destroy it, don't let it have you because if it gets you then it'll get Harry, too –*

– and Laura walked forth into the room, among the possessed, touching them, hugging this one, lovingly squeezing the hand of that one, looking into their eyes and using the power of love to bring them to her, out of their darkness and into the light with her.

15

As he shattered the bonds that held him and cast off Seed, Jamie Watley experienced a wave of dizziness and actually blacked out for a moment, just for an instant, not even long enough to collapse to the floor. Blackness flickered through him, and he swayed, but he came to his senses as his knees were buckling. He grabbed the edge of Mrs Caswell's desk and steadied himself.

When he looked around the classroom, he saw the adults and the other children in similar shaky postures. Many of them were looking down in disgust, and Jamie saw that they were staring at the slick, mucous-wet, black substance of Seed, which had been expelled from them and which writhed in pieces on the classroom floor.

Most of those masses of alien tissue seemed to be dying, and a few were actually decomposing with an awful stench. But suddenly one lump coalesced into the shape of a football. In seconds it formed a mottled blue-green-black shell, and as if bazooka-shot, it exploded up through the ceiling of the room, showering them with plaster and bits of lath. It smashed through the roof of the one-story schoolhouse and disappeared straight up into the blue October sky.

16

Teachers and kids came from all over the building to find out what had happened, and later the police came, and the following day both uniformed Air Force officers and plainclothes government men visited the Caswell house among others. Throughout, Jack would not move far from Laura. He preferred to hold her or least her hand, and when they had to separate for a few minutes, he held fast to a mental picture of her, as if that image were a psychic totem that insured her safe return.

Eventually the furor subsided, and the reporters went away, and life returned to normal – or as close to normal as it would ever be. By Christmas, Jack's nightmares began to diminish in both frequency and vividness, though he knew that he would need years to scrub out the residue of fear that was left from Seed's possession of him.

On Christmas Eve, sitting on the floor in front of the tree, sipping wine and eating walnuts, he and Laura exchanged gifts, for Christmas Day itself was always reserved for visiting their families. When the packages had been opened, they moved to a pair of armchairs in front of the fireplace.

After sitting quietly for a while, sipping at a final glass of wine and watching the flames, Laura said, 'I've got one more gift that will have to be opened soon.'

'One more? But I've nothing more for you.'

'This is a gift for everyone,' she said.

Her smile was so enigmatic that Jack was instantly intrigued. He leaned sideways in his chair and reached for her hand. 'What're you being so mysterious about?'

'The thing healed you,' she said.

His legs were propped on a hassock, as healthy and useful as they had been before his accident.

'At least some good came of it,' he said.

'More than you know,' she said. 'During those awful moments when I was trying to expel the thing from my mind and body, while I was trying to get the kids to expel it from theirs, I was acutely aware of the creature's own mind. Heck, I was *within* its mind. And since I'd noticed that you were healed and figured it must have been responsible for knitting up your legs, I poked around in its thoughts to see how it had worked that miracle.'

'You don't mean –'

'Wait,' she said, pulling her hand from his. She slipped off her chair, dropped to her knees, leaned toward the fireplace, and thrust her right hand into the leaping flames.

Jack cried out, grabbed her, and pulled her back.

Grinning, Laura held up blistered fingers as raw as butchered beef, but even as Jack gasped in horror he saw that her flesh was healing. In moments the blisters faded, the skin reformed, and her hand was undamaged.

'The power's within all of us,' she said. 'We just have to learn how to use it. I've spent the past two months learning, and now I'm ready to teach others. You first, then my kids at school, then the whole darn world.'

Jack stared at her in astonishment.

She laughed with delight and threw herself into his arms. 'It's not easy to learn, Jackson. Oh, no! It's hard. It's very hard. You don't know how many nights I've sat up while you slept, working at it, trying to apply what I learned from Seed. There were times when my head felt as if it would burst with the effort, and trying to master the healing talent leaves you physically exhausted in a way I've never been before. It hurts all the way down in your bones. There were times when I despaired. But I learned. And others can learn. No matter how hard it is, I know I can teach them. I know I can, Jack.'

Regarding her with love but also with a new sense of wonder, Jack said, 'Yeah, I know you can, too. I know you can teach anything to anyone. You may be the greatest teacher who ever lived.'

'Miss Attila the Hun,' she said, and she kissed him.

Hardshell

1

Arteries of light pulsed in the black sky. In that stroboscopic blaze, millions of cold raindrops appeared to have halted in mid-fall. The glistening street reflected the celestial fire and for a moment seemed to be paved with broken mirrors. Then the lightning-scored sky went black again, and the rain resumed. The pavement was dark. Once more the flesh of the night pressed close on all sides.

Clenching his teeth and trying to ignore the pain in his right side, squinting in the gloom, Detective Frank Shaw gripped the Smith & Wesson .38 Chief's Special in both hands. He assumed a shooter's stance and squeezed off two shots.

Ahead of Frank, Karl Skagg sprinted around the corner of the nearest warehouse just in time to save himself. The first slug bored a hole in the empty air behind him; the second clipped the corner of the building.

The relentless roar of the rain on metal warehouse roofs and on the pavement, combined with rumbling thunder, effectively muffled the shots. Even if private security guards were at work in the immediate area, they probably had not heard anything, so Frank could not expect assistance.

He would have welcomed assistance. Skagg was big, powerful, a serial killer who had committed at least twenty-two murders. The guy was incredibly dangerous even in his best moments, and right now he was about as approachable as a whirling buzzsaw. This was definitely not a job for one cop.

Frank considered returning to his car and putting in a call

for backup, but he knew that Skagg would slip away before the area could be cordoned off. No cop would call off a chase merely out of concern for his own welfare – especially not Frank Shaw.

Splashing across the puddled serviceway between two of the huge warehouses, Frank took the corner wide, in case Skagg was waiting for him just around the bend. But Skagg was gone.

Unlike the front of the warehouse, where concrete loading ramps sloped up to the enormous rolling garage doors, this side was mostly blank. Two hundred feet away, below a dimly glowing bulb in a wire security cage, was a single, man-size metal door. It was half-open but falling shut.

Wincing at the pain in his side, Frank hurried to the entrance. He was surprised to see that the handle was torn off and that the lock was shattered, as if Skagg had used a crowbar or sledgehammer. But the man had been empty-handed. Had he found a tool leaning against the warehouse wall, and had he used it to batter his way inside? He had been out of sight for mere seconds, no more than half a minute, which surely wasn't enough time to break through a steel door.

Why hadn't the burglar alarm sounded? Surely the warehouse was protected by an electronic security system. And Skagg had not entered with sufficient finesse to circumvent an alarm.

Thoroughly soaked, Frank shivered involuntarily when he put his back to the cold wall beside the door. He gritted his teeth, willed himself to stop shaking, and listened intently.

He heard only the hollow drumming of rain on metal roofs and walls. The sizzle of rain dancing on the wet pavement. The gurgle and slurp and chuckle of rain in gutters and downspouts.

Wind bleating. Wind hissing.

Frank broke the cylinder out of his revolver. He reached under his jacket and plucked four cartridges from the row of ten that were held in leather loops along the rim of his custom-designed shoulder holster. He quickly reloaded.

His right side throbbed. Minutes ago Skagg had taken him by surprise, stepping out of shadows, swinging a length of two-by-four as Mickey Mantle might have swung a baseball bat. Frank felt as if chunks of broken glass were working against one another in his deep muscles and bones, and the pain sharpened slightly each time he drew a breath. Maybe he had a broken rib or two. Probably not . . . but maybe. He was wet, cold, and weary.

He was also having fun.

2

To other homicide detectives, Frank was known as Hardshell Shaw. That was also what his buddies had called him during Marine Corps basic training more than twenty-five years ago, for he was stoical, tough, and could not be cracked. The name followed him when he left the service and joined the Los Angeles Police Department. He never encouraged anyone to use the sobriquet, but they used it anyway because it was apt.

Frank was tall, wide in the shoulders, narrow in the waist and hips, with a rock-solid body. His enormous hands, when curled into fists, were so formidable that he usually needed only to brandish them to assure an adversary's cooperation. His broad face appeared to have been carved out of granite – and with some difficulty, with much breaking of chisels and snapping of hammers. His colleagues in the homicide division of the LAPD sometimes claimed that Frank had only two basic expressions: mean and meaner.

His pale blue eyes, clear as rainwater, regarded the world with icy suspicion. When thinking, he frequently sat or stood perfectly still for long periods during which the quickness and alertness of his blue eyes, contrasted with his immobility, gave the impression that he was peering out from within a shell.

He had a damn hard shell, so his friends claimed. But that was only half of what they said about him.

Now, finished reloading his revolver, he stepped in front of the damaged warehouse door. He kicked it open. Crouched, head tucked down, holding the .38 in front of him, he went in fast, looking left and right, expecting Skagg to rush at him with a crowbar, hammer, or whatever tool the scumbag had used to get into the building.

To Frank's left was a twenty-foot-high wall of metal shelving filled with thousands of small boxes. To his right were large wooden crates stacked in rows, towering thirty feet overhead, extending half the length of the building, alternating with avenues wide enough to admit forklifts.

The banks of overhead fluorescents suspended from the fifty-foot-high warehouse ceiling were switched off. Only a few security lamps in conical tin shades shed a wan glow over the stored goods below, leaving most of the place sheathed in shadows.

Frank moved cautiously and silently. His soggy shoes squished, but that sound was barely audible over the background drumming of rain on the roof. With water dripping off his brow, jawline, and the barrel of his gun, he eased from one row of crates to another, peering into each passageway.

Skagg was at the far end of the third aisle, about a hundred and fifty feet away, half in shadow, half in milk-pale light, waiting to see if Frank had followed him. He could have kept out of the light, could have crouched entirely in the gloom against the crates, where he might not have been visible; by waiting in plain sight, he seemed to be taunting Frank. Skagg hesitated a moment, as if to be sure that he had been spotted, then disappeared around the corner.

For five minutes they played hide and seek, moving stealthily through the maze of cartons and crates. Three times, Skagg allowed himself to be seen, although he never let Frank get close.

He's having fun, too, Frank thought.

That made him angry.

High on the walls, under the cobweb-festooned eaves, were slit windows that helped illuminate the cavernous building during the day. Now only the flicker of lightning revealed the existence of those narrow windows. Although that inconstant pulse did not brighten the warehouse, it occasionally caused shadows to leap disconcertingly, and twice Frank nearly shot one of those harmless phantoms.

Easing along another avenue, scanning the shadows on both sides, Frank heard a noise, a hard scraping sound. He knew at once what it was: a crate sliding on a crate.

He looked up. In the grayness high above, a sofa-size box – visible only as a black silhouette – teetered on the edge of the crate beneath it. Then it tipped over and plummeted straight toward him.

He threw himself forward, hit the floor, and rolled just as the crate exploded against the concrete where he had been standing. He averted his face as the wood disintegrated into hundreds of splintery shards of shrapnel. The box had contained plumbing fixtures; bright, chrome-plated faucets and shower heads bounced along the floor, and a couple of them thumped off Frank's back and thighs.

Hot tears of agony burned in his eyes, for the pain in his right side flared brighter. Further abused by all of this activity, his battered ribs now seemed not merely broken but pulverized.

Overhead Skagg let out a sound that was one part a cry of rage, one part an animalistic ululation celebrating the thrill of the hunt, and one part insane laughter.

With some sixth sense Frank was suddenly aware of a murderous, descending weight. He rolled to his right, flat up against the same wall of crates atop which Skagg stood. Behind him, a second huge box crashed into the warehouse floor.

'You alive?' Skagg called.

Frank did not respond.

'Yeah, you must be down there because I didn't hear you scream. You're a quick bastard, aren't you?'

That laugh again. It was like atonal music played on an out-of-tune flute: a cold, metallic sound. There was something inhuman about it. Frank Shaw shivered.

Surprise was Frank's favorite strategy. During a pursuit, he tried to do what his prey would least expect. Now, taking advantage of the masking roar of the rain on the corrugated steel roof, he stood up in the darkness beside the wall of crates, holstered his revolver, blinked the tears of pain out of his eyes, and began to climb.

'Don't cower in the shadows like a rat,' Skagg shouted. 'Come out and try to take a shot at me. You've got a gun; I don't. It'll be your bullets against whatever I can throw at you. What better odds do you want, you chickenshit cop?'

Twenty feet up the thirty-foot-high wall of wooden boxes, with his chilled fingers hooked into meager niches, with the toes of his shoes pressed hard against narrow ledges, Frank paused. The pain in his right side tightened as if it were a lasso, and it threatened to pull him backward into the aisle almost two stories below. He clung desperately to his precarious position and squeezed his eyes tightly shut, willing the pain to go away.

'Hey, asshole!' Skagg shouted.

Yeah?

'You know who I am?'

Big man on the psycho circuit, aren't you?

'I'm the one the newspapers call the Night Slasher.'

Yeah, I know, I know, you drooling degenerate.

'This whole damn city lays awake at night, worrying about me, wondering where I am,' Skagg shouted.

Not the whole city, man. Personally I haven't lost any sleep over you.

Gradually the hot, grinding pain in his ribs subsided. It did not disappear altogether, but now it was a dull throb.

Among friends in the marines and on the police force,

Frank had a reputation for persevering and triumphing in spite of wounds that would have incapacitated anyone else. In the Nam he had taken two bullets from a Vietcong machine-gun, one in the left shoulder and one through his left side directly above the kidney, but he had kept on going and had wasted the gunner with a grenade. Bleeding profusely, he nevertheless used his good arm to drag his badly wounded buddy three hundred yards to a place of concealment, where they were safe from enemy snipers while the Medevac chopper sought and found them. As the medics loaded him into the helicopter, he had said, 'War is hell, all right, but it's also damned exhilarating!'

His friends said he was iron-hard, nail-tough. But that was only part of what they said about him.

Overhead, Karl Skagg hurried along the top of the boxes. Frank was close enough to hear the man's heavy footsteps above the ceaseless rumble of rain on the roof.

Even if he had heard nothing, he would have known that Skagg was on the move, for the two-crate-thick wall trembled with the killer's passage. The movement was not violent enough to shake Frank off his perch.

He started to climb again, feeling cautiously for handholds in the darkness, inching along the pile of plumbing supplies. He got a few splinters in his fingers, but it was easy to tune out those small, stabbing pains.

From his new position atop the wall, Skagg shouted into another shadowy section of the warehouse to which he apparently thought Frank had moved, 'Hey, chickenshit!'

You called?

'I have something for you, chickenshit.'

I didn't know we were exchanging gifts.

'I got something sharp for you.'

I'd prefer a TV set.

'I got the same thing for you that I used on all the others.'

Forget the TV. I'll settle for a nice bottle of cologne.

'Come and get your guts ripped out, you chickenshit!'

I'm coming. I'm coming.

Frank reached the top, raised his head above the edge of the wall, looked left, then right, and saw Skagg about thirty feet away. The killer had his back to Frank and was peering intently down into another aisle.

'Hey, look at me, standing right up here in the light. You can hit me with no trouble, cop. All you have to do is step out and line up a shot. What's the matter? Don't you even have the nerve for that, you yellow bastard?'

Frank waited for a peal of thunder. When it came, he levered himself over the edge, on top of the stack of crates, where he rose to a crouch. The pounding rain was even louder up here, and combined with the thunder it was enough to cover any noise he made.

'Hey, down there! You know who I am, cop?'

You're repeating yourself. Boring, boring.

'I'm a real prize, the kind of trophy a cop dreams of!'

Yeah, your head would look good on my den wall.

'Big career boost if you brought me down, promotions and medals, you chickenshit.'

The ceiling lights were only ten feet above their heads, and at such short range even the dim bulbs in the security lamps cast enough of a glow to illuminate more than half of the crates on which they stood. Skagg was in the brightest spot, posturing for the one-man audience that he believed was below him.

Drawing his .38, Frank stepped forward, out of a shadowy area into a fall of amber light.

Skagg shouted, 'If you won't come for me, you chickenshit, I'll come for you.'

'Who're you calling chickenshit?' Frank asked.

Startled, Skagg spun toward him and, for an instant, teetered on the edge of the boxes. He windmilled his arms to keep from falling backward into the aisle below.

Holding his revolver in both hands, Frank said, 'Spread your arms, drop to your knees, then lay flat on your belly.'

Karl Skagg had none of that heavy-browed, slab-jawed, mongoloid, cement-faced look that most people associated with homicidal maniacs. He was handsome. Movie-star handsome. His was a broad, well-sculpted face with masculine yet sensitive features. His eyes were not like the eyes of a snake or a lizard or some other wild thing, either, but were brown, clear and appealing.

'Flat on your belly,' Frank repeated.

Skagg did not move. But he grinned. The grin ruined his movie-star looks, for it had no charm. It was the humorless leer of a crocodile.

The guy was big, even bigger than Frank. He was six five, maybe even six and a half feet. Judging by the solid look of him, he was a dedicated, lifelong weightlifter. In spite of the chilly November night, he wore only running shoes, jeans, and blue cotton shirt. Damp with rain and sweat, the shirt molded to his muscular chest and arms.

He said, 'So how're you going to get me down from here, cop? Do you think I'll let you cuff me and then just lay up here while you go for backup? No way, pig face.'

'Listen and believe me: I'll blow you away without the slightest hesitation.'

'Yeah? Well, I'll take that gun off you quicker than you think. Then I'll rip your head off and shove it up your ass.'

With unconcealed distaste, Frank said, 'Is it really necessary to be so vulgar?'

Grinning more broadly, Skagg moved toward him.

Frank shot him pointblank in the chest.

The hard report echoed off the metal walls, and Skagg was thrown backward. Screaming, he pitched off the crates and plummeted into the aisle below. He landed with a *thunk* that cut off his scream.

Skagg's violent departure caused the crates to rock, and for a moment the unmortared wall of boxes swayed dangerously, creaking and grinding. Frank fell to his hands and knees. Waiting for the stacks to steady under him, he thought about all the paperwork involved in a shooting of this sort, the many forms required to appease the bleeding hearts who were always certain that every victim of a police shooting was as innocent as Mother Teresa. He wished Skagg had not forced the issue so soon. He wished the killer had been more clever, had managed a more involved game of cat and mouse before the climactic scene. The chase had not provided half enough fun to compensate for the mountain of paperwork ahead.

The crates quickly steadied, and Frank got to his feet. He moved to the edge of the wall, to the place where Skagg had been flung into empty space by the impact of the slug. He looked down into the aisle. The concrete floor was silvery in the glow of the security lamp.

Skagg was not there.

Storm light flickered at the windows in the warehouse eaves. At his side Frank's shadow leaped, shrank back, leaped, and shrank again, as if it were the shadow of Alice in one of her potion-swilling fits beyond the looking glass.

Thunder pummeled the night sky, and an even harder fall of rain pummeled the roof.

Frank shook his head, squinted into the aisle below, and blinked in disbelief.

Skagg was still not there.

3

Having descended the crates with caution, Frank Shaw looked left and right along the deserted aisle. He studied the shadows intently, then crouched beside the spots and smears of blood where Karl Skagg had hit the floor. At least a liter of blood marked the point of impact, so fresh that a portion had still not soaked into the porous concrete but glistened in small, red, shallow puddles.

No man could take a .38 slug in the chest at pointblank

range, get up immediately, and walk away. No man could fall three stories onto concrete and spring straight to his feet.

Yet that seemed to be what Skagg had done.

A trail of gore indicated the man's route. With his .38 gripped tightly in his right hand, Frank traced the psycho to an intersection, turned left into a new aisle, and moved stealthily through alternating pools of shadow and light for a hundred and fifty feet. There, he came to the end of the blood trail, which simply stopped in the middle of the passageway.

Frank peered up at the piled crates on both sides, but Skagg was not clinging to either partition. No offshoot passageways between the boxes and no convenient niches provided a good hiding place.

Though badly hurt and hurrying to get out of his pursuer's reach, Skagg appeared to have carefully bound his grievous wounds to control the bleeding, had literally bound them on the run. But with what? Had he torn his shirt into strips to make tourniquets, bandages?

Damn it, Skagg had a mortal chest wound. Frank had seen the terrible impact of bullet in flesh, had seen Skagg hurled backward, had seen blood. The man's breastbone was shattered, splinters driven inward through vital organs. Arteries and veins were severed. The slug itself surely had passed through Skagg's heart. Neither tourniquets nor bandages could stanch that flow or induce mangled cardiac muscles to resume rhythmic contractions.

Frank listened to the night.

Rain, wind, thunder. Otherwise . . . silence.

Dead men don't bleed, Frank thought.

Maybe that was why the blood trail ended where it did – because Skagg died after going that far. But if he had died, death had not stopped him. He had kept right on going.

And now what am I chasing? A dead man who won't give up?

Most cops would have laughed off such a thought, embarrassed by it. Not Frank. Being tough, hard, and unbreakable did not mean that he had to be inflexible as well. He had the utmost respect for the incomprehensible complexity of the universe and for the unplumbable mystery of life.

A walking dead man? Unlikely. But if that *was* the case, then the situation was certainly interesting. Fascinating. Suddenly Frank was more thoroughly involved in his work than he had been in weeks.

4

The warehouse was vast but, of course, finite. As Frank explored the gloom-filled place, however, the chilly interior somehow seemed to be larger than the space enclosed by its walls, as if portions of the building extended into another dimension, or as if the actual size of the structure changed magically and constantly to conform to his exaggerated perception of its immensity.

He searched for Skagg in aisles formed by crates and along other aisles between towering metal shelves filled with cardboard cartons. He stopped repeatedly to test the lids of crates, suspecting that Skagg had hidden in an empty one, but he found no makeshift coffin belonging to the walking dead man.

Twice he briefly suspended the search to take time to stay in touch with the throbbing pain in his side. Intrigued by the mystery of Skagg's disappearance, he had forgotten being hammered with a two-by-four. His extraordinary ability to block pain contributed to his hardboiled reputation. A buddy in the department once said that Hardshell Shaw's pain threshold was between that of a rhinoceros and a wooden fence post. But there were times when experiencing pain to the fullest was desirable. For one thing pain sharpened his senses and kept him alert. Pain was humbling as well; it encouraged a man to keep his perspective, helped him to remember that life was precious. He was no masochist, but he knew that pain was a vital part of the human condition.

Fifteen minutes after having shot Skagg, Frank still hadn't found him. Nevertheless he remained convinced that the killer was in the warehouse, dead or alive, and had not fled into the rainy night. His conviction was based on more than a hunch; he possessed the reliable intuition that distinguished great cops from good cops.

A moment later, when his intuition proved unnervingly accurate, Frank was exploring a corner of the building where twenty forklifts of various sizes were parked beside a dozen electric carts. Because of their knobby hydraulic joints and blunt tines, the lifts resembled enormous insects, and in the smoky yellow glow of the overhead lamp, they cast praying mantis silhouettes across other machinery. Frank was moving quietly through those spikey shadows when behind him Karl Skagg spoke:

'You looking for me?'

Frank whipped around, bringing his gun up.

Skagg was about twelve feet away.

'See me?' the killer asked.

His chest was intact, unwounded.

'See me?'

His three-story fall had resulted in no shattered bones, no crushed flesh. His blue cotton shirt was stained with blood, but the source of those stains was not visible.

'*See me?*'

'I see you,' Frank said.

Skagg grinned. 'You know *what* you're seeing?'

'A piece of shit.'

'Can your small mind possibly conceive of my true nature?'

'Sure. You're a dog turd.'

'You can't offend me,' Skagg said.

'I can try.'

'Your petty opinions are of no interest or concern to me.'

'God forbid that I should bore you.'

'You're getting tiresome.'

'And you're nuts.'

Skagg cracked an icy, humorless smile of the sort that earlier had reminded Frank of a crocodile's grin. 'I'm so far superior to you and to all of your kind that you're incapable of judging me.'

'Oh, then forgive me for my presumption, great lord.'

Skagg's grin faded into a vicious grimace, and his eyes widened. They no longer seemed like ordinary brown eyes. In the dark depths of them, a strangeness appeared: a hungry, chillingly reptilian watchfulness that made Frank feel as if he were a fieldmouse staring into the mesmeric eyes of a blacksnake.

Skagg took one step forward.

Frank took one step backward.

'Your kind have only one use: you're interesting prey.'

'Well, I'm glad to hear we're interesting.'

Skagg took another step forward, and a portion of a mantislike shadow rippled across his face.

Frank stepped backward.

'Your kind are born to die.'

Always interested in the working of a criminally insane mind, just as a surgeon is always interested in the nature of the cancers that he excises from his patients' bodies, Frank said, 'My kind, huh? What kind is that exactly?'

'Humankind.'

'Ah.'

'Humankind,' Skagg repeated, speaking the word as if it were the vilest epithet.

'You're not human? Is that it?'

'That's it,' Skagg agreed.

'What are you then?'

Skagg's insane laughter was as affecting as hard arctic wind.

Feeling as if bits of ice had begun to form in his bloodstream, Frank shivered. 'All right, enough of this. Drop to your knees, then flat on your face.'

'You're so slow-witted,' Skagg said.

'Now *you're* boring *me*. Lie down and spread your arms and legs, you son of a bitch.'

Skagg reached out with his right hand in such a way that for one disconcerting moment it seemed to Frank that the killer was going to change tactics and begin pleading for his life.

Then the hand began to change. The palm grew longer and broader. The fingers lengthened by as much as two inches, and the knuckles became thicker, gnarled. The hand darkened until it was a singularly unhealthy, mottled brown-black-yellow. Coarse hairs sprouted from the skin. The fingernails extended into wickedly sharp claws.

'So tough you were. Imitation Clint Eastwood. But you're afraid now, aren't you, little man? You're afraid at last, aren't you?'

Only the hand changed. No alterations occurred in Skagg's face or body or even in his other hand. He obviously had complete control of his metamorphosis.

'Werewolf,' Frank said in astonishment.

With another peal of lunatic laughter that rebounded tinnily from the warehouse walls, Skagg worked his new hand, curling and extending and recurling his monstrous fingers.

'No. Not a werewolf,' he whispered fiercely. 'Something far more adaptable. Something infinitely stranger and more interesting. Are you afraid now? Have you wet your pants yet, you chickenshit cop?'

Skagg's hand began to change again. Coarse hairs receded into the flesh that had sprouted them. The mottled skin grew darker still, the many colours blending into green-black, and scales began to appear. The fingertips thickened and grew broader, and suction pads formed on them. Webs spun into being between the fingers. The claws subtly changed shape, but they were no shorter or less sharp than the lupine claws had been.

Skagg peered at Frank through those hideous spread fingers and over the half-moon curves of the opaque webs. Then he lowered his hand slightly and grinned; his mouth had also changed. His lips were thin, black, and pebbled. He revealed pointed teeth and two hooked fangs. A thin, glistening, fork-tipped tongue flicked across those teeth, licked the pebbled lips.

At the sight of Frank's horrified astonishment, Skagg laughed. His mouth once more assumed the appearance of a human mouth.

But the hand underwent yet another metamorphosis. The scales were transformed into a hard-looking, smooth, purple-black, chitinous substance, and the fingers, as if made of wax and now brought before a flame, melted together, five into two, till Skagg's wrist terminated in a serrated, razor-sharp pincer.

'You see? No need of a knife for this Night Slasher,' whispered Skagg. 'Within my hands are an infinite variety of blades.'

Frank kept his .38 revolver pointed at this adversary, though by now he knew that even a .357 Magnum loaded with magnum cartridges with Teflon tips would provide him with no protection.

Outside, the sky was split by an ax of lighting. The flash of the electric blade sliced through the narrow windows high above the warehouse floor. For a moment a flurry of rafter shadows fell upon Frank and Skagg.

As thunder crashed across the night, Frank said, 'What the hell are you?'

Skagg did not answer right away. He stared at Frank for a long moment and seemed perplexed. When he spoke his voice had a double-honed edge – curiosity and anger. 'Your species is soft. Your kind have no nerve, no guts. Faced with the unknown, your kind react as sheep react to the scent of a wolf. I despise your weakling breed. The strongest men break after what I've revealed. They scream like children, flee in panic, or stand paralyzed and speechless with fear. But not you. What makes you different? What makes you so brave? Are you simply thickheaded? Don't you realize you're a dead man? Are you foolish enough to think you'll get out of this place alive? Look at you – your gun hand isn't even trembling.'

'I've had more frightening experiences than this,' Frank said tightly. 'I've been through two tax audits.'

Skagg did not laugh. He clearly needed a terrified reaction from an intended victim. Murder was not sufficiently satisfying; evidently he also required the complete humiliation and abasement of his prey.

Well, you bastard, you're not going to get what you need from me, Frank thought.

He repeated, 'What the hell are you?'

Clacking the halves of his deadly pincers, slowly taking a step toward Frank, Karl Skagg said, 'Maybe I'm the spawn of hell. Do you think that could be the explanation? Hmmmm?'

'Stay back,' Frank warned.

Skagg took another step toward him. 'Am I a demon perhaps, risen from some sulfurous pit? Do you feel a certain coldness in your soul; do you sense the nearness of something satanic?'

Frank bumped against one of the forklifts, stepped around the obstruction, and continued to retreat.

Advancing, Skagg said, 'Or am I something from another world, a creature alien to this one, conceived under a different moon, born under another sun?'

As he spoke, his right eye receded deep into his skull, dwindled, vanished. The socket closed up as the surface of a pond would close around the hole made by a pebble; only smooth skin lay where the eye had been.

'Alien? Is that something of which you could conceive?' Skagg pressed. 'Have you sufficient wit to accept that perhaps I came to this world across an immense sea of space, carried on strange galactic tides?'

Frank no longer wondered how Skagg had battered open the door of the warehouse, he would have made hornlike hammers of his hands – or ironlike prybars. And he no doubt had also slipped incredibly thin extensions of his fingertips into the alarm switch, deactivating it.

The skin of Skagg's left cheek dimpled, and a hole formed in it. The lost right eye flowered into existence within that hole, directly under his left eye. In two winks both eyes re-formed: they were no longer human but insectile, bulging and multi-faceted.

As if changes were taking place in his throat, too, Skagg's voice lowered and became gravelly. 'Demon, alien . . . or maybe I'm the result of some genetic experiment gone terribly wrong. Hmmmm? What do you think?'

That laugh again. Frank *hated* that laugh.

'What do you think?' Skagg insisted as he approached.

Retreating, Frank said, 'I think you're probably none of those things. Like you said . . . I think you're stranger and more interesting than that.'

Both of Skagg's hands had become pincers now. The metamorphosis continued up his muscular arms as his human form gave way to a more crustaceous anatomy. The seams of his shirt sleeves split; then the shoulder seams also tore as the transformation continued into his upper body. Chitinous accretions altered the size and shape of his chest, and his shirt buttons popped loose.

Though Frank knew he was wasting ammunition, he fired three shots as rapidly as he could squeeze the trigger. One round took Skagg in the stomach, one in the chest, one in the throat. Flesh tore, bones cracked, blood flew. The shapechanger staggered backward but did not go down.

Frank saw the bullet holes and knew a man would die instantly of those wounds. Skagg merely swayed. Even as he regained his balance, his flesh began to knit up again. In half a minute the wounds had vanished.

With cracking and wet oozing noises, Skagg's skull swelled to twice its previous size, though the change had nothing to do with the revolver fire that the shapechanger had absorbed. His face seemed to *implode*, all the features collapsing inward, but almost at once a mass of tissue bulged outward and began to form queer insectile features.

Frank did not wait to see the grotesque details of Skagg's new countenance. He fired two more rounds at the man's alarmingly plastic face, then turned and ran, leaped over an electric cart, dodged around a big forklift, sprinted into an aisle between tall metal shelves, and tried *not* to feel the pain in his side as he ran back through the long warehouse.

When that morning had begun, dreary and rainswept, with traffic moving through the city's puddled streets at a crawl, with the palm trees dripping, with the buildings all somber-looking in the gray storm light, Frank had thought that the spirit of the day was going to be as soggy and grim as the weather, uneventful and boring and perhaps even depressing. Surprise. Instead the day had turned out to be exciting, interesting, even exhilarating. You just never knew what fate had in store for you next, which was what made life fun and worth living.

Frank's friends said that in spite of his hard shell, he had an appetite for life and fun. But that was only part of what they said about him.

Skagg let out a bleat of rage that sounded utterly inhuman. In whatever shape he had settled upon, he was coming after Frank, and he was coming fast.

5

Frank climbed swiftly and unhesitatingly in spite of the pain in his ribs. He heaved himself onto the top of another three-story-high wall of crates – machine tools, transmission gears, ball bearings – and rose to his feet.

Six other crates, which were not part of the wall itself, were stacked at random points along the otherwise flat top of those wooden palisades. He pushed one box to the edge. According to the printing on the side, it was filled with twenty-four portable compact-disc players, the kind that were carried by anti-social young men who used the volume of their favorite unlistenable music as a weapon with which to assault innocent passersby on the street. He had no idea what a crate of 'ghetto-blasters' was doing among the stacks of machine tools and bearings; but it weighed only about two hundred pounds, and he was able to slide it.

In the aisle below, something issued a shrill, piercing cry that was part rage, part challenge.

Frank leaned out past the box that he had brought to the brink, looked down, and saw Skagg had now assumed a repulsive insectile form that was not quite that of a two-hundred-fifty-pound cockroach and not quite that of a praying mantis but something between.

Suddenly the thing's chitin-capped head swiveled. Its antennae quivered. Multi-faceted, luminous amber eyes looked up at Frank.

He shoved the box over the edge. Unbalanced, he nearly plummeted with it. Wrenching himself back from the brink, he tottered and fell on his butt.

The carton of portable compact-disc players met the floor with thunderous impact. Twenty-four arrogant punks with bad taste in music but with a strong desire for high-tech fidelity would be disappointed this Christmas.

Frank crawled quickly to the edge on his hands and knees, looked down, and saw Skagg's squirming insectile form struggling free of the burst carton that had briefly pinned him to the floor. Getting to his feet, Frank began to shift his weight rapidly back and forth, rocking the heavy crate under him. Soon half the wall was rocking, too, and the column of boxes beneath Frank swayed dangerously. He put more effort into this frantic dance of destruction, then jumped off the toppling

column just as it began to tilt out of the wall. He landed on an adjacent crate that was also wobbling but more stable, and he fell to his hands and knees; several formidable splinters gouged deep into his palms, but at the same time he heard at least half a dozen heavy crates crashing into the aisle behind him, so his cry was one of triumph not pain.

He turned and, flat on his belly this time, eased to the brink.

On the floor below, Skagg could not be seen from the ton of debris under which he was buried. However, the shape-changer was not dead; his inhuman screams of rage attested to his survival. The debris was moving as Skagg pushed and clawed his way out of it.

Satisfied that he had at least gained more time, Frank got up, ran the length of the wall of boxes, and descended at the end. He hurried into another part of the warehouse.

Along his randomly chosen route he passed the half-broken door by which he and Skagg had entered the building. Skagg had closed it and stacked several apparently heavy crates against it to prevent Frank from making an easy, silent exit. No doubt, the shapechanger also had damaged the controls for the electric garage doors at the front of the warehouse and had taken measures to block the other exits.

You needn't have bothered, Frank thought.

He was not going to cut and run. As a police officer he was duty-bound to deal with Karl Skagg, for Skagg was an extreme threat to the peace and safety of the community. Frank believed strongly in duty and responsibility. And he was an ex-marine. And . . . well, though he would never have admitted as much, he enjoyed being called Hardshell, and he took pleasure in the reputation that went with the nickname; he would never fail to live up to that reputation.

Besides, though he was beginning to tire of the game, he was still having fun.

6

Iron steps along the south wall led up to a high balcony with a metal-grid floor. Off the balcony were four offices in which the warehouse's managerial, secretarial, and clerical staffs worked.

Large sliding glass doors connected each office with the balcony, and through the doors Frank Shaw could see the darkish forms of desks, chairs, and business equipment. No lamps were on in any of the rooms, but each had outside windows that admitted the pale yellow glow of nearby street-lamps and the occasional flash of lightning.

The sound of rain was loud, for the curved ceiling was only ten feet above. When thunder rolled through the night, Frank heard it reverberating in that corrugated metal.

At the midpoint of the balcony, he stood at the iron railing and looked across the immense storage room below. He could see into some aisles but by no means into all - or even a majority - of them. He saw the shadowy ranks of forklifts and electric carts among which he had encountered Skagg and where he had first discovered his adversary's tremendous recuperative powers and talent for changing shape. He also could see part of the collapsed wall of crates where he buried Skagg under machine tools, transmission gears, and compact-disc players.

Nothing moved.

He drew his revolver and reloaded, using the last of the .38 cartridges from the loops on his custom-designed holster. Even if he fired six rounds pointblank into Skagg's chest, he would succeed only in delaying the shapechanger's attack for a minute or less while the bastard healed. A minute. Just about long enough to reload. He had more cartridges in the pockets of his suit coat, although not an endless supply. The gun was useless, but he intended to play the game as long as possible, and the gun was definitely part of the game.

He no longer allowed himself to feel the pain in his side. The showdown was approaching, and he could not afford the luxury of pain. He had to live up to his reputation and become Hardshell Shaw, had to blank out everything that might distract him from dealing with Skagg.

He scanned the warehouse again.

Nothing moved, but all the shadows in the enormous room, wall to wall, seemed to shimmer darkly with pent-up energy, as if they were alive and, though unmoving now, were prepared to spring at him if he turned his back on them.

Lightning cast its nervous, dazzling reflection into the office behind Frank, and a bright reflection of the reflection flickered through the sliding glass doors onto the balcony. He realized that he was revealed by the sputtering, third-hand electric glow, but he did not move away from the railing to a less conspicuous position. He was not trying to hide from Karl Skagg. After all, the warehouse was their Samarra, and their appointment was drawing near.

However, Frank thought confidently, Skagg is sure going to be surprised to discover that the role of Death in this Samarra belongs not to him but to me.

Again lightning flashed, its image entering the warehouse not only by way of the offices behind Frank but through the narrow windows high in the eaves. Ghostly flurries of storm light fluttered across the curve of the metal ceiling, which was usually dark above the shaded security lamps. In those pulses of queer luminosity, Skagg was suddenly disclosed at the highest point of the ceiling, creeping along upside down, as if he were a spider with no need to be concerned about the law of gravity. Although Skagg was visible only briefly and not in much detail, he currently seemed to have cloaked himself in a form that was actually less like a spider than like a lizard, though a hint of strange, spikey black appendages stirred in Frank images of scuttling arachnoid creatures.

Holding his .38 in both hands, Frank waited for the storm's next bright performance. During the dark intermission between acts, he estimated the distance Skagg would have traveled, slowly tracking the unseen enemy with his revolver. When again the eave windows glowed like lamp panes and the ghostly light glimmered across the ceiling, his gunsights were aimed straight at the shapechanger. He fired three times and was certain that at least two rounds hit the target.

Jolted by the shots, Skagg shrieked, lost his grip, and fell off the ceiling. But he did not drop stone-swift to the warehouse floor. Instead, healing and undergoing metamorphosis even as he fell, he relinquished his spider-lizard form, reverted to his human shape, but sprouted batlike wings that carried him, with a cold leathery flapping sound, through the air, across the railing, and onto the metal-grid balcony only twenty feet from Frank. His clothes - even his shoes - having split at the seams during one change or another, had fallen away from him; he was naked.

Now the wings transformed into arms, one of which Skagg raised to point at Frank. 'You can't escape me.'

'I know, I know,' Frank said. 'You're like a cocktail party bore - descended from a leech.'

The fingers of Skagg's right hand abruptly telescoped out to a length of ten inches and hardened from flesh into solid bone. They tapered into knifelike points with edges as sharp as razor blades. At the base of each murderous fingertip was a barbed spur, the better to rip and tear.

Frank squeezed off the last three shots in the revolver.

Hit, Karl Skagg stumbled and fell backward on the balcony floor.

Frank fished .38 cartridges out of one pocket and reloaded. Even as he snapped the cylinder shut, he saw that Skagg already had risen.

With an ugly burst of maniacal laughter, Karl Skagg came forward. Both hands now terminated in long, bony, barbed claws. Apparently for the sheer pleasure of frightening his prey, Skagg exhibited the startling control he possessed over the form and function of his flesh. Five eyes opened at random points on his chest, and all fixed unblinkingly on Frank. A gaping mouth full of rapier teeth cracked open in Skagg's belly, and a disgusting yellowish fluid dripped from the points of the upper fangs.

Frank fired four shots that knocked Skagg down again, then fired the two remaining rounds into him as he lay on the balcony floor.

While Frank reloaded with his last cartridges, Skagg rose again and approached.

'Are you ready? Are you ready to die, you chickenshit cop?'

'Not really. I only have one more car payment to make, and for once I'd sure like to know what it's like to really *own* one of the damn things.'

'In the end you'll bleed like all the others.'

'Will I?'

'You'll scream like all the others.'

'If it's always the same, don't you get tired of it? Wouldn't you like me to bleed and scream differently, just for some variety?'

Skagg scuttled forward.

Frank emptied the gun into him.

Skagg went down, got up, and spewed forth a noxious stream of shrill laughter.

Frank threw aside the empty revolver.

The eyes and mouth vanished from the shapechanger's chest and belly, and in their place he sprouted four small, segmented, crablike arms with fingers that ended in pincers.

Retreating along the metal-grid balcony, past glass office doors that flared with reflected lightning, Frank said, 'You know what your trouble is, Skagg? You're too flamboyant. You might be a lot more frightening if you were more subtle. All these rapid changes, this frenzied discarding of one form after another – it's just too dazzling. The mind has difficulty comprehending, so the result is more awesome than terrifying. Know what I mean?'

If Skagg understood, he either disagreed or did not care, for he caused curved, bony spikes to burst forth from his chest, and he said, 'I'll pull you close and impale you, then suck the eyes out of your skull.' To fulfill the second half of his threat, he rearranged his face yet again, creating a protruding tubular orifice where his mouth had been; fine, sharp teeth rimmed the edge of it, and it made a disgustingly wet, vacuuming sound.

'That's exactly what I mean by flamboyant,' Frank said as he backed up against the railing at the end of the balcony.

Skagg was only ten feet away now.

With a sigh, regretting that the game was over, Frank released his body from the human pattern that he had imposed upon it. Bones instantly dissolved. Fingernails, hair, internal organs, fat, muscle, and all other forms of tissue became as one, undifferentiated. His body was entirely amorphous. The darksome, jellied, throbbing mass flowed out of his suit through the bottoms of his sleeves, and with a rustle his clothes collapsed in a soft heap on the metal-grid floor of the balcony.

Beside his empty suit, Frank reassumed his human form, standing naked before his would-be assailant. '*That* is the way to transform yourself without destroying your clothes in the process. Considering your impetuosity, I'm surprised you have any wardrobe left at all.'

Shocked, Skagg abandoned his monstrous appearance and put on his human cloak. 'You're one of my kind!'

'No,' Frank said. 'One of your species, but certainly not one of your demented kind. I live in peace with ordinary men, as most of our people have for thousands of years. You, on the other hand, are a repulsive degenerate, mad with your own power, driven by the insane need to dominate.'

'Live in *peace* with them?' Skagg said scornfully. 'But they're born to die, and we're immortal. They're weak, and we're strong. They've no purpose but to provide us with pleasure of one kind or another, to titillate us with their death agonies.'

'On the contrary,' Frank said, 'they're valuable because

their lives are a continuing reminder to us that existence without limits, without purpose and struggle, existence without self-control is only chaos. I spend nearly all of my time locked within this human form, and with but rare exception I force myself to suffer human pain, to endure both the anguish and joy of human existence.'

'You're the one who's mad.'

Frank shook his head. 'Through policework I serve humankind, and therefore my existence has meaning. They so terribly need us to help them along, you see.'

'Need us?'

As a roar of thunder was followed by a downpour more vigorous than at any previous moment of the storm, Frank searched for the words that might evoke understanding even in Skagg's diseased mind. 'The human condition is unspeakably sad. Think of it: their bodies are fragile; their lives are brief, each like the sputtering decline of a short candle; measured against the age of the earth itself, their deepest relationships with friends and family are of the most transitory nature, mere incandescent flashes of love and kindness that do nothing to light the great, endless, dark, flowing river of time. Yet they seldom surrender to the cruelty of their condition, seldom lose faith in themselves. Their hopes are rarely fulfilled, but they go on anyway, struggling against the darkness. Their determined striving in the face of their mortality is the very definition of courage, the essence of nobility.'

Skagg stared at him in silence for a long moment, then let loose another peal of insane laughter. 'They're prey, you fool. Toys for us to play with. Nothing more. What nonsense is this about our lives requiring purpose, struggle, self-control? Chaos isn't to be feared or disparaged. Chaos is to be *embraced*. Chaos, beautiful chaos, is the base condition of the universe, where the titanic forces of stars and galaxies clash without purpose or meaning.'

'Chaos can't coexist with love,' Frank said. 'Love is a force for stability and order.'

'Then what need is there for love?' Skagg asked, and he spoke the final word of that sentence in a particularly scornful tone.

Frank sighed. 'Well, I have an appreciation of the need for love, so I guess I've been enlightened by my contact with the human species.'

'Enlightened? "Corrupted" is the better word.'

Nodding, Frank said, 'Of course, you would see it that way. The sad thing is that for love, in the defense of love, I'll have to kill you,'

Skagg was darkly amused. 'Kill me? What sort of joke is this? You can't kill me any more than I can kill you. We're both immortal, you and I.'

'You're young,' Frank said. 'Even by human standards, you're only a young man, and by *our* standards you're an infant. I'd say I'm at least three hundred years older than you.'

'So?'

'So there are talents we acquire only with great age.'

'What talents?'

'Tonight I've watched you flaunt your genetic plasticity. I've seen you assume many fantastic forms. But I haven't seen you achieve the ultimate in cellular control.'

'Which is?'

'The complete breakdown into an amorphous mass that in spite of utter shapelessness remains a coherent being. The very feat that I performed when I shucked off my clothes. It requires iron control, for it takes you to the brink of chaos, where you must retain your identity while on the trembling edge of dissolution. You have not acquired that degree of control, for if total amorphousness had been within your power, you'd have tried to terrify me with an exhibition of it. But your shapechanging is so energetic that it's frenzied. You transform yourself at a whim, assuming whatever shape momentarily seizes your fancy, with a childish lack of discipline.'

'So what?' Skagg remained unafraid, blissfully sure of himself, arrogant. 'Your greater skill in no way changes the fact that I'm immortal, invincible. For me, all wounds heal regardless of how bad they may be. Poisons flush from my system without effect. No degree of heat, no arctic cold, no explosion less violent than a nuclear blast, no acid can shorten my life by so much as one second.'

'But you're a living creature with a metabolic system,' Frank said, 'and by one means or another – by lungs in your human form, by other organs when in other forms – you must respire. You must have oxygen to maintain life.'

Skagg stared at him, not comprehending the threat.

In an instant Frank surrendered his human form, assumed a totally amorphous state, spread himself as if he were a giant manta ray in the depths of the sea, and flew forward, wrapping himself tightly around Skagg. His flesh conformed to every fold and crease, every concavity and convexity, of Skagg's body. He completely enveloped his startled adversary, sheathing every millimeter of Skagg, stoppering his nose and ears, coating every hair, denying him access to oxygen.

Within that jellied cocoon, Skagg sprouted claws and horns and bony, barbed spikes from various portions of his anatomy, attempting to gouge and tear through the suffocating tissue that bound him. But Frank's jellied flesh couldn't be torn or punctured; even as his cells parted before a razored claw, they flowed back together and knitted up instantly in the wake of that cutting edge.

Skagg formed half a dozen mouths at various places on his body. Some were filled with needle-tipped fangs and some with double rows of shark's teeth, and all of them tore ravenously at this adversary's flesh. But Frank's amorphous tissue flowed into the orifices instead of retreating from them – *this is my body, taste of it* – clogging them to prevent biting and swallowing, coating the teeth and thus dulling the edges.

Skagg assumed a repulsive insectile shape, but Frank conformed. Skagg sprouted wings and sought escape in flight, but

Frank conformed, weighed him down, and denied him the freedom of the air.

Outside, the night was ruled by the chaos of the storm. In the warehouse, where the aisles were neatly arranged, where the humidity and temperature of the air were controlled, order ruled everywhere except in the person of Karl Skagg. But Skagg's chaos was now firmly contained within the impenetrable envelope of Frank Shaw.

The inescapable embrace with which Frank enfolded Skagg was not merely that of an executioner but that of a brother and a priest; he was gently conveying Skagg out of this life, and he was doing so with at least some measure of the regret with which he watched ordinary men suffer and expire from accident and disease. Death was the unwelcome son of chaos in a universe woefully in need of order.

For the next hour, with diminishing energy, Skagg writhed and thrashed and struggled. A man could not have endured for so long without oxygen, but Skagg was not a man; he was both more and less than human.

Frank was patient. Hundreds of years of self-enforced adaptation to the limits of the human condition had taught him patience. He held fast to Skagg a full half an hour after the last detectable signs of life had ebbed from the mad creature, and Skagg was as encapsulated as an object dipped in preserving bronze or eternally frozen in a cube of amber.

Then Frank returned to human form.

Karl Skagg's corpse was in human form as well, for that was the final metamorphosis that he had undergone in the last seconds of his agonizing suffocation. In death he looked as pathetic and fragile as any man.

When he had dressed, Frank carefully wrapped Skagg's body in a tarpaulin that he found in a corner of the warehouse. This was one corpse that could not be permitted to fall into the hands of a pathologist, for the profound mysteries of its flesh would alert humankind to the existence of the secret race that lived among them. He carried the dead shapechanger outside, through the rain-lashed night to his Chevy.

Gently he lowered Skagg into the trunk of the car and closed the lid.

Before dawn, in the dark scrub-covered hills along the perimeter of the Angeles National Forest, with the yellow-pink metropolitan glow of Los Angeles filling the lowlands south and west of him, Frank dug a deep hole and slipped Skagg's corpse into the ground. As he filled the grave, he wept.

From that wild burial ground he went directly home to his cozy five-room bungalow. Murphy, his Irish setter, was at the door to greet him with much snuffling and tail wagging. Seuss, his cat, held back at first with typical feline aloofness, but at last the Siamese rushed to him as well, purring noisily and wanting to be stroked.

Though the night had been filled with strenuous activity, Frank did not go to bed, for he never required sleep. Instead he got out of his wet clothes, put on pajamas and a robe, made a large bowl of popcorn, opened a beer, and settled down on the living room sofa with Seuss and Murphy to watch an old Capra movie that he had seen at least twenty times before but that he never failed to enjoy: Jimmy Stewart and Donna Reed in *It's a Wonderful Life*.

All of Frank Shaw's friends said that he had a hard shell, but that was only part of what they said. They also said that inside his hard shell beat a heart as soft as any.

Twilight of the Dawn

'Sometimes you can be the biggest jackass who ever lived,' my wife said the night I took Santa Claus away from my son.

We were in bed, but she was clearly not in the mood for either sleep or romance.

Her voice was sharp, scornful. 'What a terrible thing to do to a little boy.'

'He's seven years old –'

'He's a little boy,' Ellen said harshly, though we rarely spoke to each other in anger. For the most part ours was a happy, peaceful marriage.

We lay in silence. The drapes were drawn back from the French doors that opened onto the second-floor balcony, so the bedroom was limned by ash-pale moonlight. Even in that dim glow, even though Ellen was cloaked in blankets, her anger was apparent in the tense, angular position in which she was pretending to seek sleep.

Finally she said, 'Pete, you used a sledgehammer to shatter a little boy's fragile fantasy, a *harmless* fantasy, all because of your obsession –'

'It wasn't harmless,' I said patiently. 'And I don't have an obsession –'

'Yes, you do,' she said.

'I simply believe in rational –'

'Oh, shut up,' she said.

'Won't you even talk to me about it?'

'No. It's pointless.'

I sighed. 'I love you, Ellen.'

She was silent a long while.

Wind soughed in the eaves, an ancient voice.

In the boughs of one of the backyard cherry trees, an owl hooted.

At last Ellen said, 'I love you, too, but sometimes I want to kick your ass.'

I was angry with her because I felt that she was not being fair, that she was allowing her least admirable emotions to overrule her reason. Now, many years later, I would give anything to hear her say that she wanted to kick my ass, and I'd bend over with a smile.

* * *

From the cradle, my son Benny was taught that God did not exist under any name or in any form, and that religion was the refuge of weak-minded people who did not have the courage to face the universe on its own terms. I would not permit Benny to be baptized, for in my view that ceremony was a primitive initiation rite by which the child would be inducted into a cult of ignorance and irrationalism.

Ellen – my wife and Benny's mother – had been raised as a Methodist and still was stained (as I saw it) by lingering traces of faith. She called herself an agnostic, unable to go further and join me in the camp of the atheists. I loved her so much that I was able to tolerate her equivocation on the subject. However I had nothing but scorn for others who could not face the fact that the universe was godless and that human existence was nothing more than a biological accident.

I despised all those who bent their knees to humble themselves before an imaginary lord of creation, all the Methodists and Lutherans and Catholics and Baptists and Mormons and Jews and others. They claimed many labels but in essence shared the same sick delusion.

My greatest loathing was reserved, however, for those who had once been clean of the disease of religion, rational men and women like me who had slipped off the path of reason and fallen into the chasm of superstition. They were surrendering their most precious possessions - their independent spirit, self-reliance, intellectual integrity - in return for half-baked, dreamy promises of an afterlife with togas and harp music. I was more disgusted by the rejection of their previously treasured secular enlightenment than I would have been to hear some old friend confess that he had suddenly developed an all-consuming obsession for canine sex and had divorced his wife in favor of a German Shepherd bitch.

Hal Sheen, my partner with whom I had founded Fallon and Sheen Design, had been as proud of his atheism too. In college we were best friends, and together we were a formidable team of debaters whenever the subject of religion arose; inevitably, anyone harboring a belief in a supreme being, anyone daring to disagree with our view of the universe as a place of uncaring forces, any of *that* ilk was sorry to have met us, for we stripped away his pretensions to adulthood and revealed him for the idiot child he was. Indeed we often didn't even wait for the subject of religion to arise but skillfully baited fellow students who, to our certain knowledge, were believers.

Later, with degrees in architecture, neither of us wished to work for anyone but ourselves, so we formed a company. We dreamed of creating brawny yet elegant, functional yet beautiful buildings that would astonish - and win the undiluted admiration of - not only the world but our fellow professionals. And with brains, talent, and dogged determination, we began to attain some of our goals while we were still very young men. Fallon and Sheen Design, a wunderkind company, was the focus of a revolution in design that excited university students as well as long-time professionals.

The most important aspect of our tremendous success was that our atheism lay at the core of it, for we consciously set out to create a new architecture that owed nothing to religious inspiration. Most laymen are not aware that virtually all the structures around them, including those resulting from modern schools of design, incorporate architectural details originally developed to subtly reinforce the rule of God and the place of religion in life. For instance vaulted ceilings, first used in churches and cathedrals, were originally meant to draw the gaze upward and to induce, by indirection, contemplation of heaven and its rewards. Underpitch vaults, barrel vaults, grain vaults, fan vaults, quadripartite and sexpartite and tierceron vaults are more than mere arches; they were conceived as agents of religion, quiet advertisements for Him and His authority. From the start Hal and I were determined that no vaulted ceilings, no spires, no arched windows or doors, no slightest design element born of religion would be incorporated into a Fallon and Sheen building. In reaction we strove to direct the eye earthward and, by a thousand devices, to remind those who passed through our structures that they were born of the earth, not children of any god but merely more intellectually advanced cousins of apes.

Hal's reconversion to the Roman Catholicism of his childhood was, therefore, a shock to me. At the age of thirty-seven, when he was at the top of his profession, when by his singular success he had proven the supremacy of unoppressed, rational man over imagined divinities, he returned with apparent joy to the confessional, humbled himself at the communion rail, dampened his forehead and breast with so-called holy water, and thereby rejected the intellectual foundation on which his entire adult life, to that point, had been based.

The horror of it chilled my heart, my marrow.

For taking Hal Sheen from me, I despised religion more than ever. I redoubled my efforts to eliminate any wisp of religious thought or superstition from my son's life, and I was fiercely determined that Benny would never be stolen from me by incense-burning, bell-ringing, hymn-singing, self-deluded, mush-brained fools. When he proved to be a voracious reader from an early age, I carefully chose books for him, directing him away from works that even indirectly portrayed religion as an acceptable part of life, firmly steering him to strictly secular material that would not encourage unhealthy fantasies. When I saw that he was fascinated by vampires, ghosts, and the entire panoply of traditional monsters that seem to intrigue all children, I strenuously discouraged that interest, mocked it, and taught him the virtue and pleasure of rising above such childish things. Oh, I did not deny him the enjoyment of a good scare, for there's nothing religious in that. Benny was permitted to savor the fear induced by books about killer robots, movies about the Frankenstein monster, and other threats that were the work of man. It was only monsters of satanic origin that I censored from his books and films, for belief in things satanic is merely another facet of religion, the flip side of God worship.

I allowed him Santa Claus until he was seven, though I had a lot of misgivings about that indulgence. The Santa Claus legend includes a Christian element, of course. Good *Saint* Nick and all that. But Ellen was insistent that Benny would not be denied that fantasy. I reluctantly agreed that it was probably harmless, but only as long as we scrupulously observed the holiday as a secular event having nothing to do with the birth of Jesus. To us Christmas was a celebration of the family and a healthy indulgence in materialism.

In the back yard of our big house in Buck's County, Pennsylvania, grew a pair of enormous, long-lived cherry trees, under the branches of which Benny and I often sat in the milder seasons, playing checkers or card games. Beneath those boughs, which already had lost most of their leaves to the tugging hands of autumn, on an unusually warm day in early October of his seventh year, as we were playing Uncle Wiggly, Benny asked if I thought Santa was going to bring him lots of stuff that year. I said it was too early to be thinking about Santa, and he said that *all* the kids were thinking about Santa and were starting to compose want lists already. Then he said, 'Daddy, how's Santa *know* we've been good or bad. He can't watch all us kids all the time, can he? Do our guardian angels talk to him and tattle on us, or what?'

'Guardian angels?' I said, startled and displeased. 'What do you know about guardian angels?'

'Well, they're supposed to watch over us, help us when we're in trouble, right? So I thought maybe they also talk to Santa Claus.'

Only months after Benny was born, I had joined with like-minded parents in our community to establish a private school guided by the principles of secular humanism, where even the slightest religious thought would be kept out of the curriculum; in fact our intention was to insure that, as our children matured, they would be taught history, literature, sociology, and ethics from an anti-clerical viewpoint. Benny had attended our pre-school and, by that October of which I write, was in second-grade of the elementary division, where his classmates came from families guided by the same rational principles as our own. I was surprised to hear that in such an environment he was still subjected to religious propagandizing.

'Who told you about guardian angels?'

'Some kids.'

'They believe in these angels?'

'Sure. I guess.'

'Why?'

'They saw it on TV.'

'They did, huh?'

'It was a show you won't let me watch. *Highway to Heaven*.'

'And just because they saw it on TV they think it's true?'

Benny shrugged and moved his game piece five spaces along the Uncle Wiggly board.

I believed then that popular culture – especially television – was the bane of all men and women of reason and good will, not least of all because it promoted a wide variety of religious superstitions and, by its saturation of every aspect of our lives, was inescapable and powerfully influential. Books and movies like *The Exorcist* and television programs like *Highway to Heaven* could frustrate even the most diligent parent's attempts to raise his child in an atmosphere of untainted rationality.

The unseasonably warm October breeze was not strong enough to disturb the game cards, but it gently ruffled Benny's fine brown hair. Wind-mussed, sitting on a pillow on his red-wood chair in order to be at table level, he was so small and vulnerable. Loving him, wanting the best possible life for him, I grew angrier by the second; my anger was directed not at Benny but at those who, intellectually and emotionally stunted by their twisted philosophy, would propagandize an innocent child.

'Benny,' I said, 'listen, there are no guardian angels. They don't exist. It's all an ugly lie told by people who want to make you believe that you aren't responsible for your own successes in life. They want you to believe that the bad things in life are the result of your sins and *are* your fault, but that all the good things come from the grace of God. It's a way to control you. That's what all religion is – a tool to control and oppress you.'

He blinked at me. 'Grace who?'

It was my turn to blink. 'What?'

'Who's Grace? You mean Mrs Grace Keever at the toy shop? What tool will she use to press me with?' He giggled. 'Will I be all mashed flat and on a hanger when they're done? Daddy, you're silly.'

He was only a seven-year-old boy, after all, and I was solemnly discussing the oppressive nature of religious belief as if we were two intellectuals drinking espresso in a coffee house. Blushing at the realization of my own capacity for foolishness, I pushed aside the Uncle Wiggly board and struggled harder to make him understand why believing in such nonsense as guardian angels was not merely innocent fun but was a step toward intellectual and emotional enslavement of a particularly pernicious sort. When he seemed alternately bored, confused, embarrassed, and utterly baffled – but never for a moment even slightly enlightened – I grew frustrated, and at last (I am now ashamed to admit this) I made my point by taking Santa Claus away from him.

Suddenly it seemed clear to me that by allowing him to indulge in the Santa myth, I'd laid the groundwork for the very irrationality that I was determined to prevent him from adopting. How could I have been so misguided as to believe that Christmas could be celebrated entirely in a secular spirit, without giving credence to the religious tradition that was, after all, the genesis of the holiday. Now I saw that erecting a Christmas tree in our home and exchanging gifts, by association with such other Christmas paraphernalia as manger scenes on church lawns and trumpet-tooting plastic angels in department-store decorations, had generated in Benny an assumption that the spiritual aspect of the celebration had as much validity as the materialistic aspect, which made him fertile ground for tales of guardian angels and all the other rot about sin and salvation.

Under the boughs of the cherry trees, in an October breeze that was blowing us slowly toward another Christmas, I told Benny the truth about Santa Claus, explained that the gifts came from his mother and me. He protested that he had evidence of Santa's reality: the cookies and milk that he always left out for the jolly fat man and that were unfailingly consumed. I convinced him that Santa's sweet tooth was in fact my own and that the milk – which I don't like – was always poured down the drain. Methodically, relentlessly – but with what I thought was kindness and love – I stripped from him all of the so-called magic of Christmas and left him in no doubt that the Santa stuff had been a well-meant but mistaken deception.

He listened with no further protest, and when I was finished he claimed to be sleepy and in need of a nap. He rubbed his eyes and yawned elaborately. He had no more interest in Uncle Wiggly and went straight into the house and up to his room.

The last thing I said to him there beneath the cherry trees was that strong, well-balanced people have no need of imaginary friends like Santa Claus and guardian angels. 'All we can count on is ourselves, our friends, and our families, Benny. If we want something in life, we can't get it by asking Santa Claus and certainly not by praying for it. We get it only by earning it – or by benefiting from the generosity of friends or relatives. There's no reason ever to *wish* for or pray for anything.'

Three years later, when Benny was in the hospital and dying of bone cancer, I understood for the first time why other people felt a need to believe in God and to seek comfort in prayer. Our lives are touched by some tragedies so enormous and so difficult to bear that the temptation to seek mystical answers to the cruelty of the world is powerful indeed.

Even if we can accept that our own deaths are final and that no souls survive the decomposition of our flesh, we often can't endure the idea that our *children*, when stricken in youth, are also doomed to pass from this world into no other. Children are special, so how can it be that they too will be wiped out as completely as if they had never existed? I have seen atheists, despising religion and incapable of praying for themselves, suddenly invoke the name of God on behalf of their own seriously ill children – then realize, sometimes with embarrassment but often with regret, that their philosophy denies them the foolishness of petitioning for divine intercession.

When Benny was afflicted with bone cancer, I was not shaken from my convictions; not once during the ordeal did I put principles aside and turn blubberingly to God. I was stalwart, steadfast, stoical, and determined to bear the burden by myself, though there were times when the weight bowed my head and when the very bones of my shoulders felt as if they would splinter and collapse under a mountain of grief.

That day in October of Benny's seventh year, as I sat beneath the cherry trees and watched him return to the house to nap, I did not know how severely my principles and self-reliance would be tested in the days to come. I was proud of having freed my son of his Christ-related fantasies about Santa Claus, and I was pompously certain that the day would come when Benny, grown to adulthood, would eventually thank me for the rigorously rational upbringing that he had received.

* * *

When Hal Sheen told me that he had returned to the fold of the Catholic Church, I thought he was setting me up for a joke. We were having an after-work cocktail at a hotel bar near our offices, and I was under the impression that the purpose of our meeting was to celebrate some grand commission that Hal had won for us. 'I've got news for you,' he had said cryptically that morning. 'Let's meet at the Regency for a drink at six o'clock.' But instead of telling me that we had been chosen to design a building that would add another chapter to the legend of Fallon and Sheen, he told me that after more than a year of quiet debate with himself, he had shed his atheism as if it were a moldy cocoon and had flown forth into the realm of faith once more. I laughed, waiting for the punch line, and he smiled, and in his smile there was something – perhaps pity for me – that instantly convinced me that he was serious.

I argued quietly, then not so quietly. I scorned his claim to have rediscovered God, and I tried to shame him for his surrender of intellectual dignity.

'I've decided a man can be both an intellectual and a practicing Christian or Jew or Buddhist,' Hal said with annoying self-possession.

'Impossible!' I said, striking our table with one fist to emphasize my rejection of that muddle-headed contention. Our cocktail glasses rattled, and an unused ashtray nearly fell on the floor, which caused other patrons to look our way.

'Look at Malcolm Muggeridge,' Hal said. 'Or C.S. Lewis. Isaac Singer. Christians and a Jew – *and* undisputed intellectuals.'

'Listen to you!' I said, appalled. 'On how many occasions have other people raised those names – and others – when we were arguing the intellectual supremacy of atheism, and you joined me in proving what fools the Muggeridges, Lewises, and Singers of this world really are.'

He shrugged. 'I was wrong.'

'Just like that?'

'No, not just like that. Give me some credit, Pete. I've spent a year reading, thinking . . . I've actively resisted the urge to return to the faith, and yet I've been won over.'

'By whom? What propagandizing priest or –'

'No one won me over. It's been entirely an inner debate, Pete. No one but me has known that I've been wavering on this tightrope.'

'Then what started you wavering?'

'Well, for a couple of years now, my life has been empty. . . .'

'Empty? You're young and healthy. You're married to a smart and beautiful woman. You're at the top of your profession, admired by one and all for the freshness and vigor of your architectural vision, and you're wealthy! You call that an empty life?'

He nodded. 'Empty. But I couldn't figure out why. Just like you, I added up all that I've got, and it seemed like I should be the most fulfilled man on the face of the earth. But I felt hollow, and each new project we approached had less interest for me. Gradually I realized that all I'd built and that all I might build in the days to come was not going to satisfy me because the achievements were not lasting. Oh, sure, one of our buildings might stand for two hundred years, but a couple of centuries are but a grain of sand falling in the hourglass of Time. Structures of stone and steel and glass are not enduring monuments; they're not, as we once thought, testimonies to the singular genius of mankind. Rather the opposite: they're reminders that even our mightiest structures are fragile, that our greatest achievements can be quickly erased by earthquakes, wars, tidal waves, or simply by the slow gnawing of a thousand years of sun and wind and rain. So what's the point?'

'The point,' I reminded him angrily, 'is that by erecting those structures, by creating better and more beautiful buildings, we are improving the lives of our fellow men and encouraging others to reach toward higher goals of their own, and then together all of us are making a better future for the whole human species.'

'Yes, but to what end?' he pressed. 'If there's no afterlife, if each individual's existence ends entirely in the grave, then the *collective* fate of the species is precisely that of the individual: death, emptiness, blackness, nothingness. Nothing can come from nothing. You can't claim a noble, higher purpose for the species as a whole when you allow no higher purpose for the individual spirit.' He raised one hand to halt my response. 'I know, I know. You've arguments against that statement. I've supported you in them through countless debates on the subject. But I can't support you any more, Pete. I think there *is* some purpose to life besides just living, and if I didn't think so then I would leave the business and spend the rest of my life having fun, enjoying the precious finite number of days left to me. However, now that I believe there is something called a soul and that it survives the body, I can go on working at Fallon and Sheen because it's my destiny to do so, which means the achievements there are meaningful. I hope you'll be able to accept this. I'm not going to proselytize. This is the first and last time you'll hear me mention religion because I'll respect your right *not* to believe. I'm sure we can go on as before.'

But we could not.

I felt that religion was a hateful degenerative sickness of

the mind, and I was thereafter uncomfortable in Hal's presence. I still pretended that we were close, that nothing had changed between us, but I felt that he was not the same man he had been.

Besides, Hal's new faith inevitably began to infect his fine architectural vision. Vaulted ceilings and arched windows began to appear in his designs, and everywhere his new buildings encouraged the eye and mind to look up and regard the heavens. This change of direction was welcomed by certain clients and even praised by critics in prestigious journals, but I could not abide it because I knew he was regressing from the man-centered architecture that had been our claim to originality. Fourteen months after his embrace of the Roman Catholic Church, I sold out my share of the company to him and set up my own organization free of his influence.

'Hal,' I told him the last time I saw him, 'even when you claimed to be atheist, you evidently never understood that the nothingness at the end of life isn't to be feared or raged against. Either accept it regretfully as a fact of life . . . or welcome it.'

Personally, I welcomed it, because not having to concern myself about my fate in the afterlife was liberating. Being a nonbeliever, I could concentrate entirely on winning the rewards of *this* world, the one and only world.

* * *

The night of the day that I took Santa Claus away from Benny, the night Ellen told me that she wanted to kick me in the ass, as we lay in our moonlit bedroom on opposite sides of the large four-poster bed, she also said, 'Pete, you've told me all about your childhood, and of course I've met your folks, so I have a good idea what it must've been like to be raised in that crackpot atmosphere. I can understand why you'd react against their religious fanaticism by embracing atheism. But sometimes . . . you get carried away. You aren't happy to just *be* an atheist; you're so eager to impose your philosophy on everyone else, no matter the cost, that sometimes you behave very much like your own parents . . . except instead of selling God, you're selling godlessness.'

I raised up on the bed and looked at her blanket-shrouded form. I couldn't see her face; she was turned away from me. 'That's just plain nasty, Ellen.'

'It's true.'

'I'm nothing like my parents. Nothing like them. I don't *beat* atheism into Benny the way they tried to beat God into me.'

'What you did to him today was as bad as beating him.'

'Ellen, all kids learn the truth about Santa Claus eventually, some of them even sooner than Benny did.'

She turned toward me, and suddenly I could see her face just well enough to discern the anger in it but, unfortunately, not well enough to glimpse the love that I knew was also there. She said 'Sure, they all learn the truth about Santa Claus, but they don't have the fantasy ripped away from them by their own fathers, damn it!'

'I didn't *rip* it away. I reasoned him out of it.'

'He's not a college boy on a debating team,' she said. 'You can't reason with a seven-year-old. They're all emotion at that age, all heart. Pete, he came into the house today after you were done with him, and he went up to his room, and an hour later when I went up there he was still crying.'

'Okay, okay,' I said. 'I feel like a shit.'

'Good. You should.'

'And I'll admit that I could have handled it better, been more tactful about it.'

She turned away from me again and said nothing.

'But I didn't do anything wrong,' I said. 'I mean, it was a real mistake to think we could celebrate Christmas in a strictly secular way. Innocent fantasies can lead to some that aren't so innocent.'

'Oh, shut up,' she said. 'Shut up and go to sleep before I forget I love you.'

* * *

The trucker who killed Ellen was trying to make more money to buy a boat. He was a fisherman whose passion was trolling; to afford the boat he had to take on more work. He was using amphetamines to stay awake. The truck was a Peterbilt, the biggest one they make. Ellen was driving her blue BMW. They hit head on, and though she apparently tried to take evasive action, she never had a chance.

Benny was devastated. I put all work aside and stayed home with him the entire month of July. He needed a lot of hugging, reassuring, and some gentle guidance toward acceptance of the tragedy. I was in bad shape too, for Ellen had been more than my wife and lover: she had been my toughest critic, my greatest champion, my best friend, and my only confidant. At night, alone in the bedroom we had shared, I put my face against the pillow upon which she had slept, breathed in the faintly lingering scent of her, and wept; I couldn't bear to wash the pillowcase for weeks. But in front of Benny, I managed for the most part to maintain control of myself and provide him with the example of strength that he so terribly needed.

There was no funeral. Ellen was cremated, and her ashes were dispersed at sea.

A month later, on the first Sunday in August, when we had begun to move grudgingly and sadly toward acceptance, forty or fifty friends and relatives came to the house, and we held a quiet memorial service for Ellen, a purely secular service with not even the slightest thread of religious content. We gathered on the patio near the pool, and half a dozen friends stepped forward to tell amusing stories about Ellen and to explain what an impact she'd had on their lives.

I kept Benny at my side throughout that service, for I

wanted him to see that his mother had been loved by others, too, and that her existence had made a difference in more lives than his and mine. He was only eight years old, but he seemed to take from the service the very comfort that I had hoped it would give him. Hearing his mother praised, he was unable to hold back his tears, but now there was something more than grief in his face and eyes: now he was also proud of her, amused by some of the practical jokes that she had played on friends and that they now recounted, and intrigued to hear about aspects of her that had theretofore been invisible to him. In time these new emotions were certain to dilute his grief and help him adjust to his loss.

The day following the memorial service, I rose late. When I went looking for Benny, I found him beneath one of the cherry trees in the back yard. He sat with his knees drawn up against his chest and his arms around his legs, staring at the far side of the broad valley on one slope of which we lived, but he seemed to be looking at something still more distant.

I sat beside him. 'How you doin'?'

'Okay,' he said.

For a while neither of us spoke. Overhead the leaves of the tree rustled softly. The dazzling white-pink blossoms of spring were long gone, of course, and the branches were bedecked with fruit not yet quite ripe. The day was hot, but the tree threw plentiful, cool shade.

At last he said, 'Daddy?'

'Hmmmm?'

'If it's all right with you . . .'

'What?'

'I know what you say . . .'

'What I say about what?'

'About there being no heaven or angels or anything like that.'

'It's not just what I say, Benny. It's true.'

'Well . . . just the same, if it's all right with you, I'm going to picture Mommy in heaven, wings and everything.'

I knew he was still in a fragile emotional condition even a month after her death and that he would need many more months if not years to regain his full equilibrium, so I did not rush to respond with one of my usual arguments about the foolishness of religious faith. I was silent for a moment, then said, 'Well, let me think about that for a couple minutes, okay?'

We sat side by side, staring across the valley, and I know that neither of us was seeing the landscape before us. I was seeing Ellen as she had been on the Fourth of July the previous summer, wearing white shorts and a yellow blouse, tossing a Frisbee with me and Benny, radiant, laughing, laughing. I don't know what poor Benny was seeing, though I suspect his mind was brimming with gaudy images of heaven complete with haloed angels and golden steps spiraling up to a golden throne.

'She can't just end,' he said after a while. 'She was too nice to j-j-just end. She's got to be . . . somewhere.'

'But that's just it, Benny. She *is* somewhere. Your mother goes on in you. You've got her genes, for one thing. You don't know what genes are, but you've got them: her hair, her eyes . . . And because she was a good person who taught you the right values, you'll grow up to be a good person, as well, and you'll have kids of your own some day, and your mother will go on in them and in *their* children. Your mother still lives in our memories, too, and in the memories of her friends. Because she was kind to so many people, those people were shaped to some small degree by her kindness; they'll now and then remember her, and because of her they might be kinder to people, and that kindness goes on and on.'

He listened solemnly, although I suspected that the concepts of immortality through bloodline and impersonal immortality through one's moral relationships with other people were beyond his grasp. I tried to think of a way to restate it so a child could understand.

But he said, 'Nope. Not good enough. It's nice that lots of

people are gonna remember her. But it's not good enough. *She* has to be somewhere. Not just her memory. *She* has to go on . . . so if it's all right with you, I'm gonna figure she's in heaven.'

'No, it's not all right, Benny.' I put an arm around him. 'The healthy thing to do, son, is to face up to unpleasant truths –'

He shook his head. 'She's all right, Daddy. She didn't just end. She's somewhere now. I know she is. And she's happy.'

'Benny –'

He stood, looked up into the trees, and said, 'We have cherries to eat soon?'

'Benny, let's not change the subject. We –'

'Can we drive into town for lunch at Mrs Foster's restaurant – burgers and fries and Cokes and then a cherry sundae?'

'Benny –'

'Can we, can we?'

'All right. But –'

'I get to drive!' he shouted and ran off toward the garage, giggling at his joke.

* * *

During the next year Benny's stubborn refusal to let his mother go was at first frustrating, then annoying, and finally intensely aggravating. He talked to her nearly every night as he lay in bed, waiting for sleep to come, and he seemed confident that she could hear him. Often, after I tucked him in and kissed him goodnight and left the room, he slipped out from under the covers, knelt beside the bed, and prayed that his mother was happy and safe where she had gone.

Twice I accidentally heard him. On other occasions I stood quietly in the hall after leaving his room, and when he thought I had gone downstairs, he humbled himself before God, though he could know nothing more of God than what he had illicitly learned from television shows or other pop culture that I had been unable to monitor.

I was determined to wait him out, certain that his childish faith would expire naturally when he realized that God would never answer him. As the days passed without a miraculous sign assuring him that his mother's soul had survived death, Benny would begin to understand that all he had been taught about religion was true, and he eventually would return quietly to the realm of reason where I had made – and was patiently saving – a place for him. I did not want to tell him I knew of his praying, did not want to force the issue because I knew that in reaction to a too heavy-handed exercise of parental authority, he might cling even longer to his irrational dream of life everlasting.

But after four months, when his nightly conversations with his dead mother and with God did not cease, I could no longer tolerate even whispered prayers in my house, for though I seldom heard them, I *knew* they were being said, and knowing was somehow as maddening as hearing every word of them. I confronted him. I reasoned with him at great length on many occasions. I argued, pleaded. I tried the classic carrot-and-stick approach: I punished him for the expression of any religious sentiment; and I rewarded him for the slightest antireligious statement, even if he made it unthinkingly or even if it was only my *interpretation* of what he'd said that was antireligious. He received few rewards and much punishment. I did not spank him or in any way physically abuse him; that much, at least, is to my credit; I did not attempt to beat God out of him the way my parents had tried to beat Him *into* me.

I took Benny to Dr Gerton, a psychiatrist, when everything else had failed. 'He's having difficulty accepting his mother's death,' I told Gerton. 'He's just not . . . coping. I'm worried about him.

After three sessions with Benny over a period of two weeks, Dr Gerton called to say he no longer needed to see Benny. 'He's going to be all right, Mr Fallon. You've no need to worry about him.'

'But you're wrong,' I insisted. 'He needs analysis. He's still not . . . coping.'

'Mr Fallon, you've said that before, but I've never been able to get a clear explanation of what behavior strikes you as evidence of his inability to cope. What's he *doing* that worries you so?'

'He's praying,' I said. 'He prays to God to keep his mother safe and happy. And he talks to his mother as if he's sure she hears him, talks to her *every* night.'

'Oh, Mr Fallon, if that's all that's been bothering you, I can assure you there's no need to worry. Talking to his mother, praying for her, all that's perfectly ordinary and –'

'Every night!' I repeated.

'Ten times a day would be all right. Really, there's nothing unhealthy about it. Talking to God about his mother and talking to his mother in heaven . . . it's just a psychological mechanism by which he can slowly adjust to the fact that she's no longer actually here on earth with him. It's perfectly ordinary.'

I'm afraid I shouted: 'It's not perfectly ordinary in *this* house, Dr Gerton. We're atheists!'

He was silent for a moment, then sighed. 'Mr Fallon, you've got to remember that your son is more than your son – he's a person in his own right. A *little* person but a person nonetheless. You can't think of him as property or as an unformed mind to be molded –'

'I have the utmost respect for the individual, Dr Fallon. Much more respect than do the hymn-singers who value their fellow men less than they do their imaginary master in the sky.'

His silence lasted longer than before. Finally he said, 'All right. Then surely you realize there's no guarantee the son will be the same person in every respect as the father. He'll have ideas and desires of his own. And ideas about religion might be one area in which the disagreement between you will widen over the years rather than narrow. This might not be *only* a psychological mechanism that he's using to adapt to his mother's death; it might also turn out to be the start of lifelong faith. At least you have to be prepared for the possibility.'

'I won't have it,' I said firmly.

His third silence was the longest of all. Then: 'Mr Fallon, I have no need to see Benny again. There's nothing I can do for him because there's nothing he really needs from me. But perhaps you should consider some counseling for yourself.'

I hung up on him.

* * *

For the next six months Benny infuriated and frustrated me by clinging to his fantasy of heaven. Perhaps he no longer spoke to his mother every evening, and perhaps sometimes he even forgot to say his prayers, but his stubborn faith could not be shaken. When I spoke of atheism, when I made a scornful joke about God, when I tried to reason with him, he would only say, 'No, Daddy, you're wrong,' or 'No, Daddy, that's not the way it is,' and he would either walk away from me or try to change the subject. Or he would do something even more infuriating: he would say, 'No, Daddy, you're wrong,' and then he would throw his small arms around me, hug me very tight, and tell me that he loved me, and at these moments there was a too-apparent sadness about him that included an element of pity, as if he was afraid for me and felt that *I* needed guidance and reassurance. Nothing made me angrier than that. He was nine years old, not an ancient guru! As punishment for his willful disregard of my wishes, I took away his television privileges for days – and sometimes weeks – at a time, forbade him to have dessert after dinner, and once refused to allow him to play with his friends for an entire month. Nothing worked.

Religion, the disease that had turned my parents into stern and solemn strangers, the disease that had made my childhood a nightmare, the very sickness that had stolen my best friend, Hal Sheen, from me when I least expected to lose him, *religion* had now wormed its way into my house again. It had contaminated my son, the only important person left in my life. No, it wasn't any particular religion that had a grip on Benny. He didn't have any formal theological education, so his concepts of God and heaven were thoroughly non-denominational, vaguely Christian, yes, but only vaguely. It was religion without structure, without dogma or doctrine, religion based entirely on childish sentiment; therefore some might say that it was not really religion at all, and that I should not have worried about it. But I knew Dr Gerton's observation was true: this childish faith might be the seed from which a true religious conviction would grow in later years. The virus of religion was loose in my house, and I was dismayed, distraught, and perhaps even somewhat deranged by my failure to find a cure for it.

To me, this was the essence of horror. It wasn't the acute horror of a bomb blast or plane crash, mercifully brief, but a chronic horror that went on day after day, week after week.

I was sure that the worst of all possible troubles had befallen me and that I was in the darkest time of my life.

Then Benny got bone cancer.

* * *

Nearly two years after his mother died, on a blustery day in late February, we were in the park by the river, flying a kite. When Benny ran with the control stick, paying out string, he fell down. Not just once. Not twice. Repeatedly. When I asked what was wrong, he said he had a sore muscle in his right leg: 'Must've twisted it when the guys and I were climbing trees yesterday.'

He favored the leg for a couple of days, and when I suggested he ought to see a doctor, he said he was feeling better.

A week later he was in the hospital, undergoing tests, and

in another two days, the diagnosis was confirmed: bone cancer. It was too widespread for surgery. His physicians instituted an immediate program of radium treatments and chemotherapy.

Benny lost his hair, lost weight. He grew so pale that each morning I was afraid to look at him because I had the crazy idea that if he got any paler he would begin to turn transparent and, when he was finally as clear as glass, would shatter in front of my eyes.

After five weeks he took a sudden turn for the better and was, though not in remission, at least well enough to come home. The radium and chemotherapy were continued on an out-patient basis.

I think now that he improved not due to the radium or cytotoxic agents or drugs but simply because he wanted to see the cherry trees in bloom one last time. His temporary turn for the better was an act of sheer will, a triumph of mind over body.

Except for one day when a sprinkle of rain fell, he sat in a chair under the blossom-laden boughs, enjoying the spring greening of the valley and delighting in the antics of the squirrels that came out of the nearby woods to frolic on our lawn. He sat not in one of the redwood lawn chairs but in a big, comfortably padded easy chair that I brought out from the house, his legs propped on a hassock, for he was thin and fragile; a harder chair would have bruised him horribly.

We played card games and Chinese checkers, but usually he was too tired to concentrate on a game for long, so mostly we just sat there, relaxing. We talked of days past, of the many good times he'd had in his ten short years, and of his mother. But we sat in silence a lot, too. It was never an awkward silence; sometimes melancholy, yes, but never awkward.

Neither of us spoke of God or guardian angels or heaven. I knew he had not lost his belief that his mother had survived the death of her body in some form and that she had gone on to a better place. But he said nothing more of that and did not discuss his own hopes for the afterlife. I believe he avoided the subject out of respect for me and because he wanted no friction between us during those last days.

I will always be grateful to him for not putting me to the test. I am afraid that I'd have tried to force him to embrace rationalism even in his last days, thereby making a bigger jackass of myself than usual.

After only nine days at home, he suffered a relapse and returned to the hospital. I booked him into a semi-private room with two beds: he took one, and I took the other.

Cancer cells had migrated to his liver, and a tumor was found there. After surgery he improved for a few days, was almost buoyant, but then sank again.

Cancer was found in his lymphatic system, in his spleen, tumors everywhere.

His condition improved, declined, improved, and declined again. However each improvement was less encouraging than the one before it, while each decline was steeper.

I was rich, intelligent, and talented. I was famous in my field. But I could do nothing to save my son. I had never felt so small, so powerless.

At least I could be strong for Benny. In his presence I tried to be cheerful. I did not let him see me cry, but I wept quietly at night, curled in the fetal position, reduced to the helplessness of a child, while he lay in troubled, drug-induced slumber on the other side of the room. During the day, when he was away for therapy or tests or surgery, I sat at the window, staring out, seeing nothing.

As if some alchemical spell had been cast, the world became gray, entirely gray. I was aware of no color in anything; I might have been living in an old black-and-white movie. Shadows became more stark and sharp-edged. The air itself seemed gray, as though contaminated by a toxic mist so fine that it could not be seen, only sensed. Voices were fuzzy, the audial equivalent of gray. The few times that I switched on the TV or the radio, the music seemed to have no melody that I could discern. My interior world was as gray as the physical world around me, and the unseen but acutely sensed mist that fouled the outer world had penetrated to my core.

Even in the depths of that despair, I did not step off the path of reason, did not turn to God for help or condemn God for torturing an innocent child. I did not consider seeking the counsel of clergymen or the help of faith healers.

I endured.

If I had slipped and sought solace in superstition, no one could have blamed me. In little more than two years. I'd had a falling out with my only close friend, had lost my wife in a traffic accident, and had seen my son succumb to cancer. Occasionally you hear about people with bad runs of luck like that, or you read about them in the papers, and strangely enough they usually talk about how they were brought to God by their suffering and how they found peace in faith. Reading about them always makes you sad and stirs your compassion, and you can even forgive them their witless religious sentimentality. Of course, you always quickly put them out of your mind because you know that a similar chain of tragedies could befall you, and such a realization does not bear contemplation. Now I not only had to contemplate it but *live* it, and in the living I did not bend my principles.

I faced the void and accepted it.

After putting up a surprisingly long, valiant, painful struggle against the virulent cancer that was eating him alive, Benny finally died on a night in August. They had rushed him into the intensive care unit two days before, and I had been permitted to sit with him only fifteen minutes every second hour. On that last night, however, they allowed me to come in from the ICU lounge and stay beside his bed for several hours because they knew he did not have long.

An intravenous drip pierced his left arm. An aspirator was inserted in his nose. He was hooked up to an EKG machine that traced his heart activity in green light on a bedside monitor, and each beat was marked by a soft beep. The lines and the beeps frequently became erratic for as much as three or four minutes at a time.

I held his hand. I smoothed the sweat-damp hair away from his brow. I pulled the covers up to his neck when he was seized by chills and lowered them when the chills gave way to fevers.

Benny slipped in and out of consciousness. Even when awake he was not always alert or coherent.

'Daddy?'

'Yes, Benny?'

'Is that you?'

'It's me.'

'Where am I?'

'In bed. Safe. I'm here, Benny.'

'Is supper ready?'

'Not yet.'

'I'd like burgers and fries.'

'That's what we're having.'

'Where're my shoes?'

'You don't need shoes tonight, Benny.'

'Thought we were going for a walk.'

'Not tonight.'

'Oh.'

Then he sighed and slipped away again.

Rain was falling outside. Drops pattered against the ICU windows and streamed down the panes. The storm contributed to the gray mood that had claimed the world.

Once, near midnight, Benny woke and was lucid. He knew exactly where he was, who I was, and what was happening. He turned his head toward me and smiled. He tried to rise up on one arm, but he was too weak even to lift his head.

I got out of my chair, stood at the side of his bed, held his hand, and said, 'All these wires . . . I think they're going to replace a few of your parts with robot stuff.'

'I'll be okay,' he said in a faint, tremulous voice that was strangely, movingly confident.

'You want a chip of ice to suck on?'

'No. What I want . . .'

'What? Anything you want, Benny.'

'I'm scared, Daddy . . .'

My throat grew tight, and I was afraid that I was going to lose the composure that I had strived so hard to hold onto during the long weeks of his illness. I swallowed and said, 'Don't be scared, Benny. I'm with you. Don't –'

'No,' he said, interrupting me. 'I'm not scared . . . for me. I'm afraid . . . for you.'

I thought he was delirious again, and I didn't know what to say.

But he was not delirious, and with his next few words he made himself painfully clear: 'I want us all . . . to be together again . . . like we were before Mommy died . . . together again someday. But I'm afraid that you . . . won't . . . find us.'

The rest is agonizing to recall. I was indeed so obsessed with holding fast to my atheism that I could not bring myself to tell my son a harmless lie that would make his last minutes easier. If only I had promised to believe, had told him that I would seek him in the next world, he would have gone to his rest more happily. Ellen was right when she called it an obsession. I merely held Benny's hand tighter, blinked back tears, and smiled at him.

He said, 'If you don't believe you can find us . . . then maybe you won't find us.'

'It's all right, Benny,' I said soothingly. I kissed him on the forehead, on his left cheek, and for a moment I put my face against his and held him as best I could, trying to compensate with affection for the promise of faith that I refused to give.

'Daddy . . . if only . . . you'd look for us?'

'You'll be okay, Benny.'

'. . . just *look* for us . . .'

'I love you, Benny. I love you with all my heart.'

'. . . if you look for us . . . you'll find us . . .'

'I love you, I love you, Benny.'

'. . . don't look . . . won't find . . .'

'Benny, Benny. . . .'

The gray ICU light fell on the gray sheets and on the gray face of my son.

The gray rain streamed down the gray window.

He died while I held him.

Abruptly color came back into the world. Far too much color, too intense, overwhelming. The light brown of Benny's staring, sightless eyes was the purest, most penetrating, most beautiful brown that I had ever seen. The ICU walls were a pale blue that made me feel as if they were not made of plaster but of water, and as if I was about to be drowned in a turbulent sea. The sour-apple green of the EKG monitor screen blazed bright, searing my eyes. The watery blue walls flowed toward me. I heard running footsteps as nurses and interns responded to the lack of telemetry data from their small patient, but before they arrived I was swept away by a blue tide, carried into deep blue currents.

* * *

I shut down my company. I withdrew from negotiations for new commissions. I arranged for those commissions already undertaken to be transferred as quickly as possible to other design firms of which I approved and with which my clients felt comfortable. I pink-slipped my employees, though with generous severance pay, and helped them to find new jobs where possible.

I converted my wealth into treasury certificates and conservative savings instruments, investments that required no monitoring. The temptation to sell the house was great, but after considerable thought I merely closed it up and hired a part-time caretaker to look after it in my absence.

Years later than Hal Sheen, I had reached his conclusion that no monuments of man were worth the effort it took to erect them. Even the greatest edifices of stone and steel were pathetic vanities, of no consequence in the long run. When viewed in the context of the vast, cold universe in which trillions of stars blazed down on tens of trillions of planets, even the pyramids were as fragile as origami sculptures. In the dark light of death and entropy, even heroic effort and acts of genius appeared foolish.

Yet relationships with family and friends were no more enduring than humanity's fragile monuments of stone. I had oncc told Benny that we lived on in memory, in the genetic trace, in the kindness that our own kindnesses encouraged in others. But those things now seemed as insubstantial as shapes of smoke in a brisk wind.

Unlike Hal Sheen, however, I did not seek comfort in religion. No blows were hard enough to crack my obsession.

I had thought that religious mania was the worst horror of all, but now I had found one that was worse: the horror of an atheist who, unable to believe in God, is suddenly also unable to believe in the value of human struggle and courage, and is therefore unable to find meaning in anything whatsoever, neither in beauty nor in pleasure nor in the smallest act of kindness.

I spent that autumn in Bermuda. I bought a Cheoy Lee sixty-six-foot sport yacht, a sleek and powerful boat, and learned how to handle it. Alone, I ran the Caribbean, sampling island after island. Sometimes I dawdled along at quarter-throttle for days at a time, in sync with the lazy rhythms of Caribbean life. But then suddenly I would be overcome with the frantic need to move, to stop wasting time, and I would press forward, engines screaming, slamming across the waves with reckless abandon, as if it mattered whether I got anywhere by any particular time.

When I tired of the Caribbean, I went to Brazil, but Rio held my interest for only a few days. I became a rich drifter, moving from one first-class hotel to another in one far-flung city after another: Hong Kong, Singapore, Istanbul, Paris,

Athens, Cairo, New York, Las Vegas, Acapulco, Tokyo, San Francisco. I was looking for something that would give meaning to life, though the search was conducted with the certain knowledge that I would not find what I sought.

For a few days I thought I could devote my life to gambling. In the random fall of cards, in the spin of roulette wheels, I glimpsed the strange, wild shape of fate. By committing myself to swimming in that deep river of randomness, I thought I might be in harmony with the pointlessness and disorder of the universe and therefore at peace. In less than a week I won and lost fortunes, and at last I walked away from the gaming tables with a hundred-thousand-dollar loss. That was only a tiny fraction of the millions on which I could draw, but in those few days I learned that even immersion in the chaos of random chance provided no escape from an awareness of the finite nature of life and of all things human.

In the spring I went home to die. I'm not sure if I meant to kill myself. Or, having lost the will to live, perhaps I believed that I could just lie down in a familiar place and succumb to death without needing to lift my hand against myself. But although I did not know how death would be attained, I was certain death was my goal.

The house in Buck's County was filled with painful memories of Ellen and Benny, and when I went into the kitchen and looked out the window at the cherry trees in the back yard, my heart ached as if pinched in a vise. The trees were ablaze with thousands of pink and white blossoms.

Benny had loved the cherry trees when they were at their radiant best, and the sight of their blossoms sharpened my memories of Benny so well that I felt I had been stabbed. For a while I leaned against the kitchen counter, unable to breathe, then gasped painfully for breath, then wept.

In time I went out and stood beneath the trees, looking up at the beautifully decorated branches. Benny had been dead almost nine months, but the trees he had loved were still thriving, and in some way I could not quite grasp, their continued existence meant that at least a part of Benny was still alive. I struggled to understand that crazy idea –

– and suddenly the cherry blossoms fell. Not just a few. Not just hundreds. Within one minute every blossom on both trees dropped to the ground. I turned around, around, startled and confused, and the whirling white flowers were as thick as snowflakes in a blizzard. I had never seen anything like it. Cherry blossoms just don't fall by the thousands, simultaneously, on a windless day.

When the phenomenon ended I plucked blossoms off my shoulders and out of my hair. I examined them closely. They were not withered or seared or marked by any sign of tree disease.

I looked up at the branches.

Not one blossom remained on either tree.

My heart was hammering.

Around my feet, drifts of cherry blossoms began to stir in a mild breeze that sprang up from the west.

'No,' I said, so frightened that I could not even admit to myself what I was saying no *to*.

I turned from the trees and ran to the house. As I went, the last of the cherry blossoms blew off my hair and clothes.

In the library, however, as I took a bottle of Jack Daniels from the bar cabinet, I realized that I was still clutching blossoms in my hand. I threw them down on the floor and scrubbed my palm on my pants as if I had been handling something foul.

I went to the bedroom with the Jack Daniels and drank myself unconscious, refusing to face up to the reason why I needed to drink at all. I told myself that it had nothing to do with the cherry tree, that I was drinking only because I needed to escape the misery of the past few years.

Mine was a diamond-hard obsession.

* * *

I slept for eleven hours and woke with a hangover. I took two aspirin, stood in the shower under very hot water for fifteen minutes, under a cold spray for one minute, toweled vigorously, took two more aspirins, and went into the kitchen to make coffee.

Through the window above the sink, I saw the cherry trees ablaze with pink and white blossoms.

Hallucination, I thought with relief. Yesterday's blizzard of blossoms was just hallucination.

I ran outside for a closer look at the trees. I saw that only a few pink-white petals were scattered on the lush grass beneath the boughs, no more than would have blown off in the mild spring breeze.

Relieved but also curiously disappointed, I returned to the kitchen. The coffee had brewed. As I poured a cupful, I remembered the blossoms that I had cast aside in the library.

I drank two cups of fine Colombian before I had the nerve to go to the library. The blossoms were there: a wad of crushed petals that had yellowed and acquired brown edges during the night. I picked them up, closed my hand around them.

All right, I told myself shakily, you don't have to believe in Christ or in God the Father or in some bodiless Holy Spirit.

Religion is a disease.

No, no, you don't have to believe in any of the silly rituals, in the dogma and doctrine. In fact you don't have to believe in *God* to believe in an afterlife.

Irrational, unreasonable.

No, wait, think about it: Isn't it possible that life after death is perfectly natural, not a divine gift but a simple fact of nature? The caterpillar lives one life, then transforms itself to live again as a butterfly. So, damn it, isn't it conceivable that our bodies are the caterpillar stage and that our spirits take flight into another existence when the bodies are no longer of use to us? The human metamorphosis may just be a transformation of a higher order than that of the caterpillar.

Slowly, with dread and yet hope, I walked through the

house, out the back door, up the sloped yard to the cherry trees. I stood beneath their flowery boughs and opened my hand to reveal the blossoms I had saved from yesterday.

'Benny?' I said wonderingly.

The blossom fall began again. From both trees, the pink and white petals dropped in profusion, spinning lazily to the grass, catching in my hair and on my clothes.

I turned, breathless, gasping. 'Benny? Benny?'

In a minute the ground was covered with a white mantle, and again not one small bloom remained on the trees.

I laughed. It was a nervous laugh that might degenerate into a mad cackle. I was not in control of myself.

Not quite sure why I was speaking aloud, I said, 'I'm scared. Oh, shit, am I scared.'

The blossoms began to drift up from the ground. Not just a few of them. All of them. They rose back toward the branches that had shed them only moments ago. It was a blizzard in reverse. The soft petals brushed against my face.

I was laughing again, laughing uncontrollably, but my fear was fading rapidly, and this was good laughter.

Within another minute, the trees were cloaked in pink and white as before, and all was still.

I sensed that Benny was not within the tree, that this phenomenon did not conform to pagan belief any more than it did to traditional Christianity. But he was *somewhere*. He was not gone forever. He was out there somewhere, and when my time came to go where he and Ellen had gone, I only needed to believe that they could be found, and then I would surely find them.

The sound of an obsession cracking could probably be heard all the way to China.

A scrap of writing by H.G. Wells came into my mind. I had always admired Wells' work, but nothing he had written had ever seemed so true as that which I recalled while standing under the cherry trees: 'The past is but the beginning of a beginning, and all that is and has been is but the twilight of the dawn.' He was writing about history, of course, and about the long future that awaited mankind, but those words seemed to apply, as well, to death and to the mysterious rebirth that followed it. A man might live a hundred years, yet his long life is but the twilight of the dawn.

'Benny,' I said. 'Oh, Benny.'

But no more blossoms fell, and through the years that followed I received no more signs. Nor did I need them.

From that day forward, I knew that death was not the end and that I would be rejoined with Ellen and Benny on the other side.

And what of God? Does He exist? I don't know. Although I have believed in an afterlife of some kind for ten years now, I have not become a churchgoer. But if, upon my death, I cross into that other plane and find Him waiting for me, I will not be entirely surprised, and I will return to His arms as gratefully and happily as I will return to Ellen's and to Benny's.

Edward Bryant

AUTHOR'S NOTE

Try this at a party, sometime.

I have and it works.

Pick somebody out of the crowd. It doesn't matter if they're a man or a woman. All that matters is that they're human. Back them into a corner. Not by the chip-and-dip table. Find a place that's quieter, less congested. If you can, try the bedroom where all the coats are stacked on the bed.

Make them tell you if they've ever killed anyone.

Don't let them weasel with their war stories and auto crashes and fatal sins of omission. Find out if they ever put the serrated blade of the bread knife between someone's ribs and then sawed back and forth, or if they know what it's like to gently wiggle the barrel of a pistol into someone's mouth and squeeze the trigger. Ask if they know what human blood really smells like. How much of it spills out of the punctured human body. What it tastes like when it isn't yours.

I'm never surprised at how many answer me honestly.

I'm never surprised at how many know.

Predators

Her nostrils were choked with the stench of bus fumes and all the other myriad odors crushed down into the streets by the winter inversion layer. Another day of looking for work in the city . . . Still no luck.

Lisa Blackwell's first reaction to the person who'd moved in upstairs was bewilderment. She could smell the fresh Dymo label on #12's mailbox in the downstairs hall. It read 'R.G. Cross.' Evidently the moving in of furniture and whatever other personal belongings had taken place earlier in the day, while Lisa had been hitting the job agencies for interviews.

The afternoon hadn't gone well. Lisa didn't like the cold, cloudy October weather – it looked as if it was going to snow. Worse, she didn't think she had uncovered any good employment leads. It had been weeks now, and the money the missionaries had given her was running out. She didn't want to check the balance in her new checking account. It was so important to make it here . . . Lisa wanted her parents to be proud.

Her apartment had been restful, a quiet refuge, with no one living upstairs. But now she had a neighbor. The first thing she learned about him – Lisa assigned him a gender upon no particularly firm evidence – was his taste in music. It was raucous and simplistic. She felt the vibration as soon as she entered her own apartment and shut the door. Then he punched the volume up. The bass line predominated. From time to time, a buzzsaw treble would slice through the bass. Lisa thought she could see the ceiling vibrate. Her ears hurt.

She decided to endure it. Surely he would get tired, leave, go to sleep, choose a more interesting album. Lisa understood that what she was listening to second-hand was heavy metal. She had learned that she preferred jazz. She loved the intricate rhythms. If worse came to worst, Lisa knew she could call the building managers and complain. That privilege had been explained to her when she'd moved in.

The next thing she discovered about her neighbor was the fact of his sexual activity. At about seven o'clock, Lisa was taking a pound of ground beef out of the refrigerator. The heavy, sweet odor hung in the air. She felt – as well as heard – the stereo upstairs turned down. Then she heard heavy steps clump out onto the third-floor landing and descend. On the ground floor, the foyer door squeaked open. Two sets of footsteps ascended. She heard voices – a treble piping mixed with the bass rumble. The door to apartment 12 banged shut.

It wasn't, Lisa thought, as though she was truly eavesdropping. The building was about fifty years old; the construction, thin to begin with, was loosening up.

The music from above started again, though the volume wasn't as loud as it had been in the afternoon. At eleven, Lisa lay sleepless on her Salvation Army Thrift Store mattress. She needed her rest. Bags beneath her eyes at job interviews . . . no! She had just decided to throw on a robe and go upstairs to ask her new neighbor to turn the volume down when the stereo abruptly shut off. Lisa curled up in a warm ball.

The respite was brief. Sounds began again from upstairs. Since the apartment layouts were identical from floor to floor, her neighbor's bedroom was directly above Lisa's own. R.G. Cross's bedsprings were not subtle. She tried to ignore the rhythm, then pulled the ends of the pillow around her head when she heard private cries.

After a time, the squeaking stopped and the thumping began. In spite of herself, Lisa wondered what *that* noise meant: a steady, muffled *flump, flump*. Something that sounded liquid spattered on the floor above. How weird *was* R.G. Cross?

She didn't wonder long. The sounds stopped for good. Exhausted, homesick, a little lonely, wondering when she would ever get a job in this strange, new city, Lisa fell asleep.

She dreamed of a warm, lazy, savanna summer, and of lush sun-dappled foliage. It was all green and golden and smelled like life itself. She wanted to be again with everyone she'd left, Lisa thought fuzzily. Mama . . .

* * *

The next day was Saturday. Lisa had no interviews, but she did have a sheaf of application forms to fill out. She hadn't gotten up until noon. Between mild depression keeping her in bed, along with the simultaneous feeling of stolen luxury, she dozed away the morning.

When her eyes finally flickered open for good, her mind registered the time as 11:56. Digital clocks amazed her with their precision. Lisa rolled over on her back and remembered vaguely having been awakened earlier in the morning by angry voices from upstairs. She slowly and luxuriously stretched, then padded toward the bathroom.

Lisa brushed her hair and cleaned her teeth. Then she put on her gloves, terrycloth robe, and slippers, and went downstairs to collect her newspaper. The stairway was chilly, as though someone had left the outer door propped open.

She encountered a tall, blond stranger in the front hall. Lisa scented him before she actually saw him. He smelled of some sharp, citrus cologne.

'Hi, there.' He shoved a large, tanned hand at her. 'You're my downstairs neighbor, right? I'm Roger.'

Lisa glanced at the mailbox and back at him. 'R.G. Cross.'

'That's me.' He grinned widely. For a second, all Lisa could see was the array of flawless white teeth. 'Mighty nice to meet you.'

His hand overpowered hers. She withdrew her fingers, sensing he could have crushed down much harder. Roger leaned back against the wall and hooked his thumbs in his jeans pockets. He was more than a full head taller than she, though Lisa could stare level into the eyes of most of the men she'd met. He had an athlete's powerful physique. He probably works out every day, she thought. His jaw was strong. Roger's eyes were a bright, cold blue; his hair, tousled and light. His grin didn't seem to vary from second to second by a single millimeter.

Roger unhooked one thumb to gesture at the mailbox. 'You must be L.P. Blackwell.'

Lisa nodded politely and started to turn toward the steps with her paper.

'What's it stand for?'

'Lisa Penelope.'

Roger stuck out one long leg so that his foot partially blocked her exit. 'Oh yeah? Could stand for a lot of other things.'

Unsure what to do now, Lisa paused at the foot of the stairs. She examined her options. The list was short.

Roger said, 'Could stand for Long Playing . . .'

She stiffened, feeling a chill of apprehension.

'Like with a record album.' He chuckled at his own joke. 'Long playing, all right. Stereo too, probably.' He smiled at her expression, then looked slowly and deliberately down the front of her to the floor, and then back up again.

'Excuse me, but I need to get upstairs.' Lisa made her voice sound as decisive as she could.

'So what's the hurry?' His voice remained warm and friendly.

'I need to fix breakfast.' She regretted saying anything the moment the words came out, but by then it was too late.

'I haven't had breakfast yet either,' Roger said. 'You like breakfast? I know I do. Best way to start the day.'

Lisa looked straight ahead, up the stairwell. She sighed and said nothing. She didn't want this to mean trouble.

'We could do it together,' said Roger. 'Breakfast. What sort of meat do you like in the morning?'

'Please move your leg.' He slowly, with great deliberation, evidently savoring the power of the moment, withdrew his foot from her path. 'Thank you.' Lisa resisted the impulse to bound up the steps two at a time.

He called after her, 'Hey, don't mind me, L.P. I'm feeling good today. Great night, last night. Now I'm just high-spirited, you know?'

Lisa fumbled with her keys. She heard slow, steady steps ascending the staircase. She practically kicked the door open when the latch clicked. Once in the refuge of her apartment, she closed and locked the door. Then she turned the dead-bolt home. She did not want trouble. She had enough on her mind already.

'Damn it,' she said under her breath. 'Damn them. Why are they like that?'

* * *

Lisa spent Saturday afternoon filling out job application forms. Unfortunately she recognized her employability problems, not the least of which was her inability to type. After two hours of laborious and exquisitely neat printing, she took a break and made a pot of rich cambric. In rapid succession, she turned on a TV movie, switched it off, picked up a new paper-back mystery she'd bought at Safeway, then put it down when she realized she wasn't concentrating on the plot.

Someone knocked at her front door.

Lisa hesitated.

Her building dated back to the late 'twenties or early 'thirties. Lisa's managers had told her that with some pride.

This was a building that hadn't been razed to make room for a modern and characterless highrise. Some of the art deco touches still remained. About half the renovated apartments had glass spy-tubes in the front doors so that the tenants could scrutinize whatever callers stood on the other side. Lisa's door had something that antedated the tubes. She could open a little hinged metal door set at face height, and look out through a grill of highly stylized palm trees cast in some pewter-colored metal.

If she opened the little door. She hesitated.

There was a second, more insistent knock. She heard the floor-board creaking of someone shifting his weight. She could hear breathing on the other side of the door.

Lisa reached for the latch of the small door and pulled it open. She looked into the apparently eternally grinning face of Roger Cross.

'Oh, hi,' he said nonchalantly.

'Hello.' Lisa made the word utterly neutral.

'Hey, listen. I want to apologize for sort of coming off the wall before. You know, stepping out of line.' Roger met her gaze directly. He reached up with one hand to scratch the back of his head boyishly, tousling the carefully styled blond hair. 'I didn't mean to come across as such a turkey. Honest.'

'It's all right,' said Lisa. She wasn't sure what else to say. 'Thanks for saying that.'

'Say, could I come in?'

He must have seen something in her expression. Roger quickly added, 'You know, just for a little while. I thought maybe we could sit down and talk. Get acquainted. You know, I really want to be a good neighbor.' The grin became a sincere smile. 'And friends.'

Lisa said nothing for a few seconds, trying to get a handle on this. 'Not – now, thanks, I'm not ready. I mean I wasn't expecting company and –'

'I don't mind a mess,' Roger said. 'You should see my place. A real sty.'

She momentarily noted his vocabulary and wondered that he knew a word like 'sty.' He definitely didn't seem rural. But then, she thought, she knew she had never met anyone like this before. 'No. Really. We – I can't.'

He switched tracks. 'Hey, L.P., you living on your own for the first time?'

Startled, Lisa said, 'How'd you know that?'

'I thought so. You look pretty young. Going to college?'

She couldn't help responding. 'No. I haven't had much formal schooling.'

'Neat accent,' he said. 'I can't quite place it. From the South?'

She nodded. 'A ways.' *Dappled sunlight on the leaves.* Lisa felt a sudden stab of homesickness like an arrow piercing her side.

'Great winters here. You come north to live so you could ski?'

'No.' It had never occurred to her to ski.

'That's why I came here. That and work. I've got a great job with an oil company. Marketing.'

Floundering, Lisa said, 'That must be . . .'

'Oh yeah, real interesting. Get to work with the public. Meet people.' The sincere smile became more engaging. 'Say, you come out here to get away from your family?'

'Uh, yes,' she said. Lisa felt more pangs, equally painful. *Food, warmth, security, all provided. Her mother's satiny touch.* She suddenly and desperately wanted to see her parents again. She wanted so much to be on her own, but she also needed to be stroked and reassured. For the thousandth time she regretted leaving home.

'I know what it's like,' said Roger earnestly. 'I've been on my own for a long time. Never knew my father. Mother died when I was real young. Really I've got no family.' His voice lowered. 'I know it gets real lonely here in the city.'

'Yes,' said Lisa. 'It does.'

'Let me make things up,' he said. 'You want some hot

coffee? I've got some great Colombian grind up in my place.'

'I drink tea.'

'Got all the Celestial Seasonings flavors. Or black, if you want it.'

'No thanks,' she said. 'I just made a pot.' Lisa turned her head and glanced across the living room at the pot of cambric slowly cooling beneath the quilted cat-print cozy. 'It'll be getting cold, so I'd better go.' She thought of the skim forming on the surface of the milk. Lisa turned toward him again. 'Excuse me, please.'

'Wait!' he said, seeming a little frantic now. 'This is important –'

'Yes?'

'Listen, how's your laundry?'

'Beg your pardon?' What *was* he talking about?

'Don't you do your laundry on the weekend?'

'Well, yes.' Lisa had lived in the apartment for little more than a month, but already discovered that she hated the laundry room. It was a dark, dank cell in the basement beneath the house next door. The laundry served both buildings, as the two were owned by the same company. The room contained two sets of coin-operated washers and dryers. All the machines were usually in use all the weekend daylight hours. It was a secluded and uncomfortable place at night.

The closest commercial laundramat was more than a mile away, and Lisa had no car.

'I'm gonna do a load sometime tonight,' said Roger. 'If I don't, no socks and underwear for Monday morning. If you want to come along and do a load too –' He spread his hands. 'I could escort you, make sure no freako jumps out and grabs you. We could get in some civilized conversation down there. Don't you need to wash some clothes?'

Of course she did. Lisa had been putting off the laundry room expedition. She really did need clean clothing for Monday. 'Thanks anyway,' she said. 'I've got to stay in tonight and work. I've got a lot to do.'

'I think you're lying,' said Roger quietly.

'I really do have –'

'*Lying*!' Roger slammed the heel of his hand against the door. It jumped and rattled in its frame. Lisa involuntarily stepped backward.

'So what's wrong with me, you black bitch?' Roger shoved his face forward so that he blocked the entire opening. It occurred to Lisa that this was like looking out of a wild animal's cage – or into one. There was a fixedness to his eyes that she wondered might be madness. She had done nothing to bring this on herself. *Nothing*!

'Listen, I'm sorry,' she said, stepping forward and flipping the little metal door firmly shut. She heard him outside, now speaking to the closed door.

'These doors are old. Not stout at all. I could kick this one down in just two seconds. Just like the big bad wolf . . .'

'Please go 'way,' said Lisa. 'I'll call the manager.'

'You think you're gold, don't you?' His voice was low and intense. She could hear him working into a frenzy. 'You think *it*'s gold.'

'Go. Please.'

'You know who I am, Lisa? I'm the boogey man. And I eat up, little girls just like that.'

Lisa decided that perhaps if she didn't answer him any more, he'd go away.

'So don't answer. I know you're there.'

She still said nothing.

'You know who you are?' Roger's chuckle decayed to something horrible. 'You're a puckered little prude. I think maybe you need to be loosened up.'

Lisa tried to back away from the door quietly, hoping none of the boards in the hardwood floor would creak.

'*I hear you*! You know what else you are, L.P.? You're a real fruitcake.'

She continued to step quietly away from the door.

Roger laughed, almost a giggle. He said, 'You're *so* weird, girl. Right out of the sticks – or is it off the plantation? Who else would wear gloves with a terrycloth robe. You –'

He said a string of things she didn't want to hear, including a few she didn't understand. Finally he seemed to run out of obscenities. Roger evidently turned away from the door and his voice became muffled. His deliberate, slow steps clumped upstairs. She heard his door open and slam shut.

Even though he was gone, she still tried to move as quietly as she could toward the couch and the tea cozy. The pot was still warm, so she poured herself a cup of well-steeped cambric. The milky, soothing scent filled the living room.

Lisa Blackwell had never before encountered anyone like Roger Cross. She had heard of them – creatures like him. A danger to their kind. She said to herself softly, 'What is wrong with him?' And was confounded by the inexplicable.

* * *

Later that evening, Lisa heard Roger go out. She listened to the sound of him descending the back stairs, past her kitchen door. Something trailed his footsteps with a series of soft impacts. It made her think of something large and dangerous, dragging its prey. Almost against her will, she went to the kitchen window and looked down as the building's rear door swung open. Roger emerged, dragging a laundry bag.

So he does have a load to wash, she thought. Not that it made any difference. The man was clearly disturbed, a defective individual. Roger rounded the corner of the adjacent house and was lost to sight.

Lisa went into the living room and looked at the number she'd written on the piece of paper taped beside the telephone. She called the managers, a married couple who lived in the house above the laundry room. She got it wrong on the first attempt and had to dial again.

Joanne, the female half of the managerial team, answered the phone and Lisa identified herself.

'Right,' said Joanne. 'You're in number ten. What can I do for you?'

Lisa hesitated, then gave the woman an abbreviated account of her encounters with Roger, leaving out most of the things he'd said that she didn't want to repeat. It was still enough to kindle concern in Joanne's voice.

'You might be interested in knowing,' the manager said, 'that you're the second complaint. I heard from the tenant in number two. Our studly friend gave her a come-on too. Nothing as jerk-off as his thing with you, but it was still scummy enough for her to mention it to me.' She hesitated. 'I only talked to the guy a little when he first came to look at the apartment. He seemed harmless enough then.'

Lisa said nothing.

Joanne volunteered, 'Listen, if you're really upset tonight, you're welcome to come over here. Joe and I have a couch you can use. You won't have to worry about that guy sneaking around your place.'

Lisa considered it. 'No,' she finally said. 'Thank you very much, but no. I'd have to go home sometime. Anyhow, I'm probably just overreacting. I'll go ahead and stay here tonight and keep my door double-locked.'

'You're sure? Really, it's no problem if you want to come over.'

'Thanks again, Joanne. I'm sure.' No, she wasn't sure, but she wasn't going to admit it. If she were going to be on her own in the city, then she'd just have to learn to cope. Breaking free. That's what she had come here for. Roger G. Cross wasn't going to spoil it for her.

'I've got an idea,' Joanne said. 'The owners'll be back from vacation Monday. First thing Tuesday morning, I'll get hold of them and explain about you and the other tenant that jerk hassled. Maybe the owners can find grounds to evict the son of a bitch, okay?'

Lisa thanked her and then kept the phone pressed to her ear long after Joanne had set down the receiver. She listened to the indecipherable whispers of the dead line, then the click and dial tone. Finally she hung up and sat there, not moving and blindly staring at the knotted fiber wall-hanging her friends at home had given her.

She realized she was tired, very tired. Stress. She had read articles about it. It was not a condition she was accustomed to in her old home. It did not please her.

In bed, she felt the cold desolation of being alone and lonely in a strange place. The feeling hadn't changed in all these weeks. She reminded herself she would keep trying.

After a long time, and not until she heard the telltale sounds of Roger Cross returning from the laundry room and closing his door, Lisa fell asleep.

She dreamed of traps.

* * *

In the morning, she woke tense, the muscles in her shoulders tight and sore. She awoke listening, straining to hear sounds from the upstairs apartment. She heard nothing other than the occasional traffic outside and the slight hum of the clock by the bed.

Lisa lay awake for an hour before uncurling and getting out of bed. There was still nothing to hear from upstairs. Finally she put on her robe and gloves and went into the living room, hoping for sun-warmth from the east windows. It was another cloudy day.

She almost missed the scrap of paper that had been slipped beneath her front door. Lisa gingerly picked the thing up and examined it curiously. It was a heart cut from a doubled sheet of red construction paper. The heart bore the inscription in wide, ink-marker slashes: 'R.C. + L.P.' She set the thing down on the coffee table and stared at it a while. Then she crumpled the Valentine into a ball and dropped it into the kitchen trash sack.

Lisa returned to the front door, opened the spy panel and

looked out. Nobody. She opened the door a crack. No one lurked outside on the landing. She quietly and quickly descended the flight to the foyer. No one confronted her when she claimed her Sunday paper from the skiff of snow sifted on the front step. Roger didn't ambush her when she returned to her own door. The building was still and quiet, just as it had been every other Sunday Lisa had lived there.

The telephone rang as she closed the door. Lisa picked up the receiver and heard Roger's voice say, 'Listen, Lisa, please don't hang up yet, okay?'

This confused her. She hesitated.

'Did you get what I left you?'

'The heart?' she said, still feeling she was lagging.

'I know you must have found it – the Valentine. I didn't want to knock and wake you up.'

She wasn't sure of an appropriate response. 'Thank you.'

'I'm really sorry about yesterday. Sometimes I get into moods, you know? I guess I was sort of on the rag.' He chuckled.

Lisa didn't answer.

'Did you like the Valentine?'

'It's – early, isn't it?'

There was an odd tone in his voice. 'You're worth anticipating, Lisa.'

'I'm going to go now,' she said.

'Don't you dare,' he said quietly. 'I need to talk to you. I want to see you.'

This was more than enough. 'Goodbye.' She set the phone down.

Lisa fixed a light breakfast – her ordinarily healthy appetite was diminished – and read the newspaper while she ate. She discovered she was reading the same headline paragraph over and over. She flipped to the comics section.

The phone rang. This time she let it ring half a dozen times before answering.

Roger. His voice was coldly furious. 'Don't you *ever* hang up on me, Lisa. I can't stand that.'

'Listen to me,' she said. 'Don't bother –'

'*Never* do that!'

'– me again,' she finished. 'Just. Go. Away.'

There was a long silence. Then it sounded like he was crying.

Lisa set the receiver down. She realized she was gripping the hand-piece as though it was a club. She willed her fingers to relax.

She paced the perimeter of the living room until she decided there were more productive outlets for her nervous energy. For part of the afternoon, she scrubbed out the kitchen and bathroom. By sundown, she'd begun to relax. Roger was apparently not home. Either he impossibly wasn't moving so much as an inch, or he'd gone out. The hardwood floor didn't squeak up there. No sounds filtered down from the bedroom. The stereo was mute.

When the telephone rang, Lisa stared at the set as though it were a curled viper. She allowed it to ring twenty times before answering. It could be an emergency. It could be Joanne or someone else. She picked up the receiver and said, 'Hello?' Nothing. 'Hello,' she said again. Someone was there. She could hear him breathing. Then the other receiver clicked into its cradle. In a few seconds more, Lisa heard the hum of the dial tone.

Roger Cross was a new listing in directory assistance. Lisa dialed the number the computer voice intoned. When she held the receiver away from her ear, she could hear the telephone ring upstairs. No one answered.

By early evening, Lisa found she was ravenous. She fixed herself a splendid supper of very rare steak and ate every morsel. She wondered if Roger were in some suburban singles bar picking up easier prey. While washing the day's dishes, she began to contemplate the unpleasant possibility of having to move to another neighborhood. It wasn't fair. She wouldn't go. She *liked* this apartment.

The phone rang. Lisa ignored it. Ten minutes later, it rang again. And ten minutes after that. Finally, she picked up the receiver with a curt '*What.*'

'Hey, don't bite my head off.' It was Joanne. The manager hadn't seen Roger all day either. She was calling to check on Lisa. Lisa told her about Roger's harassment.

'You could try calling Mountain Bell.'

'Maybe I will,' said Lisa.

'Listen, the offer's still open if you want to stay over here.'

Lisa felt stubborn. Territorial. 'No,' she said. 'Thank you.'

'Hang in there and I'll talk to the owners on Tuesday,' said Joanne.

Lisa thanked her and hung up.

By eight o'clock, Lisa was again immersed in comfortable cleaning routines. She swept all the floors. Then she gave the shower curtain a scrub-down. She dusted the shelves in the walk-in closet and put down Contac paper. Finally she returned to the bathroom and considered running a hot bath. It occurred to her she was out of clean towels. In fact, she was out of *everything* clean.

It sank home that she didn't really have anything clean and neat to wear in the morning. Lisa knew it would be an error to appear at interviews in limp Western shirts and grubby blue-jeans. She had one good wash-and-wear outfit. Her first interview was at nine; that meant she would have to catch the bus before eight. Something had to be done about the laundry tonight. Since coming to the city, she'd been called *too* clean, *too* neat. She couldn't help it.

Lisa didn't relish the idea of taking her dirty clothes and soap and bleach into that very cold night and descending to the laundry room next door, but there seemed to be no alternatives. Lisa cocked her head and glanced at the ceiling. She still had not heard a sound from upstairs. Maybe Roger had got lucky at some bar and no longer concerned himself with her. Perhaps he had drunk too much and fallen in front of a speeding truck. That thought was not without a tinge of hope.

It wasn't getting any earlier. She would need a full night's sleep.

Lisa stuffed everything she would need into the plastic laundry basket and unlocked her rear door. The back staircase was dimly lit by exit signs on each landing. The light cast her shadow weakly in front of her on the yellowed walls.

She counted. Seven steps down to the landing. Turn a blind corner to the left. Seven more steps to the first floor. Before opening the outer door, she belatedly fumbled for her keys. They were in her hip pocket.

The night was just as cold as she had anticipated. She felt the goose flesh form. The fine hairs rose on the back of her neck. The cracked concrete slab sidewalk extended the length of the apartment building. Lisa walked toward the alley, her stride faltering for a moment when she noticed the door of the garage across the alley hanging open. She thought she saw something move within the deeper darkness of the interior. She heard nothing. Probably just imagination. Probably.

She followed a branching path to the right, around a pair of blighted and dying elms. Now she was at the rear of the house where her managers lived. The building was an elaborate Victorian which had been converted into apartments sometime in the 'fifties. The original brickwork was plastered over and painted green. All the windows in the rear of the house were dark.

The long, straight flight of cement steps led to the basement and the laundry room. One, two . . . She realized she was counting the steps under her breath. . . . five, six . . . The temperature dropped perceptibly as she descended. . . . ten. A level space and then a door. The sign tacked on the outside read: LAUNDRY EQUIPMENT AND PIPES WILL FREEZE IF DOOR REMAINS OPEN.

Lisa pushed the door open. The wood had swelled and the bottom scraped the cement floor. The hall was not illuminated, but she could see light glowing from within the laundry room, ahead and to her left. The hallway was long and dusty. She scented the odor of must and mildew. Eventually the passageway ended in darkness, where Lisa knew were locked storage rooms and a barricaded staircase leading up to the rest of the house.

Her steps echoed slightly as she hefted the basket and started toward the laundry room. She felt, rather than heard, the door swing shut behind her. She didn't turn and look. Don't get paranoid, she thought.

Inside the laundry room, she set the basket down beside the more reputable-looking of the washers. The place smelled of neglect and decay. Lisa had the exaggerated feeling that even clean clothes could get dirty instantly just by being brought into this room. The brick walls showed through the crumbling plaster. The ceiling was a maze of haphazard exposed piping and conduits, ribbed from above by skeletal strips of lath.

She had loaded the washer and was adding the bleach when she heard the outside door scrape open distantly. She smelled the citrus cologne.

Lisa heard footsteps advance down the corridor toward the doorway of the laundry room. There was no place she could go, so she set down the bottle of bleach and waited.

Roger filled the doorway, grinning as happily as ever. 'Hi there, L.P.,' he said. 'I waited a long time for you. It's cold out here.' He rubbed his hands briskly. 'It gets lonely in the dark.'

'What do you want?' Lisa said.

'To get to know you.' His voice warmed like syrup heating on the kitchen range. 'I like hair that dark and sleek. I love green eyes. Too bad you don't have more on top –' his gaze flickered to her chest ' – but no one can have everything.'

She stood still, hands at her sides.

'Nice night for finishing chores.' Roger glanced at the washer. 'You might want to take those clothes out of the machine.'

'Why?' she said.

'Just spread 'em out on the floor. I think you'll be a lot more comfortable.' He made fists of his hands, then unclenched them.

'I don't think so,' Lisa said.

'Oh? Why not?' Roger's teeth shone dully in the forty-watt glow. They looked as yellowed as old ivory.

'My family taught us to fight if we were in a corner.' The words came out quietly, calmly.

'Well, I think your family is stupid.' Spreading his arms slightly, Roger started forward. He hesitated when Lisa didn't retreat into one of the corners. Then he edged off to her right. Lisa finally reacted, moving away, but still facing him, following the contour of the wall. She was slightly closer now to the door.

'Keep going,' he said.

She looked back at him uncertainly.

'It's no accident you're by the door,' he said. 'I'm fast. Very fast. You won't make it to the stairs.'

'I'm not going to run,' said Lisa.

'Oh yeah? Why not?' Roger stared at her, apparently bewildered.

'All I wanted to do was live here peacefully,' said Lisa. She sighed. 'But you had to push.' She held up her hands, palms out. Worn leather shone. 'You think I'm weird. A fruitcake, right? Well, I am weird. But I'm not like you.' She slowly began to peel off her gloves.

His eyes stayed fixed on hers. Lisa smiled sadly at him. She felt her muzzle unhinge slightly, the jaw sliding forward. Her gloves dropped to the floor, a sound as muffled as the snow that had fallen that morning. She knew he was looking at the teeth. He should have looked at her hands. Her claws.

* * *

When she returned to her apartment with her laundry, she bathed herself, and then went into the bathroom to stare at

her own face in the mirror. *Sunlight through the leafy canopy dappled patterns on her flanks*. She examined the openings in her fingertips where the claws could fully extend. 'Mama,' she whispered. 'I don't like it here.'

But she would persevere. She knew that. She would make a life for herself.

Lisa listened to the distant sirens, the drone of an airplane, a sharp noise that might have been either a backfire or a gunshot.

The city disturbed her.

She wished she felt safe.

AUTHOR'S NOTE

I suppose what you're really asking is, 'So where do you get your ideas?'

I'm not talking about stupid conversations at parties or bars, for God's sake. I never talk to you there. I never want to. I'm talking about a more intimate time, when we're even closer than during sex. I can see you, you know. It doesn't matter how dark it is or how alone in the house you think you are. I can hear you.

You lean back with the sick fascination on your face and feel the questions ooze out with the fluids. You ask: is that sorry son of a bitch just exorcizing his own fear? Or is he trying to avoid the admission that he'd do it if he just could.

It's a sucker's quiz. You'd never ask it of genuine artists. And I wouldn't answer, even if you did.

Ask the Marquis. If you could find him. De Sade was a clever magpie, plucking up lambent fragments of truth to piece into his fabricated stories. He was probably the most accomplished magpie, coming close to knowing the truth and the language of blood. But his more gifted literary progeny depend less on vivid imaginations, more on direct experience.

It's a funny thing. For the longest time as a kid, I didn't understand the difference between fiction and journalism. Everything was equally real to me. Even after one of my teachers explained the distinction, I still wondered: in fiction, didn't the storyteller have to live the story? What good were tales that were made up?

The Baku

Whatever it was, it sucked at him – not like a maelstrom tugging at his body, but rather something unspeakable syphoning the deepest pools of his mind. Somehow he knew it was feeding on him. What it drank, he didn't know. He had only the knowledge that something had fastened on him, in him. Worse, he knew also that he wouldn't remember this when he woke up.

But there were other things he would remember . . .

* * *

The sudden white light overcame him from behind. Maxwell could feel the radiance burning through the back of his head, searing his retinas, spilling out before him from the melting panes fronting his eyes. He grabbed the steel-framed Army Air Corps glasses away from his face, but he could still see his shadow stretching impossibly far across the devastated buildings and rusted automobiles.

Robert Maxwell scrambled down the rubbled slope with the rolling explosion lingering, low and gut-shakingly bass, in his ears. As the blast died, the bricks and broken paving shifted beneath his feet, some of the debris pulling loose and rolling ahead of him, each piece starting a small rockslide of its own. He almost lost his balance, but flailed his arms, catching himself.

This place stank of death. The odor was that of roasted

meat, cooked far too long and then left out in the sun for days. Everything here was a shade of gray. All he could see lay on a monochrome spectrum between white and black.

Maxwell almost made it to the bottom of the slope before his sense of balance finally betrayed him. He sprawled forward, trying to roll and diminish the impact. The leather flying jacket helped, though his left arm started to bend the wrong way sickeningly as he put out his hand to take the fall. He felt the air knocked out of him.

He lay there in the broken stones, trying to regain his breath. His left arm didn't seem to be broken, though jagged pains shot from elbow to shoulder when he moved it. Maxwell tried to sit up. He couldn't find his glasses. He did find his USAAC captain's cap and clutched it as if it were a life preserver.

When Maxwell got to his feet, he turned and looked behind him, even though he had heard nothing. He saw what he feared. There were dozens of them, perhaps more, though he couldn't tell where the mass of shadowy stick-figures ended and the deeper shadows at the top of the slope began. They were raggedy things, tattered parodies of human beings. They moved jerkily as though infirm, and the first of them was already descending the slope. The figures moved perfectly silently, barely disturbing the rubble. In fact, Maxwell wasn't sure if his pursuers' feet were touching the stones at all.

Lungs and muscles protesting, Maxwell lunged away. He could feel the sweat cake the dust on his face. Panting, he forced himself into a stumbling run. Behind him, he thought he heard whispering.

Ahead of him loomed a ruined building. Something inside his head whispered, *refuge*. He didn't know why. But he struggled toward a dark doorway, hesitated, then entered.

There were no furnishings inside the hulk, just heaps of fallen brick and charred timbers. The room had one exterior window with a few jagged shards of remaining glass. Maxwell crouched behind one of the rubble heaps and tried to control his desperate gasping. He stared toward the window. He heard the sound of whispering, soft and indistinct.

Maxwell hunched down further behind his shelter, trying now not even to breathe, but still sneaking looks at the window. He waited in horrid fascination.

The shadow figures filed past the broken glass. Maxwell recognized the language of the whispered words, even if he didn't understand them. Japanese.

The last figure passed. The whispers died. Maxwell waited.

After what he estimated to be many minutes, the man slowly arose from behind the rubble heap. Starting to turn toward the door, he stopped in shock.

The little girl looked back at him from calm black eyes. She was Japanese. She was a beautiful girl, perhaps seven or eight years old. She wore a simple white shift and had a garland of fresh flowers around her neck.

The girl smiled at him, a shy smile, and then extended one hand toward Maxwell. The fingers were closed, but as they opened, the man saw they were webbed. He also saw what lay on the girl's palm. It was a netsuke, a small carved figurine. This one was in the shape of an exotic creature with a feline body and elephantine head.

Maxwell recoiled a step. There was *something* –

The little girl said, 'Baku?'

The single word terrified Maxwell. He didn't know why.

He looked down at his hands. They were wrinkled. He hadn't realized he was so old.

He wasn't old. He was twenty, and –

He was old.

* * *

The enormous bomber roared over him, props beating back the night. Maxwell blinked. There was no shining B-29 eclipsing the moon. What he saw was the plastic model on its stand near his bed. The humped gun turrets loomed in silhouette. What he had taken to be the whirling propellers were discs of clear plastic.

The bomber was going nowhere.

Was this a dream? Where was he?

He blinked again, attempting to orient himself. The little girl –

The bedroom door banged open sharply. He stared at the figure in the doorway. It was Marge, he thought. But Marge had died. How many years ago? Ten, eleven?

'Daddy?' said the figure. *Who was this?* 'Are you okay?' She swiftly crossed the dark room toward the head of his bed.

It was his daughter. 'I'm fine, Connie,' he said. He tried to motion her away. She ignored him, sitting on the edge of the bed and snapping on the lamp.

'I don't believe you.'

Maxwell tried to force a smile. 'I said I'm okay.'

'Daddy,' said his daughter, 'I've seen more reassuring smiles on the bats I dissect in mammalogy.' She crossed her arms across the USC nightshirt.

Maxwell propped himself up on his elbows. 'Thanks,' he said wryly. 'For this, I pay the university eight grand a year on top of your scholarships?'

'Give me a break, Daddy. You're not getting bad dreams from the raw fish we had tonight at the Pacific Palace?'

'Could be,' he said. 'No reason dead fish can't have ghosts.' He was suddenly aware his daughter was looking at him peculiarly.

'Why'd you say that?'

'I'm still half asleep,' he said. 'Look, I'm probably just a little edgy about tomorrow.'

Connie smiled and touched his cheek. He felt the softness of her hand against his stubble. 'Don't worry about tomorrow morning. This isn't the 'sixties. I'll bet the police won't drop gas from helicopters. Probably won't even bring dogs.'

Maxwell said, 'I'm reassured.' He tried to stifle a yawn. It didn't work.

'Want some hot chocolate?' said Connie. She paused to cover her own mouth against a yawn. Then she pulled her blonde hair away from her face. 'Mom always fixed me a cup when *I* had nightmares.'

Maxwell shook his head. 'Who says I was having a nightmare?'

Connie's voice was light. 'I don't think what I heard was the dialogue from an erotic dream.'

He stared at her. 'What did you hear?'

'You –' She hesitated. 'You screamed.'

Maxwell looked away. 'I'm fine now. I'll be okay.'

'This wouldn't have anything to do with the siting decision and the start-up hearing,' she said.

He said nothing.

'I haven't been on your case about any of that.'

'Which I appreciate,' Maxwell said tiredly.

'I know this is a bad time.'

'Yep.' Maxwell wanted to turn off the light, keep her from looking at him.

'You probably don't want to talk about jobs and cheap power weighed against human lives.' She smiled gently, undercutting some of the effect.

'Probably not.'

She leaned toward him and kissed him on the cheek. 'Tomorrow, then.' She glanced at the clock and corrected herself. 'Later today. We'll argue over breakfast.' Connie got up from the bed. 'I think very highly of you, you know.'

Maxwell tried to smile at her. 'I love you too.'

She stared at him a moment, then turned and walked toward the door. Maxwell switched off the lamp after she exited the bedroom.

He lay there quietly in the darkness, watching the red LED digits gradually transform on the clock-face by the bed. Now they read 12:17. Beyond the clock, the model of the B-29 flew through the dark in perfect stasis.

In his head, Maxwell heard the distant, lingering thunder that accompanied the blast wave.

I'm dreaming, he thought.

* * *

The nightmare continued in the morning.

The clock read 6:41. Beyond the bedroom windows, the gray morning sky draped like a shroud over the San Fernando Valley. Maxwell eyed his image in the mirror, fidgeting with the final adjustment to his tie. He stepped back, shrugged, moved his shoulders again. The charcoal Armani suit had fit perfectly yesterday; today he couldn't seem to get it to adjust to his body. Nothing *looked* wrong. Things simply felt out of alignment.

Connie's voice drifted from the kitchen. 'Three eggs or four?'

'None.' Maxwell raised his voice. 'Dr Hansen's still trying to wean me off my cholesterol dependency.'

He abandoned the mirror. Whatever was wrong was too minute to worry about. He must be nervous. That was it. He hadn't expected to be this apprehensive about the final round of hearings.

As Maxwell passed the shelves of netsuke on the way to the bedroom door, he abruptly halted, transfixed. *That wasn't there yesterday.* Had he even looked at the figures yesterday? Slowly, he reached toward the bottom shelf, his fingers stopping just short of touching the figurine he didn't remember seeing there before. It was carved from what appeared to be very dark jade. About the length of his thumb, the creature's body was feline, long muscles clearly defined, with a muscular tail looped around it. The head was that of an elephant, the trunk symmetrically curling to echo the tail.

He hesitated until he berated himself for being a chickenshit. Maxwell slowly picked up the netsuke figure, turning it over and over in his hand, the cold stone not warming in his palm. He saw no spark of life in the creature's open eyes; just the shine of polished jade.

Maxwell replaced the figure on the shelf and continued staring at it. He reached for one of the other netsuke. When he lifted the figures he saw the slightly lighter patch where the dust had not fallen. He lifted the cat-elephant creature from its original position. There was dust beneath it.

'Daddy? Are you coming to breakfast?'

As Maxwell entered the kitchen, Connie set a plate of ham and toast down on the kitchen table beside a steaming mug of coffee.

'I probably shouldn't even let you have coffee,' said his daughter.

'My heart needs the kick-start.' He grimaced at the first hot taste of coffee, then set the mug down.

'Sit down,' said Connie.

'Don't have time.' Still with his attaché case gripped in his free hand, he turned toward the young woman. 'Listen, quick question. Did you give me a present?'

Connie looked puzzled. 'Not lately. Why?'

'There's a netsuke on the shelf I never saw before. Looks expensive. I thought maybe you knew something about it.'

She spread her hands and grinned. 'The Japanese art fairy?'

'No doubt.' Maxwell took another draught of coffee. 'The neighborhood's getting better if burglars are leaving expensive *objets d'art*.' He checked his watch, then started for the door. 'Sorry about breakfast, but thanks.' He paused to give his daughter a peck on the cheek. 'Wish me luck. See you for supper?'

'Can't, sorry. I'm going out with Paul. We'll probably eat down in Venice and then go to a movie. It'll be late. I'll let myself in.'

Maxwell said, 'When am I going to meet this mysterious young man?'

'Very soon, I think,' said Connie. 'Sorry, Daddy. He just keeps very busy.'

'Me too. Okay.' He smiled. 'Have fun. Be careful.'

'You too,' said Connie. 'Don't let them get you down.'

'The executive board of Enerco or the protestors?'

'Either one.'

'Until I make some final decision,' said Maxwell, 'nobody's going to shoot me.' He smiled to ameliorate the seriousness. As he shut the door to the garage, he realized Connie was still staring after him.

* * *

The Enerco Tower was located on Sunset, on one of the blocks where Beverly Hills segued into Hollywood. With its golden, reflective panes, the energy company shed radiance on its neighbors at all times of the day.

Maxwell squinted against the sun-glare. Enough of the smog had burned away to the east, the Enerco Tower looked spectacular. A beacon for America. That's what the PR people were currently pushing as a catch-phrase.

Then he steered the Olds into the curved drive leading to the underground parking ramp and all semblance of peace ended. The walks were choked with demonstrators. He'd seen the placards the day before, and many other days before that. 'Chernobyl, Three-Mile Island, Boca Infierna.' 'Power Now. Jobs Now.' All sides were represented. Fairness in protesting.

Maxwell was instantly recognized. The penalty of momentary stardom, he thought wryly. The Board had wanted him to travel in a chauffeured company limo with smoked glass. He'd be damned if he'd be cowed into no longer driving himself in an ordinary sedan. Listening to the voices outside, looking at the variety of faces, he wondered if he'd perhaps made a wrong decision.

Pro-nuke or anti-nuke, the faces of the demonstrators ranged from concerned to furious. No one looked bored. Certainly no compassion. A handful of company security officers tried with only moderate success to keep the demonstrators on the sidewalk. Maxwell found himself facing several determined-looking adults staring back at him through the windshield.

He lowered the window and said, 'Listen to me, please get out of the way.' If they heard him, they didn't honor his request.

The press people were there too. The reporter of a mini-cam crew got close enough to shout a question: 'Mr Maxwell, as the vice-president for development for Enerco, do you think the start-up schedule for the Boca Infierna plant'll be set today?'

Maxwell said, 'I hope so.'

One of the demonstrators shouldered past the news crew and said, 'How's it feel to be a mass murderer?'

Maxwell ignored him. He was staring at a woman standing perfectly still in the midst of the chaos. She looked Japanese, perhaps middleaged, though it was hard to tell. Her black hair was combed long and straight down her cheekbones. The left side of her face was obscured. She stood with fingers curled into fists, hands at her sides. Her eyes stared directly back into his. Maxwell blinked.

A demonstrator was screaming, '. . . killer!'

Maxwell snapped back into reality, almost as though from a dream. Or is it the other way around? he thought. He stepped on the accelerator. The Olds peeled rubber with a screech. The demonstrators scattered as the sedan tilted down the ramp and plunged into the underground parking garage.

The woman looked so familiar . . . but he couldn't place her.

Maxwell parked the car in his assigned spot and locked it. He walked across the barren concrete toward the uniformed company guard sitting by the bank of elevators.

When he was close enough, the guard called out, 'Morning, Mr Caldwell.'

'Good morning, Reuben.'

Reuben had already punched the button for him. 'Saw you on the news this morning. The President thinks mighty highly of you.'

'The president of Enerco?' Maxwell said bemusedly.

Reuben shook his head. 'No, sir! Of the whole blamed country. Said you were a hero.'

The elevator abruptly chimed and the doors slid open. Maxwell started to enter, then stopped in shock, recoiling. Distantly, he heard the clatter of the attaché case hitting the floor.

From behind him, Reuben said, 'Sir? Something wrong?'

The little Japanese girl stood there in the elevator car. Waiting. She smiled and held out her hand, displaying for him again the grotesque feline elephant form of the netsuke. The figure glowed in the grasp of the girl's webbed fingers, casting a white radiance.

'Mr Maxwell?' Reuben had come up behind him. He shouldered past Maxwell, one hand unsnapping the holster at his hip. Reuben surveyed the interior of the elevator. No one stood there. No little girl. No one. 'Are you feeling all right, sir?' said Reuben. 'Do you want me to phone upstairs?'

Maxwell shook his head violently and retrieved his case. He got into the elevator. 'I'm fine. Just fine.' He was aware of the guard staring after him until the elevator doors hissed shut.

At least the car was an express. He silently watched the illuminated floor numbers mutate one into the next, listened to the chime at each floor.

There was a janitor waiting for him at the top floor. The doors slid open and Maxwell was confronted by a young man wearing an Enerco custodian's coverall. He held a mop as if it were a practice rifle at parade rest. For some reason, Maxwell noticed it was dry. He paused, waiting for the janitor to get on the elevator. Instead, the young man stared at him.

'Mr Maxwell?' said the man. 'I'm Paul Newton. It's really important I talk to you.'

Maxwell realized how trapped he was in the elevator car. 'Mr Newton, try an appointment.'

Newton spoke rapidly, dropping the mop, unzipping the coverall and slipping out of it. He was wearing clean, well-pressed blue jeans and one of the 'Chernobyl, Three-Mile Island, Boca Infierna' T-shirts. 'Appointment? You know how much chance there is of that. Listen, your daughter says you're a good man –'

Maxwell felt like he was starting to slip into the rabbit hole. He interrupted, 'Hold on – you're *that* Paul?'

Newton said, 'Yeah, well. I guess so. We've been going to get together for a while, dinner, something like that.' He smiled cheerfully. 'But it seems like you or I always have one meeting or another going on. I guess it's the penalty of being committed.' He hesitated. 'Truth to tell, I think Connie wasn't too hot on the idea.'

Maxwell tried to move past the young man. 'Mr Newton, this isn't really the time –'

'Yeah, I know,' said Newton. 'Basically, I sneaked in here to talk to you on behalf of one of the groups you won't meet with.'

Maxwell didn't know what the hell the younger man was talking about. It evidently showed.

'PSC,' said Newton. 'People for a Safe California. We're not loonies, Mr Maxwell. Half of us want the jobs your companies'll provide. But all of us figure we have a reasonable fear we'll be fried in our sleep if anything goes wrong with Boca Infierna.'

Maxwell realized he was rising to the bait, tried to withstand the temptation to reply, couldn't. This was an objection he could at least answer. 'We're not talking Diablo Canyon. The geology for the plant looks impressive. As for the safeguards –'

'Chernobyl looked fine too.' Newton tried to block Maxwell with the mop without actually touching him. 'Listen, you're a top guy in the free world's largest nuclear power consortium. You've also got a family. You wouldn't want to lose 'em, would you?' He sounded earnest.

'Is that a threat?' said Maxwell.

Newton shook his head violently. 'I'm talking about what happens if any number of your "reasonable risks" beats the odds.'

Maxwell started past his adversary again. This time Newton let him by. 'I really do have to get to the hearing.'

'And I really care about Connie, Mr Maxwell. I care about her and me and everyone around us. I even care about you.'

Maxwell hesitated. 'I appreciate the concern. I'm not kidding about the appointment. We can talk another time.'

'Count on it,' said Newton, 'but it's gotta be soon.' He smiled at Maxwell, but concern sounded in his voice. 'You'd better get some sleep tonight. You look like you need it.'

Maxwell nodded. 'I can sleep when all this is over.'

'Good luck,' said Newton. He stuck his hand out. Maxwell hesitated, then shook it. The younger man got into the elevator with his mop and pressed the button.

As the doors closed, Maxwell thought about sleep. What he needed was rest. He wondered if Newton were just as much a visual hallucination as the little girl with the netsuke had been. Perhaps, for Connie's sake, he ought to hope so.

* * *

This was real.

Isn't it? he thought, eyes blinking, staring around his black and white world, taking in the night-obscured field of rubble. He smelled dust in his nostrils. Dust and dead meat.

Maxwell half-crouched in the desolation, looking from side to side. He saw the heaps of tumbled brick, heat-blackened, the charred timbers and stubs of rebar protruding. Slowly, he straightened. He adjusted his Air Corps hat.

The spoiled-meat smell intensified. He heard the whispers.

Maxwell turned and saw the shadow figures contemplating him from the top of the slopes. Their eyes were darker hollows in the blackness of their faces.

Hands that seemed little more than charred chicken claws extended toward him. The massed whispers raised in volume. Isolated words seemed familiar, '. . . *hibakusha* . . .' '. . . *baku* . . .' He knew they were talking to him. He didn't understand, but he could recognize the tone. Pleading . . . Something else. The fear built in him. There were so many of them. They would surround him, envelop his body, bear him down into the carpet of cinders and ash. And then –

Maxwell turned and ran. He knew how exhausted he was. Yet his twenty-year-old body kept running, the muscles straining, protesting. The energy came from somewhere. Terror.

Clawing his way across the jumble of brick and stone, negotiating the maze of isolated, fire-blackened walls, Maxwell came upon the Jeep. For just a moment, he stared at it. It looked as if it had been there for forty years. Some of the sheet metal hung ragged and loose from the frame. Yet the tires all seemed up, inflated. Without further thought, the man climbed into the front seat and twisted the ignition key.

The key? It's a miracle, he thought. It would be a miracle if the engine started.

The starter ground over and then the engine caught. It roared into life, the noise curiously flat, as though there were no echoes in the destroyed city. Maxwell jammed the shift lever into place, slipped the clutch, and felt the vehicle jerk into motion. The headlights illuminated the road ahead. He didn't remember turning them on.

The bright cones speared through the dust, into the night. The road was a straight track. Somewhere far ahead of him, the headlights beams simply dissipated. As far as he could see, the road extended toward no particular horizon.

Maxwell looked back over his shoulder. Of course he could see nothing. When he turned back ahead, he involuntarily cried out.

The little girl stood on the road in the glare of the headlights. Maxwell hit the brake with his entire weight. The Jeep fish-tailed crazily, slid to a stop with the front bumper not ten feet from the girl. Her dress was very white in the light. Maxwell comprehended the bright colors of the flower garland around her neck. The reds and yellows and pinks were the only colors here.

Dust billowed past the front of the Jeep, catching up.

The little girl smiled up at him earnestly. She extended her webbed hand. 'Baku . . .' she said. Nothing lay on her palm. She turned her hand over, made a small gesture. *Down.*

Maxwell glanced down.

It was there. It sat on the dash where one might otherwise have placed a Bakelite Jesus or a St Christopher's medal. The Baku glowed. Then it moved, starting toward him along the dash.

Maxwell acted without thinking. He reached, grabbed, hurled the figure away from him, far into the darkness. He could track it with his eyes, the increasingly bright glow trailing light like a falling star. It vanished somewhere out there in the night. It had felt warm. His fingers tingled. There was something about his hand that felt good.

Maxwell screamed.

This time the sound echoed.

* * *

If being forty years older was a dream, at least it took place in a fantasy mostly quieter than the ruined, night-time city.

Maxwell examined his reflection in the bathroom mirror. He morosely touched the deep shadows beneath his eyes, ran finger-tips across the stubble on his jowls. *I feel so tired.* He turned away and walked back into the bedroom. He glanced at the clock. He was running late. It occurred to him that he was moving stiffly, something like the shadow figures that pursued him in his waking life. Wait a second, he thought. Do I have that right?

When he passed the shelves of netsuke, he abruptly stopped. Something was wrong. His vision registered the sight of something missing.

The Baku figurine was gone. There was only an indented ring in the dust to show where it had been.

* * *

Maxwell sat at the kitchen table, hunched over his coffee. He didn't have the suit jacket on yet; it was draped over the back of his chair. He'd set his attaché case down on the floor by his feet. Connie came into the room and seemed to try to hide a doubletake. Maxwell knew he must look awful.

'Daddy,' she said, obviously concerned. 'What's wrong?'

'It's – nothing,' said Maxwell. 'It's gone, that's all.'

'What's gone?' Connie poured herself a cup from the Mr Coffee and sat down, scooting her chair in close to his.

'The Baku.'

His daughter looked relieved. 'It's around somewhere. I was trying to locate it in one of the netsuke books yesterday.' She hesitated. 'I thought I put it back exactly where I found it. Maybe not.'

Maxwell held his hands over the coffee as though he were stranded in the Arctic and the cup were the only fire.

'The Baku's not exactly the prettiest of the netsuke.'

'It's a household demon,' said Maxwell. 'I don't know which one. The Japanese have so many.'

Connie said lightly, 'Maybe whoever gave it to you broke in and stole it back.'

'No one stole it,' said her father. 'I threw it away.'

'An art object like that?' Connie looked a bit bewildered.

'It was on the dash of the Jeep.'

Her face mirrored her sudden comprehension. 'More bad dreams?'

Maxwell nodded.

Connie said, 'Last week in psych, we learned about night terrors. You know what they are?'

'No.' Maxwell didn't look up.

'Kind of weird. They're dreams that linger a long time, even after you wake up –'

Smashed glass sprayed across the tabletop. The crash jerked them both back in their chairs. The fist-sized chunk of jagged concrete and rebar skidded off the table and thunked to the floor.

'Christ!' His daughter tried to shield him from whatever was going to happen next. Maxwell struggled to extract himself. They both stared toward the shattered kitchen window.

The voice from outside sounded like a bullhorn, the tone augmented and distorted: 'Hey, Mr Maxwell, we know you're in there. Recognize the debris? That's from the V.A. hospital in Sylmar. Souvenir. Remember how that sucker came down in the quake? So what's going to happen to your power plant a ways on up the Richter Scale?'

Maxwell and Connie exchanged looks. 'Is that who I think it is?' he said.

Connie stared at him for a long several seconds. 'I'm afraid so.' She glared toward the window. 'I told him not to do this.'

'He takes orders about like you do.' Maxwell stood up and walked over to the destroyed window. There were dozens of them outside. The usual placards were in evidence. He cupped his hands and raised his voice, 'Paul Newton! You wanted to talk? Get your tail in here or forget it.'

From the number of jeers that elicited, it was evident the crowd wasn't eager for a parley. 'Okay,' came the reply. 'I'm coming in alone.'

Maxwell smiled wanly. 'It's dialogue out of a bad detective movie.'

'Thanks, Daddy,' Connie said. 'Thanks for not calling the police.'

'I may yet. Depends on how well your young man can talk.'

Someone knocked at the front door. Taking the chunk of

concrete-and-rebar in one hand, Maxwell made his way out of the kitchen. The window shards crunched under his shoes.

As he passed the hallway leading to the back of the house, he stopped, shocked. A woman stood in the corridor looking back at him. She was the Japanese woman who had stood in the crowd of demonstrators the morning before, the one who had fixed him with a silent stare before he'd driven down the parking ramp. Dressed in a somber jacket and skirt with a white blouse, she extended one hand toward him.

He saw her lips silently form the syllables, 'Ba-ku.'

Of course the Baku figurine crouched in her palm. He saw that the woman's fingers were webbed. He also saw the Baku glowing even in the daylight. It cocked its head and regarded him, the wide, round eyes shining even more brightly than the body.

He continued to hear the knocking on the front door, but now the sound rose and crescendoed like a long, echoing blast wave. The deep vibration made his teeth hurt.

The sound diminished and vanished. No one stood in the hall. There was no woman. No Baku.

I want to wake up. Maxwell shook his head as though trying to clear the remains of a particularly nasty dream.

The sound returned, but this time it was only the insistent knocking of clenched flesh on hardwood. Maxwell continued on to the door.

When he opened the door, it was, of course, Paul Newton standing there. He was wearing dark chinos and a black T-shirt depicting a fire extinguisher spraying a Bohr atom.

'Come on in.'

Newton looked down at the chunk of debris in Maxwell's hand. 'Sorry about that. Wasn't my idea.' He grinned disarmingly. 'You're in this game long enough, you learn to capitalize on the late breaks.'

Maxwell carefully set the object on the hall table with the basket for outgoing mail. 'Come on back to the kitchen. The fresh air'll be good for us all.' Leading Newton, he continued, 'I'm interested in your terming this a game, Mr Newton.'

'It's Paul, remember? I think we know each other well enough by now for that.' His tone turned serious. 'I don't think it's really a game, though it sometimes seems that way when we all get tired and turn ringy. I try, but I can't always just flatly call it what it is – life and death.' He seemed to force a smile. 'Look, in all this, I'm not trying to find a fault.'

'Pretty cute on top of your rhetoric about the Sylmar quake,' said Maxwell.

'Sorry, things are heavy enough, I need a joke. This is serious now.'

They entered the kitchen. Connie waited, pressed back against the sink. She looked tense. Trapped.

Maxwell said dryly, 'I believe you two know each other.'

'Daddy, I'm really sorry.' To Paul, she said, 'You told me you wouldn't do anything like this.'

Paul Newton spread his hands. 'It seemed like a good idea . . .'

'You promised –'

'Excuse me,' said Maxwell. 'Let's get to it.' He sat down and pulled his chair up to the table. 'What do you want to tell me, Paul? I've got to get to work soon. The hearings are moving glacially, but I think they're almost over. Tomorrow will probably do it.' He shook his head wearily. 'I hope to hell it does.'

Paul Newton sat down on the other side of the table. Glass tinkled and grated as he moved the chair up. Connie walked over and stood at his shoulder. She started to touch him, but stopped. 'This isn't the 'sixties, Mr Maxwell –'

'Paul.'

'– Paul. I'm not charging you with murdering babies with napalm or even conniving to blow up the world.'

'Thanks,' said Maxwell.

'That'd be unrealistic. What People for a Safe California are worried about are the maybe three or four million citizens who could get lunched here for the sake of your stockholders.'

'I've heard all this before,' said Maxwell. 'I know you've watched the hearings on television. I think you're the sort who does his homework. How many times can we explain that Boca Infierna is maybe the biggest nuclear power project, but it's also the safest. Every time a plant's gone down before, we've learned –'

Newton interrupted disgustedly. 'And maybe someday another power company will learn from Boca Infierna?'

Maxwell had no answer.

'I'm not willing to take the chance.'

'When we finally work through all the clichés,' said Maxwell, 'there's no final answer. None. People want the electrical power. We need it. Enerco sees the acceptable risk as very small.'

Newton said, 'I hate phrases like that. Too glib. It's not an acceptable risk to me that any of us here could get wasted at any time just 'cause something or someone screwed up down at the plant and the wind's right.' He stared Maxwell in the eye. 'I don't want our kids to glow at night.'

'Kids?' Connie said.

Newton turned his head and looked up at her. He nodded vehemently. 'Yeah, children.'

Maxwell said gently, 'It's not as though it's totally up to me.'

'But I think you've got the biggest single vote.'

'I can be overruled by the Chairman, by –'

'Horseshit,' said Newton. 'Gonna use the Nuremberg defense? Just following orders?' He looked like he was debating whether to say the next thing. 'Listen, I researched you. I know about your war record. I saw the UPI picture of you getting the medal for killing a hundred thousand people.'

Wake up. Maxwell felt like sand bags were being loaded on his back. 'That was another situation. That was *war*.'

'I'm sure that was a comforting distinction to all those people who fried in Nagasaki.'

'Paul –' Connie said.

'I was a bomber officer,' said Maxwell. 'I had a responsibility –'

'Yeah, responsibility. I'm frankly surprised a hundred thousand ghosts haven't hounded you to your grave.'

The kitchen wavered, as though Maxwell were sitting at the bottom of a swimming pool, watching everything through a dozen feet of water. He saw the darkness of the ruined city begin to flow around him.

Newton's words brought him back. 'You want to risk more? What's another few million phantoms?'

Connie's voice rose angrily, desperately. 'Stop it! My father is a good man –'

'So was mine,' said Newton. 'You wanna know what happened to *my* dad? You may have seen it, Maxwell. There's a Navy base on dry land in the middle of Idaho. It's a government graveyard for faulty and experimental and deactivated reactors.'

Maxwell nodded. 'I've seen it. Pretty bleak.'

'*Bleak?*' Newton almost spat the word. 'I bet they didn't show you the human debris. People have died there. Not many, but if one was your father, that was more than plenty. Acceptable casualties, that's the term, right? The bodies got so radioactive that only a few pounds of meat and bone were saved from the autopsy for the casket. Everything else got put in a sealed steel drum and was buried in some waste dump.'

'I'm very sorry,' said Maxwell. 'I had no idea.'

'They won't even let me see where most of him's buried.'

Connie put her hands on the young man's shoulders. He stiffened, but didn't twist away.

Maxwell said, 'I can't say it any more eloquently, Paul. I'm sorry. I'm very sorry.'

Newton rubbed his eyes and looked across at him. 'I just hope you can deal with the ghosts, man.'

The three stared at each other. Maxwell finally nodded. 'I've got to get to the hearings. They'll go on whether I'm there or not.'

Newton smiled for the first time since the front door. 'I'll give you an escort through the lines. It's a sincere crowd, but not a dangerous one.' He nodded toward the window. 'That was a fluke. I'll pay you back for whatever a glass company charges to fix it.'

Maxwell got up, shrugged on his coat, hefted the attaché case. He realized he was unconsciously straightening his tie and deliberately took his hand away from the knot. He said to Connie, 'Hold down the fort, love. I'll probably be late for dinner.'

Connie looked like she was in an agony of decision. 'I don't think I can be here tonight.'

Maxwell stared at his daughter. *A nightmare.*

'I've got to go away and think,' she said.

'Connie –' Newton started to say.

'Alone.'

No one said anything else for a moment.

Maxwell felt the fatigue sweep over him. He said, 'Will you be safe?'

'I'll be okay.'

'Promise?'

'Promise. Absolutely.' Connie tried to smile. 'Maybe I'll call.'

Maxwell watched her another few moments, then turned toward Newton. 'Okay, son. Let's run the gauntlet.'

Connie hugged him before he left. 'I love you. Don't have bad dreams, Daddy.'

This is one. 'I won't,' he said.

She squeezed his hand as if she knew he was lying.

* * *

Of course he had a nightmare.

Maxwell dreamed he was lying asleep. Barely discernible against the night, a shadowy figure bent down across the head of the bed. A shadow hand gently touched the side of

Maxwell's face. He tried to wake up, to confront the creature that was about to do – *something* to him.

The figure moved slightly and a bar of light from the window fell across its face. Her eyes. It was Connie.

* * *

He awoke from the dream for good into the nighttime city. Maxwell shook his head, attempting to clear it of the sleep fragments. He was sitting on a long, rectilinear chunk of concrete that looked to have been part of a building foundation. He stood and straightened his uniform jacket.

Maxwell stared as he realized what it was he was looking at. The wrecked B-29 thoroughly dwarfed him. Camouflaged in patches of muted black and gray, the sheet metal extended high above him. One wing crossed his vision to the side and extended far into the distance. Both huge engines on that side had torn loose from their cowlings, the prop blades twisted and corroded.

The man realized he was even with the cockpit. At that point, the fuselage was crushed down into the rubble so that the Plexiglass panes windowing the cockpit were almost low enough to touch, had he wished to. Maxwell reached out and gingerly ran his fingers over the panel below the cockpit. The metal was warm to his touch, as though the aircraft was heated from within. His fingertips traced the edges of the two black mushroom clouds painted in silhouette on the metal. Twin images. Identical victories. Two kills.

The silhouettes were abruptly hotter than his fingers could stand. He gasped and took his hand away, putting the afflicted fingers in his mouth.

Maxwell heard the whispering behind him. He also heard the voice.

'Don't fear him . . .'

It was the young girl. The necklace of flowers was still as vibrant and fresh as Maxwell remembered, the riot of colors startling in the monochrome world. She reached out toward him, fingers uncurling, revealing the Baku figurine.

'Please don't fear,' she said again.

Maxwell stepped back, flattening himself against the B-29's massive fuselage. 'Please, no . . .' He frantically looked to each side. The shadow figures, the *hibakusha*, had formed a semicircle. He saw no lane of escape. 'Please. Not . . . him.'

The girl continued to proffer the figure.

The shadow figures leaned closer. Maxwell could now make out some of their features. He closed his eyes and turned away when he saw the man whose eyes had melted and run down the sides of his charred cheeks.

He opened his eyes and saw the woman who would always smile because of the flesh around her mouth and jaw having been burned away.

'Take him,' said the little girl gently.

Maxwell stared as a shadow lengthened toward him from the Baku, just as if black ink were issuing from a spilled bottle. The edge of the darkness flowed down the little girl and crept across the intervening dust and broken stones. Maxwell wanted to run, but he looked at the creatures hemming him in and realized he simply had no further place to go.

He cowered against the crumpled metal and watched the shadow reach his shoes. It flowed up over the toes, then started to envelop him, moving up over his feet, up the ankles and legs to the chest, the neck . . . It didn't feel warm or cold. It simply felt like nothing at all. As the shadow reached his face, Maxwell was finally about to react.

'No! Damn it, no!'

With his fingers, he ripped at the shadow which had now almost completely covered him. The shadow-stuff came away in long, gossamer tatters. But the more darkness he tore away, the more new shadow flooded across him.

Finally, inevitably, it covered his face and eyes.

Maxwell heard himself scream.

* * *

He had once seen all three of George Romero's zombie movies at a USC festival screening his daughter had dragged him to one Halloween. Maxwell looked into the bathroom mirror and reflected that he looked a bit like one of the less colorful zombie characters. He ran the cordless razor over his cheeks again. He couldn't seem to get all the stubble ground down.

Finally he gave up. Giving his blue-striped tie one last tug, Maxwell picked up his attaché case and walked to the kitchen. He stopped short in surprise. The coffee maker was perking happily away. Maxwell knew he hadn't set the timer. He noticed the place setting on the kitchen table. There was a note rolled up in the coffee mug.

He picked up the note and smoothed it out. It read: 'Daddy, I had to see that you were okay, so I let myself in late last night and watched you while you slept. I fixed you something to eat and it's in the fridge. Just stick it in the microwave and nuke it for about 30 seconds. I figure you'll need all the energy you can muster today. I know this is the final day for the hearings and it's make or break for the power plant. I'll be watching the TV. I want to see you when it's over, but not right now. I hope you understand. Whatever happens today, I'll still love you.'

Maxwell convulsively crumpled the note, then flattened it on the table, reading it a second time. Finally he folded it in eighths and put the note in his coat pocket.

He went to the refrigerator to see what Connie had prepared him. She was right. He needed the energy.

* * *

The morning cloud cover and a light drizzle dimmed the golden magnificence of the Enerco spire. The weather did not diminish the numbers of demonstrators. They all were waiting as Maxwell wheeled the Olds into the circular drive and aimed for the entrance to the parking ramp. The corporate security people were forever urging him to use a driver, a company limo, Enerco security escorts, different driving routes daily, all manner of other security precautions. Maxwell turned them all down. He wasn't about to be bullied. At least that was what he told them all.

This morning he used the air conditioning and left all the windows rolled up. What he saw out the driver's side glass was silent, dream-like. It was like watching brightly colored fish swim in an aquarium. Maxwell just stared at the signs, the rude gestures, the silent frantically moving lips.

LAPD officers were on hand to keep the demonstrators from getting too close to the parking ramp. Maxwell had no trouble driving up to the incline and starting down. He parked the Olds as usual, locked it, and started for the elevator bank.

He realized with a small shock that Reuben's chair was vacant. 'Reuben?' he called. No one answered. The echo bounced three or four times across the vast underground garage. No one else seemed in evidence.

Maxwell heard a burring sound from above him. He looked up. The overhead lights started to crackle and fizz. Then they dimmed.

He reached the elevator bank and pushed the 'up' button.

The lights momentarily regained their brightness. Then they dimmed a final time and went out, starting with the tubes on the other side of the garage.

Maxwell watched the lights sequentially extinguished, the wave of darkness moving inexorably toward him. He punched the elevator button again. No bell sounded. Nothing happened.

Maxwell decided to try for his car while there was still light. He didn't make it. Total blackness descended. He felt a ringing in his ears. Lack of orientation clawed at him. He knew he was staggering, struggling for balance. He'd lost his attaché case somewhere. Carefully, he got down on his knees and felt around for it.

He finally touched the leather handle.

That's when he thought he woke up.

The lights came back up again. Maxwell realized he was still in the parking garage, but it was not the place he remembered from his dream, even though it was without color. He saw the Oldsmobile, just a few yards ahead of him. The car was covered with a thick coating of dust, the tires flat, the fenders corroded. It was part of the general wreckage that surrounded him.

Maxwell was still wearing his suit. Slowly, confused and disoriented, he got to his feet, clutching the attaché case to his chest.

'Mr Maxwell.'

It was the Japanese woman he had seen first in the crowd of demonstrators, then momentarily in the hallway of his home. She stood not more than two yards away. She wore a simple white shift in the style of that worn by the little Japanese girl. She wore a garland around her neck, but the blooms were all wilted and brown. The flowers were dead. Her glossy, black hair fell straight along the sides of her face.

Behind the woman, the rank of shadowed figures seemed to stare implacably back at Maxwell.

'Who are you?' he said shakily. He gestured. '*All* of you?'

'My name is Mariko,' said the woman. 'You know who we are.'

'I don't believe in ghosts,' Maxwell said defiantly.

'Then call us what you will. We are *hibakusha* – "sufferers." You saw none of us when you flew above our home.' The woman's voice was level, the words almost gentle.

Maxwell said softly, 'Nagasaki.'

Mariko nodded.

'You must hate me.'

'We hate no one now,' she said. 'We wish only to set you free.'

'Free?'

'Of your past, your dreams. Set you free of your nightmares.'

'By killing me?' said Maxwell. 'I guess I can't blame you.' The wind started to sweep across the rubble. Dust eddied up in front of him. He blinked.

'You don't understand, Mr Maxwell. Listen to me. All we wish to do is give you this.' She held out her hand. The Baku was in it. As before, it glowed. Also as before, it moved, looking curiously up at Maxwell from her palm.

'Won't you listen?' Mariko shook her head vehemently. 'He does not destroy. The Baku is benign. You don't recognize the devourer of nightmares?'

'Devourer?' Maxwell said stupidly. 'Nightmares?'

'He eats bad dreams. The Baku blesses any house with his presence, but only if he's accepted into it.'

Maxwell stared at the creature. The Baku stared back. The man started to reach out, but then withdrew his hand.

Mariko said, 'Please, Mr Maxwell. If you cannot accept compassion, neither can you grant it.'

He listened to her, considering that. 'He will help with the bad dreams?'

Mariko nodded.

Slowly, Maxwell reached out and took the Baku from the woman's hand. The wind continued to rise, blowing the hair away from the sides of her face. The man saw the terrible scars along her jaw.

'You were *there*,' he said.

'The little girl was.' She smiled. 'I am not a ghost, Mr Maxwell. Some of us didn't die right away.'

Maxwell looked at her, then down to the Baku in his hand. The figure was warm. It pulsed gently. 'He can eat all the nightmares of my life?'

'Up to a point.'

Something occurred to Maxwell. 'And if I feed him too many? If he can't – consume any more?'

Mariko smiled again, but bleakly now. 'You don't want to know. Don't let it happen.'

The wind wailed to a crescendo. Maxwell squinted. The

light seemed brighter around them. Mariko's image appeared to diminish.

'Choose wisely, Mr Maxwell.'

The parking garage – *changed*. Color came back. The level of light rose. Maxwell looked beyond where Mariko had stood. The Oldsmobile was no longer a rusted, decaying hulk.

He felt the object in his hand. Maxwell spasmodically closed his fingers, then opened his hand again. The Baku lay there in his palm. It was the inanimate, carved object he had first seen on the netsuke shelf.

'Mr Maxwell? Are you okay, sir?' It was Reuben.

Maxwell looked away from the Baku and saw the guard approaching. 'Yes. I'm fine.'

'They been callin' down for you, sir. I guess they really need you upstairs at the hearing.' He gently took the tip of Maxwell's elbow and steered him toward the elevators. 'Last day of the hearings, huh? Bet that's a load off your mind.'

Maxwell glanced again at the Baku. Then his fist clenched around the figure. This is the nightmare, he thought, isn't it?

He wondered where Paul Newton was, where his daughter Connie was waiting in front of a flickering television screen. He even thought about Paul Newton's father, the several pounds of him that were left, resting in a sealed drum in Idaho. He wondered how soon it would be before he again saw Mariko, how long before the *hibakusha* whispered to him just outside the range of his vision.

The level of light in the parking garage continued to rise. Maxwell looked up at one of the overheads as the light brightened, igniting into a brilliance that blinded him.

The nightmare.

Isn't it? he thought.

AUTHOR'S NOTE

If there's one thing I can't do, it's work for someone else. Writing is bad enough, since I have to deal with editors and my agent. But I'm not really working for them. They are working for me.

Before I started writing, I had lots of jobs. None of them lasted. The trouble with working is that bosses want to screw you over. They do it endlessly, finding an infinite number of new and terrible injustices to shovel on your head.

There's never any recourse.

It just isn't fair.

When I lived in Seattle, the summer before my wife died, I met a guy who had worked at the Hanford Nuclear Reservation. He'd had some sort of low-level job handling chemicals in a laboratory. There had been an accident and the man had breathed in something like fifty micrograms of plutonium oxide dust – not even enough, he told me over boilermakers, to see in a dot, if it had collected on my thumbnail.

To help my friend, the laboratory had scrubbed him, cleansing his skin as much as they could. Then they drowned him. Three times. The procedure was called a lung lavage. The doctors filled his lungs with water, drew the water out, repeated the process, did it again. Nothing got all the dust out. It was encapsulated in his cells. In his blood.

The message was there forever.

When I met him, the ex-nuclear worker was living off what his wife could make waiting tables at Ivar's Acres of Clams.

He couldn't get Workman's Comp because the government said there were no accidents like the one he'd suffered. Nuclear plants were safer than Teddy Kennedy's car at Chappaquidick. Actuarial tables would be compiled from the accidents and subsequent deaths of people like my friend. I thought about his predicament a long while.

Seattle was a rough period. I was fired from my own job at Boeing. I think I knew then that Joyce's death was in the future, but not that far away. I think my bosses knew too.

I remember the sixth of August that year. We decided to have a backyard party. Before any of the guests arrived, I got roaring drunk. I remember I wanted to hit Joyce. I wanted to beat her to death.

Then I called up the guy who'd had the lab accident to ask if he'd like to come over and light up our lives.

All I reached was his wife. He'd died that morning.

The message was clear.

Frat Rat Bash

'Scrub! you little worms. Get down there low, close to the tile! Lean into it. Scrub!' Clearly Pledgemaster Bonzer fancied himself Captain Bligh. He revelled in the role. His voice virtually dripped with excited juices as he urged the pledges on to faster and more exacting exertions. '*Scrub*, damn you!'

Scotty Turnbuckle scrubbed. Strike that. *Pledge* Turnbuckle scrubbed. Every muscle in his body ached. His head buzzed from lack of sleep. His ears hurt from the shouting of most of the active members of Tau Sigma fraternity. As for his brain – he knew his mind wasn't working properly. Six days of this. Hell Week culminated tonight, so long as the dozen pledges successfully cleaned, scrubbed and polished the abysmally filthy Tau Sigma house into a splendor worthy of hosting the annual Acapulco Bash. The GDIs called it the Frat Rat Bash.

Cleaning up was only part of it. The pledges also had to negotiate the afternoon initiation ceremonies successfully. If they made it through the mysterious rituals, they would be considered active members of Tau Sigma and worthy of participating in the evening's bacchanal. If not, then – Failure didn't bear thinking about.

Pledge Turnbuckle really did wonder at the degree to which Bonzer had it in for him. There was no question about it. All the pledges had been abased, abused, humiliated and driven during the week past. But Scotty Turnbuckle had received more than his share. It wasn't just his imagination or even a healthy dollop of self-pity. The other pledges had whispered about it during the brief and rare intervals when they thought themselves unobserved by the active members and the pledgemaster himself. Turnbuckle had heard them whisper. He resented the sick pity in their tones. He liked the other pledges about as little as he welcomed the company of the active members. He was here only because his father and older brothers had been active members of Tau Sigma. The importance of that had been made clear to him.

'Make me proud,' his father had told him when he'd gone off to be a freshman. Right. *Make us proud* was the fraternity's official motto. It was penned in Greek and framed in a smoked-glass windowbox above the hardwood mantel in the vast living room.

Turnbuckle didn't feel proud. He felt like shit. He knew it was intended he feel precisely like shit after a solid week of alternating sensory deprivation and motor overload.

'Good,' said the pledgemaster grudgingly. Bonzer loomed over them, staring at the speckled off-white patches of tile where the grime had finally begun to grind loose. 'Some of you may – and I stress the word – *may* yet see some beer and poontang at the Bash tonight.' He chuckled evilly. 'Well, beer at any rate. Those of you who make it through initiation – if any of you do – will still carry the stench of lowly pledge status with you. Soap'll do no good at all. I sincerely doubt any of the Delts'll even look at you. Tough, but that means studs like me'll have just enough to get by.' He laughed again, more a snicker.

Turnbuckle didn't look up.

'Hey, Turnbuckle, you lazy shit. Get down on your belly. Rub with your nose if you have to. Honker that size, you could squeegee windshields.' Bonzer loomed over him. Turnbuckle got down. He rubbed. Bonzer prodded him in the ribs with the pointed toe of one scuffed boot. Kicked him once. Kicked him again, harder. Said, 'Oops. IFC rules forbid hazing. Just slipped, that's all. Tripped. Sorry,

Turnbuckle, you slime.' He kicked the pledge again.

Turnbuckle bit his lip to keep from crying out, felt the tissue shred on the inside, tasted salt. Worse, felt the pity flood around him from the other pledges. With what breath remained in his bruised rib cage, he forced out, 'What are you looking at?' Nobody was looking at anything.

From upstairs, someone jacked up the volume of an endless-loop tape of the Washakie State University fight song.

Bonzer kicked him again and laughed.

'I don't need a reason to think you're a puking little worm,' said Pledgemaster Bonzer. 'None. Zero. Nada. It's all instinct.'

'But –'

'No questioning it. That's part of the discipline.'

* * *

' "Mi casa esta tu casa",' said Bonzer. 'The theme for tonight's bash. Beaner metaphor. Suppositional case, a temporary state or condition. Get those crepe streamers precise. I'll be measuring.'

They all knew he would be. He'd measured, gauged, evaluated everything they'd done all week. He even checked the mopped and wiped-down heads with an assortment of white gloves. Bonzer wouldn't let down now, nor would he allow them to let down. Not this close.

'When the house is decorated,' he said, 'then we'll see if anyone qualifies to attempt initiation. And if anyone makes it through *that*, then we'll see who all will get to help build the pinata for the Bash. That's tradition.' Another active had come up beside him and nodded vigorously, seconding Bonzer's speech.

'Everybody happy? Permission to speak.'

'Yes, Bonzer!' from a dozen throats. Croaking, dead-tired, cracking. 'We're very happy.'

'Great.' The pledgemaster idly traced his boot-toe along the side of Turnbuckle's still-prone body. 'Your enthusiasm refreshes me, takes me back to my own dear Hell Week.'

Turnbuckle thought he knew why Bonzer had it in for him.

'There was one real asshole,' his next-older brother had said. 'A little piss-ant who was a pledge when I was a senior. Arrogant little shit. Had to take him down a peg or two. Pretty decent sort by the time I graduated. You two'll get along fine if he's still there.'

* * *

The streamers crinkled crisply and precisely. The mirror ball was hung by the mantel with care. The red and green banner with WELCOME – BUENOS DIAS spelled out in block poster-board letters pinned to the dyed sheets was draped over the front door. Tatty bullfight posters had been taped to the walls of the living room. In the kitchen, the hashers were making up galvanized tubs full of taco mix and guacamole salads.

At either end of the Tau Sigma house, stereos played top-decibel, but slightly out of synch, tapes of De Falla's 'Bolero.' The idea was to keep anyone upstairs from hearing what was going on in the basement.

* * *

Turnbuckle didn't know how long he'd waited. He was blind-folded, with a stereo headset flooding a sort of Led Zep Christmas tape endlessly into his brain. He'd tried counting the cycles, mentally marking each replay of the heavy metal 'Rudolph,' but lost track somewhere after seventeen.

He flexed his toes, the only movement he could hide sufficiently to get away with. His skin burned where it had cracked and admitted the harsh cleansers. The astringent odor still seared his nostrils. Naturally Bonzer had made sure he was on the crew cleaning the kitchen ranges. While he'd been contorted on his belly, stretching to reach the back of one of the huge ovens, Bonzer had turned on the gas. The pilot had caught with a *whuff*. Turnbuckle had scrambled out, his fingertips already starting to sear.

'Keep working, slime,' Bonzer had said. 'You'll have a hot time at the Bash too.' He'd actually giggled.

Turnbuckle's kinesthetic sense told him he was by himself. The other eleven pledges had been led quietly away, one by one, to their initiation. Now he alone waited.

Finally they came for him too.

* * *

Bonzer and Turnbuckle faced each other in the dimly illuminated supply room off the back hall. There was one window, but it was screened with a square of burlap. The blindfold was off. The place stank of stale food and dead mice that hadn't been removed from the traps in the corners. This was one room the pledges hadn't been required to clean.

Turnbuckle looked around, his stinging eyes beginning to adjust to the light. In front of him, to one side of the smirking Bonzer, was a low mountain of newspapers. Beside that was a roll of cleanly shining chicken wire. And beside that, two cases of yellow boxes labeled Metylan.

'Art paste,' said Bonzer, gesturing at the cartons. 'Your special task is something of an honor, my boy. I've decided you don't even rank as a slime. You're a slime-*mold*, and mold is exactly what you're going to do.' He used his arms expressively. 'You're going to mold the centerpiece for the fun and games tonight.'

'I –'

'Shut up, slime-mold! You're going to make the piñata. You know what the design is?'

Turnbuckle shook his head miserably, mutely.

'It's going to be an ass, pledge. A huge ass. As anatomically correct as you can manage. Use your own as a model. Got it?'

'But –' Turnbuckle tried to say. He knew *nothing* about art.

Bonzer stared at him impatiently. 'Make the frame for this piñata out of chicken wire, slime. That way it'll support all the apples and oranges and beer cans and all the rest of the heavy shit. But be sure to leave a hole in the chicken wire for everything to fall through. Make the hole about five or six inches in diameter, no bigger, and put it on the bottom, right where you paint the asshole. That way everybody else can beat the shit out of it from the sides without getting any results – then *I'll* step in and use an underhand hook shot to open her up.'

Turnbuckle looked back at him silently.

'Just get started,' said Bonzer. 'Only a mere matter of hours until the Bash.' He gestured to more cartons off to the side. 'Fill it with those. There's candy, rubbers, suppositories, all that kind of shit. Do a good job.' He started for the door.

'Initiation –' Turnbuckle struggled to say.

'Oh, yeah.' Bonzer turned back from the door. 'No initiation. The other actives and I had a little talk downstairs. All the other guys made it. Good pledges, you know? But we think you need a little attitude adjustment.'

Turnbuckle stared at him.

'Do a good job with the piñata,' the pledgemaster continued, 'and we'll let you stay on as a pledge next term. Then maybe *next* year you can make it as an active. Okay by you?' He kept staring at the pledge. 'Hey, that's a question, slime-mold. You can answer me now.'

Turnbuckle couldn't say anything at all.

'Well,' said Bonzer. 'I'm guessing you're trying to find the words to express your gratitude. Get to work on the piñata. Build the ass, fill it up with goodies like I'm telling you, and maybe tonight I can line up somebody to do the same with yours.' He turned and shut the door after him.

Turnbuckle heard the key click in the lock.

* * *

Make us proud.

It was all he could make out through the buzzing in his head.

* * *

Some indeterminate time later, Turnbuckle used the cosh on Pledgemaster Bonzer. He'd made the cosh by filling one sock with stale hard candies and lumps of petrified bubble gum.

He'd heard the key turn in the lock, leapt to a position to Bonzer's blind side just inside the door, waited for the pledgemaster to enter, then slammed the improvised cosh across the base of Bonzer's neck as hard as he could swing. The Tau Sigma active plummeted forward to the cement floor as though poleaxed, landing on his face, forehead smacking against the harder surface with the sound meat usually makes impacting from a height.

Turnbuckle was on Bonzer in a frenzy, the sock rising and falling, but he abruptly realized it was all redundant. The pledgemaster was out cold, breathing raggedly and gurgling just a little. Turnbuckle used some of the filament tape that was included with the piñata supplies. He moved the active's arms and legs so that the body simulated a fetal position. Then he wound the tape round and round the man. Several loops went around Bonzer's mouth, sealing in the red cloth napkin Turnbuckle had inserted. He thought about taping the nose shut, enjoyed the fantasy for just a moment, then suddenly realized the supply room door was still ajar.

He hurried to the doorway, looked out and saw no one. He could hear 'Bolero' still playing in the background. Turnbuckle shut the door and locked it from the inside.

He turned back toward Bonzer and realized the pledgemaster looked like nothing so much as a trussed turkey at Thanksgiving.

'Piñata, my ass,' Turnbuckle muttered. Thanksgiving. He'd seen his father and brothers at Thanksgiving. They'd asked him how classes were going, but more important, how his pledgeship in Tau Sigma was progressing. Naturally, he'd lied.

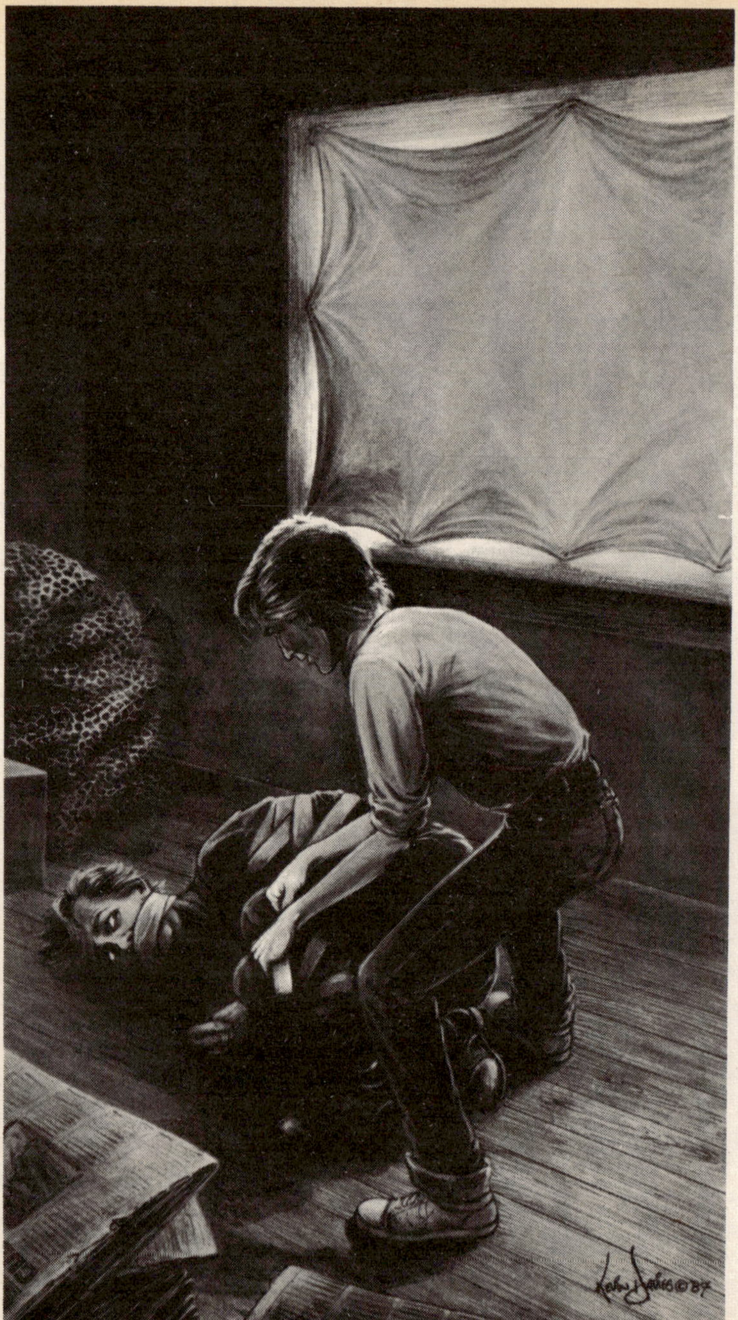

Disregarding Bonzer, Turnbuckle resumed work on the piñata. He had to admit to himself that he had done a good job constructing the outer shell. The pâpier-maché, aided by the quick-setting Metylan, was hardening nicely. The shape even *did* look like a pair of wide buttocks. And it was big, very big. Turnbuckle knew the fraternity liked a lot of goodies when they smashed open the piñata at the Bash.

The pledge stopped only to check the time on Bonzer's wristwatch. As he wrestled the pledgemaster into a position where he could read the dial, he realized the active's eyes were open and focused. Bonzer tried to say something. Only the mildest noises came past the very efficient gag.

Turnbuckle rolled Bonzer back over and returned to the piñata. Not as much time left as he'd like. He'd do what he could.

He'd make himself proud.

* * *

It took six of the newly initiated former-pledges to hoist the piñata into position and suspend it from the massive ring-bolt in the center of the living room ceiling. The bolt groaned a little, but held. Only a small amount of white plaster dust sifted to the carpet.

'Christ Almighty!' said one of the hoisters. 'What'd you stuff this thing with, fishing weights?'

'Pledgemaster Bonzer told me this was an especially big Bash. He made sure I had plenty of candy and nuts and apples and cans of beer and – all the rest. It took a lot,' said Turnbuckle.

'Good job, slime-mold,' said one of the new actives.

How quickly they forget, thought Turnbuckle.

'Great piñata. You painted in the asshole and everything.'

The buzzing in his head overcame the words around him. Turnbuckle swayed, had to steady himself with a hand against the brick fireplace.

'Take it easy, slime-mold,' said another of the new actives. 'Don't fall down and hurt yourself. You're the guest of honor at the Bash.'

'Huh?' said Turnbuckle, confused.

'Go get cleaned up,' said a former pledge-brother. 'While you're at it, see if you can run down Bonzer. We want to feed him a beer.'

'I'll see what I can do,' said Turnbuckle.

The new active gave him a good-natured shove on the way past. 'Take it easy, slime-mold. We'll give you a good time during your second pledgeship.'

The buzzing drowned out everything.

* * *

They trotted Turnbuckle out of the supply room at the climax of the Acapulco Bash. They stripped him down to his underwear in front of the entire fraternity and all the sorority dates. Everyone seemed startled that he didn't seem to mind.

Obviously the brothers of the fraternity and their dates had all taken a swing at the piñata. Turnbuckle's creation was dented and crazed with cracks. The chicken wire had apparently done yeoman's work in protecting the piñata's structural integrity. Looking at the battered, but as yet unbreached, piñata, Turnbuckle felt a joy and an excitement that gave him a sudden, sharp transfusion of energy.

They blindfolded him with a bra donated by a fetchingly blushing head cheerleader.

Then they placed him in position beneath the piñata and whirled him around three, six, ten times. He knew he was staggering. The buzzing in his head seemed to make up a song.

They put the stout wooden club into his hands and danced away out of range.

'Okay, slime-mold!' they screamed. 'Go to it! Bash it! Bust ass!' He heard a chorus of giggles. He hefted the club and the music rose to a crescendo.

It took only a few swings to find his range. Then it was all a joy. He savored the sound and feel of every impact.

Still blindfolded, he swung and struck, revelling in the sensations fed back through the wood. His muscles complained, but that was just fine.

The climax of the song in his brain came when he knew it was time to follow Bonzer's advice. He thrust the club up from below, feeling the stick slide along its prepared channel. He felt an initial resistance; then the shaft broke through.

He heard first the murmurs and mumbles, then the exclamations and finally the screams that meant that at last he'd succeeded in breaching the piñata. He felt the warm spatters on his upturned face and knew that the piñata was spilling its bounty for everyone.

Then the song was drowned out by the rising noise from the Acapulco Bash around him. Someone jerked the club out of his hands.

Turnbuckle heard the chanting. The song started to rise again. He had a feeling he knew what was going to happen next.

He had passed initiation.

AUTHOR'S NOTE

When I was a child, I ran into a lot of psychotic kids. At least that was my assumption. I had no friends. The other children were irrational monsters who hated me because I achieved more than they.

Apparently I threatened them.

It wasn't my fault I could do things better than they.

Since I had a lot of time on my hands, I learned to function quite well on my own.

When I was nine, my father took me to work with him one day. Nothing strange about that, except he was an assistant M.E. – medical examiner – for the city of Baltimore. That was not long before we moved west.

I still remember the sight of the autopsy rooms, but what I recall most are the temperature and the smell. It was cold – an absolute chill that seemed foreboding in spite of having come in from a sweltering August afternoon. And the smell. It was the first time I'd filled my nose with the fumes of formaldehyde.

My father told me that workers in a room like this were only good for about twelve years. Then the formaldehyde got to their brains. He introduced me to some of his colleagues and I speculated how long each had worked here. It was harder to tell just from their faces or how they spoke than I expected.

I looked for a slackness in their features.

Some sign that their minds had started to strip away the upper layers of intelligence.

That the beast was peeking out.

I returned frequently that summer. School was on vacation and my mother was visiting her dying sister in Cleveland. Everyone let me have the run of the place. I saw things I knew would help me out in school when the teacher asked me to write about what I'd done on my summer vacation.

Everything went smoothly until one afternoon when I walked in on one of my father's friends who had been working alone in one of the smaller rooms. Years later, I decided he must have been chopping off bits he wasn't supposed to.

And playing with them.

How was I supposed to know? It looked educational. He asked me not to tell anyone of what I'd seen. I agreed, not because I was intimidated, but because I wanted to know something more.

Many years later, at the University of Wisconsin, I briefly joined a fraternity. It seemed like a good idea at the time. Of course I learned that my new 'brothers' were no better than the boys who had made my life hellish when I was a child.

But at any rate, there were elements of the initiation ritual that reminded me of those halcyon August days in Baltimore.

Haunted

The Big Bopper boomed out 'Chantilly Lace,' and it all seemed strangely incongruous and lost among the crowd dressed in LaCoste shirts, a few Armani suits, trendy Liz Claiborne sportswear and Benetton ensembles. Angie Black paused at the front door of Boulder's L.A. Diner and felt momentarily out of place and time. She was dressed in a clean and comfortably bulky Holly Near sweatshirt and worn denim jeans. Behind her, the 28th Street traffic rumbled and ground up the shift spectrum as the lights turned green.

The hostess approached her. 'For just one?'

Angie shook her head. 'I'm meeting someone.'

From behind her, a woman's voice said, 'Angie! Hi! Come over, sit down.'

'Enjoy your lunch,' said the hostess, turning away.

Angie couldn't help staring, before catching herself. This shouldn't be the woman she was looking for. 'Um,' she said, hesitating. 'Bonnie?' The woman was just as tall and statuesque as she remembered, both physical attributes Angie lacked.

The woman took her elbow and propelled her over to a booth under a canopy of waxy green leaves. 'God, Angie, it's been such a long time. Ten years? Twelve? I never see you around Boulder anymore.'

Angie politely tried to disentangle herself. 'I'm supposed to be meeting a client,' she said to Bonnie Keller.

The other woman seated herself and looked up at

her. 'That's me,' she said. 'I'm the client.'

Angie shook her head in confusion. 'There's something here I'm not tracking.'

'Because the message on your machine said you should meet someone named Clear Brook Eversoul?' Bonnie smiled, showing flawless white teeth almost beyond counting. 'You're talking to her. To me. It's my name in the Menyata.'

'I thought the voice was familiar,' Angie said. 'I just couldn't quite place it. Too many years . . .' She slowly seated herself opposite Bonnie. 'The Menyata?'

'It's a wonderful new way of living,' said Bonnie/Clear Brook. 'Very, *very* spiritual. It's made an incredible difference in my life.'

It was all coming back to Angie why her conversations with Bonnie had rarely been the most satisfying. She recalled Bonnie's rapid-fire enthusiasms for EST, primal scream, the Maharishi, Tao, Buddhism, neo-Tao, deprivation tank, pseudo-lobotomy, Baba – too bad she hadn't stuck with them, Angie thought, Maranatha, Scientology, Illuminati Temple, Fish Worship, Unitarianism, Church of the New Way, Neolithic Regression, and ten or fifteen others.

'I don't do deprogramming,' she said.

Bonnie looked momentarily confused. 'No, that's not it. I need you,' she said, 'because I've heard you're a witch.'

A roller-skating waitress rolled up with menus.

After they'd ordered drinks, Angie said, 'I'd expect Boulder would be full of witches.'

The juke box was playing Buddy Holly and the Crickets rolling out 'That'll Be the Day.'

'It is,' said Bonnie. 'But they're mainly either the Wicca kind or else the suburban weirdos who dance naked around fires four times a year in their backyards out in Table Mesa. You know, like dilettantes.'

'Right,' said Angie, trying not to smile.

Bonnie's expression turned serious. 'You're the one I need to talk to, Angie. You can actually *do* stuff – you know, white and gray and black magic, all that stuff. You've got the power.'

Angie considered her gravely. '*Some* powers,' she said. 'It's nothing to mess around with.'

'Yes, I know, I know. I also talk to people. The right people. I know you do some things for hire. I need help, Angie. You're my friend. I'll pay you to help me.'

'Hold on,' Angie said. She put her hands across the table in the booth and took Bonnie's cold fingers. She realized the other woman was about ready to break down and cry. 'Listen,' she said. 'I'm just a person who's privy to occasional things she probably *shouldn't* screw around with. I have to earn a living, and sometimes I get to help people out. That's about it in a nutshell.'

'I need you to help *me* out, Angie.' Bonnie's dark lacquered nails dug into Angie's wrists. 'I'm going crazy.'

'How so?'

A tall werewolf slouched across the graveled parking area to the window and glanced in. It licked its lips with a shiny red tongue and moved on.

The waitress rolled up, braked to a stop without spilling a drop, and set the drinks down on the table. Angie had a Campari and tonic. The waitress set something fruity and frothy in front of Bonnie.

Bonnie took a long drink, then dabbed with a napkin, licked her lips, and said, 'Remember Danny?'

'Clay?' Bonnie nodded. Danny Clay had been a momentary star, nova-like in his intensity, in the firmament of 'sixties protest at the University of Colorado. He had done as much as anyone to weld together a diverse gaggle of politically divided activist groups into an effective demonstration and mobilization force. It had been in 1966, when the Hill had still been a reasonable microcosm of brave ideals and revolution. The Haight East.

Angie remembered –

– the cops running down Eleventh at midnight, shining

their lights under bushes, behind hedges, searching garages, knocking on doors. In the distance, dogs barked. Blocks away, flame and smoke curled from a burning bank. Angie had come out of the big turn-of-the-century house where she and about a dozen others lived, to see what was going on.

The unkempt shrubbery that bracketed the front steps had spoken to her in a loud, male whisper, interrupted by panting. 'Hey, girl. You know some magic, you might use it to get the pigs off my case.'

He should only know . . . She'd squinted into the darkness. The police on this side of the street were about two houses away. 'Maybe,' she said. 'I'd probably be more inclined, if I could see who was talking to me.'

Part of the bush moved. What she had taken to be normal shrubbery turned out to be a head of hair Bob Dylan would have been proud of. He didn't quite move into the direct glare of the porchlight. In the partial darkness, she made out dark eyes and a long straight nose. He was grinning at her. The white teeth showed up nicely in the shadows.

'This have something to do with the bank?' she said.

She had the impression of him shrugging. 'Looks like it. I didn't torch that hog-trough, but I was there. Far as the pigs are concerned, that makes it close enough for folk-rock.'

'Okay,' Angie said. 'I'm going to switch off the light. Then you better be fast.'

'Like quicksilver,' the man said.

'You got a name?'

The police were muttering around the garage of the house next door.

'You don't mind,' said the man, 'we'll rap later. Just get me inside.'

Later, Angie invited him to stay in her room and share the lumpy thrift-store mattress. His name was Danny, and he was carrying some dynamite Acapulco gold. They listened to *Surrealistic Pillow* and all her Dead albums and talked until long past the presumed departure of the police from the neighborhood. Then they made love. It wasn't terribly satisfactory for either, but Angie loved the look of his hair and his nose. *So* much like Dylan's. His full name was Danny Clay.

The next week, Danny moved in with Angie and the others. One of the others was Bonnie Keller . . .

'Oh, come on, Angie,' Bonnie had said not long after Danny's entrance into the household. 'It's not that much bread – only a hundred dollars.'

'It goes a long way toward the rent,' Angie said. 'I don't make all that much hustling pizzas. You know that.'

'But Mackinac Island is important,' said Bonnie. 'Moral Rearmament can save the world.'

'I've heard that before. About once every month or two. Just plug in different groups. Come *on*, Bonnie.'

Bonnie looked stricken. 'What am I going to do?'

'I can loan you a little, if you need it.' Danny had come into the kitchen and sat down at the table.

'No kidding? That'd be wonderful.' Bonnie smiled and – it seemed to Angie – shifted her shoulders so that her bra-less chest more advantageously filled out the peasant blouse.

'We'll talk about it,' said Danny. He flashed his patented grin, picked up the coffee pot and refilled all their cups.

Another in the group was Bud Keller. No one quite knew why he was living in the house on Eleventh instead of by himself in his own apartment. Bud was an economics major who prided himself on being even more apolitical than Angie.

That was not readily apparent when he walked in on the rest of them in the kitchen that September afternoon. He was carrying his prized Barlow knife and one of the figurines he whittled habitually. This one looked like an Easter Island head.

'Who're you?' he'd said brusquely to Danny.

Angie introduced them and started to explain why Danny was there at all.

'He's a friend of Angie's,' Bonnie said grudgingly.

'Christ,' said Bud. 'The dope's bad enough. You're bringing

revolutionaries into the house? We get busted, you know how quick we're all going to be tossed out of school on our asses?'

'I'll leave,' said Danny. He stood.

'Sit down.' Neither Angie nor Bonnie knew which of them had said it first.

'Let's talk about this,' said Bonnie.

Angie added, 'Danny didn't have anything to do with the bank-burning.'

'Right,' said Bud. 'Maybe the cops'll come around to that conclusion sooner or later. Right now, they don't seem too sure. Neither does the *Daily*.'

'I'm sure it will die down,' Bonnie said. She looked at Danny.

Angie put one hand over his wrist. 'He can stay here a while. If he wants to.'

Danny Clay smiled at Bud. 'You know, the accent's all wrong, but you could pass for a young LBJ.'

'Screw off.' Bud said to Bonnie, 'I overheard what you were saying about the Moral Rearmament conference. I'll give you some money, enough to take care of it.'

Bonnie looked momentarily confused. 'But Danny already –'

'I'll give you the money.'

She shrugged. 'Thanks.' Bonnie looked from Bud to Danny and back again.

The bank affair had died down. Angie remembered that the police had busted some black exchange students who had recently bought cami jackets and black berets. Eventually they were let go before any trial, or even indictment. In the meantime, Danny Clay graduated from the SNCC to his own organization, zeroing in on student rights and organizing protest against the widening war in Southeast Asia.

Bud, on the other hand, continued on the singleminded course that, twenty years later, ensured that he sold more Volvos and BMWs than any other dealer between Fort Collins and Pueblo.

Now, sitting in the L.A. Diner in Boulder and sipping her Campari and tonic, all Angie said was, 'I remember Danny.'

'You remember what happened to him?'

Angie nibbled at the maraschino. 'I guess as much as anybody. He split for Canada one night, right?'

'That's what people said.' Bonnie looked down at her drink.

'Right,' said Angie. 'The government was closing in. His number was up and he was headed for 'Nam if they caught him. I remember the day before he left, he said he'd never lost a lottery. He figured it must have been fixed. I told him he was paranoid. Danny was not happy.' Angie shook her head. 'I haven't thought about that in a long time. One day he was there; the next, he'd gone.'

'He's back,' said Bonnie.

'Oh?' said Angie. 'Just like *The Big Chill*. Are you getting together a party?'

Bonnie looked like someone was tramping over her grave. 'I saw him last night.'

'So how is he?' said Angie.

Bonnie's face had turned haggard suddenly, as though she hadn't gotten any sleep for a month. 'He's dead.'

A file of vampires of various genders and physiognomies straggled past on the sidewalk.

Angie nodded soberly. 'How do you know?'

'I used to see him,' said Bonnie. 'It was after Bud and I bought the old house and renovated it. I'd see Danny in my dreams, but he was always pretty far away, distant, fuzzy. He wasn't scary then.' She stared at Angie. 'There's something about him now. It's not just that Bud's gone for the week at the dealers' conference in Atlanta. It's spooky, and Danny's suddenly right there in the room and he looks . . . awful. There's something terrible going on.'

Angie looked contemplative. 'When did Danny leave? Exactly when?'

Bonnie was silent for a moment. Then she said, 'It was twenty years ago. Just twenty years ago tonight.'

'Happy anniversary.' Angie expelled her breath. 'I'm sorry. I just wasn't expecting this. I think maybe I should come over and spend the night.'

'Please. Thank you.' Bonnie smiled. It was the first smile Angie had seen in the last half hour that looked genuine. 'You'll miss all the fun down on the Mall.'

'I'm watching enough of it now.' Angie glanced out the window and saw ghosts trussed in leather and pierced with chromed spikes meandering along 28th.

The juke box blasted out Richie Valens' 'La Bamba.' Angie didn't say anything to Bonnie. Holly, the Big Bopper, and now Valens. The three musicians who'd died together when the Beechcraft Bonanza had plowed into that snowy, frozen field in 1959. Angie shivered slightly and took another sip of the Campari.

God, she hated omens.

* * *

Bonnie fixed supper back at the house on Eleventh. The outside had remained much as Angie remembered it, though the landscaping was more precise. The trim had been painted. The roof was new.

The inside had been totally redone. As Angie recalled the damp, peeling interior from twenty years before, the renovation was a blessing. The only psychedelic posters in evidence were a set of Joplin, Grateful Dead, and Quicksilver Messenger Service framed under glass and mounted above the fireplace in the spacious living room.

'Originals,' said Bonnie, waving at the posters. 'Bud bought them from someone who was liquidating the stuff from the Filmore.'

Supper consisted of brown rice, oddly shaped patties of tofu, and steamed vegetables. There was, of course, no red meat. Nor even fish or chicken. Neither woman ate much.

'Tell me about yourself,' Bonnie said, over the cinnamon dessert tea.

It wasn't that Angie had little to tell, she just was not sure if she wanted to recapitulate her past for Bonnie. She compromised by skimming over the years she had spent recognizing, defining, and developing her powers. Bonnie was sharp enough to know Angie hadn't gone off to witch-school somewhere. It had all been accomplished through trial and error, occasionally dangerous experimentation, and encountering a few mentors.

'But you're a witch,' Bonnie kept saying. 'That's so cool.' She gestured around at the interior of the house. 'You must have just incredibly sharp perceptions. Can you . . . feel anything?'

'You mean Danny?' Angie raised her eyebrows. 'Sometimes I can pick up what I guess I'd call emanations.' She shook her head. 'I'm not getting anything at all. Maybe –' She tried to smile. 'Maybe I'm just on the wrong wavelength.'

'Keep trying,' said Bonnie. 'I'm sure something will happen tonight. I know it will.' For a moment, her voice sounded almost wistful.

'You never heard from Danny?' said Angie. 'No letters? Nothing but the dreams?'

'Nothing ever. The dreams came and went, and now they're back again. Maybe the twenty years has something to do with it?' Bonnie said hopefully.

'Anniversaries can have a meaning all out of proportion,' said Angie. 'Sometimes it's only symbolic. Sometimes it's real.'

There was a silence. 'I'm not sure I want to see Danny again.'

'It sounds like you don't have a choice,' Angie said.

* * *

Bonnie hadn't wanted to go to sleep, but Angie kept feeding her homemade Margaritas, heavy on the tequila, until the first woman had started to nod. 'You know,' she said drowsily, no longer fighting it when Angie gently lay her down on the couch and pulled the comforter up around her chin, 'I always knew you fell hard for Danny.'

It was ten before midnight.

'That was a long time ago,' said Angie. 'It wasn't exactly a secret. I thought I loved him. I thought a lot of bullshit things then.' She hesitated, and then smiled. 'Actually I didn't think much of anything. I was very much involved with trying to survive, to figure out who and what I was, to find someone – *anyone*, I thought sometimes – to love me and take care of me. It was a . . . phase, a momentary aberration.' She touched Bonnie's forehead gently. 'Anyway, I'm glad Bud married you. He's been good to you, hasn't he?'

Bonnie's voice had gotten fuzzy. 'We never had kids. Danny and I wanted kids. Bud didn't.' She mumbled something else Angie couldn't understand, then said, 'Do you know I didn't want to take him away from you?'

Angie said nothing, but half-turned away.

'I'm sorry, Angie. I'm really . . . sorry. I had Bud, but I wanted Danny, I was awful.'

'Twenty years,' said Angie evenly. 'Those years cover a lot.'

'Maybe not enough.' Bonnie slowly rolled her head from side to side on the satin pillow.

'Why do you have me here?' said Angie softly.

Bonnie didn't seem to hear.

Five until the witching hour.

Angie glanced at the Betty Boop clock. It sat above the living room shelf that held the Michelob-bottle-shaped lava lamp and the small pewter figurines of Joplin, Hendrix, and Morrison. Damn it, would Bonnie ever pass out?

'Twenty years . . .' said Bonnie, slurring the words. 'Angie, I'm sorry.' Her eyes closed. 'Danny, I wanted you so much. It's taken so long to realize . . . I wanted . . .' Her voice dwindled off.

Midnight.

Angie touched Bonnie's forehead one more time. The skin felt hot. Then Bonnie's wide blue eyes snapped open. 'It's twelve, isn't it?' She sat up, looking as though she hadn't downed however many Margaritas she'd drunk.

Angie stared at her. 'Just sit still.' She flicked her lighter and ignited the wick of the single dark candle on the coffee table. 'We'll wait.'

She didn't have long to wait.

Bonnie's eyes focused. 'Look,' she said. 'The glow.'

Angie followed the line of Bonnie's gaze. 'What glow?'

'It's like a candle. It's getting brighter, colder. Over there –' She pointed. 'See? By the kitchen door?' She indicated the direction of the long staircase that wound down from the kitchen to the vast cellar that had been excavated for the original house on this site.

Angie had been down in that basement earlier in the evening, to retrieve a jar of green tomatoes Bonnie had put up after her last summer's vegetable gardening. The room had been shadowed and echoing, quite cool with moisture condensed on the stone walls and the packed earthen floor. The ancient furnace squatted at one end like an enormous spider. The rest of the room was crowded with shelves and cartons, the cardboard bulging and wilted in the damp air.

Angie had wondered if any of Danny's stuff were still down here. No one, she recalled, had claimed him as kin or friend after he'd gone north. Surely his books and manifestos, the mimeographed core of his life, were all still down here somewhere. Also the albums, the blacklight posters, the blue chambray shirts and the jeans. All here. No way he had carried everything away with him. She doubted Bonnie would have thrown it out. She had the feeling Bonnie never discarded the past.

Fleetingly she wondered what might have happened had Danny stayed with Bonnie, and she had ended up with Bud. She'd probably be driving a BMW. Angie wondered at her own flippancy. She could sense a palpable tension, but it didn't seem to her to be occult. She wasn't sure *what* it was.

'It's at the door,' said Bonnie. She began to shiver. Angie held her shoulders.

'What is?'

'The glow.' Then she said, 'It's here, it's in the room.'

Angie could not see *anything* out of the ordinary. She felt nothing other than the tension she had decided was coming from Bonnie. 'Tell me what you see.'

'He looks the same.' Bonnie started to recoil. Angie continued to hold her.

'Danny?'

'It's like the years never went by. It's him. See, Angie? Can't you see? The brown hair's the same – all curly and falling down below his collar. His eyes are so mild, so gentle. He's wearing the granny glasses. You know, like John Lennon. Oh God, he looks the same.'

'What else?' said Angie.

'The T-Shirt,' said Bonnie. She shivered more violently. 'Oh, Jesus!'

'What is it?'

Bonnie said, 'The Jefferson Airplane shirt . . . The one he loved most . . . Grace Slick signed it. The shirt . . . It's covered with blood –' Bonnie drew her knees up on the couch, hugging herself, still staring into the distance. 'The blood fans out like the patterns in a light show. It's spilling out from – from –' She hesitated. 'The knife. It's there in his chest. The blood's running down onto his legs, it's running down his jeans.'

'Oh, Danny!' Angie said under her breath. It wasn't addressed to the apparition she still could not perceive. It was just the only thing her lips could frame.

'The blood's so dark . . .' said Bonnie. 'It looks black.'

'Where is he?' Angie tried to feel Danny's presence in the living room. 'Bonnie, tell me.'

'I want to take you in my arms,' Bonnie said dreamily to the empty air. 'God, I want to warm you.'

Then the woman shook herself free of Angie's arms.

Bonnie straightened, got her legs under her, stood up.

'What are you doing?' said Angie.

'He wants me to follow him,' said Bonnie. She started to walk toward the kitchen. Without hesitation, Angie followed her. Bonnie moved somnambulistically through the door from the living room, toward the steps down into the nighted basement. The cellar door stood wide open. Angie was sure it had been shut when they had finished washing and drying the supper dishes. She still sensed no magic at work, no occult forces. Aside from what Bonnie said, Angie possessed no perception of what it was the other woman was following.

The two of them descended the steps into the basement. The only illumination spilled down from the kitchen through the stairwell. At the foot of the stairs, Angie flipped the wall-switch, but nothing happened other than a hollow click. Bonnie moved away from her through the increasingly murky shadows.

'Shit,' Angie said, and followed. It was cold down here. She could feel the chill of the packed earthen floor through the soles of her flats. Bonnie had walked to the opposite end of the basement from the furnace. Now she stood perfectly still before ranks of dark shelves, silent and staring down at her feet. Angie caught up with her and took her elbow. Bonnie's flesh felt as cold as the dirt floor. Angie could feel the skin stippled with gooseflesh.

'I'm so very sorry,' said Bonnie.

'Where is he?' Angie said.

Bonnie said nothing at all.

Angie's eyes started to adjust. She realized what filled the painted wooden shelves. It was a collection of Bud Keller's wooden carvings, all the figurines she had seen him laboriously fashion during the years on Eleventh. She could make out the tiki gods, the skeletal human figures, the masks. There seemed to be more bizarre objects crowding the darker recesses of the shelves.

She looked from the carved figures to the hard earth below.

She looked at Bonnie, who had not moved. The woman's eyes were dilated and staring.

'Bonnie?' she said. There was no reply. Angie raised her voice slightly. 'Will you talk to me?'

'Angie?' Bonnie said, voice barely audible. 'What?'

'The knife,' Angie said, no longer wanting to stare at the whittled figures, but unable to look away. 'The knife in Danny's chest. What did it look like?'

Bonnie said nothing. She began to cry.

* * *

'I don't understand this,' said Bonnie. 'I don't understand any of it.' Her eyes were red with crying, tears streaking the mascara.

With Angie's help, Bonnie had managed to totter back up the steps to the kitchen. Then she virtually collapsed. Angie had helped her reach the living room. There was no question of Bonnie's making it to the bedroom. She slumped down onto the couch and was asleep instantly. Angie sat up in one of the uncomfortable chrome-and-leather designer chairs, drank coffee, and waited. And thought.

Morning came in about seven hours. Pale first-of-November sunshine slanted into the kitchen and washed the formica table. The moment Bonnie had shown the slightest signs of stirring, Angie had taken her by the hand and led her back to the basement. This time the switch had worked and the bare bulb in the overhead had dimly banished most of the shadows.

Now the two women sat opposite one another across the kitchen table. Steam plumed up from their coffee mugs and dissipated.

'I don't understand anything,' Bonnie said again.

'I'm not sure I have anything to say other than what happened,' Angie said. 'I followed you into the basement. I've showed you where you led me.'

Bonnie shook her head mutely.

'You can dig there or not.'

'The ghost –' Bonnie said.

Angie shook her own head. She tried to make her words sound less brutal. She didn't think it worked. 'If you dig, I think you'll find Danny. He never got to Canada. That was Bud's story, remember? Bud was always convincing. I bought it just like everybody else. I was ready to believe Danny had simply run. At the time, it made sense.' She stopped talking.

'That isn't all, is it?' Bonnie's voice rose.

Angie stared past Bonnie, out the window and into the austere sunlight. Outside it looked like everything had sharp edges.

'*Angie!*'

Angie wanted to pick her words to form a syntax that was somehow less brutal. She couldn't think of another way of phrasing it. 'I'm just guessing now, but I suspect if you find Danny, you'll also find Bud's Barlow knife in his chest.'

The tears leaked down Bonnie's face. Angie shut her mouth. 'But *why*?' Bonnie said. Complete and hopeless bafflement creased her face into the mask of an older woman.

Angie shrugged carefully, softened her tone. 'It was twenty years ago,' she said as gently as she could. 'I'm not going to try to recreate what was in Bud's head. It's hard enough just to begin to recall what *I* was thinking then.'

'Bud wouldn't –'

'I think Bud *did*. Maybe he thought he'd never have you if he didn't do this thing. Maybe it was something else. It was so long ago.' A phrase of music came into her mind. 'We were so much older then!'

'But it's *Danny*, and he's *dead*!' It was almost a wail.

Angie felt like crying too. She remembered Danny that first night when she had taken him in, the night of the bank-burning. She couldn't think of anything comforting to say to Bonnie, and so said nothing.

Bonnie wept then, and Angie held her, trying to supply

soothing words and occasional tissues. She stroked her friend's hair, feeling the warm wetness when her palm brushed Bonnie's eyes. Finally the worst of the sobs subsided.

'What am I going to do?' Bonnie said. 'Tomorrow Bud's coming home. What am I going to say to him?'

Angie looked out the window again. Something crashed past the pane. Icicles falling. 'Maybe there's nothing you have to say.'

'What's that mean?'

Angie drew in a deep breath. 'Did you know?'

'No.' But Bonnie wouldn't meet her eyes.

'Did you?'

'Danny's ghost,' said Bonnie. 'He led me there.'

Angie slapped her. Once. She didn't mean to, but it happened, the flat smack echoing through the tiled kitchen. 'The ghost.' She shook her head. 'You brought me here because you thought you were dealing with the supernatural.' She laughed, and in her own ears it sounded bitter. 'There wasn't any need. I can't see your ghost. I can't hear him.'

Touching fingers to her reddened cheek, Bonnie said in evident bewilderment, 'But why not?'

'Don't you know?'

Mute, large-eyed, Bonnie said nothing.

Angie looked away toward the window and the ice outside, back at Bonnie, glanced over at the door to the cellar stairs. She wished fervently, desperately for the glint of Lennon-style granny glasses; a wisp of long, curly hair; warm, brown eyes. She wanted to see Grace Slick's looping signature on the Airplane T-shirt. Any occult sign. Anything at all.

'No,' said Bonnie. 'I don't know.'

The two women stared at each other until the coffee got cold.

AUTHOR'S NOTE

Have I ever met a witch?

Certainly I've met women – and a few eccentric men – who believed they had supernatural powers.

You can always tell.

They speak and act and even move with a sense of power, *an attitude of knowing they control the what and whom around them.*

They look at you so smugly and read your mind.

Some claim they are simply terribly accomplished at interpreting body language and nuance of expression. Perhaps that is only protective camouflage.

What is inarguable is that they use their power to influence and control human beings.

From time to time, I've felt their power. Always I have been able to resist it. Always.

Whether you believe such talent is paranormal or simply acquired and exercised through completely rational means doesn't matter. The point is that such people have sacrificed their humanity. They should not be allowed to exist.

I rarely think of the Bible *anymore but the phrase about not 'suffering a witch to live' haunts me.*

Doesn't your skin crawl at the thought of another's mind violating your own? Another's unwanted touch fouling your life?

My judgement may seem harsh at first, but I think you can see my point in making it.

Buggage

He remembered later that somewhere on the ribbon-furnace that was U.S. 380 winding across the midsection of New Mexico, he'd wished he was dead. He should have knocked on wood – had there been any – said a prayer, crossed his fingers, anything. It was just that the heat was killing and there were no rides, not since the rancher who'd picked him up in Socorro had turned off the blacktop onto a dirt track and apologetically dropped him in the middle of, if not nowhere, at least somewhere on the outskirts.

Davey Wendroff trudged toward Bingham. Sixty miles? Eighty? Beyond Bingham lay Carrizozo, more little towns, Roswell, and impossibly farther, the Texas line. Davey passed a sign that read: 'See Bottomless Lakes State Park.' Right, he thought. Bottomless. All the water in the world, and not a drop to drink. He turned to look again at the azure lake on the billboard, but the heat shimmers already obscured the image.

He shifted his shoulders, allowing the pack to ride more comfortably. Sweat ran into his left eye, the salt stinging. As he blotted it with one chambray sleeve, Davey wondered how much fluid he could lose before collapsing on the baked asphalt.

He was thirsty, hungry, tired, aching; and the hell of it was, he didn't really have any place to go. No destination. Just the homing instinct returning him to the east. In a week or two? A month, maybe? He'd be back in New Jersey. Bayonne. Home, he thought. That's a laugh and a half. Now that he thought about it, maybe he should just turn around and backtrack toward Phoenix and Vegas. Perhaps north to Albuquerque. Or south to Old Mexico.

Or maybe he simply ought to die right here. The thought was tempting; so much easier just to lie down by the road and bake to death, get nice and crispy for the buzzards, well done for the gila monsters . . . Shut up, he told himself. Keep walking. Somebody'll pick you up.

But they didn't. The few westbound cars did slow a bit so the drivers and passengers could inspect him. They'd whip past, then start accelerating in the general direction of California. The cars heading east never even slowed. The only reaction Davey elicited was from a pair of kids in the back of a station wagon who jeered in mime and laughed. Davey stared at the dot that was the image of the wagon diminishing in the east, and softly cursed. Then he untied the plastic Chlorox bottle from his belt and swigged the tepid water. Not much left. Certainly not enough for a day's hike.

A black Datsun Z-car buzzed past. Davey shook his head and watched it go. What do they think, I'm out here for a marathon? He walked a while, then stopped and rested in the hot shadow of a highway bridge across a dry wash. And then, because there was nothing else to do and he knew he really didn't want to die just yet, Davey kept on walking.

* * *

He stared toward the sun. He looked at his watch. How long had he been out here? It was after six. Eventually the sun would set and the temperature would plummet. He wondered if he could freeze to death in the desert. Davey looked around for the highway and saw not even the slightest track. There were no billboards, no cars.

His mind cleared with a sudden lucid chill. In the sun-blaze, he had wandered. He didn't know where he was. He realized he was nearing the crest of a dry hill and there was nothing around him other than the scrub and the sparse, thin grass. He'd done it! He'd finally managed to kill himself. Davey checked the water bottle. He let the few remaining drops rest on his tongue. They dried before he could swallow them.

Christ! he thought. The heat. It's never going to go down. But he knew it would. And when it did, he would probably die. He had the feeling he wasn't completely rational.

It occurred to him, upon reaching the crest of the hill, that the house below was only a mirage. That did not deter him from descending toward the weathered frame building. It was only when Davey entered the shade of the two-story building that he was sure. It had to be real. Tentatively he touched the wall with his fingers, feeling the splinters protruding from the rough boards. He slapped one palm against the wood, giggling when he felt the pain. This was real.

Appraisingly he looked up at the height of the house. The structure wasn't precisely vertical – he could see the roof-slope had a sag to it. The entire wall leaned a few degrees west, as though the house were slowly collapsing into the sun.

Davey pounded on the wall, not heeding the splinters. 'You home? Anyone home? You got some water? Please?' No one answered and finally he took his hand away from the wood and walked toward the nearest corner, searching for an entrance.

The only door was cut into the opposite side of the house. Already open a few inches, the rusting hinges yielded when Davey set his shoulder to the wood. 'Anybody here?' he said, voice faltering when he heard the absolute silence of the house's interior. For only a moment he hesitated because he suddenly *knew* there was someone there. Then he also knew that *of course* there could be no one else in this desolate place, and so he entered.

The state of what furnishings remained, and the carpet of dust covering those furnishings, offered evidence that no one had been here in quite a while. No, maybe not. Davey leaned down and examined the surface of the plank table. The dust wasn't perfectly flat. It was stippled, dimpled as though someone had pricked it thousands, millions of times with a straight pin. He shrugged and straightened.

There must be water somewhere in this house – a pump, a cistern, anything. Then he would worry about food. He passed the ruined chairs, long-ago splintered, but whether smashed in caprice or anger, he couldn't tell.

He did find a pump by the kitchen sink. It was old and iron, the metal long discolored. When Davey gingerly pulled on the pump handle, he had to break the rust-seal holding the joint. The metal shrieked, but the lever moved. After a dozen strokes, water started to pour from the spout. It was rusty and smelled vile, but the man cupped his hands beneath the flow and then drank.

The water was bad, but it didn't kill him. Davey was careful not to drink too much at once. He possessed a vague apprehension of bloating. So he regularly pumped and drank, pumped and drank, but didn't obey the impulse to guzzle his fill and be done.

He found some canned goods in the pantry, but the cans were corroded and bulging, so Davey let them go. When he searched his pack again, he found an overlooked packet of cellophane-wrapped Saltines he'd picked up at the truckstop in Globe. The crackers were a feast he thought he couldn't have imagined. He ate them a bit at a time, cleansing his palate after each small bite with the dark well-water.

His stomach wasn't satisfied, but at least his thirst was assuaged. Davey noted that it was dark outside. He knew it was the time of the new moon. He could forget about reading the ragged paperback copy of *Still Life With Woodpecker*. The candle. He had a stub of candle somewhere in his pack. He found it, realized it wouldn't provide all that many minutes of illumination, but struck a match to light the wick.

He decided he would explore the rest of the house before sleeping. There was an apparent trapdoor cut into the wooden flooring of the kitchen. It had no handle and didn't budge when Davey tried to prise it loose with his fingertips.

A narrow flight of steps led up to the second floor. Davey found two empty bedrooms linked by a hall and what was either a one-time bathroom or a very large closet. In the flickering light, he could see a wooden ladder going up to what was presumably the entrance to the attic.

It was when Davey started back down the staircase to the ground floor where he expected to make up some sort of austere bed, that he hesitated on the top step. He thought he saw something moving in the darkness. 'Oh shit,' he said under his breath. 'Oh, holy shit.' And louder, 'Somebody there?' Something moved again. It was indistinct, more the impression of movement than anything specific or visible.

'Aw, come on now,' said Davey.

And it did. He hadn't meant anything by the remark. It was said more to allay his own sudden apprehension. But something did come. What had moved in the darkness approached the bottom of the stairs. Davey still could not see anything specific. He thought he heard sounds that he couldn't identify. It was a rustling, almost the murmuring of a multitude of voices.

Davey leaned forward with the candle at arm's length, but saw nothing. The bottom step was a darker brown than he remembered, but that was all. The next step up darkened. And then the next. Davey blinked, trying to focus his eyes. Something seemed to be flowing up the stairs toward him.

It wasn't until he was well along the upstairs hall that he realized he had dropped the candle. He smashed painfully into the wall, rebounded, felt his fingers touch something he could grab. It was the ladder. Instinct made him climb.

When his head struck the attic hatch, he panicked for a moment when the door didn't give. He shoved and the hatch came loose. Davey hoisted himself into the attic.

And whatever murmured and pursued him . . . followed right up after.

It was when Davey came up against the boarded window in

the darkness of the far end, that he realized there was no way out of the attic. Whatever it was that confronted him in the night-time house was not to be eluded so easily.

'Who are you?' he said, trying not to scream the words, horribly aware that what he really wanted to say was, '*What* are you?' Nothing answered him. Nothing said a word. But something else. Something small scrabbled across the plywood sheets sagging between the beams. Soft rustlings. Hard, chitinous chitterings.

Davey never actually screamed until he felt the first touches brushing across his shoes, up his ankles, the tickling of hard little legs tangling with the hair on his shins.

Never religious, he said, 'Oh God, Oh God,' over and over again, the invocation automatic and desperate. He flailed about himself, brushing off what seemed to be ants or roaches or something else. Something small and hard and fast, a multitude of crawling things.

The true panic afflicted him when he felt the burrowings beneath his clothes, between his legs, even between the cheeks of his rear. But when he opened his mouth, this time truly to scream as he had never done before, the things inserted themselves between his lips, obstinately clinging and pushing forward past the soft tissues when he clawed at his own skin, rubbed, and beat, and slapped at that which he couldn't see. His ears, his nose, all the soft and hard places of his mouth . . . there the things penetrated and clung, and moved inward, ever inward. The violation didn't stop. He could do nothing. Bitter fluid rose in his throat, but the flood didn't stop that which crawled and skittered down to meet it.

Some corner of his mind was grateful through the outrage and the screaming when the final darkness came.

* * *

He awoke dreaming he was screaming.

Davey rocked his head from side to side, squinted his eyes

into focus, and realized that the sound coming from his throat was a dry, rasping wheeze. Morning sun splashed around him. It was already getting hot. He levered himself upright with his elbows. He was sitting on the tough scrub grass outside the house.

He had been in the attic. He remembered that. He remembered –

He remembered.

Davey's arms flailed without conscious volition, beating at himself, slapping the air, slowing, finally stopping. Without getting all the way up, he twisted and tugged, pulling off all his worn clothing. Nothing moved. No bugs. All he found to give him pause were two spots of dried blood in the seat of his cotton briefs.

He absently rubbed with a thumbnail at the dull red stain. The man suspected he didn't remember everything that had happened the previous night; but what he *could* recall . . . Davey wrapped his arms around himself and started to shake violently.

A coughing spasm wracked him. Something tickled in his throat, irritating the dry tissues. He hacked violently and brought something up. It was hard in his mouth. He put two fingers inside and extracted a small object that was shiny and black. He examined it closely, but for a moment or two it didn't register. The thing was a bit of shell, a chunk of carapace. Davey hurled it from him. 'Jesus!' The night pooled up around him and Davey staggered to his feet just so he could keep his head above the darkness.

The sun shone bright and hot. Davey steadied himself by crossing the short distance to the house and grasping the edge of the front door with both hands. The door creaked, but held firm. The smooth, weathered wood reassured him. He began to take an inventory of himself. His hunger was a dull ache. Thirst was equally pressing. Davey realized suddenly that his bladder felt about the size of a cantaloup. Some lingering sense of propriety drove him away from the front of the house and into the scrub. He gingerly picked his way with tentative bare steps and found what seemed a suitable spot to relieve himself.

Nothing happened.

The pressure seemed to grow unbearable. Davey strained. Pain zigzagged through his abdomen and he whimpered. Then it was as though a small dam were breaking, a river beginning again to flow. Yet it wasn't right. More pain – so *much* pain – rippled through him, this time centered in his penis. Davey suddenly remembered his uncle from Yonkers talking about 'passing stones.' He imagined it felt something like this. He could feel something hard and irregularly shaped slowly moving along the length, agonizing toward the tip.

When it finally appeared, Davey stared in shock. The shattered black shell was moist and shiny. The remaining leg moved weakly.

For just a moment his mind broke, dry screams ripping up from his chest.

Sorry, said a voice from somewhere.

Heedless of yucca and cactus, Davey ran blindly into the wilderness. Everything he touched tried to flay his skin from the body beneath, and he welcomed that.

Sorry, repeated the voice, *sorry – we're so sorry*.

He heard but didn't listen. All he could do was to run and run, desperate for the New Mexico sun to burn him clean. He ran until he collapsed into the dust with all the grace of a bundle of sticks coming untied.

Sorry. The voice was still with him. He shuddered and tore at himself weakly. The voice was *in* him. He wanted to believe that he was going insane.

But he couldn't.

* * *

I *am sorry* – we *are sorry*, said the voice from somewhere deep inside him, so deep, he couldn't determine any source at all. Davey started to scratch at his other arm, at his sides, his belly, his thighs. The scratching became something deeper, more frantic, violent.

Please do not hurt yourself, said the voice. *We do not want you to hurt yourself, just as we do not wish to harm you.* The man could sense a reassuring tone in the inner voice. He was not reassured.

'Just who *are* you?' He could hear the sound of his own hysteria.

The answer was from the same voice, yet changed. Davey sensed hundreds, *thousands* of voices overlaid one on the other. *We are a multitude*, said the voice(s).

Then *Call me Gregor*, said the single, unaugmented voice again.

Davey remembered the dark and the sounds and the sight of glistening shell. He made the awful connection. 'I'm hallucinating,' he said. 'It's gotta be.'

No, you are not. My designation comes from your mind, from the story by Franz Kafka. You read the book last year. It was in your literature survey course. The designation was 101. The –

'I did,' said Davey. 'God help me, I did.' He tried to concentrate, making fists of his hands so that his fingernails would not dig into his flesh. 'You – *all* of you – what are you doing inside me?' His voice wailed. 'You *are* inside me.'

I think you will find us beautiful, said the voice that had called itself Gregor. An image came unbidden to Davey's mind and he examined it. He gazed upon something like the vaulting interior of a Gothic cathedral. He saw the great inner spaces spiring upward, glistening wet. He felt the sensation of space, of breathless, soaring beauty.

'What is that?' he said, already suspecting, not wanting to know.

It is us, said the voice. *It is you. You are us. We are you.*

Davey looked inside at the vast, gaping interior of himself, at the distant bands of white enclosing this place. He knew with horrid certainty that the stripes were bone.

'What have you done to me?' His voice, stunned, could do no more than plead. 'What have you done?'

We are still doing it, said Gregor. *We will never stop. We are building a home.*

'Oh, God,' Davey moaned.

* * *

There had been more. Much more. Davey remembered it all during the year that followed.

We are here to help you. That was Gregor's favorite line. *We are here to help*. It was just like goddamned government. How many times had Davey heard similar protestations from the workers from Social Services, his councilors at school, the tax people, the bosses at his various early jobs? He hadn't been stung many times before wising up. Others' conception of 'help' tended to be different than his own.

The funny thing was, Davey grudgingly admitted to himself, the insects really *did* seem to be helping him. One of the few things he remembered his father saying was that you don't foul your own nest. The insects were behaving admirably in that respect. Davey still did not relish the thought of all those creatures dwelling inside him. He knew the first awful knowledge of violation would never go away. Not completely. But he also knew he had learned to live with it. Or at least to go on functioning.

Then: fuck it, he would tell himself about a dozen times each day. I've never had it so good.

That was absolutely true. He had to recognize it. He had never felt better physically. The insects kept the organic machine in which they lived in tip-top, fully maintained condition. Davey never got colds now. His allergies had vanished. Gregor told him he had had a pre-cancerous condition in his liver, which had been taken care of.

You will live a long and healthy life, Gregor said. *We shall ensure it.*

'But what do you get out of it?' Davey had questioned. He knew everything had a catch.

We have a home. That shall be sufficient for a while.

'And after that?' He wasn't sure he wanted to know.

We will always be here. Don't worry that we will abandon you. But we must grow and develop as a group. Eventually we will colonize.

It had an ominous ring. 'What's that going to mean?'

To you? Nothing. We have our own ways of . . . settling new territory.

That the insects did. Davey remembered the night in the old house in New Mexico only too well. He asked no more questions about the intentions of those he hosted.

The insects got him a new job. They even taught him how to dress. It wasn't quite that direct, of course. Gregor told him the flow of oxygenated blood to his brain had been made more efficient. His thoughts seemed more gathered, more cogent. The principles of computer programming that had seemed so fragmented and elusive before, now were as clear as the temperature when he walked outside in the morning. Gregor had offered invaluable advice. He caused the man to observe the more apparently successful humans around him, including their effective costumes. When Davey scanned the job openings in the newspaper, it was Gregor who suggested applying for the position at DynInfo. Gregor coached Davey when the man went in for the interview. Afterward, after the interviewer had said DynInfo would be in touch, but had also suggested strongly that Davey's job-acceptance was in the bag, Davey had stood in the men's room staring at his own reflection. The person he looked at was no longer, in any way, the image he remembered. He cautiously thought he liked the changes.

We're glad, said Gregor.

Ten months went by. Davey received two merit raises. That

was better than any other probationary employee at DynInfo. He moved to a more comfortable apartment, purchased some decent clothes, bought a sensible Nissan sedan. He took night courses at a local community college.

That was where he met Lynda Wendiger.

He first noticed her because her last name was so close to his own. It took only half a second after that to glance again, and then to stare outright. He caught her eye. She looked back at him and smiled, and so he immediately looked away.

During the break in the programming class, she deliberately sought him out as they both purchased cups of coffee from the vending machine in the lobby.

'So,' she said. 'I think we both work for the same corporation.' Both of them did indeed work for DynInfo. Lynda had been a management trainee for nearly a year. She had moved to New Jersey's Silicon Valley East from Los Alamos. Hers had been one of the 'first families' relocated to the government's research community in New Mexico when the Manhattan Project moved west toward the end of World War II.

Davey listened, but her background wasn't what he was hearing. It was the softness of her voice. The music in it.

Breathe regularly, came Gregor's inner voice. *We will help diminish the pumping of your hormones*.

Davey wasn't sure he *wanted* his pumping hormones diminished.

Relax, said Gregor.

The man couldn't. He stared at her red hair, her green eyes, kept listening to her voice even though she was no longer speaking, and wondered how it could be that he was in love. He had never been in love before. Never.

Lynda looked at him peculiarly. 'Is there something wrong?' Absolutely not. He couldn't even say the words aloud. Mute, he shook his head.

The woman smiled radiantly. 'That's good. I'm glad.' She hesitated. 'Would you like to do something sometime? Maybe go out for dinner or a movie?'

This time Davey nodded. Yes. A thousand times, yes.

'That's great,' said Lynda. 'I knew I liked you. I'm looking forward to this.'

And that's how it started.

* * *

Here's how it ended.

The courtship – Davey started thinking of the relationship that way – went on for months. He escorted Lynda to all manner of ethnic restaurants he had never been aware existed. He took her to films, first the popular first-run releases, then to a variety of classics at the revival houses. He learned about music first from accumulating compact discs, then by attending a variety of live concerts, all recommended by Lynda. They enjoyed each other's company. Davey was sure of that. Lynda told him so. He loved her and so he believed her.

He had his arguments with Gregor. The insects seemed skeptical of the whole affair. They communicated dubiously about the growing friendship between the two humans.

You don't need her, Gregor said. *You have us.*

'I know,' said Davey, 'and I appreciate it. But I think I love Lynda. I want to be with her.'

We clearly need to adjust your endocrine system and perform whatever other adjustments are necessary.

'No,' said the man. 'Even all that wouldn't do it. I can tell you that right now.'

The speaker for the insects tried another tack. *It simply isn't time yet. We are not quite ready to colonize.*

Davey recoiled in nausea. 'Absolutely not. Lynda is not to be a colony. No way.'

What could be more logical? It would be akin to your feeling of love, but even closer, more intimate.

'No!'

He received the impression of what could have been a sigh. *We love you too, you know.*

The debate continued on other occasions. The insects urged common sense and even more seductive logic. *With a base of two colonies, we could begin to grow exponentially.*

'I'm not interested,' Davey said.

It's in our nature.

'Suppress your nature.'

It's now your nature as well.

Davey was stubborn. 'You will not colonize her. You will do nothing against her.'

And so it went on.

Lynda seemed to see nothing odd in Davey. She appeared to relish every moment in his company. One Saturday night, they attended a science fiction film festival on the Rutgers campus in Princeton. They sat through a marathon triple-bill of *Them!*, *Tarantula*, and *The Giant Gila Monster*. Afterward, they followed their custom of late-night coffee and conversation. Davey discovered that the New Mexico settings for the three monster movies had somewhat set him on edge.

Lynda, on the other hand, admitted that all three had made her nostalgic. 'Have you ever spent much time in New Mexico?' she said, stirring cream into her Denny's coffee and sipping delicately.

'A little.' He committed himself no further.

'New Mexico's a strange place,' Lynda mused. 'I've always loved the weird mixture of Old West and high tech.' She added more sugar to her coffee. 'You know something? There are more people than you'd think who'd swear the movies we saw tonight are closer to documentaries than fantasies.'

'No kidding,' said Davey a bit morosely.

She nodded. 'Ever since Los Alamos and the Trinity Project, there's been a modern folklore that the radiation's done strange things to the flora and fauna.'

Davey suddenly wondered whether Lynda was somehow suspicious of his nature, actually knew something of what *really* lurked inside him.

Don't be silly, said Gregor. *How could she know?*

Davey allowed the insects to help him breathe more regularly, to calm his racing pulse. 'It makes for good horror thrillers,' he said.

She shrugged. 'I suppose. That's what everybody *knows*.' Her attention seemed to wander. She looked buried in thought.

'What is it?' he said.

'I'm changing the subject,' said Lynda.

He looked at her inquiringly.

'I like going out with you.'

'So do I,' he said sincerely.

'Things have to keep growing.'

Davey wasn't sure what she was getting at.

Lynda reached across the table and took one of his hands in both her own. Her touch was light and dry and very warm. 'We've been doing things together for months,' she said. 'You've never kissed me.' She hesitated. 'Nor done anything else.'

Davey could figure out the question implicit in her voice. 'It's just . . .' he started to say, then stopped because he was positive he would choke or stutter or somehow otherwise screw up what he wanted to say. 'I love you very much, and I've never . . .' The words trailed off.

'You've never.' Lynda smiled and her expression was warm. 'That's lovely and very dear.' Something Davey didn't remember seeing before came into her features. 'I want you to come home with me tonight. I want to make love with you.'

Yes, Davey thought. 'Yes,' he said.

No, said Gregor.

'I want to very much,' Davey said.

'Then let's go,' Lynda said. She started shrugging on her coat. 'It's getting late.'

Davey didn't remember walking out to the parking lot and starting the Nissan. All the way to Lynda's home, he argued internally with Gregor. Please, he thought. Don't fight me on this. I love her. I want her.

So do we, said Gregor, *but it's not time yet.*

Anybody else, Davey thought. Just name them. But leave me alone with her.

In a manner of speaking, said Gregor. There was a sensation of amused resignation. *Go ahead. We wish only your happiness*. Then there was a hesitation.

What? Davey thought. What is it?

Nothing. We're just – no, nothing.

You're worried about something. What is it?

No, no suspicion. Nothing at all. The communication broke up and reformed in a way Davey hadn't experienced before. *We must think*, said Gregor. *Now go ahead. We will not disturb you.*

Lynda's apartment was tastefully decorated and exquisitely clean. Lynda did not give him a tour after she locked the dead-bolt and returned from using the bathroom. She leaned against him and kissed him. Davey had only the vaguest impression of dark draperies and hardwood furniture. Then she was in his arms, lips uptilted against his own, and he felt an all-encompassing warmth suffusing his body.

After a while, she said, 'Let's go to bed.' She took him by the hand and he followed.

Her bed was wide and sloshed. 'Do you like waterbeds?' she said.

'Sure,' said Davey. He let her help him off with his shirt, as he clumsily, in turn, started undoing the many, many buttons of her white blouse.

Finally they were in the bed itself, pressed against the satin of the sheets. Lynda helped him, first sitting astride him, soothing Davey when he started to buck against her.

'Take it easy,' she said. 'There's plenty of time.'

And so there was. After a while, Lynda shuddered and sighed and smiled. She pulled him over on top of her and wrapped her legs tightly around his back. 'That's it,' she said under her breath, again and again. 'That's it.'

Davey knew he couldn't keep this up – he was far too

excited. He told her that. Her eyes opened and she stared blankly at him. 'Now!' he said. 'I –'

'Now,' Lynda answered. Her arms and legs wrapped even more tightly around him. She smiled, her lips parting, moist tongue gleaming in the light from the single candle she had lighted at the beginning.

Davey, said Gregor.

'Shut up!' Davey cried, realizing the words were aloud. He saw Lynda's green eyes widen. He couldn't help himself. 'All of you, shut up!'

Danger, Davey! We know now –

'Shut up, shut up!' He felt the first constriction around the part of him that was deep within her, felt his own climax begin to shudder outward.

No! Davey! It was like a mental scream.

He denied the voice in his head. 'Lynda!' he cried out. 'I love you.'

With her mouth wide open, she said something too, but he couldn't make it out. The he saw the blackness swelling in her gaping mouth, spilling up out of her throat. He felt that which was moving now in her vagina. 'Lynda! I love –' And then there was no more time.

He tried to recoil, but her legs and arms were strong as spring-steel.

Gregor cried out, one final despairing word:

Spiders!

AUTHOR'S NOTE

They are so damnably naive.

For many writers, it seems, the act of creating fictions, the actual sequence of putting words down on paper, is their catharsis. Writing is too sacred to be a mere confessional. I must create something, and my writing is what I build.

I build it in the hope it will withstand the attacks of those who would tear down everything they are too ignorant or too stupid to understand.

I have sat at writing classes, laughing inside, listening to the failed creators enter endless, futile debates about whether writing is a causative act or only a reflection of reality.

Fools. They finally claim it is the chicken or the egg.

I can solve the idiocy.

The chicken came first.

Think about the egg.

Think about the sharpness of the chicken's beak.

It is very sharp.

Sharp and oh, so unforgiving.

When Joyce died of birth complications along with my son, I suspected what had really happened.

I could never prove what the doctors had done.

Now I live alone.

I write my little stories, knowing how we writers are all obliged to write from experience. We are to suck the lifeblood from the lives around us in the manner of vampires. The justification is that our creations will be richer, fuller to the point of bursting. Brutal honesty is the key.

There are no experiences too dreadful to cannibalize.

Doing Colfax

'You wanna eat?' said Jeffie.

Kin stared out the passenger's window of the big old Chevy at the neon dazzle of Colfax Avenue. 'I want to do someone.'

'Aw, come on.' Jeffie put his free hand on Kin's wrist, let the fingers lie there lightly. 'Let's eat. I'm buyin'. Burgers okay?'

Kin started to turn away from the night. 'Yeah, burgers are – hold it. Look at that one.'

That one was what looked to be a teenaged girl standing by a bus bench with her thumb out. Short dark hair, shorter suede skirt, defiant stance. She stared directly into the windshield of the Chevy and smiled.

'I want to do *her*,' said Kin.

'Burgers –' Jeffie protested.

'Her.'

Jeffie braked the sedan to a stop. Kin reached back over the seat and unlatched the rear door.

The girl climbed in, set a canvas book-bag down beside her and said, 'Hi. Hey, thanks – I don't think the RTD ever stops here. Not ever.'

'How far you headin'?' said Kin.

'As far east as you're going. Anywhere on Colfax. I live out in Aurora.'

'We're going that far,' Kin said.

'That's really great,' said the girl. She leaned forward, forearms on the seat divider. 'You guys got names?'

They told her. Neither asked the girl her name. She

told them anyway. Neither Kin nor Jeffie remembered it.

The Chevy cruised along through the night. Jeffie scrupulously obeyed each speed sign. He ran no yellow lights. The girl told them about night school at Aurora. She was going to be a psychiatric social worker, or maybe just a psychologist. She had a part-time job at a Burger King. Jeffie perked up briefly when he heard that. The girl talked and talked, and finally they crossed under I-470. Though there were still plenty of lights, Jeffie sensed that the eastern plains lay close ahead. Nebraska. Kansas. He felt the oppressive freedom of all that space.

'Anywhere along here,' said the girl. She started to arrange her canvas bag.

'Naw,' said Kin, and then he was over the seat and in back with her.

'What are you –' she started to say. Kin slapped her hard across the jaw and her head fetched up solid against the window on Jeffie's side. The driver's shoulders hunched when he heard that meaty sound.

'She's just out,' said Kin. He extracted a length of coarse baling twine from under the seat ahead, let the girl's body slump over his lap, twisted her arms behind her, and bound the wrists tight. He set her upright again, wedged back into the corner between seat and window.

'Jesus, I'm starved,' said Jeffie.

Kin said, 'You just keep driving.' While he waited for her to wake up, he explored the girl's body with his hands. His fingers went up under her skirt and rolled the dark pantyhose down off her hips and legs, and finally off her feet after he pulled her flats loose. 'It's her time of the month,' he said, grimacing. 'Guess nothing's goin' right for her.'

The girl screamed. Startled, Kin jerked upright and cracked his head against her chin. He muttered something and slapped her again, but this time not as hard as before. 'Listen,' he said. 'Hey, listen to me.'

The girl stared at him and listened. Kin picked something

up off the car floor and showed it to her. 'Know what this is?'

She shook her head.

'It's a tennis ball, dummy. I don't want you to scream. And I don't want to hit you again. If you keep on yellin' like that, I'm goin' have to put this in your mouth and keep it in there with some tape. You understand?'

Her eyes widened, but she didn't say anything at all. And she didn't scream. Her eyes looked like they were all wide, dark pupil.

'If I have to do that,' said Kin, 'then maybe too I'll go on and pinch your nose shut, or maybe tape it altogether. You know what'll happen then?'

She slowly nodded, eyes still fixed on his.

'Okay,' said Kin. He started touching her again. The girl struggled against him, but almost silently. Little whimpers came out.

'How you gonna do her?' said Jeffie.

Kin looked thoughtful.

The girl briefly stopped struggling. Her eyes glistened with tears, but she seemed to pull herself together visibly. She said, '*Do* me?'

The two men stared back at her.

'Listen, you bastards. You're going to kill me, say it. Don't talk like I'm not really here.' She paused. 'I'm here. I'm real.'

They didn't say anything.

'You're not going to *do* me – you're going to *kill* me.'

Jeffie and Kin stared at each other in the rearview.

After a long pause, Jeffie said again, 'How you gonna do her?'

'This way,' said Kin. 'Best I know how.' He used the pantyhose he had tugged off the girl earlier. She struggled silently, as though using all her strength to twist away from him. Somehow she got her chin between the taut loop and her throat. Her eyes never left Kin's.

'Give me the screwdriver out of the jockey box,' said Kin hoarsely, trying to hold her body still with one arm, attempting to draw the noose tight with his other hand.

'Phillips or the other one?' said Jeffie, rummaging.

'Don't matter. Just a screwdriver.'

'Here you go.' Jeffie passed the steel tool over the seat. He winced as either Kin or the girl kicked the backrest.

Kin put the screwdriver shaft between the loop of pantyhose and the nape of the girl's neck, and began to twist. The nylon stretched, then tautened. The noose crept along the point of the girl's chin, then snapped free, digging into the flesh of her throat.

'That's it,' said Kin.

And it was.

The girl's eyes never did close, so Kin finally had to twist her head around so that she looked accusingly out at the neon night.

'We gotta dump her,' said Jeffie.

It was like Kin didn't hear him. 'I'm hungry now,' he said. 'I feel good and I'm hungry.'

'We got to –'

'I hear you, buddy. We'll do it. But I want a burger. I'm starvin'.'

'Guess it'll have to be a drive-up.'

'Guess so,' Kin agreed.

The old Chevy ghosted through the dark.

'I'm hungry too,' Jeffie finally said.

'Yeah,' said Kin. 'Let's just do some burgers.'

AUTHOR'S NOTE

Since moving to Denver, I've spent endless nights traveling the length of Colfax Avenue.

It exorcizes the pain.

It soothes my mind.

It's what I do.

DISCLAIMER

The Publisher wishes to remind you that the 'author's notes' in Edward Bryant's contribution are fiction, a complete and utter fabrication. There is absolutely no connection between the created persona in the 'author's notes' and the real mental states, attitudes, or deep personal feelings of any man or woman who actually writes dark fantasy. Honest.

Robert R McCammon

The Deep End

Summer was dying. The late afternoon sky wept rain from low, hovering clouds, and Glenn Calder sat in his Chevy station-wagon, staring at the swimming-pool where his son had drowned two weeks ago.

Neil was just sixteen years old, Glenn thought. His lips were tight and gray, and the last of his summer tan had faded from his gaunt, hollow-eyed face. *Just sixteen*. His hands tightened around the steering-wheel, the knuckles bleaching white. *It's not fair. My son is dead – and you're still alive. Oh, I know you're there. I've figured it all out. You think you're so damned smart. You think you've got everybody fooled. But not me. Oh no – not me.*

He reached over the seat beside him and picked up his pack of Winstons, chose a cigarette and clamped the filter between his lips. Then he punched the cigarette lighter in and waited for it to heat up.

His eyes, pale blue behind a pair of horn-rimmed glasses, remained fixed on the Olympic-sized public swimming pool beyond the high chainlink fence. A sign on the admissions gate said in big, cheerful red letters: CLOSED FOR THE SEASON! SEE YOU NEXT SUMMER! Beyond the fence were bleachers and sundecks where people had lolled in the hot, sultry summer of north Alabama, and there was a bandstand where an occasional rock band had played at a pool party on a Saturday night. Steam rose from the glistening concrete around the pool and, in the silence between the patter of raindrops, with his windows rolled down and the moody smell of August's last hours inside the car, he thought he could hear ghostly music from that bandstand, there under the red canopy where he himself had danced as a kid in the late fifties.

He imagined he could hear the shouts, squeals and rowdy laughter of the generations of kids that had come to this pool, here in wooded Parnell Park, since it had been dug out and filled with water back in the mid-forties. He cocked his head to one side, listening, and he felt sure that one of those ghostly voices belonged to Neil, and Neil was speaking like a ripple of water down a drain, calling 'Dad? *Dad*? It killed me, Dad! I didn't drown! I was always a good swimmer, Dad! *You* know that, don't you . . .?'

'Yes,' Glenn answered softly, and tears filled his eyes. 'I know that.'

The lighter popped out. Glenn got his cigarette going and returned the lighter to the dashboard. He stared at the swimming pool as a tear crept down his cheek. Neil's voice ebbed and faded, joining the voices of the other ghosts that were forever young in Parnell Park.

If he had a dollar for every time he'd walked through that admissions gate he'd be a mighty rich man today. At least he'd have a lot more money, he mused, than running the Pet Center at Brookhill Mall paid him. But he'd always liked animals, so that was okay, though when he'd been young enough to dream he'd had plans of working for a zoo in a big city like Birmingham, travelling the world and collecting exotic animals. His father had died when he was a sophomore at the University of Alabama, and Glenn had returned to Barrimore Crossing and gone to work because his mother had been hanging on the edge of a nervous breakdown. He'd always planned on going back to college but the spool of time just kept unwinding: he'd met Linda, and they'd fallen in love, and then they'd gotten married and Neil was born four years later, and . . .

Well, that was just the story of life, wasn't it?

There were little flecks of rain on his glasses, caused when the drops ricocheted off the edge of the rolled-down window. Glenn took them off to wipe the lenses with a handkerchief. Without the glasses, everything was kind of fuzzy, but he could still see all right.

His hands were trembling. He was afraid, but not terrified. Funny. He'd thought for sure he'd be scared shitless. Of course, it wasn't time yet. Oh, no. Not yet. He put his glasses back on, drew deeply at his cigarette and let the smoke leak from his mouth. Then he touched the heavy-duty chain cutter that lay on the seat beside him.

Today – the last day of summer – he had brought his own admission ticket to the pool.

Underneath his trousers he was wearing his bathing suit – the red one, the one that Linda said he'd better not wear around the bull up in Howard Mackey's pasture. Glenn smiled grimly. If he hadn't had Linda these past two weeks might've made him slip right off the deep end. She said they were strong, that they would go on and learn to live with Neil's death, and Glenn had agreed – but that was before he'd started thinking. That was before he'd started reading and studying about the Parnell Park swimming pool.

That was before he *knew*.

After Neil had drowned, the town council had closed the pool and park. Neil had been its third victim of the summer; back in June a girl named Wanda Shackleford had died in the pool, and on the fourth of July it had been Tom Dunnigan. Neil had known Wanda Shackleford, and Glenn remembered that they'd talked about the incident at home one night.

'Seventeen years old!' Glenn had said, reading from a copy of the Barrimore Crossing *Courier*. 'What a waste!' He was sitting in his Barcalounger in the den, and Linda was on the sofa doing her needlepoint picture for Sue Ann Moore's birthday. Neil was on the floor in a comfortable sprawl, putting together a plastic model of a space ship he'd bought at Brookhill Mall that afternoon. 'Says here that she and a boy named Paul Buckley decided to climb the fence and go swimming around midnight.' He glanced over at Linda. 'Is that Alex Buckley's boy? The football player?'

'I think so. Do you know, Neil?'

'Yeah. Paul Buckley's a center for Grissom High.' Neil glued a triangular weapons turret together and put it aside to dry, then turned to face his father. Like Glenn, the boy was thin and lanky and wore glasses. 'Wanda Shackleford was his girlfriend. She would've been a senior next year. What else does it say?'

'It's got a few quotes from Paul Buckley and the policeman who pulled the girl's body out. Paul says they'd had a sixpack and then decided to go swimming. He says he never even knew she was gone until he started calling her and she didn't answer. He thought she was playing a trick on him.' He offered his son the paper.

'I can't imagine wanting to swim in dark water,' Linda said. Her pleasant oval face was framed with pale blond hair, and her eyes were hazel, the same color as Neil's. She concentrated on making a tricky stitch and then looked up. 'That's the first one.'

'The first one? What do you mean?'

Linda shrugged uneasily. 'I don't know. Just . . . well they say things happen in threes.' She returned to her work. 'I think the City should fill in that swimming pool.'

'Fill in the *pool?*' There was alarm in Neil's voice. 'Why?'

'Because last June the Harper boy drowned in it, remember? It happened the first weekend school was out. Thank God we weren't there to see it. And two summers before that, the McCarrin girl drowned in four feet of water. The lifeguard didn't even see her go down before somebody stepped on her.' She shivered and looked at Glenn. 'Remember?'

Glenn drew on his cigarette, staring through the rain-streaked windshield at the pool. 'Yes,' he said softly. 'I remember.' But at the time, he'd told Linda that people – especially kids – drowned in pools, ponds and lakes every summer. People even drown in their own bathtubs! he'd said. The city shouldn't close Parnell Park pool and deprive the people of Barrimore Crossing, Leeds, Cooks Springs and the other surrounding communities. Without Parnell Park, folks would have to drive either to Birmingham or go swimming in the muddy waters of nearby Logan Martin lake on a hot summer afternoon!

Still, he'd remembered that a man from Leeds had drowned in the deep end the summer before Gil McCarrin's daughter died. And hadn't two or three other people drowned there as well?

'You think you're so damned smart,' Glenn whispered. 'But I know. You killed my son, and by God you're going to pay.'

A sullen breeze played over the pool, and Glenn imagined he could hear the water giggle. Off in the distance he was sure he heard Neil's voice, floating to him through time and space: 'It killed me, Dad! I didn't drown . . . I didn't drown . . . I didn't . . . I –'

Glenn clamped a hand to his forehead and squeezed. Sometimes that made the ghostly voice go away, and this time it worked. He was getting a whopper of a headache, and he opened the glove-compartment and took a half-full bottle of Excedrin from it. He popped it open, put a tablet on his tongue and let it melt.

Today was the last day of August, and tomorrow morning the city workmen would come and open the big circular metal-grated drain down in the twelve-foot depths of the deep end. An electric pump would flood the water through pipes that had been laid down in 1945, when the pool was first dug out. The water would continue for more than two miles, until it emptied into a cove on Logan Martin lake. Glenn knew the route that water would take very well, because he'd studied the yellowed engineering diagrams in Barrimore Crossing's City Hall. And then, the last week of May when the heat had come creeping back and summer was about to blaze like a nova, the pipes would start pumping Logan Martin lake water back through another system of filtration tanks and sanitation filters and when it spilled into the Parnell Park swimming pool it would be fresh, clean and sparkling.

But it would *not* be lifeless.

Glenn chewed a second Excedrin, crushed his cigarette out in the ashtray. This was the day. Tomorrow would be too late. Because tomorrow, the thing that lurked in the public swimming pool would slither away down the drain and get back to the lake where it would wait in the mud for another summer season and the beckoning rhythm of the pump.

Glenn's palms were wet. He wiped them on his trousers. Tom Dunnigan had drowned in the deep end on the fourth of July, during the big annual celebration and barbecue. Glenn and Linda had been eating sauce-sloppy barbecues when they'd heard the commotion at the pool, and Linda had screamed, 'Oh my God! *Neil!*'

But it was not Neil who lay on his stomach as the lifeguard tried to force breath back into the body. Neil had been doing cannonballs off the high dive when Tom's wife had shouted for help. The pool had been crowded with people, but no one had seen Tom Dunnigan slip under; he had not cried out, had not even left a ripple in the water. Glenn got close enough through the onlookers to see Tom's body as the lifeguard worked on him. Tom's eyes were open, and water was running between the pale blue lips. But Glenn had found himself staring at a small, circular purple bruise at the back of Tom's neck, almost at the base of the brain; the bruise was pinpricked with scarlet, as if tiny veins in the skin had been ruptured. He'd wondered what could have caused a bruise like that, but it was so small it certainly wasn't important. Then the ambulance attendants wheeled Tom away, covered with a sheet, and the pool closed down for a week.

It was later – much later – that Glenn realized the bruise could've been a bitemark.

He'd been feeding a chameleon in the pet store when the lizard, which had turned the exact shade of green as the grass at the bottom of his tank, had decided to give him a bite on his finger. A chameleon has no teeth, but the pressure of the lizard's mouth had left a tiny circular mark that faded almost at once. Still the little mark bothered Glenn until he'd realized what it reminded him of.

He'd never really paid much attention to the chameleon before that, but suddenly he was intrigued by how it changed colors so quickly, from grass-green to the tan shade of the sand heaped up in the tank's corner. Glenn put a large gray rock in there as well, and soon the chameleon would climb up on it and bloom gray; in that state, he would be invisible but for the tiny, unblinking black circles of his eyes.

'I know what you are,' Glenn whispered. 'Oh, yeah. I sure do.'

The light was fading. Glenn looked in the rear seat to check his gear: a snorkel, underwater mask and fins. On the floor-board was an underwater light – a large flashlight sealed in a clear plastic enclosure with an upraised red off-on switch. Glenn had driven to the K-Mart in Birmingham to buy the equipment in the sporting goods department. No one knew him there. And wrapped up in a yellow towel in the back seat was his major purchase. He reached over for it, carefully picked it up and put it across his lap. Then he began to unfold the towel, and there it was – clean, bright and deadly.

'Looks wicked, doesn't it?' the K-Mart clerk had asked.

Glenn had agreed that it did. But then, it suited his needs.

'You couldn't get *me* underwater,' the clerk had said. 'Nossir! I like my feet on solid ground! What do you catch with that thing?'

'Big game,' Glenn had told him. 'So big you wouldn't believe it.'

He ran his hands over the cool metal of the speargun in his lap. He'd read all the warnings and instructions, and the weapon's barbed spear was ready to fire. All he had to do was move a little lever with his thumb to unhook the safety, and then squeezing the trigger was the same as any other gun.

He'd practised on a pillow in the basement, late at night when Linda was asleep. She'd really think he was crazy if she found what was left of that tattered old thing.

But she thought he was out of his mind anyway, so what did it matter? Ever since he'd told her what he knew was true, she'd looked at him differently. It was in her eyes. She thought he'd slipped right off the deep end.

'We'll see about that.' There was cold sweat on his face now, because the time was near. He started to get out of the station-wagon, then froze. His heart was pounding.

A police car had turned into the parking-lot, and was heading toward him.

Oh, Jesus! he thought. No! He visualized Linda on the phone to the police: 'Officer, my husband's gone crazy! I don't know what he'll do next. He's stopped going to work, he has nightmares all the time and can't sleep, and he thinks there's a monster in the Parnell Park swimming pool! He thinks a monster killed our son, and he won't see a doctor or talk to anybody else about –'

The police car was getting closer. Glenn hastily wrapped the towel around the speargun, put it down between the seat and the door. He laid the chain cutter on the floorboard and then the police car was pulling up right beside him and all he could do was sit rigidly and smile.

'Having trouble, sir?' the policeman on the passenger side asked through his rolled-down window.

'No. No trouble. Just sitting here.' Glenn heard his voice tremble. His smile felt so tight his face was about to rip.

The policeman suddenly started to get out of the car, and Glenn knew he would see the gear on the back seat. 'I'm fine!' Glenn protested. 'Really!' But the police car's door was opening and the man was about to walk over and see –

'Hey, is that *you*, Mr Calder?' the policeman sitting behind the wheel asked. The other one hesitated.

'Yes. I'm Glenn Calder.'

'I'm Mike Ward. I bought a cocker spaniel puppy from you

at the first of the summer. Gave it to my little girl for her birthday. Remember?'

'Uh . . . yes! Sure.' Glenn recalled him now. 'Yes! How's the puppy?'

'Fine. We named him Bozo because of those big floppy feet. I'll tell you, I never knew a puppy so small could *eat* so much!'

Glenn strained to laugh. He feared his eyes must be bulging with inner pressure.

Mike Ward was silent for a few seconds, and then he said something to the other man that Glenn couldn't make out. The second policeman got back into the car and closed the door, and Glenn released the breath he'd been holding.

'Everything okay, Mr Calder?' Mike asked. 'I mean . . . I know about your son, and –'

'I'm fine!' Glenn said. 'Just sitting here. Just thinking.' His head was about to pound open.

'We were here the day it happened,' Mike told him. 'I'm really sorry.'

'Thank you.' The whole, hideous scene unfolded again in Glenn's mind: he remembered looking up from his *Sports Illustrated* magazine and seeing Neil going down the aluminum ladder on the left side of the pool, down at the deep end. 'I hope he's careful,' Linda had fretted and then she'd called to him, 'Be careful!' Neil had waved and gone on down the ladder into the sparkling blue water.

There had been a lot of people there that afternoon. It had been one of the hottest days of the summer.

And then Glenn remembered that Linda suddenly set aside her needlepoint, her face shaded by the brim of her straw hat, and said the words he could never forget: '*Glenn? I don't see Neil anymore.*'

Something about the world had changed in that moment. Time had been distorted and the world had cracked open, and Glenn had seen the horror that lies so close to the surface.

They brought Neil's body up and tried mouth-to-mouth resuscitation, but he was dead. Glenn could tell that right off.

He was dead. And when they turned his body over to try to pound the life back into him, Glenn had seen the small purple bruise at the back of his son's neck, almost at the base of the brain.

Oh God, Glenn had thought. *Something stole the life right out of him.*

And from that moment on, maybe he *had* gone crazy. Because he'd looked across the surface of the pool, and he had realized something very odd.

There was no aluminum ladder on the left side of the pool, down at the deep end. On the pool's right side there was a ladder – but not on the left.

'He was a good boy,' Glenn told the two policemen. There was still a fixed smile on his face, and he could not make it let go. 'His mother and I loved him very, very much.'

'Yes sir. Well . . . I guess we'll go on, then. You sure you're all right? You . . . uh . . . haven't been drinking, have you?'

'Nope. Clean as a whistle. Don't you worry about me, I'll go home soon. Wouldn't want to get Linda upset, would I?'

'No sir. Take care, now.' Then the police car backed up, turned around in the parking lot and drove away along the wooded road.

Glenn had a splitting headache. He chewed a third Excedrin, took a deep breath and reached down for the chain cutter. Then he got out of the car, walked to the admissions gate and cleaved the chain that locked it. The chain rattled to the concrete, and the gate swung open.

And now there was nothing between him and the monster in the swimming pool.

He returned to the car and threw the cutter inside, shucked off his shoes, socks and trousers. He let them fall in a heap beside the station-wagon, but he kept his blue-striped shirt on. It had been a present from Neil. Then he carried his mask, fins and snorkel into the pool area, walked the length of the pool and laid the gear on a bleacher. Rain pocked the dark surface, and on the pool's bottom were the black lines of swimming lanes, sometimes used for area swim-meets. Ceramic tiles on the bottom made a pattern of dark blue, aqua and pale green.

There were thousands of places for it to hide, Glenn reasoned. It could be lying along a black line, or compressed flat and smooth like a stingray on one of the colored tiles. He looked across the pool where the false ladder had been – the monster could make itself resemble a ladder, or it could curl up and emulate the drain, or lie flat and still in a gutter waiting for a human form to come close enough. Yes. It had many shapes, many colors, many tricks. But the water had not yet gone back to the lake, and the monster that had killed Neil was still in there. Somewhere.

He walked back to the car, got the underwater light and the speargun. It was getting dark, and he switched the light on. He wanted to make sure the thing found him once he was in the water – and the light should draw it like a neon sign over a road-side diner.

Glenn sat on the edge of the pool and put on his fins. He had to remove his glasses to wear the facemask; everything was out of focus, but it was the best he could do. He fit the snorkel into his mouth, hefted the underwater light in his left hand, and slowly eased himself over the edge.

I'm ready, he told himself. He was shaking, couldn't stop. The water, untended for more than two weeks, was dirty – littered with Coke cups, cigarette butts, dead waterbugs. The carcass of a bluejay floated past his face, and Glenn thought that it appeared to have been crushed.

He turned over on his stomach, put his head underwater and kicked off against the pool's side, making a splash that sounded jarringly loud. He began to drift out over the drain, directing the light's yellow beam through the water. Around and beneath him was gray murk. But the light suddenly glinted off something, and Glenn arched down through the chill to see what it was – a beer can on the bottom. Still, the monster could be anywhere. *Anywhere*. He slid to the surface, expelling water through the snorkel like a whale. Then he continued slowly across the pool, his heartbeat pounding in his ears and the sound of his breathing like a hellish bellows through the snorkel. In another moment his head bumped the other side of the pool. He drifted in another direction, guiding himself with an occasional thrust of a fin.

Come on, damn you! Glenn thought. I know you're here!

But nothing moved in the depths below. He shone the light around, seeking a shadow.

I'm not crazy, he told himself. I'm really not. His head was hurting again, and his mask was leaking, the water beginning to creep up under his nose. Come out and fight me, damn you! I'm in your element now, you bastard! Come on!

Linda had asked him to see a doctor in Birmingham. She said she'd go with him, and the doctor would listen. There was no monster in the swimming pool, she'd said. And if there *was* where had it come from?

Glenn knew. Since Neil's death, Glenn had done a lot of thinking and reading. He'd gone back through the *Courier* files, searching for any information about the Parnell Park swimming pool. He'd found that, for the last five years, at least one person had died in the pool every summer. Before that you had to go back eight years to find a drowning victim – an elderly man who'd already suffered one heart attack.

But it had been in a copy of the Birmingham *News*, dated October tenth six years ago, that Glenn had found his answer. The article's headline read *'Bright Light' Frightens Lake Residents*.

On the night of October ninth, a sphere of blue fire had been seen by a dozen people who lived around Logan Martin lake. It had flashed across the sky, making a noise – as one resident put it – 'like steam whistling out of a cracked radiator'. The blue light had gone down into the lake, and for the next two days, dead fish washed up on shore.

You found the pipes that brought you up into our swimming

pool, didn't you? Glenn thought as he explored the gray depths with his light. Maybe you came from somewhere that's all water, and you can't live on land. Maybe you can suck the life out of a human body just as fast and easy as some of us step on ants. Maybe that's what you live on – but by God I've come to stick you, and I'll find you if I have to search all –

Something moved.

Down in the gloom, below him. Down near the drain. A shadow . . . *something.*

Glenn wasn't sure what it was. He just sensed a slow, powerful uncoiling.

He pushed the speargun's safety off with his thumb. He couldn't see anything; dead bugs floated through the light like a dust storm, and a sodden newspaper page drifted up from the bottom, flapped in his face and sank out of sight again. Glenn's nerves were near snapping, and he thought with a touch of hysterical mirth that it might have been an obituaries page.

He lowered his head and descended.

Murky clouds swirled around him. He probed with the light, alert for another movement. The water felt thick, oily; a contaminated feel. He continued to slide down into the depths, and they closed over him. His fins stirred more pool silt, and the clouds diffused the light. He stayed down as long as he could, until his lungs began to heave, and then he rose toward the surface like a flabby arrow.

When he reached the top, something grasped his head.

It was a cold, rubbery thing, and Glenn knew it was the grip of death. He couldn't help it; he shrieked around the snorkel's mouthpiece, twisted violently in the water and caught sight of slick green flesh. His frantic movement dislodged the face-mask, and water flooded in. He was blinded, water was pressing up his nostrils and the thing was wrapped around his shoulders. He heard his gurgling underwater scream, flailed the thing off him and thrashed desperately away.

Glenn kicked to the edge of the pool, raising geysers. The

aluminum ladder was in front of him, and he reached up to haul himself out.

No! he thought, wrenching his hand back before it touched the metal - or what was supposed to pass as metal. That's how it had killed Neil. It had emulated the other ladder and entwined itself around Neil as he entered the water, and it had taken him under and killed him in an instant while everyone else was laughing and unaware.

He swam away from the ladder and clung to the gutter's edge. His body convulsed, water gurgling from his nostrils. His dangling legs were vulnerable, and he drew them up against his chest, so fast he kneed himself in the chin. Then he dared to look around and aim the light at the monster.

About ten feet away, bouncing in the chop of his departure, was a child's deflated rubber ring, the green head of a seahorse with a grinning red mouth lying in the water.

Glenn laughed, and spat up more of the pool. Brave man, he thought. Real brave. Oh Jesus, if Linda had been here to see this! I was scared shitless of a kid's toy! His laughter got louder, more strident. He laughed until it dawned on him that he was holding his facemask's strap around his right wrist, and his right hand gripped the gutter.

In his left hand was the underwater light.

He had lost his snorkel. And the speargun.

His laughter ceased on a broken note.

Fear shot up his spine. He squinted, saw the snorkel bobbing on the surface five or six feet away. The speargun had gone to the bottom.

He didn't think about getting out of the pool. His body just did it, scrabbling up over the sloshing gutter to the concrete, where he lay on his belly in the rain and shivered with terror.

Without the speargun, he had no chance. I can use the chaincutter! he thought. Snap the bastard's head off! But no, no: the chain cutter needed two hands, and he had to have a hand free to hold the light. He thought of driving back to Birmingham, buying another speargun, but it occurred to him that if he got in the car and left Parnell Park his guts might turn to jelly on the highway and Neil's voice would haunt him: '*You know I didn't drown, don't you, Dad? You know I didn't . . .*'

He might get in that car and drive away and never come back, and today was the last day of summer, and when they opened the drain in the morning the monster would go back to the lake and await another season of victims.

He knew what he had to do. Must do. Must. He had to put the facemask back on, retrieve the snorkel, and go down after that speargun. He lay with his cheek pressed against the concrete and stared at the black water; how many summer days had seen him in that pool, basking like a happy whale? As a kid, he couldn't wait for the clock of seasons to turn around and point him to this pool – and now, everything had changed. Everything, and it could never be the same again.

Neil was dead, killed by the monster in the swimming pool. The creature had killed part of him, too, Glenn realized. Killed the part that saw this place as a haven of youthful dreams, an anchor-point of memories. And next summer, when the monster came back, someone else's dreams would die as well.

He had to go down and get the speargun. It was the only way.

It took him another minute or so to make his body respond to his mind's command. The chill shocked his skin again as he slipped over the side; he moved slowly, afraid of noise or splashes. Then he put the mask on, swam carefully to the snorkel with his legs drawn up close to the surface; he bit down hard on the mouthpiece, thinking suddenly that if there was really a monster here it could have emulated the snorkel, and both of them would've gotten a very nasty surprise. But the snorkel remained a snorkel, as Glenn blew the water out of it.

If there was really a monster here. The thought caught him like a shock. *If*. And there it was. What if Linda was right? he asked himself. What if there's nothing here, and I'm just treading dirty water? What if everything I've thought is wrong – and I'm losing my mind? No, no, I'm right. I know I am. Dear God. I *have* to be right.

He took a deep breath, exhaled it. The collapsed green seahorse seemed to be drifting toward him again: was its grin wider? Did it show a glint of teeth? Glenn watched the rubber ring move through the light's beam, and then he took another breath and slid downward to find the speargun.

His thrashing had stirred up more debris. The water seemed alive with reaching, darting shadows as he kicked to the bottom and skimmed along it, his belly brushing the tiles. The light gleamed off another beercan, off a scatter of pennies left by children who'd been diving for them. Something bony lay on the bottom, and Glenn decided it was a chicken drumstick somebody had tossed over the fence. He kept going, slowly swinging his light in an arc before him.

The dirty clouds opened under his waving hand, and more metal glinted. Another crushed beercan – no, no, it wasn't. His heart kicked. He fanned the murk away, and caught sight of the speargun's handle. Gripped it in his right hand with a flood of relief. Thank God! he thought. Now he felt powerful again, and the shadows seemed to flee before him. He turned in a circle, illuminating the darkness at his back. Nothing there. Nothing. To his right the newspaper page flapped like a manta ray, and to his left the clouds parted for a second to show him a glimpse of the drain. He was in the twelve-foot depth. The deep end, that place where parents warned their kids not to go.

And about three feet from the drain lay something else. Something that made Glenn's throat catch and bubbles spill from his nostrils.

And that was when the thing that had taken the shape of a speargun in his right hand burst into its true form, all camouflage done. Ice-white tentacles tightened around Glenn's wrist as his fingers spasmed open.

The bubbles of a scream exploded from Glenn's mouth, but

his jaws clamped shut before all his air was lost. As he tried to lunge upward, a third and fourth tentacle – pale, almost translucent and as tough as piano-wire – shot out, squeezing into the drain's grate and locked there.

Glenn fought furiously, saw the monster's head taking shape from its gossamer ghost of a body; the head was triangular, like a cobra's, and from it emerged a single scarlet, blazing eye with a golden pupil. Below the eye was a small round mouth full of suction pads like the underside of a starfish. The mouth was pulsating rapidly, and began to turn from white to crimson.

The single eye stared into Glenn's face with clinical interest. And suddenly the thing's neck elongated and the mouth streaked around for the back of Glenn's neck.

He'd known that's where it was going to strike, and he'd flung his left arm up to ward off the blow an instant before it came. The mouth sealed to his shoulder like a hot kiss, hung there for a second and withdrew with a *sputt* of distaste. The monster's head weaved back and forth as Glenn hunched his shoulders up to protect the back of his neck and spinal cord. His lungs heaved; his mouth was full of water, the snorkel spun away in the turbulence. Water was streaming into his mask, and the light had dropped from the fingers of his left hand and lay on the bottom, sending rays through the roiling clouds like a weird sunset through an alien atmosphere.

The thing's head jerked forward, its mouth aiming at Glenn's forehead; he jinked aside as much as he could, and the mouth hit the facemask glass. Glenn felt tentacles slithering around his body, drawing him closer, trying to crack his ribs and squeeze the last of his air out. He pressed his left hand to the back of his neck. The monster's eye moved in the socket, seeking a way to the juices it craved. The mouth was bright red now, and deep in the folds of its white body Glenn saw a crimson mass that pulsated at the same rhythm as its mouth.

Its heart, he realized. Its heart.

The blood thundered in his head. His lungs were seizing,

about to grab for water. He looked down, saw the real speargun a few feet away. He had no time for even a second's hesitation, and he knew that if he failed he was dead.

He took his hand away from the back of his neck and reached for the gun, his own heartbeat about to blow the top of his skull off.

The creature's head came around like a whip. The suckers fixed to the base of Glenn's brain, and for an instant there was an agony that he thought would end only when his head split open; but then there was a numbing, floating, novacained sensation, and Glenn felt himself drifting toward death.

But he had the speargun in his hand.

The monster shivered with hungry delight. From between the suction cups tiny needle-like teeth began to drill through the pores of its prey's flesh, toward the spinal cord at the base of the brain.

One part of Glenn wanted to give up. Wanted to drift and sleep. Wanted to join Neil and the others who had gone to sleep in this pool. It would be so easy . . . so easy . . .

But the part of him that clung to life and Linda and the world beyond this pool made him lift the gun, press the barbed spear against the monster's pulsing heart and squeeze the trigger.

Sharp, head-clearing pain ripped through him. A black cloud of blood spilled into the water. The spear had pierced the creature's body and gone into his own forearm. The monster released his neck, its head whipping and the eye wide and stunned. Glenn saw that the spear had gone right through the thing's heart – if that's indeed what the organ was – and then he wrenched at his arm with all his remaining strength. The spear and the heart tore out of the monster's writhing body. The pupil of its eye had turned from gold to black, and its tattered body began to ooze through the drain's grate like strands of opaque jelly.

Glenn's lungs lurched. Pulled in water. He clawed toward

the surface, his arm puffing blood. The surface was so far, so terribly far. The deep end had him, was not going to let him go. He strained upward, as dark gnawed at him and his lungs hitched and the water began to gurgle in his throat.

And then his head emerged into night air, and as he drew a long, shuddering breath he heard himself cry out like a victorious beast.

He didn't remember reaching the pool's side. Still would not trust the ladder. He tried to climb out and fell back several times. There seemed to a be a lot of blood, and water still rattled in his lungs. He didn't know how long it was, but finally he pulled himself out and fell on his back on the wet concrete.

Sometime later, he heard a hissing sound.

He wearily lifted his head, and coughed more water out. At the end of the spear, the lump of alien flesh was sizzling. The heart shrivelled until it resembled a piece of coal – and then it fell apart like black ash, and there was nothing left.

'Got you,' Glenn whispered. 'Got you . . . didn't I?'

He lay on his back for a long time, as the blood continued to stream from the wound in his arm, and when he opened his eyes again he could see the stars.

* * *

'Crazy fella busted in here last night,' one of the overall-clad workmen said to the other as he lit a cigarette. 'Heard it on the news this mornin'. Radio said a fella broke in here and went swimmin'. That's why the chain's cut off the gate.'

'Is that right? Lawd, lawd! Jimmy, this is some crazy world!' The second workman, whose name was Leon, sat on the concrete beside the little brick enclosure housing an iron wheel that opened the drain and a switch that operated the electric pump. They'd spent an hour cleaning the pool out before they'd turned the wheel, and this was the first chance to sit down and rest. They'd filled a garbage bag with beercans, dead bugs, and other debris that had collected at the bottom. Now the water was draining out, the electric pump making a steady thumping sound. It was the first morning of September, and the sun was shining through the trees in Parnell Park.

'Some folks are just born fools,' Jimmy offered, nodding sagely. 'Radio said that fella shot himself with a *spear*. Said he was ravin' and crazy and the p'liceman who found him couldn't make heads or butts outta anythin' he was sayin'.'

'Musta wanted to go swimmin' awful bad. Hope they put him in a nice asylum with a swimmin' pool.'

Both men thought that was very funny, and they laughed.

They were still laughing when the electric pump made a harsh gasping moan and died.

'Oh, my achin' ass!' Jimmy stood up, flicked his cigarette to the concrete. 'We musta missed somethin'! Drain's done clogged for sure!' He went over to the brick enclosure and picked up a long-handled, telescoping tool with a hooked metal tip on the end. 'Let's see if we can dig whatever it is out. If we can't – then somebody named Leon is goin' swimmin'.'

'Uh uh, not me! I don't swim in nothin' but a bathtub!'

Jimmy walked to the edge of the low diving board and reached into the water with his probe. He telescoped the handle out and began to dig down at the drain's grate, felt the hook slide into something that seemed . . . rubbery. He brought the hook up and stood gawking at what dangled from it.

Whatever it was, it had an eye.

'Go . . . call somebody,' he managed to tell Leon. 'Go call somebody right *quick*!'

Leon started running for the pay phone at the shuttered concessions stand.

'Hey, Leon!' Jimmy called, and the other man stopped. 'Tell 'em I don't know what it is . . . but tell 'em I think it's dead! And tell 'em we found it in the deep end!'

Leon ran on to make the phone call.

The electric pump suddenly kicked on again, and with a noise like a heartbeat began to return water to the lake.

A Life in the Day of

Late! Late! Late! Late! Late!

Twelve minutes after nine on the cold face of his golden Bulova. Heartbeat drumming . . . hurry, hurry . . . pulse like a jackhammer under his skin . . . hurry, hurry . . . neck itchy with sweat in the wet August heat . . . hurry, hurry, . . . somebody gets in the way, push them aside . . . Hurry, hurry, hurry!

Johnny Strickland was almost running on the Fifth Avenue sidewalk, dodging in and out of other blurry shapes, hitting the slower ones and knocking them aside. Somebody yelled, 'Watch it, Mac!' when he shouldered the guy out of his way, but he had a long stride and he was out of range of a punch within seconds. He could almost hear time ticking past, and he kept his black briefcase in front of him like a wedge to dig a path before him. He would not now be twelve minutes late if he hadn't stayed up until after three in the morning poring over the layout roughs for Hammerstone Seafoods; he detested being late but he knew Mr Randisi would forgive him. Packed into his briefcase were dynamite ideas that would surely bring old hard-assed Hammerstone around to renewing the contract. And if these ideas didn't do the trick, he'd work all night tonight to come up with better ones. No way am I going to be left behind! he told himself, his teeth clenched and his jaw jutting out like the prow of a speedboat. No way! Those junior execs are going to be eating my dust this time next year and wondering who passed them!

He had hardly spoken to Anne this morning, had crammed a blueberry croissant into his mouth and washed it down with ebony coffee to get his batteries charged. He was in such a rush to gather all the work together and finish his report that he'd hardly had time to think; of course he'd missed his subway train by only a few minutes, and he damned himself for pausing at the apartment's front door to let Anne kiss him before he darted off to the white-collar wars.

She would have to understand that being a rising young star in one of the most muscular ad agencies in Manhattan had to come first, he reasoned as he plowed through the sidewalk crowd. Sure, she didn't understand now. She didn't see why he couldn't slow down just a *little* bit, why he couldn't take the time for a leisurely dinner with her, go out to the movies or the theater or just sit and talk like they used to. But Jesus Christ, *everybody* had time to do that sort of stuff when they were kids and just married! Now he was twenty-five years old and he was on the fast track at Kirby, Weingold and Randisi, and if he landed Hammerstone again he'd get a hoped-for bonus that would pump his pockets up to thirty thousand scoots a year. Anne didn't understand that Fletcher and Hecht and Anderson – as well as a dozen other Ivy League grads – were breathing down his neck, and the only way to keep ahead of them on that fast track was to put the pedal to the metal, the nose to the grindstone, the coals to the fire –

'*Pencils?*' a high, thin voice asked, and a tarnished metal cup full of them was shoved upward in Johnny Strickland's path.

He almost stumbled over the figure before him, cursed and drew himself up short. His hand was locked to the briefcase's grip, and a surge of fury coursed through him at being even momentarily stalled.

'Pencils, mister?' the man asked again. He was small and gnarled and as ugly as yesterday's headlines; he wore a ragged green coat, even in this stifling heat, and on his head was a filthy Mets cap. He had no legs, and he was confined to a little red wagon that looked as if it had been salvaged from the dump. He cocked his angular, grimy face in Johnny's direction, and Johnny could see that both eyes were filmed with grayish-white cataracts. Hanging on rubber bands around his neck was a crudely-lettered cardboard sign that read: I AM BLIND. PLEASE HELP ME IF YOU CAN. THANK YOU.

The beggar shook the can of pencils in Johnny's face. 'Wanna buy a pencil, mister?'

Johnny almost shrieked with frustration. The revolving doorway to the Brennan Building was little more than a block away! 'No!' he snapped. 'Move out of my way!' He started to go around the old man, but the beggar suddenly reached out and caught Johnny's trouser leg.

'Hold it. How 'bout a nice wristwatch, huh?' And he thrust his skinny right arm out of his coat sleeve; on it were maybe eight or nine watches, all of them showing different times. 'For you, wholesale.'

'I said *no!*' He pulled his leg free, started to stride on.

And he felt the beggar's claw grip his ankle, with much more strength than he would've imagined the frail-looking old man possessed. Johnny tripped, almost fell but righted himself. His face flamed with anger.

'In a hurry, ain't you?' the beggar said, and when he grinned his teeth were the color of mud. 'Businessman. Young bull, thinkin' the world's movin' in slow-motion, right?'

'Listen, I'm going to call a cop if you don't –'

'Hush,' the beggar told him, and the sound of his voice made Johnny stop speaking. 'I'll tell you somethin', and I'll tell it true: Time flies.'

'Huh?'

'Time flies,' the old man repeated. His grin widened. 'Nice watch you got on. How much it put you back?'

'It . . . was a present . . . from my wife . . .' He caught

himself suddenly, realized he was talking to this old, smelly coot like the bastard was *somebody*! My God! he thought, and dared to look at his watch again. I'm seventeen minutes late!

'Time flies,' the beggar said, and nodded. 'You remember that.' And he released Johnny's ankle with a satisfied grunt.

Johnny took three long strides, turned and shouted, 'You're a public menace, jerk!' but the old man was already pushing himself along with one hand and shaking the can of pencils in someone else's irritated face. Johnny pushed his way forward, his face red to the roots of his curly, dark brown hair, and finally shoved through the Brennan Building's revolving doors at exactly nineteen minutes after nine o'clock.

He had to endure a wry, snide glance from Peter Fletcher as he came off the elevator onto the sixth floor and hurried past Nora, the attractive auburn-haired receptionist. Fletcher was bending over the desk, making chitchat; but Johnny knew he was trying to look down her dress, and anyway Fletcher was a married man the same as Johnny. But then he was past that point of torture and striding along the corridor, past the secretaries at their desks and to his own small, windowless office. He went in, closed the door and paused for a moment to take a couple of deep breaths; he was feeling dizzy, light-headed, and he thought that his encounter with the blind pencil seller had affected him more deeply than he'd known. Jesus Christ, the cops ought to get stuff like that off the streets! That guy could've broken my leg!

He knew Mr Randisi would be calling him in a few minutes, and he'd better have the notes and outlines organized. He laid the briefcase atop his desk like a crown jewel. On the desk were files and folders from other accounts, and on the floor were stacks of newspapers, ad magazines and various other publications. Johnny was nothing if not a voracious reader, particularly if it helped his climb to the advertising stratosphere – and he planned to be in that celestial realm by the time he was thirty years old.

He started to open the briefcase, and then he realized

something was wrong. He had caught from the corner of his eye the number of the calendar that hung on the back of his door; it said *Tuesday, August 11, 1987*. But that wasn't right. No, he'd forgotten to pull the page off when he'd left the office yesterday. Probably in too much of a hurry. But that bothered him, and so he crossed the cramped little office, reached up and ripped the page away. And now the date was correct: *Wednesday, August 12, 1987*. He was a man of dates and times, and now he felt a lot better. This office was a second home to him. Small wonder, he mused as he went to his desk and sat down. I probably spend a lot more time here than at the apart –

His intercom buzzed. He quickly punched it on. 'Yes?'

'Randisi, Johnny. Got the work done?'

'Yes sir. Be there in one minute.'

'Make it thirty seconds.' The intercom clicked off.

There was no time to check the work. His heart pounding, Johnny picked up the briefcase, quickly adjusted his tie and left his office. He walked down the corridor, turned to the left and faced Mr Randisi's blonde, streamlined young receptionist. Oh, the big guys really knew how to pick 'em! he thought. But then again, she wasn't prettier than Anne. Anne was the most beautiful woman he'd ever seen, and once all this rush died down he was going to buy her flowers and take her to dinner at a real four-star res –

'He's waiting for you,' the receptionist said, and Johnny went in.

Mr Randisi, thick and gray-haired and possessor of a blue-eyed stare that could chip flint, was parked behind his dark slab of a desk. 'Got it for me, Johnny?' he asked in his hearty voice.

'Yes sir, right here.' He patted the briefcase as he put it on the blotter atop Mr Randisi's desk. 'I stayed up pretty late last night, finishing it up, so that's why I came in a little tardy this morning. Sorry. It won't happen again.' He unsnapped the briefcase and lifted its lid.

'Tardy? This morning?' Randisi's gray eyebrows knitted together. 'I thought you were at your desk at eight-thirty.'

'Uh . . . no sir. I just got in a couple of minutes ago. Sorry.' He took out the neatly-typed report and slid it across the desk. 'There you are, sir. And I can be so bold as to say, I think Mr Hammerstone's really going to jump at that program.'

'Mr Hammerstone?' The eyebrows had almost merged. 'Johnny, what in the name of Hell's half-acre are you talking about?'

Johnny had been smiling; now he felt the smile slip a notch. 'Well . . . uh . . . I mean . . . Mr Hammerstone's going to appreciate the work that all of us have put into this –'

'George Hammerstone had a heart attack in September, Johnny,' Randisi said, and his voice had turned from hearty to a bit cautious. The blue eyes bored into Johnny's face. 'We went to his funeral together. Don't you remember?'

'Uh . . . uh . . . well, I –' He found himself looking down at the typed title on the report; he saw it upside-down, and he reached out to turn it around.

The title was *Proposed Program for Weston Electronics Multi-Media Campaign*. And beneath it, in smaller letters, was *By John Strickland*.

'You look sick, Johnny,' Randisi said, and he glanced at his own wristwatch. 'Well, it's almost six now. You can go home if you like. If I have any questions about this report, I'll call you la –'

'Oh . . . my God,' Johnny whispered. He was staring at the large window that looked down on Fifth Avenue.

It was snowing outside. Big, spinning, dead-of-winter snowflakes.

He went to that window like a sleepwalker. Snow was collecting on the rooftops, and whirling in the wind. Down on Fifth Avenue, people were wearing coats, hats and gloves.

And he suddenly realized that he was not wearing the lightweight dark blue summer suit he'd hurriedly put on this morning; he was wearing a tweed coat that he'd never seen before, dark brown slacks and tan oxfords. The only thing he recognized about his outfit was his brown-striped necktie, a Christmas gift from his father-in-law two years ago.

'Johnny?' Randisi asked carefully. 'Are you all right?'

'Yes . . . I mean . . . I don't know what I mean.' He shook his head, entranced and terrified by the falling snow. 'It's August,' he said softly. 'August. I know it is. It . . . can't be snowing in August.'

There was a long, terrible silence. 'Say it's August, Mr Randisi,' Johnny whispered. 'Please, say it's August.'

'Uh . . . why don't you take a day off tomorrow.' It was a statement, not a question. 'A couple of days if you like. I know the strain of working on three major accounts at the same time must be damned heavy. I know *I* wouldn't have shouldered it when I was your age. Anyway, if the workload overflows I can shift some of it to Fletcher or Manning –'

'*No!*' Johnny spun toward the other man, and he saw Randisi's heavy-lidded blue eyes blink. 'I'm fine. Don't you worry about me, no sir! I can handle anything you throw at me, and I'll do it in half the time anybody else can!' He felt sweat on his face, and his legs were shaking. 'I'm fine,' he repeated. This time he sounded like he really meant it.

Randisi didn't move for a moment or so. His stare had returned to full wattage. 'Are you and Anne all right, Johnny?'

'Yes. Everything's fine.' He heard his voice tremble.

'I hope so. Anne's a lovely, gracious young woman. I wish to God I'd found a wife like her when I was your age, and maybe I wouldn't be up to my neck in alimony right now. My ex-wives curse my name, but my cash sure keeps 'em living in high style! Oh, my ulcers!' He grimaced and put a hand to his belly, and it was then that Johnny saw the little day-by-day calendar that sat on a corner of Randisi's desk.

The date was *Friday, January 8, 1988.*

'No . . . no,' Johnny whispered. 'It was . . . August, just a few minutes ago . . .'

'Take a week,' Randisi told him. 'Go somewhere. Relax. Forget about the accounts. I'll shift the workload to somebody else.'

'I can handle it!' Johnny protested. 'I said I'm fine!'

'And *I* said, take a week.' Randisi's tone was final. He swivelled his chair around and busied himself – or pretended to, at least – with the report Johnny had just delivered.

Johnny walked out of the office and closed the door behind him. His stomach was churning, his head pounded and he didn't know what the hell was happening to him; his insides felt compressed but his skin felt stretched. But he couldn't leave it like this, couldn't let Mr Randisi shoulder him aside and give more work – more *opportunities* – to Peter Fletcher and Mark Manning. No way! He turned abruptly and put his hand on the doorknob.

'Can I help you, Mr Strickland?'

An attractive Oriental woman was sitting at the receptionist's desk, where the streamlined blonde had been a few minutes before. She lifted her eyebrows and waited for him to answer.

He'd never seen her before in his life. 'How . . . do you know my name?'

She hesitated, looked confused, then smiled. 'You're such a kidder, Mr Strickland! Really!'

'Listen, I don't know what this game's all about but you're not Mr Randisi's secretary!' He turned the doorknob – and found the door was locked.

'Mr Randisi's gone to lunch,' the woman said, her voice cool and wary now. 'You know he goes to lunch every day from twelve until two.'

'To *lunch*? Lady, I was just talking to him! I just walked out that door!'

She glanced at her wristwatch, her face impassive. 'That door,' she said, 'has been locked for one hour and twenty-seven minutes. Mr Randisi will be back at two o'clock.'

He looked at his own Bulova. Whoever she was, she was right: it was one twenty-seven. But what day? He almost screamed and laughed at the same time. *What day?*

Because he'd realized the woman was wearing a summery pale blue pin-striped dress, and on her desk was a glass of purple flowers.

He shook his head dazedly, strode past her and into the corridor where the noise of clicking typewriters and teleprinters in the secretarial work area sounded like summer hornets. He almost collided with Mark Manning, tall and dapper, dark-haired and confident as always. 'In a hurry, aren't you, John?' Manning asked him, but Johnny swept on past the man without answering.

Turning down another corridor, he faced a window that looked toward Central Park. He heard someone give a soft, strangled gasp and realized it was his own voice.

The trees were green in Central Park. It was a beautiful day – late May or early June, he thought it might be – and the warm golden sunlight glowed in the windows of nearby buildings. Off over the park, he caught sight of a kite sailing up and up in the breeze.

Johnny staggered back along the corridor in the direction of his office. He needed a drink, a cigarette, something, anything to clear his head. He closed his door, sat behind the cluttered desk – again his gaze locked on the wicked, insane calendar. It had changed again: now it said *Monday, October 23, 1989*. He heard the sound of thunder beyond the walls.

He pressed his hand to his mouth. It was a joke! It had to be a crazy, evil joke! Oh my God, my God, what's happening to me?

And then he saw the dates on some of the newspapers and magazines that were stacked around him: 1989 . . . 1989 . . . '89 . . . '89 . . .

But there was something else on his desk too. Something even more terrible.

It was a Hallmark greeting card, and on the front were the words *With Deepest Sympathy*.

There were other cards too, and with shaking hands Johnny dared to open one of them.

The signature said *Max and Carol Davidson*. They were his parents' nextdoor neighbors in the little town of Harrington, Delaware. Just above the signature either Max or Carol had written: *Your mother was a wonderful woman, Johnny. We're going to miss her very much*.

Tears sprang to his eyes. He flung the sympathy cards aside and searched for the telephone in the jumble of papers on his desk. His hand came up with a framed photograph of Anne, buried for God only knew how long beneath a leaning tower of workpapers. He had never seen that particular picture before, and as he stared at it he realized that Anne's hair was cut shorter, and she somehow looked older, tired, maybe disappointed. He wiped tears from his eyes, found the phone and dialed their apartment.

'Yes?' she answered.

'Anne! Thank God!' he almost sobbed with relief. 'Oh Lord, I've got to tell you what's been –'

'Who is this, please?'

'It's me! Johnny!'

'I'm sorry, you must have the wrong number. Nobody named Anne lives here.'

It was not Anne's voice. This woman's voice was deeper, harsher. 'Wait!' Johnny said, before whoever it was could hang up. 'Please wait! This isn't 554-0989, is it?'

The woman paused. Then, 'Yes, it is. But I'm telling you, there's no Anne here, mister.'

'That's my number, damn it!' he almost shrieked into the phone. 'That's my apartment! What do you mean, there's nobody named Anne there! Listen, I know that place! The front door sticks when it rains, and there's a crack that looks like a dinosaur's backbone on the bathroom wall! The toilet makes a jingling noise when you flush it, and down in the front lobby, there's a mailbox with my name on it – John Strickland!'

The woman was silent. Then she said, 'Strickland? I know that name. Yes, I used to get mail for the Stricklands. Magazines and stuff. I didn't know where to send them, but the lawyer came by one day and picked some stuff up for the woman. I believe her name was Anne.'

'The lawyer? What lawyer?'

'Her lawyer, I guess. They divorced a few years ago. I don't know, I don't try to find out the life stories of the previous tenants. Listen, this is my apartment. You want to find somebody named Anne, call the Lonely Hearts Club.' And she hung up.

He sat with the receiver clenched in his fist, his eyes seeing nothing. *They divorced a few years ago. A few years ago. Years ago . . .*

He could feel the calendar calling his eye. Could sense it there, waiting for him to look. He heard the steady ticking of his wristwatch, and he kept his neck rigid so he couldn't even glance at it. Time had gone crazy. Had jumped its tracks like a runaway train, and was carrying him on a headlong journey to oblivion.

On his desk was a copy of the *New York Times*. The headline read *President Redford Oks Second Manned Space Station*. And the dateline – the hated evil dateline – said it was Wednesday, September 16, 1992.

The sunlight of dying summer painted the walls of his office. Only his office had had no windows – until now, that is.

He swivelled around in his chair and looked out over Fifth Avenue.

A new building was going up, its sides shimmering with blue glass. He could see the workmen, high up in the skyscraper's iron bones. And higher up in the sky a blimp floated past with FEDERAL EXPRESS emblazoned on its side.

The intercom on his polished walnut desk buzzed. He

turned toward it, as slowly as if locked in a nightmare. The buttons were different, and it took him a few seconds to find the right one.

'Yes,' he said tonelessly.

'Mr Kirby's waiting to see you, Mr Strickland,' said a bright, cheerful female voice.

'Tell him . . . tell him I'll be there in a few minutes.'

'Oh, no sir. He's right outside. Can I send him in?'

He thought he said yes. He didn't know for sure. Anyway, the door opened and Frederick Kirby – the commanding force of Kirby, Weingold and Randisi – came in, followed by a willowy and very attractive young blonde woman wearing a yellow VASSAR pullover and a plaid skirt.

Mr Kirby had had swirls of gray in his hair yesterday, Johnny remembered. Now his hair was totally gray, and receding in front. 'Here's our boy wonder!' Mr Kirby said; he was holding the girl by the elbow, and now he pushed her forward. 'John, I want you to meet Kim. She's just back from Europe. I told her you'd have a lot in common, since you both seem to like London so much. Don't you think she favors her father?' He smiled, showing his perfect teeth; she smiled too, but her teeth looked sharper.

'Yes sir. I . . . guess she does.'

'Yes *sir*?' Kirby laughed. 'So what's with the *sir* bit? Kim, this man before you has brought six new accounts in one year to Kirby, Weingold and Strickland. I ought to be calling *him* "sir". Now, isn't he as dashing as I told you he'd be?'

She smiled only with her mouth. Her eyes were very blue, but they were not warm. 'I've always liked older men,' she said.

'We want you to come out to the house on Saturday night for dinner. Seven o'clock cocktails. Kim's in town for a few weeks before she heads out to Hollywood for a visit, and I'd like for you two to get acquainted. That suit you, John?'

Johnny nodded. Or thought he did. Nothing was real anymore, and nothing seemed to matter worth a damn.

'Keep up the good work, John,' Mr Kirby said as he and his daughter were leaving. 'We're depending on you to bring in the Cartier account before September 1. Okay?'

'Okay,' Johnny said, and his face almost cracked when he smiled.

Before September 1, Mr Kirby had said. And then his eye was pulled to a gold-rimmed calendar that sat on the edge of the desk, exactly where it had sat when this desk had belonged to Mr Randisi.

The date was Tuesday, July 15, 1997.

Rain was running down the window. The walls of his office sparkled with awards and plaques. The telephone hummed, and when he picked it up a strident female voice said, 'Don't you hang up on me again! I swear to God I don't know why I put up with this! We're supposed to have a garden party and look at this weather! Did you order the champagne?'

'Who . . . is this?'

'Look, you can play games with the other chickies around the office, but not with me! Daddy's right down the hall, and Daddy wouldn't like to hear how you've been treating his golden girl lately!'

And then he knew. 'Kim,' he said.

'Wow! Got it right the very first time!' she said bitterly. 'I swear to God, I ought to go back to Hollywood! I could've been somebody out there! Now are you going to order the champagne or do I have to do everything?'

'Oh . . .' he said, as tears spilled down his cheeks. 'Oh, God . . . I want to go back . . .'

'Cut the crap! Oh you'd like me to feel guilty, wouldn't you? It wasn't *my* fault! Maybe I ought to go to that closet and get that gun and put it to my head, and I'd curse you to Hell when I pulled the trigger. How'd you like that, huh?'

'Please . . . please,' he begged, and he squeezed his eyes shut when he put the receiver down.

When he opened them, he was looking right at the calendar. It was Friday, March 19, 2004.

His hands were shaking. A mound of cigarette butts lay in a green onyx ashtray on his desk. And suddenly he realized he was heavy, and his shaking hands were thick. Something pounded and hurt down deep in his stomach, and when he put his hand there he said, 'Oh, my ulcers!' and his hand sank into a cushion of flab.

Time flies, he thought. And he saw the face of the pencil seller, from what seemed to be both many years ago and a flicker of time. He felt sluggish and tired, as if the gears of his brain were bogging down in dark mire. I need a drink, he thought, and he looked toward the little bar where the bottles were.

As he got up, cold sunlight sparkled on the face of his wristwatch and drew his eye there. It was no longer a Bulova; it was a Rolex, with diamonds where the numbers should be. According to the watch, it was forty-one minutes after eight. In the space of time it took Johnny to reach the bar, the light changed. The sun went away, and sleet hit the window like a scatter of birdshot. Bottles emptied and multiplied under his hand, and he could never catch any of them. He turned again toward the window, saw the sun slanting through heavy winter clouds; he went closer, and saw a building fall like dead leaves under the crash of a wrecking-ball. More new buildings were going up, and other ones were falling. Down on Fifth Avenue, the cars looked weird. Off in the distance, a bridge in the sky pulsed with brilliant blue light.

Time flies, he thought. And he saw his own face, reflected there in the glass.

It was not a face he knew. It had heavy jowls and sunken eyes, and the curly hair on its head was going gray. And worst of all – worst of all was that he could see in those staring eyes so many things that had been lost a long, long time ago. Maybe long before he was twenty-five, and hustling down Fifth Avenue with dynamite ideas crammed into a black briefcase. He glanced over his shoulder. The calendar said it was November 9, 2011. He blinked. May 28, 2017. Blinked again. February 7, 2022. *Time flies*, he thought. *Time flies*.

'I want to go back,' he whispered. His voice was harsh, used to giving orders. 'I want to go back.'

And down on Fifth Avenue, in the hot sunlight of midsummer, he saw the figure pushing itself along in a child's red wagon.

His heart leaped and labored. Something was wrong with his lungs, and his hands would not stop shaking. But he knew then what he had to do, as he strode to the door on aching legs and . . . hurry, hurry . . . out past the red-haired receptionist he'd never seen before . . . hurry, hurry . . . along the endless corridor that had STRICKLAND, MANNING AND HINES on it in iron letters . . . hurry, hurry . . . and down in the elevator . . . hurry, hurry . . . out through the glass-walled lobby and into the street where . . . hurry hurry hurry! . . . a thin cold rain was falling.

Ghosts ebbed and flowed around him, moving to spectral pulses. Things that no longer resembled cars purred and whined along the avenue. The drizzle stopped, the sun came out, a cold wind blew, a fog swept past, the sun burned hot, sleet cracked against the concrete – but ahead of him, through the hurrying ghosts, was the figure in the red wagon. Offering people pencils from a tin cup.

Johnny could feel himself aging with every step, could feel the clothes dissolving and reforming on his now-thickening, now-thinning body. Hours, days, years streaked past with every footstep. His heart felt like it might explode, and he gasped for air and prayed that he would not die of old age before he reached that figure in the red wagon.

Cold wind lifted him off his feet. Someone shouldered him aside, and he fell to the pavement. He lay there, his hands – skinny and spotted with age – thrust out before him in the ice-crusted snow. His heart kicked and pumped and his lungs wheezed like an old steam furnace about to blow.

And over the sound of his own rapidly-approaching death came the squeak of wagon wheels through the snow.

Then silence, but for the muted keening of the freezing wind.

Johnny slowly lifted his head, and looked up at the figure in the red wagon.

The old man wore a ragged green overcoat, and on his head was a cap with N.Y. Zaps on the front. But the grimy, angular face was the same, and so were the cataract-covered eyes. When he smiled, the old man's teeth were the color of mud. He rattled the can in front of Johnny's face. 'Pencils, old fella?' he asked softly.

'Please . . . please . . . let me go back . . . please . . .'

'Let you go *back*?' The old man scowled. 'Well, you were in a hurry to get here, weren't you? Lord A'mighty, you only get one trip! So here you are! Ain't you pleased at the destination?'

'I'm dying,' Johnny whispered, snow caked to his face. 'Please . . . I'm dying.'

'Like I said, time flies. Oh, something in you was dead way back then, mister businessman! Figured you'd be happy if the rest of you was the same way, too! Time flies! Don't you understand that yet?'

'Yes . . . I do understand. Please . . . I've got to get back . . . to my wife. To the way it was . . . before. I've got to get back –'

'Why?' The old man's eyes narrowed. 'Why do you have to get back?'

Johnny's eyelids were beginning to freeze together, and he could hardly make his tongue move. 'I've got to get back,' he whispered through numb lips, 'so I . . . can make the trip the way it ought to be made. Not in a hurry. Not by hurting. Just . . . knowing that . . . time flies.'

'Right you are.' The old man nodded, shook the can again. Johnny could feel his heartbeat stuttering, getting slower . . . slower . . . slower . . .

'Well,' the old man said, 'take a pencil, then.' He offered the can to Johnny, then suddenly drew it back as Johnny's gnarled fingers reached for it. 'Uh, uh,' he said. 'Not yet. First gimme that pretty watch.'

Johnny took off the diamond-studded Rolex, and the other old man slipped it on his wrist with the rest of the wristwatches. 'Nice, real nice. Don't keep time worth a damn, though. Now you take a pencil. Do it quick.'

Johnny reached up. His groping fingers found one, and he pulled it from the metal can.

And in a sweeping swirl of time the snowy avenue was gone. It was hot August again, and a twenty-five-year-old Johnny Strickland was standing on the crowded sidewalk with a pencil in one hand and a briefcase in the other. The old man in the red wagon was still before him, but now wearing the Mets cap again.

They stood staring at each other, and the crowd of people moved around them as if they were islands in a fast-rushing stream.

'Well?' the old man asked. 'What do you have to say now, young businessman?'

Johnny looked past him, toward the Brennan Building. It occurred to him that he hadn't had time to really look at Anne today, to smell the perfume of her hair, to kiss her and hold her the way he had when they were first married years – no, minutes! – ago. And suddenly he let go a joyous whoop and he flung the briefcase into the air, and as it soared higher and higher it came open and all the papers, the report, the notes, and the outlines, all of it tumbled out and sailed upward like the kites of children who know that it's never – *never* – truly too late.

'There you go,' the old man said, and he smiled.

'Thank you!' Johnny told him. 'Thank you! Thank you!' He turned and started to run along Fifth Avenue, but this time in the direction of home. A sudden thought struck him, and he turned back toward the old man in the child's red wagon.

Johnny held up the pencil. 'What am I supposed to do with this?'

'Write your life story,' the old man told him, and pushed himself and the red wagon into the jungle of legs.

Johnny ran home laughing, and he did not look back again.

Best Friends

1

He hurried across the parking-lot, through a nasty stinging rain, and into the entrance of the Marbury Memorial Hospital. Under his right arm, in a dark brown satchel, was the life history of a monster.

He shrugged droplets of water from his raincoat and left wet tracks on the jade-green linoleum floor as he approached the nurse at the central information desk. He recognized Mrs Curtis, and she said good morning and opened a drawer to get a nametag for him.

'Wet day,' she commented, her glasses resting on the edge of her nose as she watched him sign in. 'Lot of doctors going to make some money off this weather.'

'I imagine so.' He dripped a few water spots on the page and tried to brush them away before they sank through. In firm, spiky penmanship, he wrote *Dr Jack Shannon* followed by the date and time, 10/16 and 10:57 a.m., and his destination, 8th floor. He looked up the list of other names and noted that the public defender, Mr Foster, was not yet here. Should he wait in the lobby or go up alone? He decided to wait. No sense rushing things.

'Full caseload today?' Mrs Curtis asked him.

It was in her voice. She knew. Of course she knows, Jack thought. Probably the entire hospital staff knew, and certainly Mrs Curtis, who'd been a fixture behind the information desk for the six years that Jack had been coming here, would know. The newspapers had screamed the case, and so had the T.V. stations. 'No,' he said. 'Just seeing one.'

'Uh huh.' She waited for him to say more, and pretended to watch the rain falling past the picture window. The sky was gray, the rain was gray, and all the color of the forest that surrounded Marbury Memorial seemed to be shades of gray as well. The city of Birmingham lay about four miles to the west, hidden by clouds that had skulked into the valley and settled there, brooding. It was Alabama autumn at its worst, humid and heavy enough to make bones moan. Just three days ago, the air had been cool enough for Marbury Memorial's custodial staff to shut down the air-conditioners; they remained off, and the old hospital – built out of red bricks and gray stone in 1947 – held heat and dampness in its walls, exuding them in stale breaths that moved ghostlike through the corridors.

'Well,' Mrs Curtis said at last, and pushed her glasses off her nose with a wiry finger, 'I expect you've seen worse.'

Jack didn't answer. He wasn't sure he *had* seen worse; and, in fact, he was quite sure he had not. He wished Mrs Curtis a good day and walked to the lobby's seating area, facing the picture window and the grayness beyond. He found a discarded newspaper, took off his wet raincoat and sat down to kill some time, because he didn't care to go up to the eighth floor without the public defender along.

And there it was, on page one: a picture of the Clausen house, and a story with the headline *Juvenile Held in Bizarre Triple Slaying*. Jack looked at the picture as rain tapped on the window nearby. It was just a white-painted suburban house with front porch and three stone steps, a neatly-trimmed yard and a carport. Nothing special about it, really; just one of many hundreds in that area of town. It looked like a house where Tupperware parties might be hosted, where cakes would be baked in a small but adequate kitchen and folks would hunker down in front of the den's T.V. to watch football games on Saturday afternoons, in a neighborhood where everybody knew each other and life was pleasant. It looked all-American and ordinary, except for one clue: the bars on the windows.

Of course a lot of people bought those wrought-iron burglar bars and placed them over the windows and doors. Unfortunately, that was part of modern civilization - but these burglar bars were different. These were set *inside* the windows, not on the outside. These appeared to have the purpose of keeping something in, rather than keeping intruders out. Other than the strange placement of the burglar bars, the Clausen house was neither especially attractive nor displeasing. It just was.

On page two the story continued, and there were pictures of the victims. A grainy wedding photograph of Mr and Mrs Clausen, a fourth-grade school shot of the little girl. Thank God there were no pictures of the house's interior after the slaying, Jack thought; he was already having a tough enough time maintaining his professional composure.

He put the newspaper aside. There was nothing new in the story, and Jack could've recited the facts from memory. Everything was contained in the satchel, and the rest of what Jack sought to know lay in the mind of a boy on the eighth floor.

He listened to the rhythm of the hospital - the polite bing-bonging of signal bells through the intercom system, followed by requests for various doctors; the quiet, intense conversations of other people, friends and relative of patients, in the seating area; the squeak of a nurse's shoes on the linoleum; the constant opening and closing of elevator doors. An ambulance's siren wailed from the emergency entrance on the west side of the hospital. A wheelchair creaked past, a black nurse pushing a pregnant dark-haired woman to the elevators en route to the maternity ward on the second floor. Two austere doctors in white coats stood talking to an elderly man, his face gray and stricken; they all entered an elevator together, and the numbers marched upward. The daily patterns of life and death were in full motion here, Jack mused. A hospital seemed to be a universe in itself, teeming with small comedies and tragedies, an abode of miracles and secrets from the morgue in its chill basement to the eighth-floor's wide corridors where mental patients paced like caged tigers.

He checked his wristwatch. Eleven-thirteen. Foster was running late, and that wasn't his usual –

'Dr Shannon?'

Jack looked up. Standing next to his chair was a tall red-haired woman, raindrops clinging to her coat and rolling off her closed-up umbrella. 'Yes,' he said.

'I'm Kay Douglas, from the public defender's office.' She offered a hand, and he stood up and shook it. Her grip was sturdy, all-business, and did not linger. 'Mr Foster can't make it today.'

'Oh. I thought the appointment was set.'

'It was, but Mr Foster has other business. I'm to take his place.'

Jack nodded. 'I see.' And he did: Bob Foster had political ambitions. Being directly associated with a case like this, with all the attendant publicity, was not expedient for Foster's career. Naturally, he'd send an aide. 'Fine with me,' Jack said. 'Are you signed in?'

'Yes. Shall we go?' She didn't wait for him to agree; she turned and walked with a purposeful stride to the elevators, and he followed a few steps behind.

They shared an elevator with a young, fresh-faced couple and a slim black nurse; the couple got off on two, and when the nurse departed on the fourth floor, Jack said, 'Have you met him yet?'

'No, not yet. Have you?'

He shook his head. The elevator continued its ascent, old gears creaking. The woman's pale green eyes watched the numbers advance above the door. 'So Mr Foster thought this was a little too hot to handle, huh?' Jack said. She didn't respond. 'I don't blame him. The prosecutor gets all the good publicity in cases like this.'

'Dr Shannon,' she said, and gave him a quick, piercing

glance, 'I don't think there's ever been a case like this before. I hope to God there isn't another.'

The elevator jarred slightly, slowing down as it reached the uppermost floor. The doors rumbled open, and they had reached Marbury Memorial's psychiatric ward.

2

'Hiya, docky!' a silver-haired woman in a bright blue shift, Adidas sneakers and a headband called out, marching along the corridor toward him. Her face was a mass of wrinkles, her lips rubbery and daubed with crimson lipstick, 'You come to see me today?'

'Not today, Margie. Sorry.'

'Shit! Docky, I need a bridge partner! Everybody's crazy up here!' Margie looked long and hard at Kay Douglas. 'Who's this? Your girlfriend?'

'No. Just . . . a friend,' he said, to simplify things.

'Red hair on the head don't exactly mean red hair on the pussy,' Margie warned, and Kay's face flushed to a similar hue. A gaunt, elderly man dressed immaculately in a pinstriped suit, white shirt and tie strode up, making a low grunting noise in his throat. 'Stop that shit, Ritter!' Margie demanded. 'Nobody wants to hear your 'gator imitations!'

Other people were approaching from up and down the corridor. Kay retreated a pace, and heard the elevator doors hiss shut at her back. She looked over her shoulder, noting that the elevator on this floor had no button, but was summoned by a key.

'Now you're caught!' Margie said to her, with a crooked smile. 'Just like us!'

'Ain't nobody said we was gonna have us a parade this mornin'!' a mighty voice boomed. 'Give Doc Shannon room to breathe, now!' A husky black nurse with white hair, massive girth and legs like dark logs moved toward Jack and Kay. Ritter gave her one more throaty grunt, like an alligator's love song, and then obeyed the nurse.

'Docky's come up to see me today, Rosalee!' Margie protested. 'Don't be rude!'

'He ain't come up to see nobody on our ward,' Rosalee told her. The black woman had gray eyes, set in a square and rugged face. 'He's got other business.'

'What other business?'

'Rosalee means Dr Shannon's on his way to see the new arrival,' said a younger man. He sat in a chair across the corridor, turned to face the elevator. 'You know. The crazy fucker.'

'Watch your mouth, Mr Chambers,' Rosalee said curtly. 'There are ladies present.'

'Women, yeah. Ladies, I'm not so sure.' He was in his mid-thirties, wore faded jeans and a blue-checked shirt with rolled-up sleeves, and he took a draw on a cigarette and plumed smoke into the air. 'You a lady, miss?' he asked Kay, staring at her with dark brown, deep-socketed eyes.

She met his gaze. The man had a brown crewcut and the grizzle of a beard, and he might have been handsome but for the boniness of his face and those haunted eyes. 'I've been told so,' she answered, and her voice only quavered a little bit.

'Yeah?' he grinned wolfishly. 'Well . . . somebody lied.'

'Show some respect now, Mr Chambers,' Rosalee cautioned. 'We want to be courteous to our visitors, and all those who don't care to be courteous might have their smokin' privileges yanked. Got it?' She stood, hands on huge hips, waiting for a response.

He regarded the cigarette's burning end for a few seconds in silence. Then, grudgingly: 'Got it.'

'How're you feeling today, Dave?' Jack asked, glad the little drama had been resolved. 'You still have headaches?'

'Uh huh. One big fat black bitch of a headache.'

'*Out.*' Rosalee's voice was low this time, and Jack knew she meant business. 'Put your cigarette out, Mr Chambers.'

He puffed on it, still grinning.

'I said put the cigarette out, please sir.' She stepped toward him. 'I won't ask you again.'

One last long draw, and Dave Chambers let the smoke leak through his nostrils. Then he opened his mouth and popped the burning butt inside. Kay gasped as the man's throat worked. A little whorl of smoke escaped from between his lips. 'That suit you?' he asked the nurse.

'Yes, thank you.' She glanced at Kay. 'Don't fret, ma'am. He does that trick all the time. Puts it out with his spit before he swallers it.'

'Better than some of the pigshit they give you to eat around this joint,' Dave said, drawing his legs up to his chest. He wore scuffed brown loafers and white socks.

'I think I'd like some water.' Kay walked past Rosalee to a water fountain. A small woman with a bird's-nest of orange hair followed beside her like a shadow, and Kay tried very hard not to pay any attention. Foster had told her Marbury Memorial's mental ward was a rough place, full of county cases and understaffed as well, but he'd voiced his confidence that she could handle the task. She was twenty-eight years old, fresh from a legal practice in south Alabama, and it was important to her that she fit in at Foster's office. She'd only been on the job for two months, and she presumed this was another one of the public defender's tests; the first test, not three weeks ago, had involved counting the bullet holes in a bloated, gassy corpse dredged up from the bottom of Logan Martin Lake.

'Good water. Yum, yum,' the woman with orange hair said, right in her ear, and Kay gurgled water up her nose and dug frantically in her purse for a tissue.

'Dr Cawthorn's already in there.' Rosalee nodded toward the white door, way down at the end of the hallway. At this distance the doorway seemed to float in the air, framed between white walls and white ceiling. 'Been there for maybe fifteen minutes.'

'Has he pulled the boy out of containment yet?' Jack asked.

'Doubt it. Wouldn't do that without you and the lawyer there. She *is* a lawyer, ain't she?'

'Yes.'

'Thought so. Got the lawyer's look about her. Anyways, you know how Dr Cawthorn is. Probably just sittin' in there, thinkin'.'

'We're late. We'd better go in.'

Margie grasped at his sleeve. 'Docky, you watch out for that fella. Saw his face when they brung him in. He'll shoot rays out of his eyes and kill you dead, I swear to God he will.'

'I'll remember that, thanks.' He pulled gently free, and gave Margie a composed smile that was totally false. His guts had begun to churn, and his hands were icy. 'Who's on security?' he asked Rosalee.

'Gil Moon's on the door. Bobby Crisp's on desk duty.'

'Good enough.' He glanced back to make sure Kay was ready to go. She was wiping her nose with a tissue and trying to get away from the small orange-haired woman everyone knew as 'Kitten'. He started for the door, with Rosalee at his side and Kay lagging behind.

'Better not go in there, Dr Shannon!' Dave Chambers warned. 'Better stay away from that crazy fucker!'

'Sorry. It's my job,' he answered.

'Fuck the job, man. You've only got one life.'

Jack didn't reply. He passed the nurse's desk, where Mrs Marion and Mrs Stewart were on duty, and continued on toward the door. It seemed to be coming up much too fast. The documents and photographs in his satchel emerged from memory with startling clarity, and almost hobbled him. But he was a psychiatrist – a very good one, according to his credentials – and had worked with the criminally insane many times before. This ought not to bother him. Ought not to. Determining whether a person was fit to stand trial or not was part of his job, and in that capacity he'd seen many things that were distasteful. But this . . . this was different.

The photographs, the circumstances, the plain white house with burglar bars inside the windows . . . very different, and deeply disturbing.

The white door was there before he was ready for it. He pressed a button on the wall and heard the buzzer go off inside. Through the square of glass inset in the door, Jack watched Gil Moon approach and take the proper key from the ring at his belt. Gil, a barrel-chested man with close-cropped gray hair and eyes as droopy as a hound's, nodded recognition and slid the key into the lock. At the same time, Rosalee Partain put her own key into the second lock. They disengaged with gunshot cracks, so loud they made Kay jump. Steady! she told herself. You're supposed to be a professional, so by God you'd better act like one!

The door, made of wood over metal, was pulled open. Gil said, 'Mornin', Dr Shannon. Been expectin' you.'

'Have fun,' Rosalee said to Kay, and the nurse relocked the door on her side after Gil had pushed it shut again.

He locked his side. 'Dr Cawthorn's down in the conference room. Howdy do, miss.'

'Hello,' she said uneasily, and she followed Jack Shannon and the attendant along a green tile-floored corridor with locked doors on each side. The light was fluorescent and harsh, and at the corridor's end was a single barred window that faced gray woods. A slender young black man, wearing the same white uniform as Gil Moon, sat behind a desk at the corridor's mid-point; he'd been reading a *Rolling Stone* magazine and listening to music over headphones, but he stood up as Shannon approached. Bobby Crisp had large, slightly protuberant dark brown eyes and wore a gold pin in his right nostril. 'Hi, Dr Shannon,' he said, glanced quickly at the red-haired woman and gave her a nod of greeting.

'Morning, Bobby. How goes it?'

'It goes,' he answered, with a shrug. 'Just floating between the worms and the angels, I guess.'

'Guess so. Are we all set up?'

'Yes sir. Dr Cawthorn's waiting in there.' He motioned toward the closed door marked *Conference*. 'Do you want Clausen out of containment now?'

'Yes, that'd be fine. Shall we?' Jack moved to the conference room, opened it and held it for Kay.

Inside, there was gray carpet on the floor and pine panelling on the walls. Barred windows with frosted glass admitted murky light, and recessed squares of fluorescents glowed at the ceiling. There was a single long table with three chairs at one end and a single chair down at the other. At one of the three sat a bald and brown-bearded man wearing horn-rimmed glasses and reading from a file folder. He stood up when he saw Kay. 'Uh . . . hello. I thought Mr Foster was coming.'

'This is Kay Douglas, from Foster's office,' Jack explained. 'Miss Douglas, this is Dr Eric Cawthorn, head of psychiatric services.'

'Good to meet you.' They shook hands, and Kay propped her umbrella up in a corner, took off her damp raincoat and hung it on a wall hook. Underneath, she was wearing a plain dark pinstriped jacket and skirt.

'Well, I guess we're ready to proceed.' Jack sat down at the head of the table and put his satchel beside him, popping it open. 'I've asked that Clausen be brought out of containment. Has he been difficult?'

'No, not at all.' Cawthorn took his seat. 'He's been quiet since they brought him in, but for security reasons we've kept him suppressed.'

'Suppressed?' Kay sat down opposite Cawthorn. 'What's that mean?'

'Straitjacketed,' he answered. His pale blue eyes cut quickly to Jack and then returned to the woman. 'It's standard procedure when we have a case of vio –'

'But you said Mr Clausen's been quiet since he was given over to your custody. How do you justify a straitjacket for a quiet patient?'

'Miss Douglas?' Jack brought a folder up from his satchel and put it before him. 'How much do you know about this case? I know Foster must've briefed you, you've seen the newspaper stories. But have you seen the police photographs?'

'No. Mr Foster said he wanted a fresh and unbiased opinion.'

Jack smiled grimly. 'Bullshit,' he said. 'Foster knew you'd see the pictures here. He probably knew I'd show them to you. Well, I won't disappoint him . . . or you.' He opened the folder and pushed a half-dozen photographs across the table to her.

Kay reached out for them. Jack saw her hand freeze in mid-air. The picture on top showed a room with furniture shattered into pieces, and on the walls were brown patterns that could only be sprays of blood flung by violent motion. The words HAIL SATAN had been drawn in gore, the letters oozing down to the baseboard. Near those words, stuck to the wall, were yellow clots of . . . yes, she knew what they must be. Human tissue.

With one finger, she moved the top picture aside. The second photograph drove a cold nail through her throat; it showed a pile of broken limbs that had been flung like garbage into a room's corner. A severed leg was propped up not unlike the umbrella she'd just put aside. A smashed head lay in a gray puddle of brains. Fingers clawed upward on disembodied hands. A torso had been ripped open, spilling all its secrets.

'*Oh*,' she whispered, and tasted hot bile.

And then the conference room's door opened again, and the boy who had torn his mother, father and ten-year-old sister to pieces walked through.

3

With no hesitation, Tim Clausen went to the chair at the far end of the table. Gil Moon and Bobby Crisp walked on either side, though the boy did indeed wear a tightly-cinched straitjacket. He sat down, the fluorescents blooming in the round lenses of his glasses, and smiled at his visitors. It was a friendly smile, with not a hint of menace. 'Hi,' he said.

'Hello, Tim,' Dr Cawthorn replied. 'I'd like you to meet Dr Jack Shannon and Miss Kay Douglas. They're here to talk to you.'

'Of course they are. Nice to meet you.'

Kay was still stunned by the pictures. She couldn't bear to look at the third one, and she found it hard to look into the boy's face, as well. She had read the case file, knew his description and that he'd just turned seventeen, but the combination of the photographs and Timothy Clausen's smiling, beatific face was almost more than she could take. She pushed the pictures away and sat with her hands tightly clenched in her lap, damning Foster for not preparing her more thoroughly. This is the second test, she realized. He wants to find out if I'm made of ice or crap. Damn him!

'I like your hair,' Tim Clausen said to her. 'The color's pretty.'

'Thank you,' she managed, and shifted in her chair. The boy's eyes were black and steady, two bits of coal in a pale face marked here and there with the eruptions of acne. His hair was light brown and had been cropped almost to the scalp. Beneath his eyes were the violet hollows of either fatigue or madness.

Jack had been examining the boy as well. Tim Clausen was a small boy for his age, and his head was oddly shaped, the cranium bulging slightly; he seemed to hold his neck rigid, as if he feared he couldn't balance the weight of his head. The boy looked at each of them in turn – long, cool appraisals. He did not blink.

'You can leave him with us,' Cawthorn said to the two attendants, and they moved out of the conference room and closed the door. 'Tim, how're you feeling today?'

His smile broadened. 'Almost free.'

'I mean physically. Any aches or pains, any complaints?'

'No sir. I'm feeling just fine.'

'Good.' He took a minute to look through the notes he'd written. 'Do you know why you're here?'

'Sure.' A pause.

'Would you like to tell us?'

'No,' he replied. 'I'm tired of answering questions, Dr Cawthorn. I'd like to ask some. Can I?'

'What kind of questions?'

Tim's attention drifted to Kay. 'I want to know things about these people. The lady first. Who are you?'

She glanced at Cawthorn, and he nodded that she should comply. Jack had gathered the photographs back and was studying them, but listening intently. 'As Dr Cawthorn said, my name is Kay Douglas. I'm representing you with the public defender's off –'

'No, no!' Tim interrupted, with an expression of impatience. 'Who *are* you? Like: are you married? Divorced? Have any kids? What religion are you? What's your favorite color?'

'Uh . . . well . . . no, I'm not married.' Divorced, yes but she wasn't about to tell him that. 'No children. I'm –' this is ridiculous! she thought. Why should she be telling private things to this boy? He was waiting for her to continue, his eyes impassive. 'I'm Catholic,' she went on. 'I guess my favorite color's green.'

'Any boyfriends? You live alone?'

'I'm afraid I don't see what this has to do with –'

'It's not fun to answer questions, is it?' Tim asked. 'Not fun at all. Well, if you want me to answer *your* questions you'll have to answer *mine* first. You live alone, I think. Probably dating a couple of guys. Maybe sleeping with them, too.' Kay couldn't control her blush, and Tim laughed. 'I'm right, huh? Knew I was! Are you a good Catholic or a bad Catholic?'

'Tim?' Cawthorn's voice was gentle but firm. 'I think you're overstepping a little bit now. We all want to get this over as soon as possible, don't we?'

'Now you.' Tim ignored Cawthorn, his eyes aimed at Jack. 'What's your story?'

Jack put aside a photograph that showed gory finger-paintings on the kitchen wall of the Clausen house. 'I've been married for fourteen years, my wife and I have two sons, I'm a Methodist and my favorite color is dark blue. I have no extramarital lovers, I'm a basketball fan and I like Chinese food. Anything else?'

Tim hesitated. 'Yes. Do you believe in God?'

'I believe . . . there's a supreme being, yes. How about you?'

'Oh, I believe in a supreme being. Sure thing. Do you like the taste of blood?'

Jack made sure he kept his face emotionless. 'Not especially.'

'My supreme being does,' Tim said. 'He likes it a lot.' He rocked back and forth a few times, and the straitjacket fabric rustled. His heavy head wobbled on his stalky neck. 'Okay. Just wanted to find out who my interrogators were. Shoot.'

'May I?' Jack inquired, and Cawthorn motioned for him to go ahead. 'Tim, what I'm trying to determine, with the help of Miss Douglas and the public defender's office, is your mental state on the night of October 12th, between the hours of ten and eleven. Do you know what incident I'm referring to?'

Tim was silent, staring at one of the frosted-glass windows. Then: 'Sure. That's when they came. They trashed the place and split.'

'In your statement to Lieutenant Markus of the Birmingham police department, you indicated "they" came to your parents' house, and that "they" –'He found a photocopy of the statement in his satchel and read the part he sought: 'Quoting, "they did the damage. I couldn't do anything to stop them, not even if I'd wanted to. I didn't. They came and did the damage and after they were through they went home and I called the cops because I knew somebody had heard the screaming.'' End quote. Is that correct, Tim?'

'Guess so.' He kept staring at a fixed spot on the window, just past Jack's shoulder. His voice sounded thick.

'Would you tell me who you meant by ''they''?'

Tim shifted again, and the straitjacket rubbed on his back-rest. A scatter of rain pelted the windows. Kay could feel her heart pounding, and she had her hands folded tightly on the table before her.

'My friends,' Tim said quietly, 'My best friends.'

'I see.' He didn't really, but at least this was one step forward. 'Can you tell me their names?'

'Their names,' Tim repeated. 'You probably couldn't pronounce them.'

'You pronounce them for me, then.'

'My friends don't like for just anybody to know their names. Not their real names, at least. I've made up names for them: Adolf, Frog and Mother. My best friends.'

There was a moment of silence. Cawthorn shuffled his notes and Jack studied the ceiling and formulated his next question. Kay beat him to it: 'Who are they? I mean . . . where do they come from?'

Tim smiled again, as if he welcomed the query. 'Hell,' he said. 'That's where they live.'

'By Adolf,' Jack said, measuring his words, 'I presume you mean Hitler? Is that right?'

'I call him that, but that's not who he is. He's a lot older. But he took me to a place once, where there were walls and barbed wire and bodies were getting thrown into furnaces. You could smell the skin cook, like barbecue on the Fourth of July.' He closed his eyes behind the round-lensed glasses. 'I got a guided tour, see. There were Nazi soldiers all over the place, just like in the old pictures, and there were chimneys spouting brown smoke that smelled like hair on fire. A sweet smell. And there were people playing violins, and other people digging graves. Adolf speaks German. That's why I call him Adolf.'

Jack looked at one of the photographs. It showed bloody swastikas on the wall over the disemboweled torso of a little girl. He felt as if he were sweating on the inside of his skin, the outer surface cold and clammy. Somehow – without any weapons or implements that the police could identify – the boy sitting at the far end of the table had ripped his parents and sister to pieces. Just torn them apart and thrown the pieces against the walls in an orgy of violence, then marked the walls with HAIL SATAN, swastikas, weirdly animalistic faces and obscenities in a dozen languages, all in fresh blood and inner matter. But what had he used to pull them apart? Surely human hands weren't capable of such strength, and on the corpses were deep bite marks and evidence of claws at work. Eyes had been gouged out, teeth had been knocked from gaping mouths, ears and noses had been chewed away.

It was the worst case of pure savagery he'd ever seen. But what kept knocking against the walls of his mind were those scrawled obscenities – in German, Danish, Italian, French, Greek, Spanish and six more languages including Arabic. According to the boy's school records, he'd made a low 'C' in Latin. That was it. So where had those languages come from? 'Who taught you Greek, Tim?' Jack asked.

The boy's eyes opened. 'I don't know Greek. Frog does.'

'Frog. Okay. Tell me about Frog.'

'He's . . . ugly. Like a frog. He likes to jump, too.' Tim leaned forward slightly, as if confiding a secret, and though he sat more than six feet away Kay found herself recoiling three or four inches. 'Frog's very smart. Probably the smartest one. And Frog's been everywhere. All around the world. He knows every language you can think of, and probably some you don't even know.' He sat back, smiling proudly. 'Frog's neato.'

Jack eased a Flair pen from his shirt pocket and wrote ADOLF and FROG at the top of the police statement, connecting them to the word 'they' with an arrow. He could feel the boy watching him. 'How'd you meet your friends, Tim?'

'I called them. They came.'

'Called them? How?'

'From the books. The spell books.'

Jack nodded thoughtfully. The 'spell books' were a collection of paperback volumes on demonology the police had found on a shelf in Tim's room. They were tattered old things the boy said he'd bought at flea markets and garage sales, the newest one copyrighted in the '70s. They were by no means 'forbidden' literature, just probably the kind of books that had sat in drugstore racks and been spun round a thousand times. 'So Adolf and Frog are demons, is that right?'

'That's one name for them, I guess. There are others.'

'Can you tell us exactly when you first called them?'

'Sure. Maybe two years ago. More or less. I wasn't very good at it at first. They won't come unless you *really* want them, and you've got to follow the directions right to the letter. If you're a hair off, nothing happens. I guess I went through it a hundred times before Mother came. She was the first one.'

'She?' Jack asked. 'Adolf and Frog are male, but Mother is female?'

'Yeah. She's got jugs.' Tim's eyes darted to Kay, back to Jack again. 'Mother knows everything. She taught me all about sex.' Another furtive glance at Kay. 'Like how a girl dresses when she wants to get raped. Mother says they all want it. She took me places, and showed me things. Like one place where this fat guy brought boys home, and after he was through with them he set them free because they were all used up, and then he put them in garbage bags and buried them in his basement like pirate treasure.'

'Set them free?' Jack repeated, his mouth had gotten very dry. 'You mean . . .'

'Set them free from their bodies. With a butcher knife. So their souls could go to Hell.' He looked at Kay, who could not restrain an inner shudder. She cursed Bob Foster right down to his shoelaces.

Hallucinations, Jack jotted down. Then: *Fixation on Demonology and Hell. Why?* 'You said a little while ago, when Dr Cawthorn asked you how you were feeling, you felt "almost free". Could you explain that to me?'

'Yeah. Almost free. Part of my soul's already in Hell. I gave it up on the night when . . . you know. It was a test. Everybody gets tested. I passed that one. I've got one more – kind of like an entrance exam, I guess.'

'Then all your soul will be in Hell?'

'Right. See, people have the wrong idea about Hell. It's not what people think. It's . . . a homey kind of place. Not a whole lot different from here. Except it's safer, and you get protected. I've visited there, and I've met Satan. He was wearing a leather jacket, and he said he wanted to help me learn how to play football, and he said he'd always pick me first when it came to choosing up teams. He said he'd be . . . like a big brother, and all I had to do was love him.' He blinked behind his glasses. 'Love is too hard here. It's easier to love in Hell, because nobody yells at you and you don't have to be perfect. Hell is a place without walls.' He began to rock himself again, and the straitjacket's fabric made a shrieking sound. 'It kills me, all this stuff about rock and roll being Satan's music. He likes Beethoven, listens to it over and over on a big ghetto blaster. And he's got the kindest eyes you ever saw, and the sweetest voice. Know what he says? That he feels so sorry for new life born into this world, because life is suffering and it's the babies who have to pay for their parents' sins.' His rocking was getting more violent. 'It's the babies who need to be freed most of all. Who need love and protection, and he'll wrap them in swaddling leather jackets and hum Beethoven to them and they won't have to cry any more.'

'Tim?' Cawthorn was getting alarmed at the boy's motion. 'Settle down, now. There's no need –'

'YOU WON'T CAGE ME!' Tim shouted, and his pale face with its encrustment of acne flooded crimson. Veins were beating at both temples. Kay had almost leaped from her skin, and now she grasped the edge of the table with white fingers. 'Won't cage me, no sir! Dad tried to cage me! He was scared shitless! Said he was going to burn my books and get me thinking right again! Won't cage me! Won't cage me, no sir!' He thrashed against the straitjacket, a sheen of sweat gleaming on his face. Cawthorn stood up, started for the door to call in Gil and Bobby.

'Wait!' the boy shouted: a command, full-voiced and powerful.

Cawthorn stopped with his hand on the tarnished knob.

'Wait. Please. Okay?' Tim had ceased struggling. His glasses were hanging from one ear, and with a quick jerk of his head he flung them off. They skidded along the table and almost into Kay's lap. 'Wait. I'm all right now. Just got a little crazy. See, I won't be caged in. I *can't* be. Not when part of my soul's already in Hell.' He smiled slickly and wet his lips with his tongue. 'It's time for my entrance exam. That's why they let you bring me here . . . so they could come too.'

'Who, Tim?' Jack felt the hairs creeping at the back of his neck. 'Who let us bring you here?'

'My best friends. Frog, Adolf and Mother. They're here too. Right here.'

'Right *where*?' Kay asked.

'I'll show you. Frog says he likes your hair, too. Says he'd like to feel it.' The boy's head wobbled, the veins sticking out in his neck and throbbing to a savage rhythm. 'I'll show you my best friends. Okay?'

Kay didn't answer. At the door, Cawthorn stood motionless. Jack sat still, the pen clamped in his hand.

A drop of blood coursed slowly from the corner of Tim's left eye. It was bright red, and streaked scarlet down his cheek, past his lip to his chin.

Tim's left eyeball had begun to bulge from its socket.

'Here they come,' he whispered, in a strangled voice. 'Ready or not.'

4

'He's hemorrhaging!' Jack stood up so fast his chair crashed over. 'Eric, call the emergency room!'

Cawthorn ran out to get to the telephone at Bobby Crisp's desk. Jack crossed the room to the boy's side, saw Tim hitching as if he couldn't draw a breath. Two more lines of blood oozed from around the left eye, which was being forced out of its socket by a tremendous inner pressure. The boy gasped, made a hoarse moaning sound, and Jack struggled to loosen the straitjacket's straps but the body began to writhe and jerk with such force that he couldn't find the buckles.

Kay was on her feet, and Jack said, 'Help me get this off him!' but she hesitated; the images of the mangled corpses in those photographs were still too fresh. At that moment Gil Moon came in, saw what was happening and tried to hold the boy from thrashing. Jack got one of the heavy straps undone, and now blood was dripping from around the boy's eye and running out his nostrils, his mouth strained open in a soundless cry of agony.

Tim's tongue protruded from his mouth. It rotated around, and Tim's body shuddered so fiercely even Gil's burly hands couldn't keep him still. Jack's fingers pulled at the second buckle – and suddenly the boy's left eye shot from its socket in a spray of gore and flew across the room. It hit the wall and drooled down like a broken egg, and Kay's knees almost folded.

'Hold him! Hold him!' Jack shouted. The boy's face rippled, and there came the sound of facial bones popping and cracking like the timbers of an old house giving way. His cranium bulged, his forehead swelling as if threatening explosion.

Cawthorn and Bobby returned to the room. The doctor's face was bleached white, and Bobby pushed Jack aside to get at the last buckle.

'Emergency's on the way up!' Cawthorn croaked. 'My God . . . my God . . . what's happening to him?'

Jack shook his head. He realized he had some of Tim Clausen's blood on his shirt, and the dark socket of the boy's ruined eye looked as if it went right down into the wet depths of the brain. The other eye seemed to be fixed on him – a cold, knowing stare. Jack stepped back to give Gil and Bobby room to work.

The boy's tongue emerged another inch, seemed to be questing in the air. And then, as the tongue continued to strain from the mouth, there was a sound of flesh tearing loose. The tongue emerged two more inches – and its color was a mottled greenish-gray, covered with sharp glass-like spikes.

The attendants recoiled. Tim's body shuddered, the single eye staring. The head and face were changing shape, as if being hammered from within.

'Oh . . . Jesus,' Bobby whispered, retreating.

Something writhed behind Tim Clausen's swollen forehead. The spiky tongue continued to slide out, inch after awful inch, and twined itself around the boy's neck. His face was gray, smeared with blood at nostrils and lips and empty eyehole. His temples pulsed and bulged, and the left side of his face shifted with a firecracker noise of popping bones. A thread of scarlet zigzagged across his pressured skull; the fissure widened, wetly, and part of his cranium began to lift up like a trap door being forced open.

Kay made a choking sound. Cawthorn's back thumped against the wall.

Dazed and horrified, Jack saw a scuttling in the dark hole where the left eye had been. The hole stretched wider, with a splitting of tissues, and from it reached a gnarled gray hand about the size of an infant's, except it had three fingers and three sharp silver talons and was attached to a leathery arm that rippled with hard piano-wire muscles.

The boy's mouth had been forced open so far the jaws were about to break. From the mouth emerged spike-covered buttocks, following its attached tail that had once been – or had appeared to be – a human tongue. A little mottled gray-green thing with spiky skin and short piston-like legs was backing out of Tim Clausen's mouth, fighting free from the bloody lips as surely as a new birth. And now the creature on the end of that muscular little arm was pushing itself out too, through the grotesque cavity that used to be Tim Clausen's eyesocket, and Jack was face-to-face with a scaly bald head the size of a man's fist and the color of spoiled meat. Its other arm appeared, and now a thorny pair of shoulders, the body pushing with fierce energy and its flat bulldog nostrils flared and spouting spray. Its slanted Chinese eyes were topaz, beautiful and deadly.

Gil was jabbering, making noise but no sense. The bald head ratcheted toward him, and as its mouth grinned with eager anticipation – like a kid presented with a roomful of pizzas, Jack thought crazily – the close-packed teeth glinted like broken razors.

And something began to crawl from the top of the boy's skull that almost stopped Jack's laboring heart. Kay felt a scream pressing at her throat, but it would not come out. A spidery thing, gleaming and iridescent, its six-legged form all sinews and angles, pushed its way from the skull's gaping trapdoor. Mounted on a four-inch stalk of tough tissue was a head framed with a metallic mass of what might have been hair, except it was made of tangled concertina wire, honed to skin-slicing sharpness. The face was ivory – a woman's face, the visage of a blood-drained beauty. Beneath silver brows her eyes were white, and as they gazed upon Jack and the body struggled out the creature's pale lips stretched into a smile and showed fangs of saw-edged diamonds.

Cawthorn broke, began laughing and wailing as he slid down to the floor. Out in the corridor, the buzzer shrilled; the emergency staff had arrived, but there was no one to unlock the door on this side.

The squatty spike-covered beast was almost out of the boy's mouth. It pulled free, its webbed feet clenching to Tim's face, and swivelled its acorn-shaped head around. The eyes were black and owlish, its face cracked and wrinkled and covered with suppurating sores that might have been Hell's version of acne. Its mouth was a red-rimmed cup, like the suctioning mouth of a leech. The eyes blinked rapidly, a transparent film dropping across them and then lifting as it regarded the humans in the room.

Tim Clausen's head had begun to collapse like a punctured balloon. The bald-headed, muscular thing – Adolf, Jack realized – wrenched its hips loose from the eyesocket; its chest was plated with overlapping scales, and at its groin was a straining red penis and a knotty sac of testicles that pulsed like a bag of hearts. As the creature's leg came free, Tim's mouth released a hiss of air that smelled of blood and brains and decayed matter – an odor of fungus and mold – and in the scabrous sound there might have been a barely-human whisper: '*Free*.'

The boy's face imploded, features running together like wet wax. The spidery metal-haired demon – Mother, Jack knew it could only be – scrabbled onto the boy's shoulder and perched there as Tim's head turned dark as a wart and caved in. What remained of the head – flaccid and rubbery – fell back over the shoulder and hung there like a cape's hood, and whatever Tim Clausen had been was gone.

But the three demons remained.

They were holding him together, Jack thought as he staggered back. He bumped into Kay, and she grasped his arm with panicked strength. After they killed the boy's parents and sister, Jack realized, they were hiding inside him and holding him together like plaster and wire in a mannequin. Shock settled over him, freighting him down. His mind seized like rusted cogs. He heard the insistent call of the buzzer, the emergency crew wanting to get in, and he feared his legs had gone dead. *My best friends*, the boy had said. *I called them. They came.*

And here they were. Ready or not.

They were neither hallucinations nor the result of psychotic trance. There was no time to debate the powers of God or the Devil, or whether Hell was a territory or a termite in the house of reason: the demon Tim had named Adolf leaped nimbly through the air at Gil Moon and gripped the man's face with those three-fingered silver claws. Gil bellowed in terror and fell to his knees; the demon's claws were a blur of motion, like a happy machine at work, and as Gil shuddered and screamed and tried to fight the thing off the demon ripped his face away from the skeletal muscles like a flimsy mask. Blood spattered through the air, marking the walls with the same patterns as at the Clausen house. Adolf locked his sinewy legs around Gil Moon's throat, the three toes of the demon's bare feet curling and uncurling with merry passion, and Adolf began to eat the man's shredded face. Gil's bony jaws chattered and moaned, and the demon made greedy grunting noises like a pig burrowing in slop.

Bobby Crisp ran, releasing a shriek that shook the windows. He did not stop to open the door, but almost knocked it off its hinges as he fled into the hallway. Jack gripped Kay's hand, pulling her with him toward the door. Mother's ashen, lustful face followed him; he saw her tongue flicker from the pale-lipped mouth – a black, spear-tipped piece of pseudo-flesh that quivered in the air with a low humming sound. He could feel the tone vibrate in his testicles, and the tingling sensation slowed him a half-step. Kay's scream let go, with a force that rattled her bones; once uncapped, the scream would not stop and kept spilling from her throat. A form leaped at her head. She ducked, lifting an arm to ward it off. The creature Tim had called Frog hopped over her shoulder, its spiky tail tearing cloth from her jacket just above the elbow. A whiplash of pain jarred her scream to a halt and cleared her head, and then Frog had landed on Dr Cawthorn's scalp. 'Don't leave me . . . don't leave me,' he was babbling, and Jack stopped before he reached the doorway – but in the next instant it was obvious that help was much too late.

Frog leaned forward and attached that gaping leech-mouth to Cawthorn's forehead. The creature's cheeks swelled to twice their size, its tail snaking around and around Cawthorn's throat. Cawthorn gave a guttural cry of pain, and his head exploded like a tire pumped beyond its limits, brains streaking the walls. Frog squatted on the broken skull, its cheeks becoming concave as it sucked at flowing juices.

Jack pulled Kay out of the room. Up ahead, Bobby Crisp was racing toward the locked security door, shouting for help. He tripped over his own gangly legs and fell heavily to the floor, scrambled up again and limped frantically onward. Now there was a pounding on the other side of the door, and Jack could see faces through the glass inset. Bobby was searching wildly through his ring of keys as Jack and Kay reached him. He tried to force one into the lock, but it wouldn't go. The second key he chose slid in but balked at turning. 'Hurry!' Jack urged, and he dared to look over his shoulder.

Mother was scuttling along the hallway toward them, moving about as fast as a prowling cat. Her mouth opened, and she made a piercing shriek like claws scraped across a blackboard. As if in response to her alarm, Frog bounded out of the conference room, its ancient and wrinkled face smeared with Cawthorn's brains.

'Open it!' Jack shouted, and Bobby tried a third key but his hand was shaking so badly he couldn't get it into the lock. It was too large, and would not fit. It dawned on Jack with terrifying force that if Gil had been on door duty, the proper key would still be on the dead man's ring, and Bobby might not have one. He glanced back again, saw Mother about twenty feet away and Frog leaping past her. Adolf strode from the conference room like a two-foot-tall commingling of gnarled man and dragon.

'Lord Jesus!' Bobby Crisp said as the fourth key engaged the tumblers and turned in the lock. He wrenched the door open – and Frog landed on his shoulder, sharp little talons in the webbed feet digging through his shirt.

He screamed, thrashing at the demon. Jack could smell the reek of Frog's flesh: a musty, cooked-meat odor. Through the open door, two white-uniformed men from the emergency room stood wide-eyed and astonished, a gurney table between them. Rosalee had seen, and so had Mrs Stewart, and both of them were too stunned to move.

Jack grasped Frog with both hands. It was like touching a live coal, and the spiky tail whipped at him as he tore Frog off Bobby's back. Most of the attendant's shirt and hunks of skin ripped away. Jack's hands were pierced by the spikes on the thing's body, and he threw the demon with all his strength against the opposite wall. It folded into a ball an instant before it hit, its head retracting into its body; it made a wet splatting sound, fell to the floor and immediately reformed itself, poising for another leap.

But Bobby was out the door and so was Kay, and Jack lunged through and slammed the door shut behind him, leaving bloody handprints against the white. There was the *wham!* of impact as Frog hit the door on the other side. 'Lock it! Lock it!' Jack shouted, and Rosalee got her key in and twisted it. The lock shot home, and the door was secured.

Bobby kept running, almost colliding with Mrs Marion and Dave Chambers. 'What's your hurry?' Dave called. Bobby reached the elevator, which the emergency staffers had left open, got in and punched a button. The doors closed and took him down.

'Doris!' Rosalee hollered to Mrs Marion. 'Bring some bandages! Quick!' She grasped Jack's wrists and looked at his palms. There were four or five puncture wounds on each hand, and much of the skin had been scorched raw. The worst of the pain was just now hitting him, and he squeezed his eyes shut and shuddered. 'They got Cawthorn and Gil Moon. Tore them up. Three of them. They came out of the boy. Out of the boy's head. Tore them to pieces, just like the boy's family . . .' A wave of dizziness almost overcame him, and

Rosalee clamped her husky arms around him as his knees crumpled.

'What . . . what *was it*?' Mrs Stewart had seen the beast with the eyes of an owl and the body of a frog, but her mind had sheared away from the sight. She blinked, found herself watching drops of blood fall from the fingers of the red-haired woman's right hand and spatter to the floor. 'Oh,' she said, dazed. 'Oh dear . . . you're hurt . . .'

Kay looked at her hand, realizing only then that Frog's tail had cleaved a furrow across her arm. The pain was bad, but not unbearable. Not considering what might have happened. The image of Cawthorn's exploding head came to her, and she allowed the fretting nurse to guide her along the corridor to a chair without really knowing where she was going or why. One of the emergency staffers broke open a medical kit and started examining Kay's wound, asking her questions about what had happened; she didn't even hear them. The other man swabbed disinfectant on Jack's hands – which sent new pain through him that almost curled his hair – and then helped Rosalee bind them in the bandages Mrs Marion had brought.

Something crashed against the door. It shivered from the blow.

'Docky?' Margie was standing next to him, her face pallid and her eyes darting with fear. 'Docky . . . what's in there?'

Another blow against the door. The floor trembled.

'God Almighty!' the man who'd helped bandage Jack's hands said. 'That felt like a sledge hammer!'

'Stay away from the door!' Jack warned. 'Everybody! Stay away from it! Rosalee . . . listen . . . we've got to get the patients off the ward! Get them downstairs!'

There was a third impact against the door. The glass inset cracked.

'I told you, didn't I?' Dave Chambers stood in the center of the corridor, calmly smoking a cigarette, his eyes narrowed. 'Told you not to go in there. Now look what you've stirred up.'

'Hush!' Rosalee snapped at him – and then Mrs Marion screamed, because the rest of the door's glass inset was smashed out and a small gray claw with three silver talons stretched through, swiping savagely at the air. 'Oh . . . Lordy,' Rosalee breathed.

Jack watched, helplessly, while Adolf's arm, shoulder and head squeezed through the opening. Margie made a croaking noise. The cigarette dropped from Dave's fingers. The demon struggled to get its hips free, then leaped to the floor and stood there grinning, its baleful topaz eyes full of greedy expectation.

And now Mother was pulling herself through the opening, inch by awful inch, her barbed-wire hair gleaming under the fluorescents.

They're going to kill us all, Jack thought; it was a surprisingly calm realization, as if his mind had been pushed to its limit and would accept no more panic. Everyone on the floor was going to die – and then, most probably, the things would start with the patients on the next floor down as well.

It dawned on him that if a hospital was indeed a universe all its own, then this one had just been claimed for destruction.

Mother got her head through, and the spider's body plopped to the floor beside Adolf.

5

Kay moved: not running wildly along the corridor, as was her first impulse, because with the elevator gone and the stairwell door surely locked the corridor was just one long dead end. She leaped out of her chair, past the nurse and two emergency staffers to the gurney table; she simply did it because she saw it had to be done, and she'd come to the same recognition of doom as Jack had. 'No!' she said, and shoved the gurney forward. Its wheels squeaked as it hurtled toward Mother and Adolf.

But they were much too fast to be caught by those wheels. Mother scuttled to one side and Adolf sprang to the other, and now Frog was squeezing through the inset like a blob of jelly from a tube. The gurney slammed into the door and bounced off.

Adolf made a grating-glass noise that might have been a cackle.

There were no screams, just a long swelling of breath that caught and hung. 'Move everyone back,' Jack said to Rosalee. She didn't budge. 'Get them down the stairs!' he demanded, and finally she made a choked sound of agreement, grasped Margie's arm and began to retreat along the corridor. The others followed, not daring to turn their backs on the creatures. Dave Chambers just stood gaping for a moment, then he too began a stiff-legged retreat.

Frog thrashed in the door's inset, its front legs clawing. The bastard's stuck! Jack realized, but it was little consolation. Mother took a slithery step forward, and Adolf clambered up onto the gurney and squatted there as if in contemplation.

Jack knew there were no weapons on the eighth floor: no knives, no bludgeons, certainly no guns. The most dangerous item up here was probably a toilet plunger, and he doubted that would do much harm to Tim Clausen's best friends. Frog was still trying to get its bulbous buttocks through the opening. Mother was advancing steadily but with caution, and Adolf's eyes ticked back and forth with murderous intent.

'Help us! Please help us!' someone shouted. Jack saw Mrs Stewart at the nurse's station, the telephone in her hand. 'We're on eight! For God's sake, send somebody to help –'

Adolf's muscular legs uncoiled, and the demon jumped over Jack and Kay, hit the floor running and had scampered up onto the nurse's desk before Mrs Stewart could finish her plea. With one swipe of a claw, Adolf opened the woman's throat. Her vocal chords rattled, and the phone fell from her twitching fingers. Adolf clung to the front of her uniform as

Mrs Stewart writhed in agony, and his razorblade teeth went to work on the ravaged throat.

'GET OFF HER, YOU SHIT!' Rosalee hollered, and whacked Adolf with a broom she'd plucked from a corner. The broom did no damage even though it was swung with a mighty vengeance, but Adolf ceased his chewing and regarded her as if admiring a new steak. Mrs Stewart crumpled, strangling, and Adolf leaped to the desktop.

'Jack! Look out!' Kay cried; he whirled around as Mother scuttled toward his legs, and without thinking about it he kicked the thing as if going for a field goal. The demon gave a moist grunt and rolled like a tumbleweed against the wall, then immediately righted herself and came at him again. Jack retreated, but the demon was coming on too fast, and he saw the wicked glitter of her diamond teeth. She was almost upon him, about to scurry up his left leg.

A chair flew past him, nearly clipping his shoulder, and crashed into Mother. She shrieked, a noise like air escaping a hole in a balloon. Some of her legs were already struggling to shove the chair off and the others pulling her out of Jack's range before he could deliver another kick. Two legs quivered and slid uselessly along the floor, leaving a smear of brown fluid.

'I busted it!' Dave Chambers shouted. 'Knocked the shit out of it, didn't I? Doc, move your ass!'

Rosalee swung the broom at Adolf again. The demon caught it, and for a few seconds they pulled it back and forth between them, until Rosalee yanked at it and Adolf let go. She squalled and staggered, falling with a jolt that shook the floor. Adolf tensed to leap upon her.

But the elevator suddenly opened, and a stout middle-aged man in the brown uniform of a security guard stepped off. He wore a badge and holster with a .38 revolver in it, and he stopped dead in his tracks as the demon's head swivelled toward him.

The guard gasped, 'What in the name of everlovin' Jesus is –'

Adolf jumped. Cleared Rosalee, who screamed and scurried away on her hands and knees, and plunged his claws into the man's chest. The talons ripped through the shirt, and the demon flailed at the man like a living chainsaw. Most of his chest was a wet, gaping cavity within the seven or eight seconds it took for Adolf to finish with him, and the guard toppled forward onto his face. His legs remained inside the elevator, and the doors kept thumping against them, opening and trying to close again.

Adolf perched on the dead man's back, licking his talons. His gaze found Rosalee, who had crawled about ten feet away, and she knew she was next.

'Hey, freak!' Dave bellowed. He had another chair, was thrusting it at Adolf like a lion tamer. The demon's eyes fixed on him, and a terrible grin flickered across its mouth. 'Come on, prick!' Dave stepped between Adolf and Rosalee, a sheen of sweat shining on his face; his own smile was maniacal. 'Rosalee, you'd best get off your butt now. Best get those people down the stairs.' His voice was calm: the voice of someone who had chosen suicide. 'Doc, you and the lady haul your asses and get off the ward!'

Rosalee stood up. Adolf hissed at her, and Dave feinted with the chair to get the thing's attention again. Jack and Kay moved past him, as Mother slowly advanced along the corridor, dragging her broken legs. 'I know you, don't I?' Dave asked the male demon. 'Sure I do. I've seen you at night, when I try to sleep. Oh, you're a sly little bastard, aren't you? You get in my head when I'm dreamin', and you make me crazy. That's why I'm here – because of you.'

Adolf swiped at the chair, left three furrows across one of the wooden legs.

'You want to jump, huh? Want to get those hands on ol' Dave's neck? Except you know I won't go lightly. I'll knock your eyeballs out, friend.' Dave glanced quickly to his right; about twenty feet away, Rosalee had slipped her key into the stairwell's door and was unlocking it. 'Hurry!' he said, then cut his gaze down the other direction. The spider with the marble-white face of a woman and barbed-wire hair was creeping inexorably up on him. The third demon was still struggling to get free of the door, and was just about to pop its butt loose.

Adolf sprang forward. Dave planted his legs and swung the chair. But Adolf drew back at the last second, and the chair's legs hit empty air.

'Maybe I can't kill you,' Dave said, 'but I'll break your bones – or whatever's holdin' you together. Maybe that makes you think a little bit, huh?'

Rosalee was getting the patients, the two emergency staffers and Mrs Marion through the door into the stairwell. Jack hesitated, watching Dave as Mother slowly advanced on him. 'Dave!' he shouted. 'We'll keep the door open for you! Come on!'

Dave laughed harshly. 'You're nuttier'n a Christmas fruit-cake, Doc,' he answered. 'You want these things runnin' all through the hospital? Man, *I'm* not even that crazy! You get through that door and make sure it's locked.'

Kay gripped Jack's arm. Everyone had gone down the stairwell except her and Rosalee. She pulled at him. 'We've got to get downstairs . . . got to call the police . . .' Her eyelids were fluttering, and Jack recognized that deep shock was finally settling in. He wanted to go, because in all his life no one had ever accused him of being a hero – but the sight of a mental patient wielding a chair against two demons from Hell would not let him descend the stairs. It would be easy to give up Dave Chambers; what was the measure of the man's life, anyway? But Jack could not leave him alone up here, though his brain screamed for escape and he knew Dave was a heartbeat away from being torn to shreds. After they finished with Dave, they would find a way down to the next floor where they could go from room to room. If they were going to be stopped, it had to here and now.

'Take her,' Jack said to Rosalee. 'Lock the door behind you.'

'No! Dr Shannon, you can't –'

'Do what I said.' His voice cracked, and he felt his courage leaking out. 'If they get off this floor . . .' He let the thought remain unspoken.

Rosalee hesitated – but only for a few seconds, because she saw his mind was made up. She said, 'Come on, miss. Lean on me, now.' She helped Kay down the stairs, and then the door swung shut in Jack's face. Rosalee turned her key on the other side, and the lock engaged with a small click of finality.

6

'Doc, you're crazy!' Dave yelled. 'You should've been up here in a rubber room with us nuts a long time a –'

Adolf jumped at Dave's legs. The man backpedalled and swung the chair; it struck the demon's shoulder and knocked the thing sprawling against the wall. Mother was almost at Dave's feet, and Jack saw Frog suddenly heave loose from the door's inset and fall to the floor. Frog started bounding toward Dave, covering three or four feet at a leap. Dave saw it coming too, and he wheeled toward Frog to ward the beast off.

'Look out!' Jack warned, but he knew he was too late. Adolf had already leapt at the man, was scrabbling up Dave's leg. Mother pounced like a cat upon Dave's ankle, and the diamond fangs ripped through his white sock. It turned crimson. Dave whacked at Mother with the chair, missed, was off-balance and falling as Adolf plunged his claws into the man's chest and opened him up from breastbone to navel. Dave's strickened face turned toward Jack, and Jack heard him gasp: '*The gun.*'

Then Dave hit the floor, with Adolf pinned and struggling beneath him, and a tide of blood streamed across the linoleum.

The gun, Jack realized. The gun in the security guard's holster.

He didn't remember taking the first step. But he was running toward the elevator, where the guard lay dead, and it occurred to him that his ravaged hands might not be able to hold the gun, or that it might be unloaded, or that he might not be able to pull it from the holster in time. All those things whirled through his mind, but he knew that without the gun he was meat to be devoured by Tim Clausen's best friends.

Tail lashing, Frog bounded from the floor at him before he could reach the elevator. He ducked, slipped in Dave Chambers' blood and fell as Frog leaped over his head. The end of the beast's tail slashed his left ear, and then he was skidding across the floor on his chest and bumped against the guard's corpse. He saw Adolf pulling his legs from underneath Dave, saw the demons' eyes widen with realization. Jack got one hand around the revolver's butt, popped the holster open with the other and drew the gun loose. The safety! he thought, and spent precious seconds fumbling to release the catch.

And then Mother was right in his face, the mouth opening with a hiss and the fangs straining. Her legs clutched at his shoulder, a breath of corruption washing at his nostrils. The fangs glittered, about to strike.

He pressed the revolver's barrel against her forehead and forced his index finger to squeeze the trigger.

Nothing happened.

Just an empty click.

Adolf cackled, wrenching his legs free and standing up.

Frog was bounding back along the corridor.

Mother grinned.

And Jack pulled the trigger again.

This time it fell on a loaded cylinder. The gun went off, almost jumping out of Jack's grip.

A hole in Mother's forehead sprayed brown fluid. Her grin turned to a rictus of what might have been agony, and she scurried backward. Adolf's cackle stopped cold.

Jack fired again. A piece of Mother's head flew off, and she was shrieking and dragging herself around in a mad circle. Frog leaped, landed on the side of Jack's neck with a wet grunt. He pressed the gun into its gelatinous, meaty-smelling body and shot – once, twice. Frog split open, oozing nastiness, and slithered away from him.

Jack tried to take aim at Mother again, but she was running like a wind-up toy gone berserk. A scrape of metal drew his attention. He looked at the opposite wall: Adolf was frantically pulling at a small metal grill. The vent! Jack thought, and his heart stuttered. If that bastard got into the vent . . .!

He fired at Adolf's back. At the same instant the .38 went off, Adolf wrenched the grill open. His left arm disappeared at the elbow in a mangle of tissue and fluid, and Adolf's body was slammed against the wall. The demon's head turned toward Jack, eyes ablaze with hatred. Jack pulled the trigger once more – and hit the empty cylinder again. The bullets were gone.

Adolf flung himself headfirst into the vent. Jack shouted 'NO!' and scrambled across the dead guard, over the bloody floor to the vent; he shoved his arm in, his hand seeking. In the tube there was a scuttling, drawing away and down. Then silence but for the rattle of Jack's lungs.

He lay on his stomach, not far from the corpse of Dave Chambers. The ward smelled like a slaughterhouse. He wanted to rest, just curl his body up and let his mind coast down a long road into darkness – but Adolf was still in the hospital, probably following the vent's pipe to the lower floors, and he could decide to come out anywhere. Jack lay shivering, trying to think. Something Tim Clausen had said . . . something about . . .

He feels so sorry for new life born into this world, the boy had said. *It's the babies who need to be freed most of all.*

And Jack knew why Tim's best friends had allowed him to be brought to the hospital.

All hospitals have a maternity ward.

There was a soft hiss beside his left ear.

Mother crouched there on trembling legs, part of her head blasted away and her face dripping brown ichor. Her tongue flicked out, quivering toward Jack, her eyes lazy and heavy-lidded. They were sated, hideous, knowing eyes; they understood things that, once set free, would gnaw through the meat and bone of this world and spit out the remains like gristle on barbarian platters. They were things that might rave between the walls of Jack's mind for the rest of his life, but right now he must shove away the madness before it engulfed him; he knew - and was sure Mother did, too - that Adolf was scrambling down through the vent toward the second floor, where the babies were. Mother leered at him, her duty done.

Jack got his hand around the .38's barrel and smashed the butt into her face. The wet, obscene skin split with a noise like rotten cloth. Barbed wire cut through Jack's bandaged fingers, and he lifted the gun and struck again. Mother retreated only a few paces before her legs gave out. Her eyes collapsed inward like cigarette burns. The mouth made a mewling noise, the diamond fangs snapping together. Jack lifted the gun and brought it down, heedless of the barbed-wire hair. Mother's head broke like a blister, and out of that cavity rose an oily mist that swirled up toward the ceiling and clung there, seething like a concentration of wasps. It bled through the ceiling tiles, leaving a stain as dark as nicotine and then it - whatever it had been - had escaped.

Mother's body lay like a rag. Jack pushed it aside and crawled to the elevator. The doors were still thumping impatiently against the guard's legs. Jack struggled to slide the corpse out, aware that each passing second took Adolf closer to the maternity ward. He got the legs out of the elevator, caught the doors before they closed and heaved himself inside, reaching up to hit the 2 button.

The doors slid shut, and the elevator descended.

Jack stood up. His legs immediately gave way again, and he fell to his knees. The front of his shirt was reddened by gore, the bandages hanging from his bloody hands. Black motes spun before his eyes, and he knew he didn't have much time before his body surrendered. The old gears and cables creaked, and the elevator jarred to a halt. Jack looked up at the illuminated numbers over the door; the number 5 was lit up. The doors opened, and a gray-haired doctor in a white lab coat took one step in before he saw Jack on the floor and froze.

'Get out,' Jack rasped.

The doctor hesitated perhaps three seconds, then retreated so abruptly he hit an orderly in the hallway and knocked over a cart of medicines and sterilized instruments. Jack pressed the 2 button once more, and the doors closed. He watched the numbers change. As the elevator passed the third floor, Jack thought how sensible it would be to stay here all the way down to the lobby and scream for help once he got there. That was the thing to do, because he had no gun, no weapon, nothing to stop Adolf with. He was bloody and balanced on the edge of shock, and he knew he must've scared the doctor half to death. A grim smile lifted the corners of his mouth, because he knew there was no time to get to the lobby; by then, Adolf might have reached the maternity ward, and the thing's remaining claw would be at work amid the new flesh. Already there might be a pile of infant limbs scattered on the floor, and each second ended another life. No time . . . no time . . .

Jack struggled to his feet. Watched the number 2 light up. The elevator halted, and the doors opened with a sigh.

There were no screams, no frantic activity on the second floor. As Jack emerged from the elevator, the two nurses on duty at the central station gaped up at him. One of them spilled a cup of coffee, brown liquid surging across the desk. Jack had never been to the maternity ward before, and corridors seemed to cut off in every direction. 'The babies,' he said to one of the nurses. 'Where do you keep the babies?'

'Call security!' she told the other one, and the woman picked up the telephone, pressed a button and said in a quavering voice, 'This is second floor. We need security up here, *fast*!'

'Listen to me.' Jack knew Rosalee and the others must be still trying to explain what had happened, and they wouldn't understand where Adolf was headed. 'Please listen. I'm Dr Jack Shannon. I've just come from the eighth floor. You've got to get the babies out of here. I can't tell you why, but –'

'Luther!' one of the nurses shouted. 'Luther!' The other woman had backed away, and Jack saw they both thought he was out of his mind. 'I'm not crazy,' he said, instantly regretting it; such a statement only made things worse. The nurse who'd called for Luther said, 'Settle down, now. We're going to get somebody up here to help you, okay?'

Jack looked around, trying to get his bearings. A waiting-room was on the left, people staring at him like frightened deer ready to bolt. On the right a sign affixed to the wall read MATERNITY and aimed an arrow down the corridor. Jack started along the hallway, one of the nurses yelling at him to stop and the other too scared to speak. He passed between rooms, leaving drops of blood on the floor and startling nurses and patients who saw him coming; they scattered out of his way, but one nurse grabbed his shoulder and he shoved her aside and kept going. A signal bell was going off, alerting security. He hoped these guards were quicker on their feet than the one upstairs had been.

He rounded a corner, and there was the large floor-to-ceiling plateglass window where babies were displayed in their perambulators, the boys bundled up in pale blue and the girls in pink. Several friends and relatives of new parents were peering in through the glass at the infants as the maternity nurse continued her duties within. One of the visitors looked up at Jack, and the woman's expression changed from delight to horror. It took two more seconds for all of them to be aware of the bloodied man who'd just lurched around the corner. Another of the women screamed, and one of the men bulled forward to protect her.

Jack slammed his hand against the window. The nurse inside jumped, her eyes stunned above her surgical mask.

'Get them out!' Jack shouted – but he knew she couldn't hear, because some of the babies were obviously crying and he couldn't hear those sounds, either. He tried again, louder: 'Get them out of –'

A pair of arms tightened around his chest from behind like a living straitjacket. 'Hold it, buddy. Just hang loose. Guards are gonna be here right soon.'

Luther, Jack thought. An orderly, and the size of a football linebacker from the thickness of those arms. The man had lifted him almost off the floor. 'You and me gonna take a walk back to the elevators. Excuse us, folks.'

'No! Listen . . .' The pressure was about to squeeze the breath out of him. Luther started dragging him along the corridor, and thrashing was useless. Jack's heels scraped the floor.

And there came another, higher scraping sound as well. Then the double crack of screws being forced loose. Jack's spine crawled; at the baseboard of the wall directly opposite the infants' nursery was a vent grill, and it was being pushed open from the other side.

Jack fought to get loose, but Luther hadn't seen and he clamped his grip tighter. The blood roared in Jack's head.

The grill came open with a squeal of bending metal, and from the vent leaped a small one-armed figure with burning topaz eyes. Adolf's head turned toward the horrified knot of ward visitors, then toward Jack and the orderly; the demon gave a grunt of satisfaction, as if expecting that Jack would be there. Luther's legs went rigid, but his grip didn't loosen from around Jack's chest.

Adolf sprang at the plate-glass.

It hit with a force that shook the window, and the glass starred at the point of impact but did not shatter. Adolf fell back to the floor, landing nimbly on his feet. The woman was still screaming – a thin, piercing scream – but her protector's nerve had failed. Behind the glass the maternity nurse had come to the front of the room in an effort to shield the babies. Jack knew she wouldn't last more than a few seconds when Adolf broke through the window.

'Let me go, damn it!' he shouted, still struggling. Luther's arms loosened, and Jack slid out of them to the floor.

Adolf shot a disdainful glance at him, like a human might look at dogshit on the sole of a shoe. He jumped at the window again, hitting it with his mangled shoulder. The glass cracked diagonally, and at the center of the window a piece about the size of a man's hand fell away. Adolf clawed at the hole, talons scraping across the glass, but couldn't find a grip. The demon rebounded to the floor again but was leaping almost as soon as he'd landed. This time his claw caught the hole, and he kicked at the glass to finish the job.

The corridor was full of screaming and the crying of babies. Jack lunged forward and grabbed the demon's legs, and as he wrenched Adolf out of the widening hole a large section of the window crashed down, glass showering the nurse as she threw her body across the first row of perambulators.

The demon twisted and writhed in Jack's grip with the agility of a monkey. Jack slung Adolf against the wall, heard the crunch of its skull against the plaster; it got one leg free, contorted its body at the waist and the smashed head - half of it pulped and leaking - came up at Jack's hand. The razorblade teeth flashed before they snapped shut on Jack's index finger. Pain shot up his forearm and into his shoulder, but he kept his hand closed on the trapped leg. Adolf's teeth were at work, and suddenly they met through the flesh; the demon's head jerked backward, taking most of Jack's finger between the teeth.

Jack's hand spasmed with agony. The remaining four fingers opened and Adolf leaped to the floor.

The demon staggered, and Jack fell against the wall with his bitten and throbbing hand clutched to his chest. He hit an object just behind him, as Adolf swiped at his legs with the remaining claw and shredded the cuff of his trousers.

Then Adolf whirled toward the broken window once more, tried to jump for the frame, but the muscular legs had gone rubbery. The demon reached up, grasped an edge of glass and began to clamber over it into the nursery.

Jack looked at Luther. The man – crewcut and husky, his face sallow and gutless – had backed almost to the corridor's corner. The nurse with the surgical mask was still lying across the first few infants, one arm outthrust to ward off Adolf's next leap. Adolf was almost over the glass, would be in the nursery within the following few seconds and the thing was hurt but he would not give up before he'd slaughtered his fill. His head cocked toward Jack, and the oozing mouth stretched wide in a grin of triumph.

There was something metal pressed into Jack's spine. Something cylindrical. He turned, saw it was a fire extinguisher.

Adolf jumped from his perch on the edge of glass. Landed on the nurse, and began to slash at her back with long strokes that cut away her uniform and flayed off ribbons of flesh.

The fire extinguisher was in Jack's hands. His good index finger yanked the primer ring. There was a hiss as the chemicals combined, and the cylinder went cold. The nurse was screaming, trying to fight Adolf off. She slipped to the floor, and Adolf clung to the side of a perambulator, started drawing himself up and into it with his claw, the razor teeth bared. He reached for the pink-clad baby's skull.

'Here I am!' Jack yelled. 'Ready or not!'

Adolf's misshapen head cocked toward Jack, teeth three inches away from infant flesh.

Jack pulled the cylinder's trigger. Cold white foam erupted from the nozzle, sprayed through the window in a narrow jet and struck Adolf on the shoulder and in the face. The baby squalled, but Adolf's caterwaul was an aural dagger. Blinded by the freezing chemicals, the demon toppled to the floor on his back, claw slashing at the air. Jack kept the spray going as Adolf tried to rise, fell again and started crawling across the floor, a little foam-covered kicking thing.

'Put it down!' someone shouted, to Jack's left. Two security guards stood there, and one of them had his hand on the butt of his pistol. 'Put it down!' he repeated, and half-drew the gun from its holster.

Jack ignored the command. He knocked out the rest of the window's glass with the cylinder and stepped into the nursery, aimed the nozzle at Adolf and kept spraying as the creature writhed at his feet. Jack felt his mouth twist into a horrible grin, heard himself shout 'Die, you bastard! Die! Die!' He lifted the cylinder and smashed it down on the body; then again, striking at the skull. Bones - or what served as bones - cracked with brittle little popping sounds. Adolf's claw struck upward, blindly flailing. Someone had Jack's arm, someone else was trying to pull him away, the nurse was still screaming and the place was a bedlam of noise. Jack shook off one of the guards, lifted the cylinder to smash it down again, but it was snatched away from him. An arm went around his throat from behind.

Adolf's head - one eye as black as a lump of coal and the face mashed inward - surfaced from the chemical foam. The single topaz eye found Jack, and the razor teeth gleamed behind mangled lips. Adolf's claw locked around Jack's left ankle, began to winnow through the flesh.

Jack pressed his right foot against the grinning face and stomped all his weight down with the force of fury behind it.

The demon's skull cracked open, and what came out resembled a lump of interwined maggots. Jack stomped that too, and kept stomping it until all the wriggling had ceased.

Only then did Jack let himself fall. Darkness lapped at his brain, and he was dragged under.

7

He awakened in a private room, found his hands stitched up, freshly-bandaged and immobilized. Minus one index finger,

which he figured was a cheap price. His left ankle was also bandaged, and he had no sensation in his foot. Dead nerves, he thought. He'd always believed a cane made a man look distinguished.

He didn't know how much time had passed, because his wristwatch had been taken away with his bloody clothes. The sun had gone down, though, and the reading light above his bed was on. The taste of medicine was in his mouth, and his tongue felt furry. Tranquilizers, he thought. He could still hear rain tapping at the window, behind the blinds.

The door opened, and a young fresh-faced nurse came in. Before it closed, Jack caught a glimpse of a policeman standing out in the corridor. The nurse stopped, seeing he was awake.

'Hi.' Jack was hoarse, probably from the pressure of that arm around his throat. 'Mind telling me what time it is?'

'About seven-thirty. How are you feeling?'

'Alive,' he answered. 'Barely.' The nurse looked out through the door and said, 'He's awake,' to the policeman, then she came to Jack's bedside and checked his temperature and pulse. She peered into his pupils with a little penlight. Jack had noted there was no telephone in the room, and he said, 'Think I could get somebody to call my wife? I imagine she'd like to know what's happened to me.'

'You'll have to ask the lieutenant about that. Follow the light, please.'

Jack obeyed. 'The babies,' he said. 'They're all right, aren't they?'

She didn't answer.

'I knew he'd go for the babies. I knew it. I remember what the boy said, that Satan –' He stopped speaking, because the nurse was looking at him as if he were a raving lunatic and had taken a pace away from the bed. She doesn't know, he thought. Of course not. The security would have clamped down by now, and the shifts had changed. All the blood had been cleaned up, the bodies zippered into bags and spirited to the morgue, the witnesses cautioned and counselled, the relatives of the dead consoled by hospital administrators, the physical damage already under repair by workmen. Jack was glad he wasn't director of public relations at Marbury Memorial, because there was going to be hell to pay.

'Sorry,' he amended. 'I'm babbling.'

She gave him the choices for dinner – chopped steak or ham – and when he'd told her what he wanted she left him. He lay musing that seven hours ago he'd been fighting a trio of demons from the inner sanctum of a young boy's insanity, and now he was choosing chopped steak over ham. Such was life, he thought; there was an absurdity in reality, and he felt like the victim of a car crash who stands amid blood and wreckage and frets about what television shows he's going to miss tonight. Demons or not, the world kept turning and chopped steaks were being cooked down in the kitchen. He laughed, and realized then that the tranquilizers in his system were either very potent or else the shock had really knocked his train off the tracks.

It wasn't long before the door opened again. This time Jack's visitor was a man in his mid-forties, with curly gray hair and a somber, hard-lined face. The man was wearing a dark blue suit, and he looked official and stiff-backed. A policeman, Jack guessed. 'Dr Shannon,' the man said, with a slight nod. 'I'm Lieutenant Boyette, Birmingham Police.' He pulled out his wallet and displayed the badge. 'Mind if I sit?'

'Go ahead.'

Boyette positioned a chair close to the bed and sat down. He had dark brown eyes, and they did not waver as he stared at Jack Shannon. 'I hope you're up to some questions.'

'I suppose now's as good a time as any.' He tried to prop himself up on his pillows, but his head spun. 'I'd like to call my wife. Let her know I'm all right.'

'She knows. We called her this afternoon. I guess you'll understand we couldn't tell her the whole story. Not until we figure it out ourselves.' He took a little notebook from the inside pocket of his coat and flipped it open. 'We've taken statements from Miss Douglas, Mrs Partain, Mr Crisp, and the maternity ward staff. I expect you'll agree that what happened here today was . . . a mite bizarre.'

'A mite,' Jack said, and laughed again. Now he knew he must be doped with something very strong. Everything was dreamlike around the edges.

'From what we can tell, you saved the lives of a lot of infants down on two. I'm not going to pretend I know what those things were, or where they came from. It's all in Miss Douglas' statement about what happened to Dr Cawthorn, Mr Moon and the others. Even the psychiatric patients gave statements that corroborated Mrs Partain's. Hell, I kind of think some of them were so shaken up they got their wits back, if that makes any sense to you.'

'I wouldn't doubt it. Probably the same effect as a shock treatment. Is Miss Douglas all right?'

'She will be. Right now she's in a room a few doors down.'

'What about Rosalee?'

'Mrs Partain's a mighty strong woman. Some of the others – like Mr Crisp – might wind up on mental wards themselves. He can't stop crying, and he thinks he feels something on his back. I guess it could've been worse, though.'

'Yes,' Jack agreed. 'Much worse.' He tried to move his fingers, but his hands had been deadened. He figured the nurse would have to hand-feed him the forthcoming chopped steak. A weariness throbbed deep in his bones: the call of the tranquilizer for sleep.

It must have shown in his face, because Boyette said, 'Well, I won't keep you long. I'd like to know what happened after Mrs Partain locked you and Mr Chambers on the eighth floor.' He brought out a pen, poised to jot notes.

Jack told him. The telling was hard and got more difficult as his bruised throat rasped and his body and brain yearned for rest. He trailed off a couple of times, had to gather his strength and keep going, and Boyette leaned closer to hear. 'I knew where Adolf was headed,' Jack said. 'The babies. I knew, because I remembered what the boy said. That's why I went down there.' He blinked, felt the darkness closing in again. Thank God it was all over. Thank God he was alive, and so were the babies. 'What . . . what floor am I on?'

'Three.' Boyette's brow was furrowed. He had leaned very close to the bed. 'Dr Shannon . . . about the bodies. The demons, or *things*, or whatever the hell they were.'

'Demons, yes. That's right. They were holding the boy together.' Hard to stay awake, he thought. The sound of rain was soothing, and he wanted to let his eyes close and drift away and in the morning maybe the sun would be out again.

'Dr Shannon,' Boyette asked, 'we only found two bodies.'

'*What?*' Jack asked – or thought he'd asked. His voice was almost gone.

'We found the body of the one in the nursery. And the one that looks like a spider. We wrapped them up and got them out of here. I don't know where they were taken, and I don't want to know. But what happened to the third one? The one you called "Frog"?'

'Shot it. Shot it twice. It split open.' His heart had kicked, and he tried to lift himself up but could not move. 'Killed it.' Oh God, he thought. 'Didn't I?'

'There was only the one that looks like a spider up on eight.' Boyette's voice sounded very far away, as if at the end of an impossibly long tunnel. 'We searched the entire floor. Took the place to pieces. But there's no third body.'

'There is . . . there is,' Jack whispered, because whispering was all he could do. He could no longer hold his head upright, and it slid to one side. His body felt boneless, but a cold panic had flooded him. He caught sight of something across the room, near the door: a vent grill. What if Frog had recombined itself? he thought through the brain-numbing frost. What if Frog had crawled into the vent on the eighth floor? But that was over seven hours ago! If Frog was going to the maternity ward, why hadn't it struck there already? 'The ducts,' he managed to rasp. 'In the ducts.'

'We thought of that. We've got people taking the ducts apart right now, but it's going to be a long job. There are two possibilities, the way I see it: either that thing got out of the hospital, or it died in the ducts somewhere. I want to believe it died, but we'll keep looking until we find the body or we take the whole system apart – that could be days.'

Jack tried to speak, but his voice was gone. There's a third possibility, he'd realized. Oh, yes. A third possibility. That Frog, the smartest of Tim Clausen's best friends, is searching from floor to floor, room to room, peering through the grills and scuttling away until it finds who it wants.

The one who killed its own best friends.

Me.

But maybe it died, Jack thought. I shot it twice, and it split open. Yes. Maybe it died, and it's lying jammed in the duct and very soon someone will remove the screws and a gelatinous thing with staring eyes and a mouth like a leech will slide out.

Maybe it died.

Maybe.

'Well, I can tell you're tired. God knows you've had one hell of a day.' Jack heard the chair scrape back as Boyette stood up. 'We'll talk again, first thing in the morning. Okay?'

Jack trembled, could not answer. Could only stare at the grill.

'You try to sleep, Dr Shannon. Good night.' There was the sound of the door opening and closing, and Lieutenant Boyette had gone.

Jack struggled against sleep. How long would it take Frog to reach his room in a methodical, slow search? How long before it would come to that grill, see him lying here in a straitjacket of bandages and tranquilizers, and begin to push itself through the vent?

But Frog was dead. Frog had to be dead.

The sun would be out in the morning, and by then the third

of Tim Clausen's best friends would be lying in a garbage bag, just limp wet flesh conjured up by infernal madness.

Jack's struggling weakened. His eyelids fluttered, and his view of the vent went dark.

But just before he drifted off to a dreamless sleep he thought the young nurse must have come in again, because he was sure he smelled the meaty odor of chopped steak.

More compulsive fiction from Headline:

DEAN R KOONTZ

THE TERRIFYING BESTSELLER

WATCHERS

"Dean Koontz is several steps beyond Stephen King in the ability to make you look over your shoulder to be sure something's not following you" ***The Weekly.***

They escape from a secret government laboratory: two mutant creatures, both changed utterly from the animals they once were. And no one who encounters them will ever be the same again:

A lonely widower; a ruthless assassin; a beautiful woman; a government agent.

Drawn together in a deadly hunt, all four are inexorably propelled towards a confrontation with an evil beyond human imagining.

"His best story yet . . . this is the sort of thoroughly frightening and entertaining tale that has its readers listening for noises in the night" ***Publishers Weekly.***

FICTION/GENERAL 0 7472 3061 7 £3.50

More compulsive fiction from Headline:

A SCALPEL-EDGED MEDICAL THRILLER BY

HAROLD L. KLAWANS

SINS OF COMMISSION

One by one the patients were dying – in agonised convulsions that made death even crueller than nature intended. Step by step the terror spread – until no one in Chicago's largest medical centre could feel safe from danger . . . or suspicion.

Enter Dr Paul Richardson, top neurologist, to follow a deadly trail through a labyrinth of laboratory secrets and human shame . . . to the shattering truth about a medical evil that was turning a prestigious hospital into a horrifying arena of intensive fear.

Also by Harold L. Klawans from Headline
INFORMED CONSENT

FICTION/MEDICAL THRILLER 0 7472 3090 0 £2.99

More Thrilling Fiction from Headline:

DAVID MORTON

THE HYENA RUN

AN ACTION-PACKED ADVENTURE IN THE AFRICAN BUSH

Joe and Ellie Lejeune, with their two children, Ben and Cassie, were just an ordinary family of tourists enjoying the excitement of a holiday drive across the rough terrain of Zimbabwe.

Until they arrived at a roadblock on a deserted section of road...

Until they were forced out of the car at gunpoint and marched into the bush, where Joe was shot and left for dead...

Until Joe came to in a hospital in Harare: a man obsessed, desperate, who would stop at nothing to find his missing family...

The search takes him down the lethal trail from Zimbabwe to Mozambique and to South Africa – and entangles him in a web of lies, double-dealing and violence; for Joe is simply a pawn in the deadly power struggle for this war-torn corner of Africa ...

FICTION/THRILLER 0 7472 3163 X £3.50

Headline books are available at your bookshop or newsagent, or can be ordered from the following address:

Headline Book Publishing PLC
Cash Sales Department
PO Box 11
Falmouth
Cornwall
TR10 9EN
England

UK customers please send cheque or postal order (no currency), allowing 60p for postage and packing for the first book, plus 25p for the second book and 15p for each additional book ordered up to a maximum charge of £1.90 in UK.

BFPO customers please allow 60p for postage and packing for the first book, plus 25p for the second book and 15p per copy for the next seven books, thereafter 9p per book.

Overseas and Eire customers please allow £1.25 for postage and packing for the first book, plus 75p for the second book and 28p for each subsequent book.